THE BOOK OF KOLI

Everything that lives hates us, it sometimes seems. Or at least they come after us like they hate us. Things we want to eat fight back, hard as they can, and oftentimes win. Things that want to eat us is thousands strong, so many of them that we only got names for the ones that live closest to us. And the trees got their own ways to hurt us, blunt or subtle according to their several natures.

By M. R. Carey

The Girl With All the Gifts
The Boy on the Bridge

Fellside

Someone Like Me

The Rampart trilogy
The Book of Koli
The Trials of Koli
The Fall of Koli

By Mike Carey

Felix Castor
The Devil You Know
Vicious Circle
Dead Men's Boots
Thicker Than Water
The Naming of the Beasts

THE BOOK OF KOLI

M. R. CAREY

orbit

www.orbitbooks.net

ORBIT

First published in Great Britain in 2020 by Orbit

1 3 5 7 9 10 8 6 4 2

A CIP catalogue record for this book is
available from the British Library.

ISBN 978-0-356-50955-6

Typeset in Bembo by Palimpsest Book Production Limited,
Falkirk, Stirlingshire
Printed and bound in Great Britain by Clays Ltd, Elcograf S.p.A.

Papers used by Orbit are from well-managed forests
and other responsible sources.

MIX
Paper from
responsible sources
FSC® C104740

Orbit
An imprint of
Little, Brown Book Group
Carmelite House
50 Victoria Embankment
London EC4Y 0DZ

An Hachette UK Company
www.hachette.co.uk

www.orbitbooks.net

For AJ

1

I got a story to tell you. I've been meaning to make a start for a long while now, and this is me doing it, but I'm warning you it might be a bumpy road. I never done nothing like this before, so I got no map, as it were, and I can't figure how much of what happened to me is worth telling. Monono says I'm like a man trying to cut his hair without a mirror. Too long and you might as well not bother. Too short and you're probably going to be sorry. And either road, you got to find some way to make the two sides match.

The two sides is this: I went away, and then I come home again. But there's more to the story than that, as you might expect. It was a hard journey, both ways. I was tried and I was tested, lots of times. You could say I failed, though what I brung back with me changed the world for ever. I met the shunned men and their messianic, Senlas, who looked into me with his hundreds of eyes. I crossed the ruins of Birmagen, where the army of the Peacemaker was ranged against me. I found the Sword of Albion, though it was not what I was looking for and it brung me as much harm as good. I fought a bitter fight against them I loved, and broke the walls that sheltered me so they'd never stand again.

All this I done for love, and for what I seen as the best, but that doesn't mean it was right. And it still leaves out the reason why, which is the heart of it and the needful thing to make you know me.

I am aiming to do that – to make you know me, I mean – but it's not an easy thing. The heft of a man's life, or a woman's life, is more than the heft of a shovelful of earth or a cord of timber. Head and heart and limbs and all, they got their weight. Dreams, even, got their weight. Dreams most of all, maybe. For me, it seems dreams was the hardest to carry, even when they was sweet ones.

Anyway, I mean to tell it, the good and the bad of it all together. The bad more than the good, maybe. Not so you can be my judge, though I know you will. Judging is what them that listen does for them that tell, whether it's wanted or not. But the truth is I don't mainly tell it for me. It's rather for the people who won't never tell it for themselves. It's so their names won't fall out of the world and be forgotten. I owe them better, and so you do. If that sounds strange, listen and I'll make it good.

2

My name is Koli and I come from Mythen Rood. Being from there, it never troubled me as a child that I was ignorant what that name meant. There is people who will tell you the rood was the name of the tree where they broke the dead god, but I don't think that's to the purpose. Where I growed up, there wasn't many as was swore to the dead god or recked his teaching. There was more that cleaved to Dandrake and his seven hard lessons, and more still that was like me, and had no creed at all. So why would they name a village after something they paid so little mind to?

My mother said it was just a misspeaking for Mythen Road, because there was a big road that runned right past us. Not a road you could walk on, being all pitted stone with holes so big you could lose a sheep in them, but a road of old times that reminds us what we used to be when the world was our belonging.

That's the heart of my story, now I think of it. The old times haunt us still. The things they left behind save us and hobble us in ways that are past any counting. They was ever the sift and substance of my life, and the journey I made starts and ends with them. I will speak on that score in its place, but I will speak of Mythen

3

Rood first, for it's the place that makes sense of me if there's any sense to be found.

It is, or was, a village of more than two hundred souls. It's set into the side of a valley, the valley of the Calder River, in the north of a place called Ingland. I learned later that Ingland had a mess of other names, including Briton and Albion and Yewkay, but Ingland was the one I was told when I was a child.

With so many people, you can imagine the village was a terrible big place, with a fence all round it that was as high as one man on another man's shoulders. There was a main street, called the Middle, and two side streets that crossed it called the Span and the Yard. On top of that, there was a score of little paths that led to this door or that, all laid with small stones trod down until they was even. None of the houses was built within fifty strides of the fence. That was Rampart law, and never broke.

I'm Koli, like I already said. Koli Woodsmith first, then Koli Waiting, Koli Rampart, Koli Faceless. What I am now don't really have a name to it, so just Koli. My mother was Jemiu Woodsmith, that was Bassaw's daughter and had the sawmill over by Old Big-Hand stream. I was raised up to that work, trained by Jemiu how to catch wood from a live tree without getting myself killed, how to dry it out and then steep it in the poisonous soup called stop-mix until it was safe, and how to turn and trim it.

My father was a maker of locks and keys. I am dark brown of skin, like he was, not light like my mother and my sibs. I don't know what my father's name was, and I don't think my mother knowed it either, or if she did she never told me. He journeyed all the way from Half-Ax to put new locks on the doors of Rampart Hold, and he billeted for the night in my mother's mill. Two things come of that night. One of them was a brand-new lock on our workshop door that would stand against the end of the world. The other one was me. And there's at least one of the two my mother never had no cause to regret.

So my mother and my father had just the one night of sweetness together, and then he went back home. Half-Ax being so far

4

away, the news of what he had left behind him probably never got there. Or if it did, it didn't prompt him to return. I come along nine months after that, dropping out of Jemiu's belly into a big, loud, quarrelsome family and a house where sawdust settled on everything. The sound of the saw turning was my nursery song, you could say, and my alarum too. The fresh-cut wood was stacked in the yard outside the house so it could dry, and the stacks was so high they shut out the sun at noon-day. We wasn't allowed to go near the piles of fresh wood, or the wood that was steeping in the killing shed: the first could strike you down and the second could poison you. Rampart law said you couldn't build nothing out of wood unless the planks had steeped in stop-mix for a month and was dead for sure. Last thing you wanted was for the walls of your house to wake up and get to being alive again, which green wood always will.

My mother had herself five children that lived to be born, a thing she managed without ever being married. I heard her say once that though many a man was worth a tumble, there wasn't one in a hundred was worth living with. I think it was mostly her pride, though, that got in the way of her marrying. She never liked much to pull her elbows in, or bow to another's will. She was a fierce woman in all ways: fierce hard that she showed on the outside; fierce loving underneath that she mostly hid.

Well, the mill did well enough but it was not a Summer-dance and there was times when Jemiu was somewhat pressed to keep us fed. We got by though, one way and another, all six of us bumping and arguing our way along. Seven of us, sometimes, for Jemiu had a brother, Bax, who lived with us a while. I just barely remember him. When I was maybe three or four Summers old, he was tasked by the Ramparts to take a message to Half-Ax. He never come back, and after that nobody tried again to reopen that road.

Then my oldest sister Leten left us too. She was married to three women of Todmort who was smiths and cutlers. We didn't get to see her very much after that, Todmort being six miles distant from Mythen Rood even if you walk it straight, but I hoped she was happy and I knowed for sure she was loved.

And the last to leave was my brother Jud. He went out on a hunting trip before he was even old enough to go Waiting, which he done by slipping in among the hunters with his head down, pretending like he belonged. Our mother had no idea he was gone. The party was took in the deep woods – ambushed and over-whelmed by shunned men who either would of et them or else made shunned men out of them. We got to know of it because one woman run away, in spite of getting three arrows in her, and made it back to the village gates alive. That was Alice, who they called Scar Alice after. They was not referring to the scars left by the arrows.

So after that there was only me, my sisters Athen and Mull, and our mother. I missed Leten and Jud very much, especially Jud because I didn't know if he was still alive and in the world. He had been gentle and kind, and sung to me on nights when we went hungry to take my mind away from it. To think of him being et or eating other people made me cry sometimes at night. Mother never cried. She did look sad a while, but all she said was one less mouth to feed. And we did eat a little better after Jud was gone, which in some ways made his being gone worse, at least for me.

I growed up a mite wild, it's got to be said. Jud used to temper me somewhat, but after he was gone there wasn't nobody else to take up that particular job. Certainly my mother didn't have no time or mind for it. She loved us, but it was all she could do to keep the saw turning and kill the wood she cut. She didn't catch all the wood herself, of course. There was four catchers who went out for her from November all the way through to March, or even into Abril if the clouds stayed thick. This was not a share-work ordered by the Ramparts, but an agreement the five of them made among themselves. The catchers was paid in finished cords, one for every day's work, and Jemiu paid them whether the day's catch was good or bad. It was the right thing to do, since they couldn't tell from looking which wood was safe and which was not, but if the catch was bad, that was a little more of our wood gone and nothing to show for it.

Anyway, Jemiu was kept busy with that. And my growed-up sisters Athen and Mull helped her with it – Athen with good grace; Mull with a sullen scowl and a rebel heart. I was supposed to do everything else that had got to be done, which is to say the cooking and the cleaning, fetching water and tending the vegetables in our little glasshouse. And I did do those things, for love and for fear of Jemiu's blame, which was a harder hurt than her forbearing hand.

But there was time, around those things, to just be a child and do the exciting, stupid, wilful things children are bound to do. My best friends was Haijon Vennastin, whose mother was Rampart Fire, and Molo Tanhide's daughter that we all called Spinner though her given name was Demar. The three of us run all over Mythen Rood and up the hills as far as we could go. Sometimes we even went into the half-outside, which was the place between the fence and the ring of hidden pits we called the stake-blind.

It wasn't always just the three of us. Sometimes Veso Shepherd run with us, or Haijon's sister Lari and his cousin Mardew, or Gilly's Ban, or some of the Frostfend Farm boys that was deaf and dumb like their whole family and was all just called Frostfend, for they made their given names with movements of their hands. We was a posse of variable size, though we seemed always to make the same amount of noise and trouble whether we was few or many.

We was chased away by growers in the greensheds, shepherds on the forward slope, guards on the lookout and wakers at the edge of the wold. We treated all those places as our own, in spite of scoldings, and if worse than scoldings come we took that too. Nobody cut us no slack rope on account of Haijon's family, or Demar's being maimed.

You would think that Haijon, being who he was and born to who he was, might have put some swagger on himself, but he never done it. He had other reasons for swaggering, besides. He was the strongest for his age I ever seen. One time Veso Shepherd started up a row with him – over the stone game, I think it was, and whether he moved such-and-such a piece when he said he didn't – and the row become a fight. I don't know how I got into it, but somehow I did. It was Veso and me both piling onto Haijon, and him giving it back as good as he got, until we was all three of us bloodied. Nobody won, as such, but Haijon held his own against the two of us. And the first thing he said, when we was too out of breath and too sore to fight any more, was "Are we going to finish this game, or what?"

My boast was I was fastest out of all of us, but even there Haijon took some beating. One of the things we used to do, right up until we went Waiting and even once or twice after, was to run a race all round the village walls, starting at the gate. Most times I won, by a step or a straw as they say, but sometimes not. And if I won, Haijon always held up my hand and shouted, "The champion!" He never was angry or hurt to lose, as many would of been.

But of course, you might say, there was a bigger race where his coming first was mostly just assumed. For Haijon was Vennastin.

And Vennastins was Ramparts.

And Ramparts, as you may or may not know, was synced.

That's what the name signified, give or take. If you was made a Rampart, it was because the old tech waked when you touched it. Ramparts got to live in Rampart Hold and to miss their turn on most of the share-works that was going on. But we relied on them and their tech for defending ourselves against the world, so it seemed like that was a fair thing. Besides, everyone got a chance to try out for Rampart, didn't they? Somehow, though, it was always Vennastins the old tech waked for and answered to. Except for one time, which I'll tell you of in its place. But the next thing I'll tell is how Demar come to be Spinner.

3

From when I was ten Summers old to when I was twelve, Lari Vennastin had a needle that she kept as a pet. She fed it on stoneberries and rats taken out of traps. She even give it a name, which was Lightning. She shouldn't of been let to do it, and certainly nobody else would of been, but Ramparts made the law in Mythen Rood or in this case kind of forgot to.

The needle was only a kitten when Lari found it, and crippled besides. Something had bitten it and took off most of its foreleg. Then the same something must of spit it out or flung it away, so it fell inside the fence. You might of thought it had fell out of a tree except of course that was all cleared ground up there by the fence and any trees that tried to root in would of been burned.

The needle was just lying there, not moving at all except that you could see its chest going up and down as it breathed. Haijon lifted up his boot to tread on it, but Lari called out to him to let it be. She carried it home and tended to it, and somehow it lived. And it kept right on living, though there was plenty of arguments in the Count and Seal to put it down. Ramparts was hard to argue against, and Lari was the sweet and savour of her mother's life.

Anyway, after a while we got so used to having that needle around that we kind of forgot what it was. Maybe it was on account of Lightning having only the three legs, and hopping around in a funny-looking way. But it also had, like all its kind do, a mouth with rings of teeth that pointed backwards and inwards and a jaw that hooked and unhooked like a ratchet so when it hunted it could eat whatever it catched. Maybe we figured if Lightning ever turned mean we'd be able to outrun it. Only that's not how it happened.

One day a gang of us was playing bolt-the-door on the gather-ground. We was running around like we was crazy people, and Lightning was running with us, getting more and more excited. Demar made a run from one end of the ground to the other, dodging round three or four that tried to catch her. When she got to the mark, she jumped up high and waved her arms around, yelling free-come. And we all come, laughing and cheering her.

Then suddenly Lari's needle was on the end of Demar's arm. It just jumped up, gaped its mouth wider than a water bucket and closed it again around Demar's wrist.

We didn't know what to do. Some of us was screaming and crying out, standing there like we was frozen. Demar didn't make a sound, though her teeth was clenched tight. Her legs give way under her and she went down slowly onto her knees. Her face was white as choker-blossom.

Haijon and me come running, from the two sides of her. But when I got there, I didn't have nothing I could do. I just kneeled down next to Demar and grabbed a hold of her other hand, gripping it tight, like I could draw some of her pain from out of her by touching her.

"Your father," Haijon said to her. "Your father's knives." He said it like the words was being squeezed out of him. Like the needle was biting on him too, and words was spurting up out of him the way blood comes out of a wound. I seen right away that it was a good thought, but it needed more than just the thinking; it needed us to take her, fast. And out of the two of us, he was the stronger.

"Lift her up," I said. "I'll take Lightning."

Demar seen what we was thinking to do, and she give herself

up to it. When Haijon scooped her up in his arms, she let herself go all soft and limp. I grabbed the needle, holding it gentle as a baby though right then I hated it like the dead god's hell.

We run together across the gather-ground and down the hill to Molo Tanhide's drying shed, which was where he would surely be on a day as hot as that one was. And I suppose he heard the shouts and screams because he come out to meet us, stepping out of the dark heat of the shed with his face red and his hand wiping across his brow.

He took it all in, right in that moment – the needle hanging off of Demar's arm, and us carrying her. Demar was his onliest child, and he brung her up all on his own after his wife, Casra, died. She was everything in his life that mattered. He stepped back inside for about a half of a heartbeat and come out again with a knife in his hand. It was his finest knife, ground so fine you couldn't hardly see the blade edge-on.

We laid Demar down in front of him, and he went to work. Haijon held her, and I held Lightning, as hard and fast as we could.

Knives and wild beasts was Molo's study. He knowed to slice down through the needle's throat and then work in a circle, too fast for it to shift its grip or bite down harder. He peeled it off Demar's right hand like a glove, and he done it near perfect.

But near's as much as saying not. He took Demar's first finger, her pointing finger, with it.

He dumped the dead needle, inside out, on the steps of Rampart Hold, like he was giving back to the Ramparts what was theirs. Lari come out to fetch it. She was rocking the dead beast like a baby in her arms, and crying like a baby herself, and cursing Molo for a lawless and a shunned man and Dandrake knows what else. But Catrin Vennastin, that was Rampart Fire, had the sense to see what was what. She dragged the bloody thing out of her daughter's arms and flung it back down on the ground. "Should of drowned it when she brung it in," she muttered. And to Molo Tanhide she said, "Bring your daughter inside, and I'll sew her up."

"Thank you, Dam Catrin," Molo says, "but I'll sew her my own self." And he did, careful enough that you could barely see the scar.

Only a little pucker where the missing finger used to be. The rest of Demar's hand healed up well enough, though it had a kind of a stippled look to it, like sacking-cloth, where all them thin, sharp teeth had bit into her.

A year passed, without any apology or make-right to the Tanhides from Rampart Hold, nor no public check for Lari. Then one day when we was out playing we passed a little stoneberry bush that had rooted inside the fence and not been burned out yet. "Them berries is all but ripe," Lari says. "Lightning would of et the lot of them." Then she gives Demar a look, and says, "If your daddy hadn't of killed him."

Demar only shrugged her shoulders, but Haijon was red-faced. "Her daddy done what had got to be done," he told his sister, looking as solemn-stern as their mother in that moment.

"He could of cut her hand off," Lari said, "and left Lightning alive. A maimed hand's not good for nothing anyway."

Lari was knowed to be mean from time to time, but it was probably being checked by Haijon in front of all of us that made her so stupid mean that day. Haijon took a step towards her, like he was going to hit her, but Demar got in first. She drawed back her right hand, the one with just the three fingers on it, and she smacked Lari Vennastin in the head so hard that Lari spun round before she fell down.

"Well now," she says. "It seems like a maimed hand is still good for one thing, Lari. It's good for to play spinning top."

After that, we called Demar Spinner. And she liked the name, and took it to herself, though her father's name being Tanhide chimed kind of strange with it. "I won't have that name for long," she said, when Veso Shepherd tried to make a joke out of it. "I'll be Spinner Waiting soon enough."

For our fourteenth year was upon us. It was almost time for us to be who we was going to be. Which I'll tell right soon, I promise, after only one more stepping sideways to talk about how we lived. It was a long time ago after all, and you might not have the sense of it.

4

Everything that lives hates us, it sometimes seems. Or at least they come after us like they hate us. Things we want to eat fight back, hard as they can, and oftentimes win. Things that want to eat us is thousands strong, so many of them that we only got names for the ones that live closest to us. And the trees got their own ways to hurt us, blunt or subtle according to their several natures.

There's shunned men too, that live in the deep forest and catch and kill us when they can. Nobody knowed back then who they was, whether they was just the faceless that had been throwed out of other villages or if they had got a village of their own that was hid somewhere, but they were monstrous cruel and worse than any beast.

Against these things, we of Mythen Rood, like every settlement of humankind, put up walls, hollowed out stake-blinds, set sentries, tried every way we could to pitch our own hate against the world's hate, giving back as good or bad as we got. We digged ourselves in and weathered it, for what else was there to do?

Each season brung its own terrors down on us. In Winter, the cold could freeze your fingers off if you weren't wary, and snow fell

13

on top of snow until you couldn't make your way without web-spreads or walkers. The snow was mostly just water set hard, but sometimes it had silver in it and that was dangerous. If you drunk snow-melt and didn't sieve out the silver first, it could make you sick in your stomach. Old ones and babies could even die of it.

In Spring the snow thawed, which was a mercy, but sometimes – maybe one time in four or five – it would be a choker Spring, and you would get something else coming alongside the thaw. Of all our mortal threats, I was most mightily afraid of the choker seeds, because they attacked so fast and was so hard to fight. If a seed fell on your skin, you had only got a few seconds to dig it out again before the roots went in too deep. After that there wasn't nothing anyone could do for you save to kill you right away before the seedling hollowed you out.

In Mythen Rood, our answer to that was to try to stop the seeds from falling in the first place. As soon as the warmer weather come, Rampart Fire (which in my day, like I told you, was Catrin Vennastin) would send out runners to check the choker trees for blossom. If they found any, she would strap on the firethrower and walk the forest. Rampart Remember would plot her route and ten strong spearmen would journey at her side while she burned out the blossoms before the trees could seed. The spearmen was to kill or fend off any beasts that might come, watching Catrin's back and her two sides while she played the firethrower across the branches and seared the seeds inside their pods. Against the choker trees themselves there wasn't any protecting that would avail, so Catrin and her spearmen only went out on days when the clouds was thick and heavy, and if the sun gun to show through they run as fast as they could for the clear ground.

Summer was hardest, because most things was woke and walking then. Knifestrikes flying straight down out of the sun so you couldn't see them coming, molesnakes out of the ground, rats and wild dogs and needles out of the forest. Anything that was big and come by its own lonely self was give to Fer Vennastin to deal with. Fer was Rampart Arrow. She would take the creature down with one of her smart bolts. And if it was a drone that come, dropping out of the sky and throwing out its scary warning, one of Fer's bolts would oftentimes do for that too. But she only just had the three of them, which meant someone always had to go out to bring the bolt back afterwards. We couldn't afford to lose none.

If wild dogs or rats or knifestrike swarms come, we had a different way, which was Rampart Knife. Loop Vennastin had that name when I was younger, then Mardew passed the test and it was give to him when Loop died. When a swarm attacked, Rampart Knife would stand up on the fence or the lookout and carve the beasts into pieces as they come. Then we would cook and eat the meat as long as there was no worms or melters in it. Wormed meat or melted meat we kept well clear of, for even if you digged out what you could see there was always more you couldn't.

I got to say, our fights against the rats was far between. Mostly it was hunters that seen them, a pack of ours crossing paths with a bunch of theirs in the deep woods and both going on their way, but watching each other out of sight with spears all up on our side and teeth and claws out on theirs.

Lots of people wondered how the rats could come through the forest even in the warmest weather, for it was plain they didn't fear the sun. Then one time Perliu Vennastin, Rampart Remember, talked to the database about it. The database said the rats had got something inside them that sweated out onto their skin when the sun come out and kind of stopped the choker trees from closing tight on them, or choker seeds from breaking open on them and growing down into their bodies.

I guess I don't need to tell you how wonderful a thing that would of been for us, to be able to walk through the forest without fear. Trees was our biggest problem, always, and the reason why we lived the way we did. The reason why there was a clear space inside the fence, fifty strides wide, that we burned with fire and sowed with salt. The reason why we never went out to hunt except on days when there was rain or overcast, and why the dog days of Summer meant dried meat if you was lucky, root mash

15

and hard tack if you wasn't. The reason why we seen the world as being made up out of three parts, which was the village, the little strip between the fence and the stake-blind that we called the half-outside, and everything else beyond.

Choker trees growed fast and tall, and they growed in any ground. The onliest way to keep them back was to uproot or burn out every seed that fell. If a seed landed in the ground, and no one seen it, it would be three feet high by lock-tide and taller than a man come morning.

I know it wasn't always like that. If you're going to tell a story about the world that was lost, you'll most likely start it with "In the old times, when trees was slow as treacle . . ." But our trees wasn't like that at all. Our trees was fast as a whip.

If you come across one tree by itself, that didn't matter so much. You might get a whack, but you could pick yourself up from that. If you was out in the forest though, and the clouds peeled off and the sun come through with no clearing close by, then Dandrake help you. The trees would commence to lean in on you from every side, and pretty soon there'd be no room for you to move between them. Then they'd close in all the way and crush you dead.

Rampart Remember had the knowing of this, but like all things he got out of the database, it was told partly in the old words that we couldn't figure no more. He said there was a time, long ago, when there wasn't hardly no trees at all. They had all died, because the earth wouldn't nourish them nor the rain wouldn't fall. So the men and women of that time made some trees of their own. Or, as it might be, they made the trees that was there already change their habits. Made them grow faster, for one thing. And made them take their nourishment in different ways, so they could live even in places where the soil was thin, which by that time was most places.

When the trees first took it on themselves to move, they wasn't hunting. They was just reaching for the sun, which was the most of their meat and drink. But as soon as they moved, creatures of all kinds got trapped between them and crushed. And the trees liked the taste of the dead beasts and the dead men and women.

16

They relished the nourishment them dead things brung with them. There was already plants and flowers a-plenty that had that craving, sundews and flytrappers and such. Now the trees got it too. And being changed so much already, by the hand of human kind, they took it on their own selves to change some more.

They got better at knowing where the beasts was. Better at trapping them, and killing them, and feeding on what was left. And by then the learning that had unlocked the changes in the first place was lost, so it was not easy to stop what had been started. People had got to live with it, and they have lived with it ever since.

When I heard these things for the first time, they made my head spin. It was hard to fathom that the men and women of the old times had such knowing and such power. They was lords of trees, is what they was. They could say "grow" and then "stop growing", and the trees would do as they was told, like you can make a dog or a horse do. It wasn't with words that they done it, Rampart Remember said. They done it with things called genetic triggers. Nobody in Mythen Rood knowed what them things was, but most agreed they could of been put to less reckless use.

But I have gone a long way about to get to my point, which is that the story the database told about the rats, and how their sweat stayed on their skins and stopped the trees from coming too close, was big news to us. When Rampart Remember told it in the Count and Seal, there was a plan put together and voted on to make cloaks out of dead rats' skins so hunters could go into the forest even on sunny days. It got so far as Molo Tanhide making one of these cloaks with skins some hunters took after a fight. But he refused flat-out to put it on and try it.

So Catrin asked for volunteers, offering double rations for a month, then for two months and in the end for three. Ulli Trethor, as was crippled and on lowest share, put up his hand at last and said he would go, but Catrin changed her mind then. I think she seen how it would look if Ulli died, and she didn't want to have no part in it after all.

For a while after that we had trouble with the rats. They knowed we killed some of theirs, and would attack our hunters in the woods every time they seen them. Nobody died, that I remember, but men and women would come back with rat bites on their arms or shoulders, or their legs gashed with rat claws. It got so fresh meat was scarce for a year or more until Catrin bought peace at last with a gift of cured hides and glasshouse onions.

Summer was like a siege, it sometimes seemed. Hunting was hardest then, and shunned men was hungriest and most desperate. The fences made a difference, and so did the stake-blind, and Ramparts made the biggest difference of all, but whenever you was outside your house you felt like something was about to jump on you and bear you down or bear you away. And if you went outside the gates, then Dandrake watch your back.

So it was in the days of best weather that we stayed inside the most. Sometimes we played in what was called the broken house, which was a ruin on the south side of the village right up by the wall. There was lots of houses left empty in the village, which I think was because we was fewer than we used to be, but the broken house was the biggest, having been a worship place either for the dead god or more likely for Dandrake. It was tall enough that it could of been used as another lookout, except that the floors was somewhat fallen in and it didn't look out on nothing except the side of a hill. The walls was part-way broke and tumble-down, which meant they was good for climbing. We would scramble up them, turn and turn about, and scratch lines on the stone to show how far we got.

Or we would sneak into the Underhold sometimes, which was as inside as you could get. There was a little window round the back of Rampart Hold that was loose in its frame, so you could lift the whole thing out and slip inside, if you was small enough. I think Dam Catrin and them knowed it was there, but they never minded enough to fix it. There was never any prisoners stowed down there, though there was places for them, and the stores was locked away in rooms we couldn't get to apart from a big bushel of apricots that had been soaked and baked and set out to dry for Winter. We run through the tunnels and corridors and played hide and go seek or blind man's touch for hours and hours.

One time when we was playing in the Underhold, I hid somewhere I wasn't supposed to. There was a door that was really two doors, one set right behind the other. The outside one was just bolted shut but the inside one had a lock plate on it the size of a man's head. I unbolted the outside door, slipped inside and drawed it closed again.

Haijon was really mad when he finally found me. "If my ma seen you there, she'd smack you till your head rang," he said. "And we'd none of us get to play down here no more."

"Why's that then?" Spinner asked. "Is there something bad behind that door?"

Haijon shrugged, trying to turn it. "There's nothing special," he said. "It's more stores, is all. Honey and curd, and dry biscuit. But she'd think we was trying to raid the larder."

Spinner looked at me and rolled her eyes. Haijon was never a good liar, especially when it was about something that mattered. I think we both knowed what was in that storeroom, though we never spoke about it. And I knowed one thing more – a secret thing, that I seen when I looked at the second, inside door. But something made me keep that secret to myself, thinking there might be trouble if I spoke it loud. In the end the trouble come anyway, but that telling will have to wait for now.

Oftentimes I come home late from these games. Jemiu would be all in a rage with me then, and we would argue, her saying I should stay home and do the work that had got to be done, me saying I was close enough to Waiting, and thence to man, that I could do as I liked. I should of knowed better. Jemiu's rage wasn't because I was slacking; it was because when I stayed out so long she didn't know but what something bad might have fallen on me. She always showed her love in a hard way, like I said.

And then the days drawed in at last and Summer ended. Falling Time was a time for rebuilding the fences, catching wood for building and laying in as much food as we could against the lean days to come. We marked the end of Summer with the Summer-dance, and the end of Falling Time with the Salt Feast. Both of them days was greatly looked forward to.

So that was our life, and it seemed like nothing would ever happen to change it. But it's when you think such thoughts that change is most like to come. You let your guard down, almost, and life comes running at you on your blind side. Because life is nothing but change, even when it seems to stand still. Standing still is a human thing, like a defiance we throw, but we can never do it for long.

5

I got to be fifteen at last, which is a time in a boy or girl's life when everything changes. In Mythen Rood it worked like this: from your fifteenth year-day to the next Midsummer, you lost your family name and took the name of Waiting in place of it. Until that time was passed, you left your family and went to live in the Waiting House, which was to the setting side of the gather-ground, right next door to Rampart Hold. I guess it was put there to say that any of them that went Waiting might be Ramparts themselves after they took the test.

The Waiting House was enormous. There was twelve beds in the boys' sleep room and twelve more for girls. Maybe if I had thought about that I might of come to some conclusions about how many people there used to be in Mythen Rood in times past and how few was left now. But a boy of fifteen Summers doesn't have no sense that what's passed has got a bearing on what's still here. For me, that thinking come later, in a very different place, and it didn't come for free.

In my year, anyway, there was just the three of us. Veso Shepherd would of been the fourth, but because he wouldn't agree to go Waiting under the girl's name his mother put on him, Rampart law said he couldn't go. Veso said he was happy for it. Rampart law at least let him stay what he was, though it didn't seem to allow him much respect. His mother was somewhat crueller, being a believer in Dandrake's hard lessons.

Anyway, Haijon went Waiting first, and he had the house to himself. By the time I come along in Abril and Spinner in May, he had changed the place around to his liking. There was a stone-game board drawed out across the floor of the boys' sleep room, and pictures of eagles and tree-cats on the walls. Haijon drawed in chalk that someone – I think it was his aunt Fer – had brung back from a hunt. Drawing was another thing he was good at. Seeing the size of him, and the size of his hands in particular, you wouldn't of thought he could have such a skill. He just had the one colour of chalk, which was white, but he made it look different by drawing the lines various ways, so you got the sense of an eagle's feathers or a tree-cat's fur.

"Thank Dandrake you come," he says to me the day I walked into the house with my bedroll under my arm. "I was like to die from the boredom." But he said it with a grin on his face. The first thing he done – after we give each other our secret sign, which was the thumb of one hand hooked into the thumb of the other hand – was to show me everything in the house from top to bottom like it was a big adventure we was sharing, which I guess is how I seen it too.

Jemiu had not been so happy to see me go. She held me hard and told me to take good care of myself and do as I was bid. There was tears in her voice. I remembered how she never cried for Jud when the shunned men took him, but she almost cried for me when I went Waiting, even though I was the fourth of her children to go (and should of been the fifth, only Jud didn't live long enough).

"I just got a fear on me," she said. "A bad thought. I hate to let you go, Koli, and that's the truth of it." She give me some nuts and an apple wrapped in an oil-leaf, and kissed me on my cheek. It was the only time she ever kissed me that I can remember. It made me want to cry too, though being growed to Waiting age I would of been ashamed.

My sisters, Athen and Mull, took turns to hug me and wish me luck. Athen said it was nothing and would be over soon, which of course it had been for her, but at the back of everyone's mind was: what if I was a Rampart, not a Woodsmith, and never come home at all? And I'm shamed to say that thought excited me. I seen myself in my mind's eye with old tech in my hand, standing on the outside fence with shunned men lying dead around my feet. And I seen Spinner watching me, her eyes all bright with love she was too shy to speak. She was the furnishing of a lot of my thoughts back then. I was a boy of fifteen after all.

So I said goodbye, with something of sadness and something of hunger, and walked to the Waiting House. It was no more than five hundred steps but it felt like I was going into another world. In a way I was, for younger children never got to set foot inside the house. It was a thing forbid.

I hadn't never seen anything like the inside of the Waiting House. I had been in Rampart Hold for public meetings – in the Count and Seal, I mean, not in the residence – and the Waiting House was not so big as that. But then we was only two boys, not a whole village, and for two boys to have such a space all to themselves was a new and wonderful thing. It must of been strange even for Haijon, who lived in Rampart Hold. For me, it was like a dream that stayed with me even when I was awake.

We was spared from all share-works, and our food – the same meals as was served to the Ramparts – was brung to us at sunrise and lock-tide. We didn't have nothing to do but play games, make up songs and stories and run mad through the place. Mostly we played the stone game, of course, but sometimes also we would do make-believe stuff. We pretended the house was a wilderness we was exploring, or we played forest-wake, where all the chairs and tables was trees and if we touched them they would wake and whelm us. It was a good time, and I remember it with wonder now. It's hard to credit how little I thought about things back then.

About the test I was going to face, and what it might mean. About Haijon, and who he was besides being my friend. About the Ramparts, and what their expectations might be for their son. Must be, I should say.

And though I said we was alone, there wasn't no rule forbidding family visits – except for little ones, who wasn't allowed to set foot in the Waiting House until they went Waiting themselves. My mother was mostly too busy with her work, but she come once or twice a week and she brung me news of the village. She brung me presents too: raspberry curd that she laid down the year before and only just opened, and a whistle that she carved out of cherry wood. Athen and Mull come too, as often as they could, but they never stayed for long. I think the Waiting House brung back too many memories for them.

Then Spinner went Waiting, and we didn't have the house to ourselves no more. For as soon as there was boys and girls together, of course there had got to be someone set to watch us. So on the day Spinner walked in through the door, Shirew Makewell come to live in what was called the turn-key room, just inside the door of the Waiting House. She trusted us though, and besides she was oftentimes busy with work that mattered more than making us behave, so we was still left alone together a lot of the time. Nor our pastimes didn't change much, Spinner being as much for games and songs and stories as either of us. More, maybe.

She had a knack for music too, and she showed me how to play the whistle my mother give to me. How to hold it, and coax the notes from it, and how to cut or strike the sound with a little shift of my fingers. When I had picked it up before, I only just blowed on it and set it down again, but Spinner teached me to draw tunes out of it, which was an amazing thing to me.

I think that time, when she was teaching me, was when I first come to love her. What she done with Lari after she lost her finger had made me admire her something keen, and besides that the shape of her face and her body's gracefulness had made their way long before from my eye to my inside longings. But that's not love,

24

though it's sometimes mistaken for it. Living with Spinner so close, for so long, I got to see who she was, and I liked what I seen more than I could ever tell you.

Most of all I liked to hear her tell stories. These weren't stories like Rampart Remember told in the Count and Seal, but things she made in her own head, all crazy and without a shape. They had monsters in them, and places and things from the old times, and her and me and Haijon as the heroes of them. Oftentimes they started with us getting out of the village somehow to rescue a child as had gone missing or it might be to explore or to find something that was lost. One time she told about how we went to Half-Ax and found my brother Jud living there. Another time it was her father, Molo, as had been pinned by a choker tree and couldn't get home. Then there was one where we went and crossed the Fathom and the Curtain, and got took by the wizard Stannabanna, the lord of all shunned men and faceless, that lived under the ground of Skullfield and only come up to waylay travellers and eat their eyes and tongues. The odds was always fearful and we come close to losing every time, but at the last moment we would always make it good by some trick or other.

And sometimes she told tales of London, and of London's heroes, that was the Parley Men. They was the guards that was set on the treasure house of London, the Palace Westernmost, where the riches of the king was piled high. Them riches included a great store of tech, and they was never broke into because the Parley Men was the fiercest fighters you ever seen. Their ghosts guard the treasure still, and they'll kill any that come to take it.

When Spinner was telling, Haijon and me would listen without a word. Sometimes Shirew Makewell would walk by the door and hear her, and linger to see how the tale come out. When the story was done, the two of us boys would whoop and slap the floor to show we liked it. Shirew didn't go in for that kind of display, but oftentimes she nodded and once she said bravo. That means a good story in a language of the old times.

I think Spinner liked me too. Well, I knowed she did, but I was far from knowing if it was as much as I liked her. Certainly I didn't dream of telling her I loved her. I thought of telling Haijon, since I told him everything else that went through my head, but whenever I was close to saying it, I held back somehow. It was a secret thing that I folded down into my heart and kept a watch on. And like the secret about the door in Rampart Hold, it had a big bearing on how my life went.

Anyway, the time went by fast and soon it was time for our testing. It's not likely you'll remember what that was, or what it meant, so I will say it straight.

It meant your name and your fate, for the rest of your life.

6

We had an abundance of old tech in Mythen Rood, but most of it wouldn't wake or work for us. The few things that did work we took good care of, seeing they made such a difference to whether we lived or died.

There was the firethrower. This was a thing like a musical instrument that you held in both your hands, only instead of making music it made a kind of long rope of fire that crawled through the air like a snake. The fire-snake burned whatever it touched, and clung to it so it would keep on burning for the longest time. You couldn't even put the flames out with water, though you could smother them with earth if you had enough of it to hand. The heat of the flames was so great you could feel it from a hundred paces off.

Whoever held the firethrower was Rampart Fire.

There was the bolt gun. This was like the firethrower only a lot smaller, and you just held it in one hand, not two. The way of it was a lot harder to figure, at least for them as was watching from far off. The bolt gun fired bolts that was like little stubby arrows of shiny metal, with no fletches to them. Somehow you was able to tell the gun before you fired it which thing the bolt should kill, and the bolt went to that thing and killed it. There wasn't no question of missing your shot, nor of wounding. The thing that got struck by the bolt was dead, sure enough. But if the thing run away between you telling the gun and firing it, the bolt would fly on after them until it hit. Then you had got to chase it down and find it, for otherwise the bolt would be lost, and the bolts was too precious to lose. We only had but the three of them.

Whoever held the bolt gun was Rampart Arrow.

There was the cutter. In my thinking this was the most fearsome weapon of the three. It wasn't like a knife at all, though it seemed to work a little bit like one, as though it had a knife in its family somewhere and had learned the way of it. To look at, though, it was a glove you put on your hand, with a flat bar across the knuckles. The bar was dull metal when you put the glove on, but it commenced to shine soon after, and once it was shining you could use it. You pointed at the thing you wanted to cut, and it got cut. It might be small like a bug or a knifestrike or big like a young tree. Either way, it got cut right through. The only thing you could see when this was happening was a kind of a ripple in the air, like the ripples you get in water when you drop a stone in. The ripple went from the glove all the way to the thing that was cut, and sometimes a good way beyond it.

Whoever held the cutter was Rampart Knife.

Last of all there was the database. This was a little thing like a stick, black and very shiny. It didn't look like nothing at all, but there was something inside it that was alive and knowed a lot of stuff. You could ask it questions and it would answer you, though oftentimes it used ancient words that no one knowed the meaning of.

Whoever held the database was Rampart Remember.

It was just them four, but there could be more than four Ramparts at a time. The old tech either knowed you or it didn't, and that was all there was to it. If it knowed you, and would answer to you, then you was said to be synced and you went to live in Rampart Hold. At the time I'm telling of, all our Ramparts was Vennastins except for Gendel, that was Fer Vennastin's husband and had the family name of Stepjack. Gendel was synced to the bolt gun, but Fer was Rampart Arrow for she tested before him – just like Haijon's cousin Mardew didn't get to be Rampart Knife until Loop Vennastin, that was Perliu's brother and Fer and Catrin's uncle, died.

If you're thinking it's strange that being a Vennastin and being synced with the tech should chime together so much, well, you would not be the onliest one. It was a thing that was oftentimes thought and sometimes said out loud. But no, Perliu said, it was not strange at all. The database told of times when there was other Ramparts. He said most of the families in the village had been Ramparts at one time or another, some of them using tech we didn't even have now on account of it got lost, or using the tech that don't wake no more for anyone. Those things all got names, so they must of worked at least once. They was called things like the light-and-dark, the wise doctor, the farsight, the swallow, the music, the mask, the signal. But nobody in Mythen Rood knowed what it was they used to do.

And back in the world that was lost, Perliu said, everyone was synced. Tech was wherever you went, in everyone's houses or in their stow-sacks or even just out on the street. People was like trees in them days, taller than anything and striding over the world. They was so big and so strong, nothing could of brung them down excepting only their own selves, which was what done it in the end. Either that or the dead god or Dandrake struck them down for sinfulness, if you got faith in things of that kind.

So it was just hap and stance that all our Ramparts was Vennastins, Perliu said. It was different once, and would be again. In the meantime, he said, we had got to be thankful there was Ramparts at all, given how bad a thing it would be if there wasn't none. Everyone got a try at waking the tech, and there wasn't nobody had a better chance than anyone else. The testing was right in front of everyone and we all could see it was fair.

That much was true. What was also true, though Perliu didn't say it, was this: Vennastins had got all the power in their hands, so why would you want them to be riled with you? Better to keep your head down, when all was said. Better to let things roll on in the direction they was going, since if you got in their way they was like to roll on anyway and leave you broke behind.

7

The testing was done in the Count and Seal, in Rampart Hold. At least, that was how it was in my year. When I was younger, I remember it happening outside, on the gather-ground. But then there was a time when a big horn-headed thing, one of the unlisted, got inside the fence and run into the crowd. Rampart Arrow brung the beast down before it killed anyone, but Deeley Pureheart got gored and two other people was hurt fending it off of him. Afterwards everyone said it was foolish for the whole village to meet out in the open, and we moved the testing indoors. We didn't stop holding the Summer-dance or the Salt Feast though. There would of been great unrest if anyone had said to do that.

When testing day come, Haijon and me waked up to find our white testing shirts laid out beside our bunks. We put them on and went into the kitchen, where Spinner was already sitting down in her own white shirt, eating a plate of pancakes and honey piled up higher than I ever seen. There was twice as many left on the platter, along with bread and warm milk and duck eggs and slices of pink-white meat, hot and steaming off the stove-top.

"I started without you, sleepyheads," Spinner said, through a mouthful of something. "You gonna have to race to catch up."

"No need to race," Shirew Makewell said. She was at the stove, frying up more meat. "You can have anything you want, and as much as you want. This is your day, remember."

"Well then," Haijon said, sitting down. "I think I'm gonna have some of everything, Shirew. Starting with this bread, which smells like it's got spike-seed in it." I sat down too. Haijon had took the seat next to Spinner, so I was opposite. That was okay though. It meant I got to look at her face while I was eating.

The bread did have spike-seed in it, and it tasted so good it kind of made you sigh through your nose when it was in your mouth. The meat was good too. I was thinking it would be chicken but it was pig. Pig was a Salt Feast thing, for at Salt Feast they cooked a whole pig in the firepit and everyone got to eat as much of it as they could hold. So the taste of pig was a holiday taste to me in any case, but somehow this was even better. The meat had been sweetened, kind of, in some way I never knowed before.

"Did you taste this?" I asked Haijon. "It's god-food."

"It's just bacon," Haijon said. "Spinner, did you get one of these eggs? You can dip your bread in it, look."

He showed her how to do it and she copied him, the two of them laughing when she spilled the yolk on her fingers and licked it up so as not to waste it. "You can be Rampart Breakfast," Spinner said to Haijon, "since you know so much about it." Then she said eggs used to be all white inside until the people of the old times used their tech to put gold inside them. "See, that's why you Vennastins always pass the test. You eat eggs every day, and all that metal builds up inside you. The tech's just recognising its own self."

Haijon bridled a little. It was a joke that kind of had an edge to it. Leastways, it pricked him a little. "We don't always pass," he said. "My uncle Vergil didn't." Which was true. Vergil had lost an arm to a choker seed just before his fifteenth year-day. He was as close to dying as a word is to a whisper, and couldn't go into the Waiting House. The next year, being on his feet again and supposed to be well, he went Waiting and was tested, but nobody thought he could be a Rampart. He was like the ghost of himself, pale-faced and solemn-quiet and almost not there at all. When he failed his test, people was sorry for him but also mostly relieved. Ramparts is meant to be strong, and that terrible wound had washed Vergil halfway out of the world. He didn't have no strength that anyone could get a glimpse of.

But he was the onliest Vennastin to fail the test. And though Perliu said other folks had been Ramparts, as far back as anyone could figure it was Vennastins and more Vennastins and occasionally their wedded kindred. Like I said already, Spinner was not the onliest one by any means to wonder why that might be.

"So that's one against all the rest," she said now. "I'd still put odds on you to pass, Jon, if anyone would fade the wager. I'm gonna watch what you do and see if there's a trick to it."

"There's no trick," Haijon says, mightily put out now. "Why would you say that?"

"There's always a trick," Spinner says to him. "Look at this."

She lifted up her knife and passed her hand over it a few times with the fingers all spread out. "Idowak, bidowak," she says in a really low voice like as it was a man speaking. "Ansum, bansum." She brung the knife down so it touched her fork, then when she lifted it up again the fork was stuck to it. Not stuck like glue, because it slid a little as she moved the knife this way and that way, but it didn't drop.

Haijon and me was sitting there with our mouths wide open, like two jump-frocks. Shirew turned round and seen it too, and she near to dropped the pan and all the bacon in it, which would of been a shame.

"How you doing that?" I says to Spinner.

"I got magic in my hands," she tells us. "Didn't you know?" She was putting a grave face on, but she couldn't keep it up no more and a laugh burst out of her. "It's not old tech or nothing. It's just a thing metal does, sometimes, if you stroke it or smack it against other metal. My father showed me. It happens to his knives when he strops them. For a while after he's finished, if he puts them down close together they find each other and latch on. Not every time, but oftentimes."

She put her hand on Haijon's arm. "I'm sorry I said the testing was a trick," she said. "That's near to saying your family is dishonest, which I didn't mean and wouldn't ever think."

It was a sweet apology, and furthermore I seen now how Spinner did the thing with the knife and the fork to turn Haijon's thoughts away from the hurt she done him. I admired her cleverness in that, which was not a sly cleverness but a thoughtful and a gentle one. That Spinner could be gentle or fierce by turns whenever there was need for one or for the other was part of who she was, and part of why I loved her.

Haijon said he knowed she never meant it, and went back to eating.

"And I'm gonna be soulful sorry," Spinner went on, "when I go to live in Rampart Hold and they throw you out for failing your test."

She timed it just right. Haijon had his mouth full of bread and bacon and he spluttered it all over the table in laughing. That made the two of us laugh like fools too, and even Shirew, though she said we was ungovernable and that Haijon was going to have to clean the table when we was done even if it meant going late to the Count and Seal.

She was only joking, of course. Nobody ever come late to their testing, or left it early. It was fixed like a star in the sky, if anything that's only human could be said to be like that.

8

The Count and Seal was a room that didn't have no corners to it. It was shaped like a circle. If that sounds strange, it's because you're imagining the Hold to be a wooden house with beams and timbers. That's my fault, for I never said no different.

Rampart Hold wasn't made out of wood; it was made out of stone. It was one of three buildings from the old times that was still standing in Mythen Rood, the other two being the lookout and the broken house. Rampart Hold stood three floors above the ground, and went down a considerable way under it. Its walls was grey, and grey slates made up the roof, that was long enough to fit four chimneys all in a line. You could tell it was a house from the old times because of all the windows it had, letting light into every room. Perliu said it was called the Little Stub once, which you might think was said as a joke because it's so much bigger than any other house in the village. But I been to Birmagen and London and Baron Furnace, and I seen how big we used to build before we lost the knowing of it. Rampart Hold wouldn't of been anything much at all in the old times.

To us, though, it was as big as big could get. It looked like part of a mountain got broke off and made into a house. There was a room you went into right away when you come in the door. It was all shiny wood that had got patterns in it, squares inside squares, and it had wooden stairs like the stairs up to the lookout, except that this wood had such a high shine to it you could see your face inside it looking back at you like in a mirror.

Only Ramparts and their kindred was supposed to go up those stairs. The top part of the house was family rooms, and it was called the residence. Even Vergil lived in the residence, for though he was no Rampart he was still Perliu's son, Catrin and Fer's brother. He was still Vennastin, and this at a time when Rampart and Vennastin had almost come to be like two ways of saying the same thing.

For the rest of us, when we come into Rampart Hold we would go on past them stairs, along a long, low corridor and into the Count and Seal. It was a room in the shape of a circle, like I already said, and it was bigger than you can imagine. There was rows of seats that was in circles too, and a round window in the ceiling. It was like whoever built the room had spun himself round and round for a long time beforehand and couldn't see nothing but circles any more.

Also there was more of the shiny wood here, but with years and years of meet-days and testing days it was all scuffed and the shine wore away so you could only see it in a few places like on the edges of things or high up on the walls.

But the main thing was that the room went down as it went into the middle. I don't know how to say it better than that. The seats went higher and higher around the sides, almost up to the ceiling, but the middle dropped away so it was below where you come into the room. That kind of made it be the natural place where you looked, no matter where you was sit. Your eye was drawed to it. There was a platform there that we called the middle round. It was another place where only Ramparts got to stand, at least on meet-days. In a testing it was different, because it was where the testing got to happen.

On meet-days there wasn't no furniture in the middle round. On testing days there was three tables stood there, kind of like three sides of a square, only the sides wasn't flat but opened out a little ways. The middle table had the tech that was already woke up and working: the firethrower, the bolt gun, the cutter and the database. The other two tables had all the things, more than you could count, that was old tech but didn't never do nothing no matter who touched it.

I seen this lots of times when other people was testing. In fact I seen it fourteen times exactly, once for every Summer up to this one, only the earliest times I was too young to remember it. So I knowed what was going to happen, right down to the last, least thing. Shirew Makewell had coached us in what to say, but we had all the words solid in our heads before we ever started so she didn't waste too much time on that. Mostly she told us how to look and how to be once we was in the Count and Seal.

"There'll be more than two hundred people there, all looking at you," she says to the three of us, "but don't you be minding that. Don't you look at them at all, or think about them. They're there for you, not the other way round. When Rampart Fire speaks to you, you say your part the way you learned it and you come forward when she bids you. After that, it's all just doing what you're told to and keeping a hold on yourself after."

It was good advice, and kindly meant, but on the day of my testing it went out of my head as soon as I stepped in the room. Actually it didn't stay even that long. When we was walking along the corridor toward the big doors (there was two doors to the Count and Seal) and hearing all the people inside, my whole head emptied out like a downturned bucket. I stumbled along behind Haijon, through the doors and into the room, and I bumped into his back when he stopped.

It's the testing, I thought. This is the time. This is the test. And my legs sort of losed their strength so I all but fell down.

Haijon stepped to the side so we was all in a line like we was supposed to be. The Ramparts was in the middle round, all in a line too except that Catrin was out in front a little way. On testing day, Rampart Fire spoke for the village.

"Who is it comes into this chamber?" she asks us.

I risked a look up at the faces all around. That was just what Shirew told us not to do, and she was right. So many people! Everyone I knowed. Everyone as had ever been in my life from before I even knowed my own name right down to the here and now. I seen my mother there, and Athen and Mull to either side of her. It was like my eyes knowed how to find them, even in all that great, breathing, shifting press of life. And I got some strength from seeing them, though also a kind of dizzy strangeness as though I was there with them looking down on my own self as well as being where I was.

It was only then I realised how come I could hear everyone breathing. It was because there was stone silence in the room. I don't think I was the only one thinking Haijon would answer first, but he never done it. I looked at Spinner and Spinner looked at me. Haijon didn't look at either of us. He was standing with his head down and his hands all clenched in fists. If I had to say what he looked like, he looked like he was afraid, only I never knowed Haijon to be afraid of anything.

"It's me," Spinner says, finding her voice first. "Demar Waiting, come to be tested."

"It's me," I says, and barely got my name out. "Koli Waiting. I come to be tested."

"It's me, Haijon Waiting," Haijon says at last. "Come to be tested."

"Stand forward on your name, and come down," Rampart Fire told us. Then to the whole room she says, "These who are Waiting will be known, by your will and with your blessing." She didn't say knowed, she said known, just like she'd said chamber instead of room. It was how they said those things in the old times, and it made her words seem heavier somehow. Like they was hard, solid things and kept right on standing there in the air after she was done saying them.

There was a murmur as everyone said yes or aye or yay or I bless it, after their fashion. Some of them made the Dandrake sign of two fingers folded. I seen Jarter Shepherd, Veso's mother, make

38

it, and I seen Veso turn away like he didn't want to look at that. He had good reason.

Catrin bowed her head like she took all them ayes and yays solemn serious.

"Demar Waiting," she says. "Come to the Count and Seal."

Demar walked down into the circle and stood right dead in the middle of it, facing Catrin. She had her arms at her sides and her back was straight. She didn't seem to be shaking at all, nor she didn't look at nobody except Catrin.

"What do you see here?" Catrin asks.

Spinner give the looked-for answer. "I see the tech of the old times."

"Will it wake for you?"

"I do not know, but mean to try."

"And if it wake for you?"

"Use it for the good of all."

"Choose well."

That was all the speaking. And for the choosing, Shirew told us to decide before we come there. "You don't want to freeze when Rampart Fire invites you and make her have to say it twice. Nobody will blame you for it, but you'll look foolish in front of everyone and you'll blame yourself after."

Spinner picked up the firethrower. It was a bold choice, but lots of people done the same before her. It was the biggest of the waked tech by far, and there was something about it that drawed the eye and kept it. The sleekness of the metal was a part of it, dark green except for the grip which had an edge of shiny grey. Not silver, for it wasn't bright: it was grey metal that was as lustrous as silver. On its side there was a name in old-times writing. Nobody in Mythen Rood could read it, but Rampart Remember had learned it from the database. The word was Phoenix, with some numbers after it. It was hard to figure what the database said oftentimes, for it speaked at great length in strange words of the world that was lost, but the gist of it was that Phoenix was a place a long way away, a village bigger than

39

Mythen Rood, that got burned down lots of times but always builded itself up again afterwards.

Spinner lifted the firethrower the way you might lift a newborn baby, with one hand on the grip and the other under it, cradling the weight. The weight seemed to be less than she was expecting, for she bent her knees a little when she first picked it up, but then straightened again. Her face was lit up with the wonder of it. Everyone I ever seen take the test got that look as soon as the tech was in their hands.

"Acknowledge," Spinner said. She might of waited a while to savour that feeling, but again most of them that was tested went at once to the word. They needed to know.

The firethrower didn't say nothing.

"Accept command," Spinner said, which was the second ancient word. And still the firethrower was silent.

"New user," Spinner said. The firethrower didn't wake, and didn't answer her. Her back was to me, so I couldn't see what was in her face right then. I seen in the set of her shoulders, though, that putting the firethrower down was going to be harder and heavier than picking it up.

Catrin seen it too, and took it from her as gentle as anything. "Demar Waiting," she said. "Wait no more. Woman of Mythen Rood you are, and will be, under what name you choose."

"Spinner Tanhide," Spinner said.

"Spinner Tanhide," said everyone in the room all at the same time.

Spinner stepped off to the side a little way to make room for me, and Catrin called me in the same words she used before.

"Koli Waiting, come to the Count and Seal."

I come to her, looking at my feet the whole way in case I tripped over them. Even when I was standing right in front of her, I didn't seem able to look up.

"What do you see here?"

"I see the tech of the old times," I answered her.

"Will it wake for you?"

"I do not know, but mean to try."

40

"And if it wake for you?"

"Use it for the good of all."

"Choose well."

I had told Shirew I meant to choose the firethrower, but now that Spinner had done it I changed my mind. I picked up the bolt gun instead. The handle of it fitted to my hand so snug I wanted to laugh, almost, which there was no law said you couldn't but would of been a shocking thing and not soon forgiven. The metal felt cold like snow against my skin, though the room was warm from all the people that was in there. And it was smoother than anything I'd ever held. Like a shiny pebble dipped in water, but smoother even than that.

I lifted it up high, like as it was a lit torch at lock-tide, and me standing at the gate. I said, "Acknowledge," just as loud as I could. Then I waited.

Nothing happened, though I give it a good long time. I heard one of the seats creak, and someone made a noise in their throat like they wanted to cough but couldn't because of the seriousness of it. Rampart Fire looked at me, expectant, and after a few seconds more she nodded. Meaning I should get to it.

"Accept command," I said.

What followed was more of that same nothing. I made myself believe I could feel the gun moving, waking up, but it was only my hand getting sweaty and slipping on the grip because of the smoothness of it.

"New user," I whispered. I only just could get the words out.

I realised something then that I never knowed before, though I've proved it many times since. The world isn't nothing next to the stories we tell ourselves. It bends to any shape we want it to. I seen this moment in my thoughts a thousand times before my testing day finally come, and there wasn't one of those times where the tech didn't wake for me. I had heard Catrin hail me a Rampart, in dreams and wakeful wondering every day and every night since I first went into the Waiting House, as though she said it so loud I had heard the echoes before the words was ever said.

41

But if the world bends easy, which it does, sometimes it will whip back like a green branch and hit you in the face. That's what it done to me then, so I was left standing like a fool with no ideas in my head, not even the idea of where I was and what come next.

You might wonder at this. After all, I told you enough times already that all our Ramparts was Vennastins, save for one man, Gendel, that was closest kin to them. Who was I to think I might beget a miracle? No one, is the answer. I was the smallest speck of dust in a world that was a thousand thousand times bigger than I even knowed it was, and I didn't have no right to be treated like anything bigger than that.

But it's when we're smallest, when we're young, that we most have the thought of ourselves as mightily important. A child – any child, I think – believes he stands plum in the middle of everything, and the sun at noon-day seeks him out so it will know where the zenith is.

Or if it's not so for every child, at least it was so for me.

"Koli Waiting," Catrin Vennastin said. "Wait no more. Man of Mythen Rood you are, and will be, under what name you choose."

I was like to forget my name for a moment.

"Koli Woodsmith," I said.

"Koli Woodsmith," said everyone else, and I felt the sorrowing burden of it fall heavy across my shoulders. The burden of being nothing very much after all, and having no part to play in the larger doings of the world.

Spinner took my hand and pulled me back to take my place next to her. Otherwise I would of kept on standing there at the table, blocking Haijon's way to it. She give my hand a squeeze, for solace, no doubt seeing my sadness on my face. And it did solace me, her being one of the onliest things outside my silly dreams that was real to me right then (though in truth I built other, sillier dreams on her).

Haijon was speaking his piece. His mother was asking him to choose.

He choosed the cutter, slipping his right hand into it even though when he played the stone game he throwed with his left.

"Acknowledge," he told it.

The bar of metal that sit over his clenched fingers went from dull grey to shiny silver. The cutter made a sweet chiming noise, like a bell.

"Haijon Rampart," Catrin said, "wait no more."

Spinner was the first to cheer, but she was only a second or so ahead of the rest of the people in the room. A new Rampart was good news for everyone. The best news, because the tech was only ours as long as there was someone it would wake for, and without the tech we would not thrive.

I cheered too, for the same reason and for one more on top of that. Haijon was my friend and I was truly happy for him, even while I was still grieving on my own account.

That happiness wouldn't last though. And nor would our friendship. I hold myself to blame for both those things, though not for the worse things that come after.

9

Everything changed for me after my testing, but not on that day. That day was celebration and holiday.

After all the cheering died down, Catrin hugged her son to her and said something to him that nobody else in the room could hear. She was smiling, holding to the back of his head like a mother would hold onto a newborn baby, and the smiling and the holding told me it was his mother spoke to him then, not Rampart Fire. And what she said was not for us.

So then we went from the Count and Seal into the recepting room, where beer and food was laid out for all that had come and where everyone could welcome us – Spinner and me no less than Haijon – into the life that we would own from then on. Into being fully growed, and being counted as one instead of just a little less than one.

Jil Reedwright had brung her pipes, and Mordy Holdfast his stringer, so there was music and also dancing. What I remember most about that day – or at least, after the moment when my name got spoke – is that I danced with Spinner three times, the piping fast and wild, my hand on her waist as she galloped and swung. I had liked dancing well enough before then, but this dancing seemed to come out of my heart in all directions into my body and into the world. I forgot my sorrow at not being found to be Rampart and just enjoyed being me.

At the end of the third dance, when Spinner kissed me tender on the cheek, I had no sense of it coming. "I love you, Koli," she whispered in my ear. "You're my best of friends."

I kissed her back. She was taller than me, so I had to lean in and stretch up to do it, which made her laugh. "Should I lift you up?" she asked, teasing me. I would of been happy if she did, but I made pretend I was bigger than I was, pulling myself up onto the tips of my toes and pushing out my chest. "I'll lift you, Spinner," I said. "In one hand. And spin you over my head."

"And when your back is broke, I'll have nobody to dance with," she said, laughing that much harder.

"You'll have me," Haijon said. He come up between us and put his hand on her shoulder. "I'd only be doing it for Koli, mind. So he didn't feel so bad about letting you down."

"Such a good man," Spinner said, clasping her hands to her chest like she was marvelling at him. "Ramparts is just the best of us, and that's all there is to it."

She was teasing him like she teased me, but Haijon nodded, all serious. "Of course we are," he said. "I'll show you."

He danced her away.

He didn't dance her back again.

45

10

So Summer went on and I was stepping into my growed-up life. I had got to put my shoulder to the running of the mill now, just like Mull and Athen, and besides that take my part in all the share-works that was going on.

This being after the year's turning, the worst of the Summer's dangers was done with, but there was plenty of clearing still to be done inside the fence. There was also a pair of molesnakes that nested in one of the glasshouses and spawned before anyone saw they was there. Rampart Fire burned the litter out, but everyone in the village stood around in a ring to kill the fry as they scuttled away.

Haijon was Rampart Knife, in that share-work. It was the first time I seen him use the cutter, and he used it as well as ever his cousin Mardew did. But Mardew held out his hand straight after, and Haijon give the cutter back in view of everyone. The rules don't bend on such a thing. The tech belongs to them that wakes it, but that's in order of testing. If it waked to you first, then you get to keep it as long as you live. There isn't anyone can claim it off of you. Mardew had been training Haijon in the cutter's mysteries, and he let him handle it on this occasion to get the feel of it, but it was still his and he made sure everybody seen that.

There was a share-work rebuilding the outer lookout too. This was a building that stood on top of Cloughfoot Hill a hundred feet from the village. It was outside the fence but inside the stake-blind, which we called the half-outside. The outer lookout was different from the lookout inside the village – not so tall, but because it was up on a rise in the ground it still let you see further to the north and west than the main lookout did. We was meant to keep this area clear just like we did the ground behind the fence, but we had missed our mark a few times. Trees had grown into the wall of the lookout and they was starting to push the stones out of true. The Count and Seal decided it was time to make repair before the whole thing toppled down, but they made it a third choice – which is to say you could do it if there was nothing more urgent that had got to be done.

I put twenty days or some into that work, across July and August, hefting stones or mixing mortar as it might be needed. I liked it, mostly. Not so much at the start of the day, when the tower had a leftover stink from something that was sleeping up there, but that never lasted too long. It was a change from sawing wood, and though the work was hard I liked to see the wall growing up taller with each day's labouring. Also, there was echo birds nesting in the roof of the lookout that cried back everything we said. So we would teach the birds to cry that Beren Sallow wet his pants, or Lari and Ban was tumbling, or whatever. The birds was so quick to pick up a cry, they would even join in with us if we striked up a song.

Spinner was there for a lot of those days too, and we worked together most companionable. I kept almost telling her how I felt about her, but not quite getting to it because a hillside in the Summer heat with ash-paint caking on your skin and sweat all stinking you up didn't feel like the place for it.

I might of done it, all the same, if something else hadn't of happened instead. One day we was working side by side, just the two of us, and talking away like the words was going to spoil if

47

we didn't get them said. It was the end of the day and we was the only ones there, which often happened. We seemed neither of us to be so very keen to go back at the end of each day's work, her to the tannery and me to the mill.

The leaves that was left from those young trees was hanging down between us and the fence, but Mardew had cut the roots into pieces and then we had dug them out, so they couldn't do us no harm now. The leaves was just like a curtain. We was as alone as we had ever been in our lives.

I don't even remember what it was we was talking about, except that it was nothing much. All I was thinking of was how good it was to be with Spinner. To be close enough that I could smell her sweat, as though in a way I was breathing her into me.

I reached out my hand to grab hold of a bucket or something, and it touched her side. I started back, sudden like. I wasn't meaning to touch her without no leave nor warning, and I didn't want her to think I was.

Spinner turns to look at me. "What was that, Koli?" she asks me, putting her hands on her hips.

"It was . . ." I stammered. "It wasn't anything."

"Then why'd you jump back like you was burnt? I'm not hot to touch." She put her hand on my cheek. "See? That doesn't hurt now, does it?"

I didn't know what to answer. I covered her hand with mine, and kept on looking in her eyes. It didn't hurt, but it did burn somewhat.

She leaned in and kissed me on the mouth. There was a salt taste on her lips, from her working and sweating hard. It's nothing much to tell, but I wondered at it. That Spinner had a taste, and I had tasted it.

She put her hand over mine, and then stroked it along my arm. Her skin looked so light next to mine. Like my brown arm was a branch of a tree, and her pink-white fingers was like the blossom of the same tree, moving in the wind.

And shortly after, I stopped thinking at all. I had kissed girls before, in the Summer-dance, and I had kissed a boy, that was Veso Shepherd. Veso hadn't decided back then whether his love was for women or men, and he put both to the test somewhat. I had even tumbled with a girl once, when the fire was dying down and everyone took hands and walked off into the dark to carry on the dancing without any music. This was different though. For me it was, anyway. When Spinner took me into her, I was taken in whole and delivered to some other place. I don't know how to say it better than that.

Afterwards we lay naked on our own shed-off clothes, arms around each other, and commenced to talk again.

"I been thinking about doing that a long while," Spinner said. "And I'm glad I did."

That give me a glow in my heart. I said I had been thinking about it too. "Yes," Spinner said. "I knowed that, Koli. You didn't think you was hiding it, did you? Dandrake help you if you ever need to keep a big secret."

You might think that would of been a good time to tell my feelings, but I was sure in my heart that it wasn't. It would of been like I was just trying to thank her for the tumble, and not meaning it. The words didn't come out anyway.

Spinner seen I was abashed, and laughed me out of it. She kissed me, and I kissed her just as readily, and so we went back and forth a while until we both seen the sun was almost touching the ground and it was past time to go back inside the fence. We walked those hundred feet hand in hand, like lovers, but parted just before the gates and walked in like friends, our arms swinging at our sides.

It was one of the best days I had ever lived through, but I wonder still whether that coming together, sweet as it was, was the thing that kept me from speaking out when words might still of been to the purpose.

Probably not, I'm bound to say. The general belief was that Haijon was strongest out of all of us and I was fastest, but my best skill was always standing too long and deciding too late.

We said goodbye at the water tower, and I watched Spinner

cross the gather-ground to the tannery before I turned onto the path that led down to the mill. I was angry with myself, a little, that I didn't speak to her, but I promised myself I would take the next chance. Tomorrow would do, I thought. And like most people who think that, I was dead wrong. There's only ever one day that matters, and it moves along with you.

11

I worked the next two days at the lookout, but Spinner never come. I stayed late each day, hoping I might see her again.

At the end of the second day, Haijon come walking out of the gates and climbed the hill to where I was sitting on the steps of the lookout. He brung a jug of beer that he dangled from one hand. "I thought this was a share-work, Koli," he says, "yet here you sit on your own. So I brung you a little something to share."

He sit down next to me, uncorked the jug and took a deep swig – then wiped the neck and handed it to me. I drunk deep. It was cold out of the ice house, and went down well. "Well, you can lend a hand if you want, Haijon," I said, with a belch in the middle of the words. "There's a shit bucket down there that won't empty itself."

Haijon grinned. "I'm Rampart Breakfast, not Rampart Shit-Bucket. Each man got a skill that's his alone to tend and master, Koli. I'm thinking you might found yours."

We drunk the beer and we joked about who had the most reason to empty the bucket, while the sun dropped down out of the sky and lights gun to be lit over in the village. We could see the glow of them between the leaves, almost like stars.

51

"I wanted to ask you something," Haijon says to me.

"Go ahead," I told him.

He give me a funny smile. Like he knowed I was going to laugh at him and he thought he might as well see the funny side of it too. "I think I might want to get married."

I didn't laugh at all. My thoughts was mostly dwelling on Spinner, and on the sweetness of being held by her. I couldn't see no downside to marriage right then, as young as we was. "You should do it," I said. "No girl is like to turn up her nose at being pair-pledged to Rampart Breakfast."

"This girl might, Koli," Haijon says. "She is as strong-willed as a boar with its back up. But I think I might ask her anyway. If so be the chance comes up. Maybe at next Summer-dance."

"That's a long time to wait, Haijon. Some other man might jump in and win her heart before you stake your claim." Then I suddenly thought of a girl we both knowed who was strong-willed, and a chilly feeling come over me. "What's her name anyway?" I asked him.

"It's Spinner," he said. "I know, it seems crazy to think that way. We all been friends so long, it's almost impossible to think of being something else instead. Only it wouldn't be instead, Koli. It would be on top of that. We'd still be friends, but we'd be wedded too. Do you think I'm wandering in my wits?"

I had looked away as soon as he speak her name. I looked away still. "I don't know," I said. "Maybe."

"But she's the best there is, isn't she? And we been through everything together. We tested together, even. I'm making up my mind to it, even as I say it."

"You can make up your mind to it," I said. "But maybe think it over before you do it." I give a grin that was probably a mite sickly. "You know she and your sister don't get along. You want to bring them under the same roof?"

"Lari?" Haijon looked at me blank, like I was just making sounds that wasn't words. I think I was, really. "Lari won't have a say in it, Koli. This is my heart, and my choosing."

"Well, yes, it's your heart," I said. "And that's a really important thing, Haijon. It's not to be decided on a heel-turn."

He frowned, like he was swallowing this down and it didn't want to go. "I thought you said I should move fast in case some other man asked her before I did."

That was when I thought it was someone else! I thought. I near to yelled it in his face. "Just wait until you're sure," I said. "Then when you're sure, ask her."

"You think she'll say yes?" he asked me, all anxious.

"I don't know, Haijon." *But I hope not.* "All you can do is ask." *I hope not.* "And, you know, stand by her choice, whatever it happens to be." *I hope not I hope not I hope not.*

Haijon clapped me on the shoulder. "Thanks, Koli," he said. "I'm glad I asked you. I'm glad someone other than me knows it. It was bouncing around inside my head until I thought I would go crazy from it. But now there's two of us knows it, it's a lot easier."

He left me the jug, and the secret of his heart's choosing, and walked on back to the gate.

I drained the jug dry before I got up.

12

Then Molo Tanhide, that was Spinner's father, took sick. His lungs had always been bad, on account of the chemicals he mixed up in his vats. He was a dyer as well as a tanner, and both jobs involved strong brews and sour, steaming air. Now Molo couldn't hardly catch a breath at all, and it was a painful thing to see him try. He kept his mouth wide open while his throat worked and his hands twitched and shaked. And yet his chest barely moved, this while. There was not much air going in there, for all the effort he put into it.

The hope was that Molo would last until the end of the Summer. There was a wandering doctor that come to Mythen Rood in Falling Time. Her name was Ursala-from-Elsewhere, and she brung strong medicines. But Falling Time was a long way off and Molo's sickness growed on him fast and hard. In the meanwhile, Shirew Makewell done what she could. So did Rampart Fire, declaring the tannery a share-work so Spinner could tend to her father while others done what was needful at the vats.

I went there every day to drop off food for her and sometimes to help her mix the dyes or soak the hides, although I was not let off from my duties elsewhere and could sometimes only stay for a little while.

Haijon had more time to spare, since Ramparts did not have to heed the call to share-work. His sole, single duty was learning the cutter, and even that he could only do when Mardew let him borrow it. So a lot of times when I come to the tannery I found him already there.

It should of been like old times, when the three of us was shut up in the Waiting House together, but it never was. There was too much between us now, though it did not ever get said out loud. He loved Spinner and I loved her too. I've taxed my thoughts with wondering whether either of them knowed how I felt, but I can't answer that. Seeing how hard it was for me to speak for my own self, I won't presume to speak for anyone else. Anyway, I found Haijon's always being there a burden, and I don't doubt he thought the same thing every time I come along. For each of us would rather of been with Spinner alone.

Alone is the wrong word though, with Molo in the next room dying slowly. His breathing, like the sounds of a man put to torture, was the background to all we said and done. Sometimes I sit and talked with him while Spinner worked, though not as often as I should of done. I was fifteen years old, I thought myself in love and in all respects I was as shallow as a puddle.

Summer ended, which we always greeted with relief. The forest was less likely to move now, meaning that hunters could go more freely and fresh meat become a possible thing again even for them as kept no ducks or chickens.

One morning in October, the bell on the gather-ground rung when we Woodsmiths was at breakfast. It rung in the two-then-one peal that meant a death, not the wild jangle that meant a danger. My mother set down the apple she was eating and was out of the door without looking back. We all followed right behind her, Mull stopping only a moment to take the porridge pot off the fire. It sounds cold, but it was one of my mother's sayings that them as waste good food is cursed to starve. It was something my sister done without even thinking of it, nor it didn't mean no disrespect for the dead, whosoever it was.

On the gather-ground, Catrin was standing on one side of Spinner, and Haijon on the other. The other Ramparts was all there too, which was unusual. Spinner's eyes was all red from crying, so I knowed right away before a word was said.

"Molo Tanhide died in the night," Catrin told us. "Spinner found him this morning, not moving. She fetched Shirew Makewell and Shirew called him dead. His goods is passed to Spinner since she was his onliest kin. Anyone that wants to speak against that should speak it now."

Nobody said a word.

"Good then," Catrin said. "The laying out of the body and the cleaning of Molo's room is share-works. I want three souls for each. Tonight we'll drink and sing his good passage, and tomorrow, assuming there's clouds in the sky, we'll have the burial."

We all waited to be dismissed.

"One more thing," Catrin said. "Glad tidings on the back of sad ones. My son, Haijon, and Spinner Tanhide are pair-pledged and mean to be wed. I hope you'll give them your good wishes."

Cheers went up on all sides. I think it was only me that stayed silent. My mother studied my face a while, then put her arm across my shoulders and give me a squeeze.

"There's other hens in the yard, Koli," she murmured.

My heart was freighted too heavy to answer.

13

I will pass over the wake, if you don't mind. Wakes has always struck me strange, and this one was stranger than any I ever went to. I was grieving a double grief, and one of them (the selfish and stupid one) I could not speak.

Everyone else was in a more mixed-up place than that, being sad for Molo and happy for his daughter being taken into the Ramparts. Nothing could go ill for her now. She was gathered up, and safe, at the very moment when she might otherwise of been most sadly lost and alone. It was a good end, like the last words of a story. *And so they lived after, long and happy, until they died.*

How could I not want that for her? How could I put my own self and the things I dreamed of before Spinner's coming down, light and easy, in a bed all of softest duck-feathers?

I could not rejoice, and I will not disguise it. I thought of things that had passed between us and my heart said no. This thing could not be. It could not be her bedtime-story happiness, because she was meant to be happy with me and she must know that. What she had with Haijon was different and less.

I was not so lost to sense that I thought like this all the time. Only I could not put it wholly out of my mind, nor bring myself to be joyful over something that seemed like a bad mistake, a thing gone where it wasn't meant to go.

We buried Molo in the little plot in the half-outside where all our dead was laid. Catrin said some words over him, and Spinner done likewise. They was Dandrake words, which come as a surprise to me. I never knowed until then that Molo believed in Dandrake. I knowed Spinner didn't, and thought that must of been on account of how she was raised.

But it struck me strange for another reason too. Molo was ever a kind-hearted man, and Dandrake's teachings don't incline much in that direction. They come down to us from around about the time when the old world fell to pieces, and they have got that flavour running all through them. Most especially in the seven hard lessons, which Catrin spoke at Molo's burying.

"The first lesson is that god isn't looking at us no more.

"The second, that he won't look again until all men and women live by the right.

"The third, that them as won't live by the right themselves got to be made to do it by pain and preaching, and by the marks of godhead made in their mortal flesh."

And so on. It only gets worse from there, so I stopped listening.

Dandrake lived by his own rules, if the stories are true. He roused up his followers to a holy war, and marched them south to London. They was going to whelm the city, kill the king along with all his Count and Seal, and build the holy kingdom of Shrewshalem right here in Ingland. They didn't get there though. They had got to cross the Fathom and the Curtain first, and that was no easy thing. The king's men met them there and sowed the land with their blood, in the place that's now called Skullfield, and that was how they knowed they wasn't yet righteous enough to get the job done. As for Dandrake, they never found his body, so either he was took up to Heaven to be with the dead god and the ever-living, or else he found some other way out of that situation. Such as, it might be, running away.

It's hard to say, now, how much of this happened and how much was made up later, by them as took Dandrake's words and kept them. I know this much though: anyone who talks about the right way to live, as if there was only just the one, is blind in one eye or maybe both and is not worth listening to.

I seen Spinner a few times after Molo died. I was one of the three that volunteered to clean and tidy at the tannery, so I was oftentimes in her company. She said she was glad I was there, for she could cry around me without feeling foolish and smile without feeling heartless and unnatural.

"You ain't nothing of that kind," I says. "You got every good thing in your heart, Spinner, and nothing else."

"Nobody's altogether good, Koli," she told me. But she hugged me, and I hugged her back, and I think she took some comfort from me. Selfish though I was, I was glad to give it.

Spinner give me something in return too. Right after we spread the room with rue and rosemary for the soul-send prayer (another Dandrake ritual that I did not have no patience for), she opened up a cupboard and handed me a pair of boots that was inside.

"Here, Koli," she said. "I want you to have these. My da was working on them right up to when he died, and I finished them last night. I can't think of nobody I'd sooner give them to."

The boots was lovely things, made of tawny leather that was soft but strong, and finished with stitches so fine you almost couldn't see them. The laces was leather too, and topped with weighted rings of white iron.

"I can't take these, Spinner," I said.

She kissed me on the cheek. "Yeah, you can," she said. "You got to, for they're a remembrance of my da, and I know you would want to honour him."

Which I did, but I knowed even then that I wouldn't never think of Molo when I put them boots on, but of Spinner's hand sewing the last stitches.

We walked out of the tannery side by side, and she shut the gate behind us. "It's so strange," she said, "to think I'll only come back here to work from now on, and not to live. It's like there's two of me, and one of them is dead."

I knowed that feeling well enough. I felt the same way after Jud got took away, and it lasted a long time. But life is a lot stronger in us than we think, and always pulls us back even when our hearts is pulling the other way. I told Spinner that, and she said she believed it.

We said goodbye at the door of Rampart Hold, and I watched her go inside.

"Thank you for the boots," I called, but I said it as the door closed and she didn't hear me.

And now I think the time is come for me to talk about Ursala.

14

Ursala come to Mythen Rood in Spring and again in Falling Time. In Falling Time, she always come between the yellowing of the leaves and the first snow. That was a wide window, but then she walked a wide range – all across the valley and the hills around it, to Tabor in the east and Burnt Lea in the far west. She even went as far as Half-Ax, back when that road was still open. Nobody ever wandered so far or seen so much – or so I thought then. Every year we thought she might not come back, having met something on the road that was too much for her, but every year she turned up the same as always. "She never yet promised Catrin a time," my mother said. "She never promises anything. But if you made a wager on her you wouldn't lose by it."

I remember what it felt like, as a child, to see her walking up the straight street to the gather-ground. To see *them*, I should say, for Ursala-from-Elsewhere didn't come alone. She come with her striding friend, the drudge, which was a piece of tech the like it's not easy to describe.

The drudge was like a horse, if a horse was made all of metal and didn't have no head. Four limbs it had, and a wide, rounded body with signs all on it from the before-times. And over that, a great number of bags and harnesses that Ursala had set upon it, some big and some small, that it bore in patience. It did all things in patience, following where its mistress led at the same steady pace and never once faltering.

Also it had a gun, set in its back, that turned and quartered all the time and looked in every direction. That gun, and the drudge's perfect aim with it, was the reason why Ursala could walk the roads alone and not get killed or et. I don't know that anyone ever seen it fire, but then I never seen any woman or man offer slight to Ursala, or gainsay her. You would have to be a reckless wight indeed to do such. She weared a bracelet on her wrist that was the same grey as the cutter blade, and like the cutter blade it was said to turn silver when Ursala bared it and looked at it a certain way. It was tech, and it was called the mote controller. It made the drudge mind her and obey her.

Ursala was from elsewhere, and she looked it. She was tall and thin as a willow stick, her face all sharp and the bones of her body plain to see in the strange, tight weeds she wore. Her eyes was green, with darker green painted over the lids of them, as shiny as oil on water. Her skin was a darker shade than anyone's, even mine and Athen's. Her long, black hair was wore in a kind of braid down her back, with beads wove into it. She had a way of holding herself, flicking her cloak to make it hang the better and looking at you straight all the while, like as if to say "I'm a queen, where I come from. What are you, now I'm standing here?"

She was different when she was doctoring, and different again when she was drinking, but no matter what she done there was not much that was warm in her and not much that was bending. In her doctor work, she was patient and steady and used her voice to calm you, but I never seen her touch anyone outside of what was needed to find a hurt or tend to it, and even then she done it with a set face and a frowning look.

When she was drinking, she was wont to talk to herself inside her tent, like she was keeping up two sides of an argument. She liked wine a whole lot, and drunk it whenever it was put in front

62

of her, but it didn't seem to make her happy. And if it fretted her to be with people when she was sober, she just plain couldn't bear them when she was in her cups.

It was no secret that Catrin Vennastin misliked Ursala, very strong. Nobody knowed why exactly, but it almost seemed to me like there didn't need to be a reason. They was just opposites, not in anything they said and done but in who and what they was. Catrin was strong and fixed. Ursala was strong and wandering. I don't know how to say it better than that.

And anyway, long and short of it, it didn't matter. Ursala was needed, lots of ways. Mostly she was needed to doctor. Shirew Makewell did well enough for the hurts of the everyday. She could bind or burn a wound, dig out a choker seed, set a limb, put a poultice on a scald. But Ursala could see the places inside you that was hurting, and she could go inside you to make them right again. She done this with a machine that was inside the drudge, that she called a dagnostic.

I'll tell you a story to show how that worked. When Athen was eight she had terrible pains in her stomach, bad enough to make her scream if you even touched her there. She had had the pains before, and they had gone away in their own course. This time, they didn't go away but got worse, and Athen sickened. She was burning up from the inside, though our mother sponged her with cold water every few minutes. Her breath come less and less until you couldn't hardly see her chest move. Jemiu thought she would die. She didn't say it, but I seen in her face that she thought it. No tears, just the hard set of facing into a grief that hasn't quite come yet.

But Ursala turned up at the village gate when Athen was in the third day of this. Jemiu begged her to come straight to see her, which she did. Normally the first thing Ursala did when she was inside the gates was to sit and have parley with Dam Catrin, telling her how things stood in the other villages and in the valley as a whole. This time, when she heard how it was with Athen, she left the Ramparts waiting and come straightway to our house. She brung the drudge too. It smashed the lintel of the door in coming inside. A crowd come along behind it, there being many in the village who wanted to see this, but Jemiu turned them away at the door and bid them keep respect.

Ursala led the drudge to Athen's bed and there she put her hands on the drudge's flank and opened it up like as it was a cupboard. The sight made Mull and me gape our mouths open, for inside the drudge there was nothing but lots and lots of tech, with shining wires that trailed out of it and lights that was shining and moving. This was the dagnostic, which I hadn't ever seen before that time. Ursala touched some of the wires to Mull and they seemed to go into her. Jemiu went pale and her hands was shaking, but not a word come out of her.

Ursala tugged her sleeve up then, and I seen the mote controller on her wrist. It was glowing silver, like I had heard tell it did, but also there was signs and symbols of the old times running all over it like ants, almost too quick to see.

"This is septicaemia," Ursala said. "Her appendix has burst, and the poison is spreading infection through her body cavity. The only option is to clean it out, but at this stage I can't make any promises. I'll do my best to save her. And your best is to leave me to do it."

It sounds cruel, writ down like that, but Ursala didn't say it cruel. She said it in the way Molo Tanhide skinned that needle when it was wrapped around his daughter's hand: like she knowed how much it hurt but she wasn't going to dance around it or shy away from it because that would only make the damage that much more.

She was in Athen's room for some while, a lot more than a glass's turning, but somehow when she was in there the time didn't seem to pass. When she come out again, to us it was like we was all of us still in the same moment somehow. Ursala had blood on her, a lot of it, and so did the side of the drudge that was now closed shut again. Jemiu looked at her, pleading, but couldn't bring herself to ask. So I said it instead. "Is she alive?"

Ursala nodded, and my mother let out the sob that had been inside her all this time. "She is," Ursala said, "and I have good hope she'll stay that way. Put this tincture under her tongue tonight and again tomorrow. Then when she wakes, boil some tea from willow bark and let her drink it, hot or cold as she prefers. That will ease the pain."

My mother wrung Ursala's hand and thanked her many times. Ursala bore this patiently, but I could see she didn't like any of it – not the touching, nor the gratefulness. She had done what she had come to do, and now she wanted to go on her way.

My mother offered payment in cured wood or food or the valley scrip that we sometimes – though less and less often – used for trade with the other villages along the Calder. Ursala bore this as long as she could, then took her hand away with some brusque word. "It's my calling, Dam Woodsmith, and it's also part of my contract with the village. The Ramparts pay me well. There's no need for you to pay me too." When Jemiu still insisted, Ursala finally took some jars of preserves and a string of beads my mother had from my father the one time they were together. She done it with reluctance, and afterwards she went away with her back bent and her shoulders hunched, like our thanks was a burden to her.

Athen lived. She slept for a day and a night, and when she woke up she was her own self again, with all that pain and weakness nowhere to be seen.

Haijon told me Catrin tried to buy the dagnostic off of Ursala more than once, offering her all kinds of treasure in return. She even offered the bolt gun or the cutter, Haijon said, though not the firethrower. Ursala give her the same word each time, and the word was no. That may of been the reason Catrin was so far from liking Ursala, despite her being of so much service to us all.

Which I begun to tell but got pulled aside by what I had to tell you about Athen's sickness. It wasn't only doctoring that Ursala did, though doctoring was a big part of it. She carried messages from other villages too, and brung warnings of things we needed to be ware of. Like a great pack of wild dogs on one occasion, and the creep-blight on another. If Catrin hadn't burned the blight at Burley Carr and turned it aside, it might of been inside the fence before we knowed it threatened.

And there was one other thing Ursala did, which was that she told which marriages would be fruitful and which wouldn't ever. She used the dagnostic for this, and also she used a knife she kept on her belt in a sheath of white leather, cutting the hands of the man and the woman who wanted to pair-pledge and letting the dagnostic taste the blood off the blade.

You would think these questions would be asked and answered in private, but in fact this was done on the gather-ground. It was done there for two reasons, I think. The first was that — except in emergencies, such as that time with Athen — the drudge was not an inside-of-doors kind of thing. If it walked down the steps of the Count and Seal, there wouldn't be no steps left when it got to the bottom. And the second was that Catrin, along with most other people in Mythen Rood, believed the issue of children being born or not being born or being born wrong was a problem for the village as a whole. After all, the children would belong to the village when they come, and with each year that passed there was fewer and fewer being born alive. It mattered to everyone to roll that particular stone up the hill instead of down, as they say.

If the news was bad, Ursala give her verdict as gentle as she could. "It doesn't mean you won't have any children," I heard her say to one couple — I think it was Vuru Cooper and Werian Strong, if you remember them names. "It just means they're that much less likely to be born alive and healthy. The probabilities are against you. But the probabilities can't take away your choice."

Maybe that was true. The probabilities, whoever they were, didn't have no say in the matter. Catrin stood firm on the yes or no of it, and if the dagnostic said no then that pair-pledge was set aside. Catrin said Mythen Rood couldn't afford no barren ground.

On this occasion when Ursala come, there was three pledges she had to decide on. Haijon and Spinner's come first, and she pronounced that there was no problem with their pairing. I told myself I was happy for them, but a part of me had been hoping for a different outcome and was cast down when the answer come. For now there was nothing in the way of it. Spinner would marry Haijon and go into Rampart Hold. I had losed any chance of being with her, and it seemed to me then that there wasn't any way of being happy without her. So I did what fools always have done since time was time, which is I pissed in my own milk and then complained about the taste of it.

Not that I spoke aloud, of course. Most people in the village was in a joyful frame of mind. Them other two couples I spoke of got good outcomes too, so there was going to be three weddings coming soon and nobody grieving on account of their hopes being dashed down. Everyone was most especially happy for Spinner, who had lost her father but now was getting a new family just pat when she needed one.

So my sullenness was inward, and for the rest I put a brave face on it. And maybe in time I would of swallowed my disappointment and done what most everyone else does in such a case, which is get on with living and with forgetting what can't be mended.

Maybe not though. For I had got an idea rooted in my deepest heart that give me torment. It was that Spinner loved me as much as I loved her, and had only gone pair-pledge with Haijon because he was a Rampart and her eyes was dazzled. It speaks ill of me, I know, to think such disrespect of her, but that was what my hurt and pride had fixed on.

It's a curious thing, when I think on it now, that I felt so trapped and so despairing of my station. The burden of my fears was that this place and these feelings I was stuck in wouldn't ever change as long as I lived. Yet it was but three weeks later that the gates of Mythen Rood closed behind me for the last time as I walked into exile.

But I am running out in front of my own story again, and this is a time when I have got to be most careful to get it right, since what happened next was to matter so much both to the boy I was and to the man I am.

I remember there was a day, maybe two or three days after Ursala sampled Haijon and Spinner and spoke them sound, that I went out of gates by myself. This was not exactly a thing forbid, but only because there wasn't no need for it to be. You wouldn't forbid someone to hold their hand in a fire, or to catch a choker seed as it fell. The woods just wasn't anywhere to be by yourself if you meant on the whole to stay alive.

This was Falling Time though, which was a safer season than most, and I didn't go beyond the stake-blind, only into the half-outside. I walked up to the high lookout that I had a hand in building up on top of Cloughfoot. The building was mostly finished now, with only the armouring still to be done. And the track up there was wide and clear on account of all the coming and going that had been done when we was putting up the walls.

I just went up there to be alone for a while. I was going to say I wanted a quiet place to think in, but the truth is that my thoughts had soured in my head and I wanted as little to do with them as I could manage.

So I sit there for about an hour, on the wall at the top of the lookout, with my feet dangling over the drop. The forest was close at hand, like an army that was creeping up to the gates of the village but had been seen doing it and now was pretending to be still. For some of that time I thought about leaning forward until I fell, but I only thought it idly. Unhappy though I might be, yet I hadn't come to the point where my life felt like a burden to me. I was just catched in a snare, is all, and running in tight circles, but since I made the snare myself there wasn't none but me could get me out of it.

When the sun come close to touching the tops of the trees, I thought it best to go. Night was still a ways off, but there are plenty of things that like to hunt in the cool that comes around lock-tide, and the shadows would just go on getting darker and more numerous from here on.

I had not come out by the gate and I didn't go back by it. There would of been questions to answer both ways. Instead I went by what we called the grass-grail. This was a place on the fence where it had been cut ever so careful to be like a ladder you could climb if you was cut off from the gate. Nobody was supposed to use the grass-grail unless they was pressed hard and close and didn't have no other choice – for shunned men or faceless might see you do it, and use our secret way for their own purposes.

And shunned men was rampant that year. Three hunting parties was attacked over the Summer, and one man struck dead – though them that was with him saved him from being took away by the shunned men and et. It had got so bad that Catrin was talking about making up a red tally, which is a war party, to find where they lived and burn them out once for all.

So it was a wrong thing I was doing, climbing the grass-grail with light still in the sky and nothing threatening. I guess I done it with somewhat of bitterness and defiance in my heart.

Then dropping down on the inside of the fence I found myself almost face-to-face with Ursala. I had forgot that this was where she put up her tent when she was with us. She done her doctoring in the gather-ground, but she retired to this much quieter place to sleep.

Right now, she was sitting out in front of her tent, which was all different greens and browns so you thought you was looking at part of a forest. She was boiling a stew over a little fire. It was just starting to steam, and it had a good, spicy smell to it. She didn't lift up her head to look at me as I jumped down, and I had hope for a second she never seen or heard me, though my feet hit the earth with a loud thump and raised up some dust.

I was making up my mind to walk right by her, pretending I was just taking myself for a stroll around the inside of the fence, when she spoke up.

"Well now," she said, still stirring the pot. "That's a strange thing to see. When a man comes into his own house he usually chooses to enter by the door. It's thieves and cut-throats, by and large, who climb over the wall."

I didn't know what to say. I hadn't done nothing that was so

69

wrong, really – except to use the grass-grail in front of someone that was not one of ours, which was meant to be forbid. Being out alone, like I said, would not be favourably looked on but it wasn't any crime.

I opened my mouth at last to say some of these things, though I didn't know for sure what words would come out. But before I said anything at all, the tocsin bell over on the gather-ground gun to sound. It wasn't the slow peal that meant a death, but the quick, shapeless jangle of an alarum.

And just as soon as it sounded, I seen what it was sounded for. A dark shape shot over us, high up in the sky but very clear to see with the brightness of sunset behind it. Then it come back on a big, wide loop, and swung right down towards the part of the fence where we was. As it dropped, it stopped being one thing and broke up into three. It was three things all moving tight together at first but now spreading out wide. They was drones. And they was lit up underneath with red light, which meant they was armed and ready to kill.

One of the three shot away towards the gather-ground and Rampart Hold. The second done much the same, except it stayed closer to the line of the fence so it would pass by the well-head.

The third come down right between me and Ursala, floating about ten feet above us.

"Disperse," it said. It sounded like someone had nailed together a voice out of the sounds a bunch of stones made when they fell into a bucket.

"Disperse, or you will be fired upon. You have thirty seconds to comply."

15

Maybe I should of told you more about the drones when I was numbering the things that hated us. I mentioned them in some kind, when I said there was weapons left over from the Unfinished War that was still dangerous, but I didn't take it any further than that saying.

The drones was a fear that was ever on our minds when we walked abroad, though they come but seldom and they give us warning before they attacked. It's hard to describe what they was like. When they was in the air they looked like insects, almost, if you can imagine an insect that's as big as a man's head and shoulders. They was dark and quick and dreadful, with an angry buzz like a hornet whether they moved or was still. And a tail like a hornet too, which was what they killed you with. But I seen a few of them after they fell to the ground, and on the ground they looked like nothing much at all. Some wires, metal rods, a sprinkle of broken glass.

The way you knowed a drone was coming was that it told you. It would drop down from out of the sky, fast as a stone, but stop dead ten or twenty feet above the ground. And it would speak a word. "Disperse." Then you knowed you just had got a few seconds to dive under cover and hope it didn't follow you or fire on you, for if it did you would most likely be dead.

If the drones didn't give their warning, they would of killed most every time. The warning, which was always the same, give us a chance to raise the alarum. Ramparts would come running then from wherever they was and whatever they was doing, carrying their name-tech with them.

They all knowed their places and their parts. Rampart Arrow would stand in the middle, with Fire on one side and Knife on the other. She would let fly with a bolt. She didn't need to aim, for that was not how the bolt gun worked, but she did point the gun at the drone for a second or two so it knowed what its target was. Then she pulled the trigger and off went the bolt.

Sometimes it hit the drone on the first pass, and that was a great good fortune. Most often, though, the drone would see the bolt coming and swing away, nearly too fast to see. Then there would be a kind of a skirmishing and snaking around in the sky, with the bolt chasing the drone and the drone flying every which way so as not to be hit, and once that was happening both Rampart Fire and Rampart Knife come into the picture. Rampart Fire would cut loose with the firethrower, making a kind of roof of fire over the village, or at least the part where the drone was. The fire was to keep it from coming down low and attacking.

If it did come down through the fire and didn't melt or fall apart, then it would be close enough for Rampart Knife to have at least a chance of hitting it. The last chance, so to speak, for if he missed then that day would be someone's funeral day. But most often the sheet of flame kept the drone high up in the sky until the bolt done its work. One or two drones come down on us every year in the times I'm speaking of, and there was only two times in all them years that they killed anyone.

But then, there had never been a time when three drones attacked us at once.

Some things come on you too fast for you to understand them when they're happening. And when you try to understand them

72

afterwards you put them together any way you can, but you get it wrong. In your mind there's a moment here and a moment there, but no sensing what went with what. That's how it was for me right then.

There was a drone standing in the air in front of me, close enough for me to touch. It had already spoke, so I ought to be running, except there wasn't nowhere I could run to. Nothing was close by except Ursala's tent, and that wouldn't offer no help at all when the drone struck.

I heard the handclap sound of the bolt gun being fired, and another sound that was like a hammer hitting a nail – the quick little taps you give when the nail is almost all the way in and you want to seat it solid without bruising the wood. The sky turned orange-yellow-white, sheets of fire rolling out like flags far away over us.

Our drone tilted in the air a little, then steadied itself. The tiny little cylinder that was its stinger flicked from Ursala to me and back again, and there was some sounds from inside it like someone was humming in there while they worked.

Ursala hadn't moved until then, but now she did. She bent down slowly and picked up a stick from the fire, one that was burning good. Then she took up a rock in her other hand. She had builded up a circle of biggish stones around her firepit, and it was one of them she grabbed a hold of now. It must of been hot to the touch but she didn't flinch or make a sound.

She walked right towards the drone.

I give a yell like I was warning her. Like she was sleep-walking or something and I had got to wake her to the danger. "Get away from there!" or some such.

She answered me without turning around. The words come out kind of in a growl, so though they was low I could make them out even over the shouts and screams that was coming from the gather-ground.

"Stand in the fire, boy."

I thought I must of misheard. The whole thing was like a dream, but that was the strangest of all. Anyway my feet weren't likely to move right then even if I told them to.

Ursala took one step after another. She was turning her hands slowly, the hand with the burning branch and the hand with the rock. The drone shifted in the air. I would of swore it was turning tight little circles too, following the movements of Ursala's hands.

I had heard stories about witches. I thought I was looking at a witching right then. The time must of run out for us and yet the drone didn't fire. What it did was come down to meet Ursala as she come, like as if she'd whistled it to her. She was holding the burning branch out in front of her now, still circling and circling. The hand with the rock was drawed back, and I seen the muscles in her arm bunch up.

That part I got pretty much straight in my mind, as you can probably tell. But after that my remembering is all tangled up again. Mardew Vennastin come running right by me, his shoulder hitting me hard and making me stagger. I seen his hand was up and the cutter was in it. I seen the bar of the cutter was shining silver, so the blade was ready to be sent out to cut something.

He was resting the cutter hand on his other hand to steady it. His head was tilted to one side, so he could sight along the line of his arm. And Ursala was stood in front of him, right between him and the drone.

I don't remember deciding to move. I almost don't remember moving at all, but my hands was around Mardew's arm, most sudden, and I was pulling it down towards the ground. Mardew sweared a terrible oath and snatched his hand free again, which didn't cost him no effort at all for I was not what you would call strong.

Then there was a sound like a bushel of eggs all cracking at once.

Mardew brung the cutter up again, only there was nothing now to aim at. He lowered his hand back down to his side, very slowly. There was a look on his face that was kind of wildered and kind of sour, all at once.

The drone was on the ground at Ursala's feet, bent almost in two. The rock was still in her hand.

"Put that thing back on safety, Mardew Vennastin," she says. "Before you slice your own foot off." She said it the same way she told me to jump in the fire, without turning her head but still knowing in some way he was there.

Mardew looked like he was going to answer her, only he couldn't find the words. He turned on me instead, his face all alight inside with strong feeling, most of which was anger.

"Do you want to tell me why you laid hands on me, boy?" he asked me. He spit out the words like he didn't like the taste of them. I didn't either, come to that. Mardew was only two years older than me, and I was done with my Waiting, so that "boy" didn't sit right at all.

He shoved me in the chest with the hand that didn't have the cutter on it. "I'm a Rampart about his duty," he says. "You know what happens to people who get in the way of me?"

I stammered out a sorry that I didn't really mean, and he roared at me, "Sorry don't help. I'm bringing it to the Count and Seal and you'll be whipped for it. Damn fool boy!"

He was wild, all right. He would of said more, or maybe done more, but then he looked all around at the people that had come up behind him from the gather-ground. I never even seen they was there until then, and I don't think Mardew did either. One of them was Haijon. Another was my mother, her face very pale.

"The boy was helping me," Ursala said, all quiet-like, "to bring down this drone."

"That's Rampart work," Mardew said.

"Usually it is," Ursala agreed. "But as you can see, I had this under control."

"My cutter would of handled it."

"Your cutter is a formidable weapon, Rampart Knife. And at full strength, pointed straight ahead of you instead of upwards . . . well, I have no doubt it would have done the job. But there are houses over there." Ursala raised up her hand to point. "And the well too, unless I'm mistaken, with a crowd of people all round it. The drone was far too low for you to hit it without hitting anything else."

"I never harmed anyone yet," says Mardew.

Ursala smiled without no warmth in it. "And your record stands unsullied. I think you should thank this boy for stepping in when he did."

Mardew hesitated, looking from Ursala to all the people that was standing around. I could see there was things he wanted to say but thought better of before they was spoke. I didn't see no thanks in his eyes when he turned his face my way again. "You watch yourself," he says to me at the other end of a long, hard stare. "And don't you come by me."

"You're very welcome," Ursala said.

Mardew walked away without another word. My mother grabbed me then and hugged me close. I seen Haijon over her shoulder, looking at me as if he was somewhat troubled by what had passed. But he give me a nod and he locked his thumbs in our secret sign.

I nodded back.

"You're coming home," Jemiu said to me. "And you're staying home. You been a big enough idiot for one day." And she dragged me away.

The last thing I seen as I went was Ursala picking the broke drone up off the ground and carrying it into her tent.

16

When Jemiu called me an idiot, she didn't mean no harm by it. The plain truth is that there's people who think before they do and people who do before they think. Most times, as you probably seen, I was the former kind. This time I was not, and I got a taste of what can come from that – enough to confirm me in my regular path.

But here I was again, in the bad place I already told you of. Brooding on what I'd lost, or thought I'd lost, and wistful of things I couldn't have. It's a curious thing, how a blessing or a curse can come to you without you knowing it. Looking back now, I see that Ursala's friendship has meant more to me than almost anything in my life, but still it come at a time when I was least like to profit by it.

It didn't come right away, neither. Jemiu was as good as her word and kept me to it at the mill, brewing stop-mix, racking the steeped wood to dry, squaring planks on the lathe, cleaning the blades of the three big saws, sweeping the mill floor, and on and on. I breathed more sawdust than air, in that time.

This was not laid on me as a chastisement. Far from it. Jemiu wanted to keep me from any bad effects springing from my recklessness, and she thought hiding me out of everyone's sight was the best way of achieving that. I knowed, though, that out of sight was not the same as out of mind. Athen and Mull went into the village most days, and they told me that what happened on the day the three drones come was still much talked of.

Then Haijon paid me a visit, and he told me the rest of it, starting with what happened on the gather-ground, where the two other drones was brung down. Rampart Arrow took one of them clean, and Rampart Fire sent up a blaze to protect against the other.

"But it was too fast," Haijon said. "It come down low even while she was firing. Come right under the fire and was there in the midst of everyone. Fer didn't have time to launch a second bolt, and my ma was facing the wrong way. It might of killed the both of them, except that Ursala's drudge was sat there on the gather-ground where she left it at the end of each day's doctoring.

"The drudge had its legs folded under and it looked like it was asleep. But it unfolded right quick. Its gun spun round and tracked the drone, and then it sent off a volley. It wasn't like the bolt gun. It was a whole lot of shots that kind of chased each other across the sky and then went off one after another like green twigs cracking in a fire. I never seen the like of it. The drone was stuck in the middle of all that and the next thing we seen it was on the ground in a hundred pieces."

That must of been the other sound I heard, that was like a hammer knocking a nail in.

Haijon leaned in close. "Here's the strangeness of it though, Koli. We looked for bullets or bolts afterwards, and there wasn't none. There was just little white chips on the ground, like broke-off bits of bone. Whatever the drudge was shooting, I don't think I want to know about it."

"So Ursala brung down two out of the three drones, one way and another," I said, ignoring the fireside tale though another time I would of relished it.

"I guess she did," Haijon says back to me. "She still went meddling in Rampart business though, and my ma only took it halfway well. The drones was took down, but not in the right way."

"The right way?" I says. "What's the right way, Haijon?"

"The right way is the way that don't shake people's faith in us. In Ramparts, I mean. Loss of faith might bring more harm than the drones in the long run. That's what my ma says anyway."

"More harm how?"

"Like, in how we live, and how we make our minds up about things." Haijon shrugged, like he didn't get it either. "She says mostly people kind of dawdle themselves to death. Something bad happens and they're not nearly quick enough in dealing with it. Sometimes Ramparts just got to be on it fast, but sometimes what they got to do is make everyone else be faster. Tell them what to do and whip them up into doing it.

"So anything that makes people slower in doing what Ramparts tell them to do is bad, she says. Ursala done a good thing, no doubt about it. But she don't have to live with the effect of it, and we do. She should of thought more about how it looked. Especially when she talked back to Mardew like that in front of everyone. Mardew didn't like that at all, and neither did my ma."

"But still," I said, kind of looking for the common ground I thought had got to be there between us, "people is alive who would of died. Me, for instance. That drone was standing as close to me as you are now."

"You got to think of the long run," Haijon says again.

I kept my silence after that. It seemed to me that us all still drawing breath was a bigger and more important thing than Catrin being the one to thank. But I didn't want to have a fight with Haijon about it. I still counted him a friend, and I took it kindly that he come to see me even though Ramparts in general was hard down on me right then.

"Listen," he said. "Spinner and me, we're to be wed on the Salt Feast. I was thinking you'd be with me on my fasting, Koli, and carry the cutter for me at the wedding, but that's not possible now. I hope you won't take it bad if I choose Veso Shepherd instead."

"I won't take it bad," I told him. I meant it too. Veso would be joyed by it, and it would do a lot to quiet them in the village that was down on him just for being who he was. Anyway, I wasn't going to be at the wedding at all if there was any way out of it. That Haijon and Spinner was going to be together was something I couldn't halt or hinder. I had got to make my peace with it. But standing right by while the two of them kissed and swapped promises felt like more than I could bear.

Haijon read my face, but he read it wrong. He thought the sadness he seen there was for me being passed over in favour of Veso, when it wasn't Veso's place but his own I was wishing to fill in that ceremony. He put a hand on my shoulder. "Let's get out of here," he said. "It's been a while since I raced you round the walls. A married man can't do that, but I didn't get married yet."

A race sounded good. I was full sick of the mill yard by this time. I hesitated a moment, thinking of what Jemiu would say when she found me gone, but then I thought of how these would likely be the last good days of Falling Time, with all the snows and sleets to come, and my mind made itself up.

"Let's put a wager on it," I said. "Winner gets a handful of apricots from the Underhold. Loser got to steal it."

Haijon give out a laugh. "I'll take that bet," he said, "for I won't be the one paying."

"Might be hard for you to get in that window now in any case, Rampart Breakfast," I said. I held up my hands to take the measure of his shoulders – then I brung them down and measured his stomach too, making it out to be wider.

"Oh, now you made this be personal," Haijon says with a laugh. "Come on, Koli, let's see what you got. Three goes two goes one. Run!"

I run, but I didn't run well. You can only do that when you can stop thinking about anything except running, and I was poorly placed to do that right then. I losed the race by ten clear strides. But Haijon let me off from stealing the fruit, for this wasn't a good time for me to be seen sneaking into the Underhold, or out of it. Catrin was not like to listen to reason in any such trespass. I was for doing it in any case, not wanting to slip sideways out of a bet, but when I walked around to the back of Rampart Hold I seen some of the upstairs windows open and my courage was bowed down a little. If someone was inside there looking out, they was bound to see me.

"We can go best out of three," Haijon said, and we parted on that understanding.

I walked back along the line of the fence, which took me past Ursala's tent. I didn't see her there, but the drudge was set beside the tent with its four legs folded under it. I was not used to seeing it any place other than the gather-ground, so I slowed down to look.

A hand lifted up the tent-flap. The nails was painted bright red, so I knowed it was Ursala's hand. Her voice sounded out of the deep dark, for so it looked to me. "Come along in, Koli Woodsmith. I'd like a word."

17

I just stood there for a moment, wondering if I could walk on and make pretend I didn't hear. It shames me now to remember it, but I thought of Ursala as somewhat to be feared. Nobody knowed where she lived, or how she come to know so much about so many strange things. There was stories about vengeances she took on them who tried to rob her or cheat her, and the vengeances was truly terrible. I had been mostly bent to disbelieve them, but that was before I seen her charm a drone out of the sky. Now I didn't know what to believe.

"There's nothing to be afraid of," Ursala said, as if I'd been speaking all this aloud. She sounded angry, or at least rate not minded to be patient. "I won't hurt you, boy. Come inside, and be quick about it. If one of your Ramparts sees us, they'll think we're plotting treason."

I didn't know what kind of thing treason might be, but I seen the drift of what she was saying – that Catrin was displeasured with the both of us and would not greatly favour the thought of us doing each other kindnesses. I still misgived a little, in my thoughts, but I bent my head and stepped inside the tent.

Once I was in there, I looked around in wonder. It wasn't dark at all, but had seemed so because there was a double skin on the tent-flap. I was in a space that was brighter than the outside. It was like the tent's walls was shining, almost, and I had to squint my eyes where I had thought I'd be hard pressed to see anything at all.

I put out my hand before I even thought about it. The tips of my fingers tingled, and somehow they didn't quite touch the cloth, but was stopped a little way before.

Ursala seen the dazzled look on my face. "The same tech as your cutter," she said. "It can be a wall as well as a knife. I can dial down the brightness if it bothers you."

I mumbled something not very much to the purpose, and turned my head away. But everywhere I looked, there was strange marvels.

There was a thing like a cooking pot, only its sides was made of glass and you could see the water boiling inside — boiling fit to bust, though there was no fire under it. There was a kind of a thing like three burning sticks in a fire that was throwing heat out into the tent — only the sticks didn't ever burn through; they just glowed bright red and stayed the same. Strangest of all, there was a picture like you might put on your wall, only it was on the floor at Ursala's feet. And it wasn't a picture of anything you might recognise. It was signs of the old times, black and spindly like ants, that moved around when Ursala touched them. She had sit down and was poking at the picture with both her hands. The signs run up and down the screen, but mostly up.

"I've just got to finish this," she says to me without looking up. "God help me."

I guessed that when she said god she meant Dandrake, for he was the main god everyone went to when it come to swearing. If she meant the dead god, it was strange she didn't give him his full name.

She give a sigh as she poked at the little picture. I plucked up my courage and asked her what she was doing.

"Maths," she said. That wasn't a word I knowed, and I suppose she seen that in my face. "This is a computer," she said, nodding at the little picture. "It's for working things out when they're too hard to work out in your head."

She poured some wine out of a leather skin into a tin cup that seemed already mostly full. The wine spilled a little down the side of the cup. For some reason, that made me think of Ursala's shirt, all covered in blood, on the day she took away Athen's sickness and saved her from dying. It made me be less afraid of her.

"Would you like some?" she asked me, holding up the skin. "I don't have another cup, but you can swig from the neck."

"No, thank you kindly," I said. I hadn't ever had no head for drink, the few times I tried it. Mostly it just made me dizzy, and being in the hot tent surrounded by all these wondrous things was doing that already. "What is it you're puzzling out?"

Ursala didn't answer. She give the little black signs another long, hard look, then she waved her hand over the thing she called a computer and the signs was gone. There was just a pattern there now, made of bright colours shifting all the time like leaves moving in the wind.

She give me a shrewd look, like we each of us knowed the same thing and knowed that the other knowed it too. "She can't hear us," she said. "Your Rampart Fire, I mean. Not in here. And I'm keeping my eyes open, though it might not look it, just in case she comes by. When she's in her current mood, it pays to be a little paranoid. Go ahead and sit down."

"All right then," I said. I had not been thinking about Catrin Vennastin, but I liked that she couldn't come by without us knowing it. I didn't think to doubt what Ursala said about that. Not now I'd seen some of what she could do.

There was pillows to sit on, and a steel box set down between them to make a table. There was more boxes besides, all over the floor of the tent, so I had got to be careful where I put my feet. I sit where Ursala bid me.

"You're sure you won't help me along with the wine?" she said.

"If I empty this skin myself, I'm going to be more dead than alive tomorrow."

"You don't got to empty it," I says. It come out before I knowed. I was thinking of my mother, who had a store of sayings against strong drink, otherwise I would not of been so bold.

But Ursala just gave a laugh, like I had said it to be funny and she got the joke. "Oh, trust me," she said. "I do. I've been sitting here crunching numbers for the last three hours, and they came out even worse than I was expecting. Drowning my sorrows feels like the least of a whole lot of evils right now."

When Ursala was doctoring and needed to ask you questions about what you was feeling, she talked like anyone else did. The rest of the time, though, she talked like this. I can set her words down in their right sense now, on account of some things that happened to me later: back then the best I could do was to run along next to her meanings like a man who's trying to get up onto a horse but can't fix his foot in the stirrup.

"What was you eating again?" I asked her, picking up the part of what she said that I could understand.

She give me a blank look for a moment or two before she got what I meant. "I wasn't eating anything. Crunching numbers means counting things up. Working out the answer to a problem."

"I'm sorry to hear you got a problem, Dam Ursala."

"I don't, Koli. You do. Mythen Rood does. But it's beyond my skill to fix it, so it's best not to talk about it. If you refuse to drink alcohol, how about some tea?"

"Tea would be good," I said.

Ursala cast around in among them boxes until she found the one she was looking for, though it didn't look no different to the rest as far as I could see. She opened it up and took some dried leaves out of it, then dropped them in another tin cup and poured water out of the bubbling pot in on top of them.

I was still thinking about what Ursala just said, and about what Haijon said to me not so long before. It was the same thing twice, really: that Catrin Vennastin was angry, and that they both was a

85

little afraid of what she might do. And I thought about one other thing that hadn't struck me strange until now.

"Most days you leave your drudge up on the gather-ground," I said.

Ursala was swirling the cup in her hands to speed the flavour. Her movements was a little clumsy, like when she poured the wine. I wondered how full the wineskin had been when she sit down, and how full it was now. But there was nothing in her voice to say she was sotted. "Yes," she said, "most days I do. Sometimes, though, I keep him close by me. When I need a visual aid. He reminds people that while I travel alone and may seem weak, I have resources that are not immediately obvious."

"You never struck me as weak," I said, once more grabbing onto a word or two while the rest run right by me.

Ursala lifted up one eyebrow. "I'm inside your gates. Depending on your hospitality and subject to your laws. Weakness is a matter of context, Koli Woodsmith. Until it becomes a matter of logistics." She set the cup down in front of me. "Would you like some honey in that?" she asked me. I liked honey any way I could come by it, was the honest answer. I nodded and she pushed over a jar that was on top of the table. The honey was thick, brown and mostly solid, so I had got to push the spoon in hard. I got a big scoop of it, then waited to be told it was too much, but Ursala didn't seem to mind. I dropped it in my tea and stirred it around.

"I was hoping to see you before I left," she said as I was doing this. "There being some unfinished business between the two of us."

"What business is that?" I asked.

"You saving my life."

"I didn't do nothing," I mumbled, sipping at the tea (though it was still too hot) to keep from having to look at her. I was not even halfway comfortable to be in this quiet, private place with her. With someone I had thought I knowed but really understood no more than I understood the world that was lost. Ursala-from-Elsewhere. Where was Elsewhere, now I thought on it? And how did its people come to be so wise and so strange?

"You stopped Mardew Vennastin from cutting me in two," Ursala said. "That's very far from nothing. Can I tell you a secret?"

I nodded. "Surely."

"I don't like people very much. I'm all in favour of them as a concept, but I don't get on with them at all when I have to mix with them. Having to talk to you now, at such close quarters . . . well, it's not pleasant, frankly. And being in debt to you is considerably worse."

She rummaged around in among the boxes, opened one up and held it out to me. There was little pieces of cake in it, cut off square with a knife and sitting in a bed of their own crumbs. I could see they was made with raisins. I took one and et it in two bites. Ursala watched me do it, her face all thoughtful and serious.

"So tell me, Koli Woodsmith," she said, as I licked my fingers clean, "is there something I can do for you? Something I can give you, whether it's goods or money, that will make your life easier? Because that would resolve the whole issue, and we could both go our separate ways again."

I squirmed on the cushion somewhat, trying to make sense of this. Ursala was looking at me hard, and I could not sit easy under that stare. "I don't think you owe me anything, Dam Ursala," I said he hasn't said this before. "If I helped you, you done the same for me right after. You done it twice over, for you broke the drone in pieces and you made Mardew stand down when he was gonna get me brung up before the Count and Seal."

Ursala's look never shifted. "Generally," she said with a coldness in her voice, "it's the one at the sharp end of the debt who has the clearest sense of it. You'll have to indulge me, Koli. Let me reward you so I can go back to not thinking about you at all."

Well, I was not one to kick at a reward, but it was not easy to answer her. I never really seen myself as needing anything, excepting to be a Rampart, which was only a foolishness, and to be with Spinner, which now she was pair-pledged was worse foolishness still. Except that I had whipped it up so much inside my head that all I could see was the froth.

I thought about the place where those two things – being a Rampart and being with Spinner – seemed to come together. Ursala's tech was as good as Rampart tech or maybe better, and would make a villager be a Rampart the second he could call it his. For a second, or maybe a bit longer than a second, I wondered whether I could ask her if she had some other thing like the water-boiler or the computer or the drudge's dagnostic. Something like those things, only smaller, that she could bear to be parted from. But it was like asking to be made a king such as they had in the world that was lost, with a palace and servants and wives and an army of soldiers. The words wouldn't come out of my mouth, for I didn't want to seem so greedy nor so stupid.

And once I seen that, I seen too that there wasn't nothing else I wanted, except maybe another piece of cake and some more tea with honey in it.

But just as I was opening my mouth to say that, another idea struck me. I considered, and Ursala seen me do it. "What is it?" she says.

"You know lots of things, Dam Ursala," I says to her. "More than anyone I ever met."

She shaked her head, it seemed with sadness. "I know a little more than you do," she said. "Not much. Not nearly enough."

She was being honest, or thought she was, but all the same what she was saying wasn't anywise true. I learned since then, and paid a price to learn it, that them as lay claim to great wisdom most often got nothing in their store but bare scrapings. And by the same token, them as think they're ignorant think it because they can see the edges of what they know, which you can only see when what you know is tall enough to stand on and take a look around. I had no idea of this back then, but I still knowed that Ursala was a lot cleverer than me and I believed that the things I wanted to know about must surely lie in her telling.

"Will you answer some questions I got?" I asked her. "I'd see that as a great kindness and a full reward, though I'll say again you don't got nothing to pay me back for."

She looked surprised at that. She didn't answer right away, but took a long swig of her wine and then filled it up again from the skin. She huffed out a breath, which I seen people do oftentimes after they drunk too much. It's like the wine or the beer turns into fumes inside them, and the fumes start filling up their head. That's what it feels like too in my experience.

"What kind of questions?" she says to me then.

"Mostly about tech," I told her. "About how you come to know so much about it, and maybe . . ." I thought most carefully about my words. "Maybe where a man could go to find it. For you got some I never seen before, and you seem to know a lot about how it works. More than Ramparts, maybe." I said that last part to please her, hoping it would put her in the right mind to say yes, but also I believed it to be true. The things I was seeing all around me here, that Ursala used so lightly, was a store of treasure like I never dreamed of.

Ursala set the wineskin down but kept her hand on it, tapping her thumb against the neck of it while she thought. "Well," she says, "here's the problem. Some questions are easy to ask, but hard to answer. Often, you can start out on an explanation only to find that it doesn't make sense unless you explain a second thing, and then a third, and so on. You've pulled on a loose thread, and instead of snapping off clean it just keeps unravelling. I'll tell you what I can, Koli, but that's not the same as telling you all I know. Very far from it. Is that acceptable?"

It made me feel good how she asked me that. Like we was two people of weight and solemn mind, striking a bargain. "Yes," I said. And I used her word because I liked the sound of it. "That's acceptable, Dam Ursala."

"Then go ahead and ask."

I meant to ask straight out where I might find myself some tech like hers, but what come out of my mouth was a different question. I think it was something I hadn't ever stopped thinking about since I seen it, and now it was sitting right behind my tongue, like they say. "How did you bring down that drone with just a rock and a stick?"

"Seriously?" Ursala said. "That's what you want to know?"

"To start with. Please."

"The drones are very old. They were built hundreds of years ago, and nobody has ever inspected or repaired them in all that time. When they were new, they had a dozen different targeting systems – line of sight, sound, vibration, body heat, god knows what – so they could switch between them at need. Over time, those systems have degraded. Some of them are permanently offline. The thermal imaging, though, is very robust." She looked at my face and she seen the blankness there. "The heat," she said. "It's easiest for them to hunt you by the heat of your body. So when I picked up the burning branch and moved it around in front of me, I confused it. I was blurring my heat signature so I didn't look quite so much like a human target any more. And when I told you to go stand in the fire, it was for the same reason. You didn't do it, but my trick with the burning stick worked, fortunately. The drone came in closer to try to resolve the anomaly, and . . . Well, that was when I deployed my secret weapon."

"The rock?"

Ursala nodded, her face all serious but with a smile underneath somehow. "The rock, yes."

That give me a lot to chew on. Like most people, when I thought of tech I mostly thought about it as a kind of magic. I knowed it was men and women like us that made it, but that was in the old times. We was fallen a long way from what we was in them days, and we had lost the lore of such makings. But Ursala seemed to know a lot of things nobody else did. I seen I was right to take my reward in questions.

"Where does your tech come from?" I says to her.

Ursala shaked her head. "I could give you a name, but the name wouldn't mean anything to you. It came from the place where I was born and grew up."

"Elsewhere?"

"Elsewhere just means far away, Koli. And what's far to one man is no distance at all to another. It was a town called Duglas. There was a great deal more tech there than there is here, and we had ways – limited, but reliable – of making more."

"You could *make* tech?" That thought was astonishing to me, but seeing there was more tech in Ursala's tent than in the whole of Mythen Rood I was ready to believe it.

"Make it, or change it to suit our needs."

"Where did you get that knowing, Dam Ursala?"

"The same place you get yours. From our parents, and people of their generation, who got it from the generation before, and so on. The difference was that we were in better shape to start with. The world went through some bad times many years ago. Bad times that turned into worse times, and then worse still. When they were getting really bad, a lot of precious things – equipment, information, personnel – were evacuated from the mainland in the hope that they'd survive. Some of them ended up in Duglas, and we kept them safe there for as long as we could. For centuries, actually. Our records go back a long way.

"But Duglas fell in the end, and her people were scattered. I'm part of that diaspora. The last part, possibly. Certainly nobody ever answers when I call."

"But could somebody go there?" I tried not to let my hope-fulness show in my face or my voice, but it was hard to hide. "I mean, there might be tech there still that was left when . . . when whatever happened . . ."

I let them tail off, for Ursala was shaking her head again before I even got through them. Her face was stern, like she wanted to put that thought a long way out of my mind. "Nothing was left standing," she said. "And nobody was left alive. If I thought there was any chance of either, I would have gone back myself. Or I would have tried at least, though it's not a journey I'd undertake lightly. For one thing, it's across thirty miles of ocean."

"What's Ocean?"

"Like a forest, but made of water. And with things in it that you don't want to meet."

I tried to imagine that, but couldn't. Mostly the water I'd seen

91

was puddles after rain. Howsoever deep they were, they weren't so bad that you couldn't wade across them – or walk around them, if you wasn't sure how deep they was in the middle. There was also the lake at Havershar, where we would fish in Spring and Falling Time. You could cross Havershar in half an hour, in a little corkle boat that was light enough to carry on your back. I thought if Ursala only pointed me in the right direction I might prove her mistaken.

Right now, though, I just stopped making pretence and asked straight out. "Do you know anywhere else I could find some tech?"

"No, I don't," Ursala said with some considerable force behind the words. "It's been so long, most of it is in pieces now, or rusted away, or buried, or in the hands of people like the Vennastins. And though I'm in your debt, Koli, such equipment as I have myself I need to keep. I can't work without it."

That was me done then. I didn't have no other idea in mind for what to ask. But I seen from Ursala's face she was thinking on something. I had a hope, and though I was fixing to thank her for the tea and the raisin cake and get myself out of there, I stayed where I was and waited.

"Have you ever operated any of the tech from the old times?" she asked me. Like as you might say, did you ever put a ladder up against the moon and climb up there, when it was full and the light was good?

I laughed, thinking she meant it as a joke. "No, Dam Ursala, I did not."

"Then did you watch closely when someone else was using it? There's a point to the question, Koli. Don't laugh."

"No," I said again. "I mean, I seen the Ramparts at work often-times. But not what you'd call close."

"Let me show you something then."

She picked up the computer and tilted it so I could see the moving, changing pattern that was on it.

"That's very pretty," I said.

"Isn't it?" Ursala said. "Now watch."

She touched her hand to the edge of the computer, and of a sudden the pattern was gone. The picture had turned black as night, and at the same time there was a sound like a dead twig snapping. It happened so quick it brung me bolt upright. I thought Ursala had broke the picture on purpose, and I was shocked at the awfulness of such a thing. That anyone might do that to a piece of tech.

But then she touched the same place and the pattern come right back again, between me opening my mouth to yell and me getting the words out. So the words, when they come, was all stammering and weak. "You . . . you . . ." I said, pointing at the computer like the world's biggest fool. Then: "What did you do to it?"

"I turned it off and then on again," Ursala said. "There's a place at the corner there that moves under your finger. One touch depresses it, just a little, and a second touch releases it. Makes it stand out again. The picture only comes when the switch is depressed."

She couldn't make me understand just by telling it. She had to make me touch the place – the switch – for myself, again and again, making the shiny leaves go and come back each time. My hands was shaking when I did it. Apart from that one time, at my testing, I had never touched tech. Only Ramparts got to touch tech. *Koli Rampart*, I said inside my head, and almost said it out loud too, for it felt like a thing that needed to be said at such a time, when such an impossible thing was happening.

"It's called a switch," Ursala said, "because that's what it does. To switch a thing is to swap it for something else. In this case, you're swapping between the computer's sleeping state and its waking state."

That word made the connection in my mind. We always said *waked* for when the tech answered to someone or lit up or did what it was supposed to do when their hands touched it. That's what had just happened. The tech had waked for me. But it had only waked because I touched the switch.

"But . . . then . . ." I said. Tried to say. "When we're tested . . .

93

is that . . . ?" I struggled with the words, for I was struggling with the idea of it. My first thought was that the computer was of a different kind from Rampart tech, since it seemed it would wake for anyone. Then another thought come on the heels of that, which was that waking might not be what I believed it was.

I was pushing it away from me, because it was too big to think about. But as much as I pushed, it just kept coming back. Was testing just a trick after all, like Spinner said that time and then unsaid right after? Was there a switch on the bolt gun? On the cutter? On the firethrower? Did the Vennastins make the tech answer to them by knowing where the switch was and finding it with their fingers when they picked it up? And did Garan, that was Rampart Fire before Catrin was, tell it to her, and to her sister Fer? Did Loop tell it to Mardew, and Catrin to Haijon?

My mouth had locked itself shut, but my mind went racing on. It jumped right over that hedge and landed in the thistles and ropeknot on the other side.

"There's more to it than that," Ursala said. No doubt she was reading in my face the fight I was having, and guessed the reason for it. "There's another part of the tech, buried deep inside, that's called the battery. It stores power. Energy. The tech will only switch itself on if the energy is there. And the energy comes from sunlight – among other places. You see this?" She showed me the other side of the computer. There was a black strip there that was shinier than the rest of the thing, though it all had the polish and the smoothness to it that only old tech has ever got. "That's called a photo-voltaic strip. When it's placed in the light – out in the sun, for preference – it turns the light into electrical energy. The energy that makes tech do all the things it does. It needs to sit out in the sun for at least an hour, the first time it's used, and then to be taken out at intervals after that to charge it up again. Otherwise it will deactivate."

"De . . . action . . . ?"

"Switch itself off. Go dark and refuse to work." Ursala give a curse and flicked her finger hard against the side of her head, like

94

she was angry with her own mind. "I've said way too much. I shouldn't have talked to you while I was drunk."

"I'm happy you did," I said, though that was only somewhat true. My thoughts was still in too much of a boiling for me to know what I thought or felt. I think Ursala knowed that too, for she shaked her head at them words.

"But since I've got this far," she said, "there's one more thing you have to know, Koli. In case you were thinking of trying something stupid and reckless. Even if you found some tech and powered up the battery and found the switch, it would still be only fifty-fifty that it would work for you."

"Fifty-fifty?" I felt like an idiot, breaking in all the time with these questions about the words she was using, but by now this was a thing I felt like I couldn't just halfway understand. I had got to know it all.

"Fifty-fifty means one chance in two. It might work for you, but it's just as likely that it wouldn't. The reason why . . . well, it's a big secret here, though in other places I've been it's well known. I suspect you could get yourself into a lot of trouble, here in Mythen Rood, if you even spoke about it."

I didn't care, right then, about any trouble. I wanted to know. I couldn't bear for this secret, whatever it was, to pass out of my hands when I was this close to hearing it.

My life has had any number of bends in it, where I was going one way and then suddenly found myself heading in another with no chance or thought of going back. And most of those times I only seen the bend after, when I was looking over my shoulder at it, as you might say. When it was too late to do anything but live with it.

This time, though, I seen the bend coming. I knowed in the heat and heart of me that this day, this talk, was going to be a kind of switch, and would turn something on that couldn't never be turned off again while I lived.

And so it was, and so it did.

18

I come home after talking to Ursala, my head still full of all the things she told me — and especially that last thing. I didn't tell you that yet, but I will soon. It will make more sense in its right place.

When I got to the mill, Jemiu was standing at the front door of our house with her hands on her hips and her face like a threatening sky. But when she seen the look I was wearing she changed at once and was afraid for me.

"What happened?" was her first words. She must of thought from my smacked-in-the-mouth stare that someone died, or else that I was took bad in a way that might not mend. And if that was what she thought then she wasn't wrong, but I couldn't tell her. It was hard enough knowing it my own self.

"I run the walls with Haijon," I said, which was true, though it seemed a long time ago now. "And I think maybe I pushed myself too hard. I'm winded."

"Well, you're an idiot," Jemiu said. I expected no less, and I only throwed out that bait so her worrying for me would be turned right back into being angry again. Spinner was right about me and secrets: I never could hold one safe for very long, if my life depended on it. In fact, when my life come to depend on it was when I failed most woefully of all. So I did not mind Jemiu giving me rough words as long as she didn't press me harder on where I'd been.

"Get off to bed," she says to me now. "And tomorrow you mind you stay home. There's ten cord of timber to be steeped, and as much again to be cut square. You'll help Mull and Athen."

"Sorry, Ma," I said. "I'll do that."

She gun to relent a little then. She told me I was an idiot one more time, but she said there was bread and soup waiting for me in the kitchen, and probably enough life left in the cinders to warm the soup again. "Though the pot's dry as Midsummer from all the warmings it already had."

I slipped away to the kitchen, and I sit there a while thinking. I didn't have the stomach to touch that soup. My mind was in two pieces that was fighting each against the other. What Ursala said was too terrible to be true, yet it made some other things, that was vexing me already, in some ways better. I had failed the test, but suppose it wasn't me that failed but the test that was wrong and bad its own self? Then I had got a right to be tested again, didn't I? I had got a right to be tested on an equal foot with them that passed.

With Haijon.

Whatever I did (and I was already thinking what I might do) I had to start with him. If what Ursala said was true, then I couldn't be friends with him no more. We had got to be enemies. I didn't want that, yet a part of me was inclined to welcome it.

If Haijon had lied, then I would shout out the lie to everyone in the village, and Spinner would shun him. Everyone would shun him. Vennastins would be shamed too, since the lie would belong in equal parts to all of them. Ramparts would fall.

And what then, Koli? I asked myself. What happens to Mythen Rood if the Ramparts fall? I was checked somewhat in my recklessness by that question, but other reckless thoughts come in its wake. It was like Ursala dropped a big stone into my heart, and what was in there had got to come slopping out one way or another.

I lay waking all night, and worked all the next day. Jemiu was watching me close the whole time. It was not just to make sure I kept at it. I thought that at first, but there was a look on her face said it was something else besides. I think it was the state I was in the night before when I come home. It was still in her mind, and it had lit a suspicion there. She was keeping me home to keep me from something worse, though she had no real idea what that thing might be.

That was the day Ursala left the village. She had told me she would, and though I was sorry I didn't get a chance to say goodbye to her, yet I felt in another way like we had said all that had got to be said. I had asked her for answers and she give me more answers than I could rightly cope with. Now her road lay to the south, down the valley, to Ludden and then on to Sowby or Burnt Lea, places that was only names to me.

I throwed myself into the steeping and the cutting with a will, hoping some of the things I was feeling would come out of me along with the sweat. I never leaned on the long-soled plane harder than I leaned on it that day, or the next day. Jemiu left me alone at last, satisfied that I was deep into what I was doing.

Nor I never meant to deceive her, think what you might. It was myself I was striving with all that time, and I had no thought for any other. Excepting Haijon. Him I thought on a great deal.

On the third day, I picked up the water buckets and shrugged the yoke on across my shoulders. "I'll do that," Athen says to me. "You're better with the plane than I am."

"If I plane another plank, I'll be crying splinters," I said. "I want a change from it, Athen, and this is as good as any."

I seen the doubt in her face. She read me almost as well as my mother did. "Did someone hurt you, Koli?" she asked. "If I didn't know you was as gentle a one as ever walked, I'd say there was blood in your eye."

"There's sawdust in my eye, is all," I said. "And I'll walk it out and sweat it out, and be back betimes."

She give it up, and kissed me on my cheek. "Go the right way then," she said. Which was a peculiar thing to say when I was only going to the well. But I believe she seen deeper into me, like I said.

I left the buckets and the yoke by the well and went on to the gather-ground. That was the most likely place for Haijon to be, and there I found him, practising with the cutter while his cousin Mardew watched him with a shrewd, mistrustful eye as if he meant to steal it. I sit down to watch, some ways off, at the corner of the ground nearest the tocsin bell.

Haijon seen me after a while, and he waved to me. I waved back, though I didn't feel much like it.

"Hey, Koli," he called out. "Watch this!"

He leaned down, grabbed a rock off the ground and throwed it into the air. Then he pointed the cutter straight up, took aim and fired. Only he must of done something to the cutter's beam I never seen before. It hit the rock as it was falling and bounced it straight back up again. The rock come down a second time, and boom! It hit the beam and shot back up.

He bounced it three times, and then he done something that surprised me even more. The fourth time the rock come down, he got the cutter right under it and made it stop dead in the air, about ten feet or so from the ground.

He looked round, like as to say "How is that then?" and laughed when he seen the wonder on my face. I never knowed the cutter could do something like that. I never knowed it could do anything but cut. But I remembered what Ursala said about how the inside walls of her tent, that you couldn't rightly touch with your fingers, was somewhat the same as the cutter beam. So maybe there was more to the cutter than anyone knowed.

Haijon slipped his wrist out of the cutter and give it back to Mardew, who had been watching all this show with a sour sort of scowl on his face. If I was made to guess, I would say that Haijon was showing better with the cutter than Mardew expected, and that sit ill with him.

Haijon come over and clapped me on the shoulder. "You want

to race again, Koli?" he asked me. "I'll give you a start as far as that tree, if you want. Knowing how lazy you are in the afternoons, and all."

He was meaning to invite me to a trial of insults as much as to the race. I couldn't take either one right then. "Let's just walk a ways," I said. "To the lade, maybe."

"What's at the lade?" Haijon says.

"Nothing I know of. But it's a place to walk to that isn't here."

He nodded slowly. "I hear that song," he said. "Okay, let's walk."

We headed up the Middle, that was busy with people going to and fro. I seen Mardew turn around to keep us in his eye the whole way. There wasn't nothing friendly in the look he give me.

The lade was a kind of an open space just inside of the gate, like the gather-ground but much smaller, with walls that was long stakes hammered into the earth. I told you that no houses was builded so close to the fence, but the lade was not a house, nor nobody was meant to live there. It was just a circle of cleared ground with a wooden bench and an iron drink trough in it. It was meant to be a place where visitors could wait until they had said what their business was and got a yes or a no. But since we didn't get no visitors except only once in a bloomed moon, the lade was not much used. The bottom of the trough was rusted almost through, and there was green stains down the sides of it. I would not of drunk from it even on a dare.

When we got there, Haijon climbed up on the bench and sit on the back of it, since there was two planks missing from the seat. I stayed standing. I couldn't find a way, at first, into what I wanted to say. But since the tech was at the heart of it all, it wasn't that hard in the end to sneak around to it. "How'd you make the cutter do that?" I asked him. "Did Mardew teach you?"

Haijon laughed like that was a big joke. "Mardew teached me everything he knows," he said. "Took about an hour, but some of that time he was off taking a shit. Koli, there's more to the cutter than anyone guessed before. So much more. You seen what it does. But it's how it does it that's the amazing thing." He held up his hand like he still had the cutter on it, clenched up in a fist and pointing at the sky. He kind of made pretend with his other hand of what the cutter was doing. First of all, he stretched out all his fingers and held them tight together in a line. "See, it makes a kind of invisible knife that goes out in front of you, like this. You can't see it by looking at it, but you know it's there because it makes the air go wavy, kind of. Like the twists and ripples you get over a puddle when the sun's cracking down on it.

"But it don't have to be a knife, really. You can sort of decide the shape of it by how you move your hand. You can narrow it right down so it's like . . ." He curled up his pointing finger and folded his thumb around it, leaving just a tiny hole in the middle. "Like that. You know? Like that drill thing you use to put neat little holes in a plank of wood."

"An auger."

"Yeah, like an auger. Or you can flatten it out into a shovel. Or you can make it really wide, and then if it hits you it's more like being punched real hard than being stabbed with a knife. That was what I was doing with that stone – hitting it with a wide beam."

"How about when you held it still?"

Haijon shrugged. "I don't even know the words for that," he said. "It's like the widest field of all. Only you drive it in soft, so it don't hit the thing you're pointed at, it just kind of slides around it. I only just figured how to do it."

He looked up at me, and maybe he seen in my face some of what was in my heart. "You gonna sit down?" he asks me. He scooted to one side, leaving room for me to get up on the bench next to him, only I didn't do that. I didn't move at all.

"Why'd you choose the cutter, Haijon?" I asked him.

He looked surprised. "What?"

"Why'd you choose the cutter? Why not the firethrower, like your ma? Keep it going down through the family, like? Wasn't that a thing you felt like doing?"

He was looking at me strange, and I didn't blame him. My voice must of gone real hard when I come up to the point at last, and

Dandrake knows what my face looked like. The whole time Haijon was telling me about the things he could make the cutter do, I was thinking of Ursala's words and kind of hating him. Kind of running forward into that hate, and holding back at the same time, and not knowing which was worse.

"What's the matter with you, Koli?" Haijon asked me.

"There isn't nothing that's the matter with me. Just you answer, now. Don't try to get out of it."

Haijon blinked, like something got in his eye. "Get out of what?" he says. "What are you talking about?"

"The cutter, Haijon! I'm talking about the dead-god-damned cutter!"

He come down off the bench. "What's the matter with you?" he asks again. "Did I say something to cross you, cos if I did I don't remember it."

"A shit on what you remember," I shouted at him. "Why the cutter? Why was it the cutter you choosed?"

He shaked his head, like he was giving up on all this. "I'm going back inside the fence," he said, "and leaving you to your sulks."

I punched him in the face. I done it without even thinking. First thing I knowed about it was Haijon putting his hand up to his nose and bringing it away bloody.

"Oh," he says. "Like that?" And he hauled off and hit me back. It wasn't like he let go of his temper or nothing. It was more like something had wobbled out of balance and he had got to tilt it back again. Just the one punch, about as hard as the one I give him. It landed on my cheek and made my whole head ring – but Haijon outweighed me by a good twenty pounds and could of knocked me off my feet without trying.

The next thing I was up at him like a madman, swinging with both fists. He held me off with his left hand on my chest, leaning his head away from the punches so they just landed on his arms and shoulders and done very little to discomfort him.

"Koli, stop it!" he said. "Stop doing this!"

I stopped, and he let go of me. Then I jumped at him again

and tried to wrestle him down. I had even less luck with that than I done with the punching. Haijon got me in a lock and pushed me down so I was on my stomach in the grass, one arm folded under me and the other held in both of his hands so I couldn't move it at all.

"You're gonna get hurt," he shouted, like I wasn't trying to hurt him, or like that wasn't a thing that mattered much.

"Tell me the truth!" I yelled back, though the force of that yell was only felt by worms in the ground. "When did you see it? When did you touch it? Dandrake choke you, Haijon, what did Catrin teach you? What did she tell you to do?"

There was just silence, for a moment, from up on top of me. Haijon still kept me pinned in the same way, his knee in my back but not hard enough to hurt – only to stop me trying to get up, and getting my arm broke in the bargain.

"Oh," he said. "That. How'd you even know about that?"

I gun to cry then. I hadn't wanted to think it, but here was Haijon telling me it was true. It was true, and it was the worst thing that could be.

"If I let you up," he said, "are you gonna come up swinging?"

"No," I said. I didn't have no fight left in me. Haijon got off of me and took a step away. After a while I rolled over onto my back and sit up, rubbing my arm to get the feeling back.

He looked at me in wonder. "What in hell are you crying for?" he asked me. "I didn't hardly touch you."

"Tell me," I said. I was too angry right then to be ashamed that he seen me crying. This was the onliest thing that mattered, and I had got to hear it all.

Haijon wiped some more blood from his nose, which was still streaming. "There isn't hardly anything to tell. I know it was breaking the rules, but it's not like it was important. Are you gonna make a big song about such a stupid little—"

"You better just tell me, Haijon," I said. "Tell me, or tell the Count and Seal."

He blinked. "The Count and Seal? Are you mazed, Koli?"

"Tell me!"

"All right. The day before I went into the Waiting House, my ma asked me if I wanted to see the tech up close. I knowed I wasn't supposed to, and I said no at first. I thought it might be bad luck or something. But she said it wasn't anything. She asked me which one I was gonna try with, and when I said the cutter she went and brung Mardew into the room. She got him to take off the cutter and give it to me so I could try it on."

I waited, but he didn't say no more. "And?" I said. "Then what?"

"Then I give it back. What, Koli? You think Mardew let me stroke my dick with it or something? I only just weared it on my hand for a second or two, and then Ma made me give it back."

That left me facing every way but the right one, as they say. I tried to figure it, but I couldn't. "There's got to be something else," I said. "Something . . . what did she say to you? What did she do, right after?"

"She didn't do nothing. I think she went out of the room with Mardew, when he went. Then she come back and told me not to talk about it, which I didn't have no idea of doing until now. Koli, why does any of this matter? I wasn't supposed to touch the tech before I was tested, I know that. It's meant to be the first time, and it wasn't. For me it was the second time. But why are you saying it like it was something I should be shunned for? Go ahead and tell the damn Count and Seal. They can dock my ration, if it makes you feel better. Only it's a stupid thing for us to fight over. The stupidest thing I ever heard of."

I run out of words, of a sudden. I had charged into this because I felt like I needed to know, and what I found wasn't what I had been looking for. I was ashamed now of what I had been thinking about Haijon, who was my friend and deserved better of me.

But also I seen clear as day what Catrin done, and what she deserved.

And between them two things I couldn't speak at all, not even to tell Haijon I was sorry. I got up onto my feet again and put a hand on his shoulder, but he shrugged it away. "Dandrake's balls,

Koli, I don't know what's in you these days. You take Ursala's side against my ma, and now you're working up into a rage against me over nothing. Unless it's because I passed the test and you didn't, or I put Veso on the rush-walk in place of you. And if it's either of those things, then you can go dance with Dandrake as far as I care."

He was almost crying his own self by this time. He walked past me, banging me with his shoulder on the way, and kept on going until he turned the corner of a wall and I losed sight of him.

I stayed where I was. I knowed right then what it was I was going to do, and it was big enough so I couldn't see past it or around it.

19

Here's what Ursala told me. I'll tell it plain, in her words, and leave you to paint the rest yourself. What it done to me to hear it. What it made me think about the Vennastins and the way they ruled over us all. What it made me think about Haijon, until I learned better.

So this is me going back to that night in Ursala's tent when I asked her to tell me what she knowed about the tech of the old times and how it worked. And when she said there was one thing more, that was a secret and not to be talked about — or at least not in Mythen Rood, though there was places she'd been to where it was knowed by all.

I asked her to tell me what the secret was. I promised not to give it away, or let anyone know who it was that told me. I meant it too. I thought I could throw the bolt on my loose tongue if I needed to, in spite of what Spinner said the day we tumbled. I thought I had the trick of hiding what needed to be hid.

All right then, Ursala said. And she laid it out for me: the big lie, and all the little lies that had been piled on top of it. She brung me out of a fool's paradise into a colder place, and it was all at my asking so the only fool was me.

"The tech of the old times," she said, "if it was dangerous or valuable, had a whole suite of security features. Safeguards designed to make sure it couldn't be used by anyone except its legal owners.

"Those safeguards got stronger and stronger over time. At first it was most likely to be what they called a password. If you picked the tech up or tried to switch it on, it would ask you for a secret word that the tech's owner had made up beforehand. Just like when you come to the gates of a village at night when it's too dark for the gate-watch to see you clearly. She'll shout, 'Who is it goes there?' and you'll have to answer with your name. Only the password wouldn't have been your name, because that would be too easy to guess. It would be the name of a pet you used to have, or the name your mother called you when you were a baby, or a word that didn't exist at all until you made it up. Do you understand, Koli?"

I nodded. I didn't think Mythen Rood gates opened after dark for anyone, but I understood how it worked for hunters and wood-catchers when they whistled to each other over dead ground and knowed who it was on account of the whistles all being different. I thought it couldn't be too far removed from that.

"Okay. Well, the safeguards became more sophisticated – cleverer – over time. You might be able to guess someone's password if you knew them well enough. Other things would be harder to guess. Some tech would open if you drew a shape on it, or answered some questions, but again it was only a matter of a thief making the right guesses and she could get past the safeguards and use your tech.

"The solution, in the end, was to make the tech itself be a sort of gate-watch. When you picked it up, it looked at you and decided whether or not to let you in."

"Tech ain't got no eyes," I said. Then I thought of the bolt gun, and how the bolts chased the thing they was aimed at. "Most tech doesn't, anyway."

"That's true. But it wasn't always a question of looking at your face. You see this?" Ursala held up her hand with all the fingers spread out wide. "The lines on your fingertips, they're different from anyone else's. So there might be a pad or strip somewhere on the tech that could take the imprint of your fingertips and check them against its memory to see if it knew you. If you matched, it would work for you. If you didn't, it shut you out. The patterns of colour in your eyes could be used in the same way. They're unique too.

"But the best method, and the one that became pretty much universal in the end, was what they called bio-sampling."

"I don't know what that is," I said.

"It's very hard to explain. Suppose I said that the tech tastes the sweat on your skin. And everyone tastes different."

"Okay," I said. I was thinking of Spinner's sweat that day in the lookout when we kissed and when we tumbled. How it had made me feel to smell and taste her, and how different it was from any smelling or tasting the world had put my way before or since.

"It wasn't really sweat that the tech was testing," Ursala said. "It was something else that was even harder to fake. Something called DNA. It's in every part of your body, invisible, and that includes the surface of your skin. The tech was so clever it could examine your DNA quicker than you could blink your eyes. And there was no arguing against what it decided. It knew exactly who you were. You were either on the nice list or the naughty list. And if you were on the wrong list then the very best that would happen to you was that the tech wouldn't wake up. If you were unlucky, it would wake up and scream an alarm, or send a shock through you that would knock you out."

She was in full flood, her eyes all shining as she talked, but when she stopped she lost the sense of where she was and sat still, staring at the table. I think the wine had something to do with it – and maybe the fear that had made her drink the wine in the first place. The fear that Catrin Vennastin might come against her in the dark.

I asked a question, aiming to start up that flood again. "But the first time you picked up that tech," I said, "it wouldn't know you. How could it? Ursala, I seen tech decide for itself to let someone use it, when they picked it up for the first time. It happened to my friend Haijon. I was there."

Ursala give a shrug, like that wasn't nothing, but her face was sad. "What you saw wasn't what you thought you saw, Koli," she said. "In the world that was lost, it was just a matter of following the instructions. You took the tech out of the box, powered it up and configured it. It woke up knowing there was a user nearby. All you had to do was introduce yourself.

"And after that . . . well, any authorised user can register someone else. You tell the tech to accept and log the next person who picks it up – to put them on the nice list – and then you hand it over."

I was still struggling, but now I was trying not to believe what Ursala was telling me. It was too awful if it was true. If it was true, then nothing else was.

"But the Ramparts . . ." I said. Then I started again: "I didn't see no . . ." Okay, that wouldn't do it neither. "Nobody done any of that when we had our testing in the Count and Seal. The tech was just set there, on the table, and we choosed what to touch. There wasn't anybody telling it who was who, or giving it orders. We would of seen. Everybody would of seen."

Ursala smiled, kind of cold, like I was helping her argument – holding the plank so she could nail it in, as they say. "Yes. You would have seen. So all of that gets done earlier. By the time you come to the testing, Catrin Vennastin has already decided which way it will go, for each and every one of you."

I seen it then. But I didn't know until Haijon told it to me just exactly how Catrin done what she done.

Which one you like, Haijon? Which one you think you're like to go for? Let me fetch it for you, so you can take a good look at it. So you can hold it, and so it can get the heft of you. Because I already told it the next one to pick it up would be a friend.

Haijon was innocent of it, at least, but that was what must of happened, just the same. I seen how Catrin made him into a Rampart. That was when the anger took me, and it just got worse and worse until me and him had that fight.

109

It wasn't like I stopped being angry after that neither. I just turned it another way. I got to feeling heedless of my future, since the onliest future I could see was being trod on by Ramparts until the day I died. Well, Dandrake could eat that and shit it out again. If rules was being broke, I could break them too. If Catrin could bend the tech to her own wish and her own winning, there wasn't a damn thing to stop me doing the same, and standing up as tall as anyone. Only trouble was, I didn't have any tech right then to work with.

So I thought I would go and steal some.

20

Breaking into Rampart Hold was real easy in the end. Also, it was the hardest thing I ever done.

That loose window was still where it had always been. All I had to do to get down into the Underhold was to wait until dark and sneak across the gather-ground while the lookout's back was turned. And once I was in, I knowed where to go.

What made it hard was the thinking about it. This wasn't like when we was kids, and sneaked in through that window to play blind man's touch down in the dark. This was me going up against the Ramparts. And not just the Ramparts but my own mind, that had steeped in all the old rules the way green wood steeps in stop-mix.

I choosed my moment, four turns of the glass past midnight when the old lookout was ready to come off the tower and most likely not so wide awake as they ought to be. I climbed out of bed, put my day clothes on again and slipped out of the house. But I stopped along the way to take the workshop key off its big hook and put it in my pocket. No one heard me go. I hoped nobody would hear me come back neither, but if they did I had already made up a story to explain what I was doing – that I heard someone moving around outside and went to see who it was.

It was a clear night, with a full moon. Anyone with any sense in their heads would of seen that and gone back to bed, but I had made up my mind to this course and it wasn't in me to put the business off even to the next night. It was now or never, as they say, and never wasn't a thought I could bear to think.

But I wasn't so stupid neither as to cross the gather-ground with that moon shining down on me like a lantern. I stood in the shadows under the tocsin bell until a cloud come over, and then I took my chances. I didn't run, though something in me surely wanted to. I knowed running would make my footsteps sound out louder, and I'd stand out that much more from the dark if someone was looking. I moved slowly, so a watching eye might not see me move at all.

But there wasn't no watching eyes, or at least none that seen me, for I made it to the back wall of Rampart Hold with no ruckus raised. The cloud was still favouring me so I didn't tarry. I found that loose window, right where it had always been, and eased it out of its frame. I set it next to me, up against the foot of the wall.

When I joked with Haijon that he might be too big now to go through the gap, I hadn't ever thought that might go for me too. I had slid through it just as easy as a rat when we was children, and I didn't feel I'd growed so very much bigger since. But it was a tight fit, and my feet scuffled on the stones a little as I pushed to get through. Then when I come down inside I landed badly and fell over on my back, knocking down a broom that was standing against the wall.

My heart was climbing up my throat with both hands as I crouched there, listening. This was the top level of the Underhold. Right over my head was the Hold its own self, where Ramparts was sleeping now and everything was still as stone. Someone must of heard me, I thought, for the noise had been so shocking loud in my ears.

But no one come, and by and by I picked myself up off the floor. My skin was still tingling with fear, and if anyone had touched

112

me I would of run up the wall onto the ceiling and kept on going. But since they didn't, I went down the stairs, feeling my way in the dark.

I could of brung a candle and a tinder-box with me, but I was scared the shining would be seen out of the window, or maybe even through the boards in the ceiling if anyone was still awake in the house up above me. In any case, I knowed my way by feel. I had played a thousand games of blind man's touch down here, and all them games was in my feet and in my fingers.

I went down past two levels of stores, and then I come at last to that door I hid behind five Summers past – the door that was two doors, one behind the other. I drawed back the bolt on the outside door, and I found the handle on the inside one. It didn't give when I turned it, being locked.

I took out the key I brung with me, my ma's workshop key, feeling all over the lock plate with my other hand until I found the keyhole. I tried the key, and it slid right in. When I turned it, I felt the wards turning with it, and I heard the click as they give.

I breathed out a big breath right then, that was like a sigh. I hadn't knowed for sure it would work; I only hoped. The first time I seen the lock, I reckoned it to be the exact twin of the lock on Jemiu's workshop door. It was my da who made both after all, and put them there. I was thinking he might of used the same key for both plates, rather than cast another while he was here. Catrin would of skinned him if she found him out, but like I said he didn't stay but a single night. It seemed like a good bet he never told the woman that was paying his hire that he put in a second lock for the woman who tumbled him.

There was nothing but pitch dark on the other side of the door. I stepped forward, my hands held out in front of me, going an inch at a time in case I tripped. I touched nothing for a long way, then suddenly my fingers was stroking cold metal. I slid them over the shape of it and found a row of shelves about an arm's length deep and maybe twice as wide. The shelves was filled with stuff of every size and shape.

113

All my guesses was working out, one after another. This was the tech that never yet worked for anyone, or else had stopped working long before. The tech that only come up above the ground once a year on testing day.

I run my fingers over all the things that was there, feeling the strange shapes and the strange smoothness of their surfaces. The men and women who made these things was dead and buried long years before I was ever born. I felt, just for a second or so, that I was buried with them, and when I reached around to find the door it would be gone because this was a grave instead of a room. I had to go back and make sure the door was open, and I took the key out of the lock so nobody could shut me in.

It was around about then I had a thought that might of done some good if I had it an hour before. I should of brung a bag. Without one, the most I could take was what I could hold in my hands. My plan was to take as many bits of tech as I could carry and try them out one by one in the hope of finding one that would wake for me. If I did find one, I would bring all the others back the next night, hoping that the Ramparts wouldn't miss the one I took. Then I could say I found it in the woods. It was a thing that had sometimes happened, though not in my lifetime.

It waked when I touched it, I'd say, *so that makes me a Rampart*. It was a flat lie, but it seemed a small one next to the lies the Ramparts themselves was telling every time they used their tech and every testing day. I felt ashamed, but I was angry enough to get myself past that feeling. And there was a thought under everything else that pushed me on, though I tried my best not to think it. It was that Spinner had choosed Haijon instead of me because he was a Rampart, and if I become a Rampart too then she might change her mind after all.

What with these hopes and dreams and tangled-up thoughts, and fearing to be catched, and not having a bag, I stood there for a long time like I had put down roots and would be found in full flower when the weather turned.

What pulled me out of that was a shout from outside that give

114

me such a shock I all but yelled my own self. I thought someone had found the window out of its frame and set up a hue. I was so panicked by it I took to my heels, though there was nowhere to run to. I missed the open door in the dark and banged into the wall, which set me down on my tail.

My head was ringing like the tocsin bell, and there was lights in my eyes that was kind of dancing. They'll get me for sure if I just lie here, I thought, but when I tried to get up my legs didn't seem to have no bones in them. Then there was another shout in a different voice, and I realised it was just the lookouts calling the change, the one of them as she went and the other one as she come.

I had been in here much too long, in other words. I crawled over to the back wall again and grabbed an armload of stuff from off the bottom-most shelf. I didn't try to choose, which wouldn't of been much use in the full dark. I just took what come. Then I put myself up on my two feet again somehow and got myself out of there. Remembering to lock the door and take the key, which if I left it behind would of been like an echo-bird shouting out "Koli Woodsmith done this!" for all the village to hear.

Coming back out of the Underhold was not half so easy as going in. I forgot where the stairs was at first. I had got to free one hand up to feel along the walls, so now I was just holding the tech all cradled in my other arm. A couple of times I dropped something and had to go back for it. I was scared past anything that I might of broke the tech. That instead of making myself a Rampart I was just making myself a wrecker and a reaver. I was moaning, kind of, in my throat, and my knees was shaking so much I must of looked like I was bit by a knifestrike and took the poison.

But I found the stairs at last, and I stumbled and scrambled my way up them to the landing where the window was. I dropped the tech out onto the grass outside, one piece at a time. There was seven pieces, I knowed now, for I counted them as they passed out of my hands. They might of broke then too, from hitting the ground or from landing on top of each other, but

115

there wasn't no other way to do it. I needed both hands and both feet to climb back out.

I done it slowly, scared of making a sound. The new lookout had only just come on, so she would be wide awake, and there was no way now to lie about what I done or why I done it. There was the tech lying right by to accuse me.

Once I was out, I had to go down on my knees and pick up all the tech, one piece at a time. The moon was down, which was a help in one way as I wasn't in full view, and a hindrance in another as I couldn't see. I swear to Dandrake, I almost forgot to breathe when I was groping around for those precious things, waiting all the time for a light to go on inside the house or for the lookout to shout a challenge.

None of them things happened. I picked up all the tech and I creeped away on my toes' tips across the gather-ground.

And home, where the door was still unlocked as I had left it, I hanged up the workshop key on its hook.

I stowed the tech under my bed, where no one was like to look.

I undressed and climbed back under the covers.

I guess I don't need to tell you how much sleep I got.

21

The next day I worked in the shed and in the mill yard, and said not a word to anyone. My ma was approving of the work I done but a mite troubled by my silence.

"What bit you on the tongue, Koli?" she asked me.

"Nothing bit me," I mumbled. "I'm just tired, is all it is."

"He sneaked out in the night," Athen said. "I think he got a sweetheart."

She only meant it as a joke, but it give me great dismay that she heard me go out. And the dismay come out as anger, like it will for anyone from time to time. "A man can't even take a walk but women watches him," I shouted, and throwed down the long-soled plane with a great clatter.

"You just wish women watched you," Mull said. "Act your age now, and go back to work."

"And pray that plane isn't broke," Jemiu put in. "For if it is, I'll take a broom to you and turn your face into something worth watching."

"Looks like someone already did," Athen says. I didn't realise until then that I took some bruises when I run into that wall in the Underhold. They had flowered up in the night, so now there was a line, all purple and yellow, down from my left eye to my chin. It seemed like I was raising a cry against my own self, every way I could.

"Did you get in a fight?" Jemiu asked me, giving me a harder look.

I put on a kind of a smile, or the closest I could get to one. "I did, Ma, if you want to know," I says. "I got in a fight with a door, and the door give me a smack when I wasn't looking. But I'm gonna win next time. I'm gonna wait till it's bolted and drub it good."

Jemiu laughed, and so did my sisters. I took up the plane again and put my back into it, hoping they would let it lie there, which I'm happy to say they did.

In the afternoon, when things was a mite quieter, I went and looked at the tech for the first time since I took it. You might wonder that I didn't steal a look as soon as the sun was up, but there was a kind of a fear on me that pushed me away from it. What I had done in the night seemed more like a dream than a real thing now that it was daylight again, and the tech was the onliest thing that would prove it true. It was like the longer I stayed away from it, the longer I could make pretend I wasn't a thief or a law-breaker and hadn't done any such crazy thing.

But when I kneeled down and looked under the bed, there it was. There wasn't no denying it, or making it be something different than it was. So I might as well go forward, for there certainly wasn't no chance of going back. I took the seven pieces out from under the bed to get a better look at them.

Now I seen my mistake, very clear. When I seen the tech on testing day, it had seemed to me to be all kinds and shapes and sizes and conditions of things all throwed in together. But that was in the hot moment, as they say. I was seeing something different now.

The seven pieces of tech I had took was all the same. They was seven little silver boxes, maybe a hand's length from top to bottom and half that much across. They was very thin, but they was made of white metal and had some weight and solidness to them. They all had the smoothness and the coldness that the bolt gun had when I picked it up on my testing day. They was shiny and lustrous and altogether beautiful.

But they was just the same thing seven times over, like I said. When the tech was took up and brung down again, the officers of the Count and Seal must of tried to keep like with like and same with same. That cast my spirits down, for it seemed my chances of carrying out my plan was a lot less than if I had got seven different things made in seven different ways.

I say they was the same, but that's a loose speaking. They was all the same shape and size, with three of the things that Ursala called switches on them, all in a line along the bottom. Also they all had a kind of a glass plate set into them on one side, that I would of called a window except you couldn't see nothing through it but black. Maybe it was one of those things Ursala told me about that soaked up the sun and stored it inside the box so it could do whatever it was made for.

They was all made that way, like I said. But underneath this sameness there was small differences to be seen. Two of the boxes had got a little twist of string hanging off of them, where the other five didn't. And one of them had a star shape stuck on the back, with a little a picture of a horse, only the horse had a horn in the middle of its head and was smiling, which is a thing I never seen a horse do. Also, one of the seven had some signs from the old times across the bottom of it under the switches. I couldn't read back then so I had no idea what the letters said. I didn't think of them as saying anything at all, but only as shapes, like the signs that was moving on Ursala's computer when she done the maths on it.

I looked at the little boxes a long while, with my thoughts running every which way inside my head. I was struck and dazzled by them being there, in my hand, in my room. I felt like I was different, somehow, when I was holding them – like some of their smoothness and coldness had come off onto me. But at the same time, I was thinking: I should of taken something from off of every shelf. It would of been easy to do, and better.

And I was wondering mightily what the boxes might do if they woke. They didn't look like no weapons, but nor did the cutter until you seen how it worked. If my plan come to pass and I was made a Rampart, what Rampart would I be?

I used up most of an hour in this dreaming, and only come out of it when I heard Mull call for me to come and help her carry some planks to the steeping trough. Quickly I gathered up all the boxes and done what I meant to do in the first place. I set them out in a line on the ledge next my window. Not in front of the window, but beside it. There was a kind of a gable there, so nobody would see them even if they come in the room, and the tech would get all the light there was. The sun was shining fit to bust right then. I think I said before that these were the last clear days – a time my ma sometimes called the engine Summer, though what engine she meant I never heard her say.

I figured I would give them silver boxes a day to charge up with sun energy, or maybe two days, and then I would start in trying to wake them one at a time. I'd keep on going for maybe a week, pressing the switches and trying to make the boxes say accept or acknowledge or such. Then if nothing happened I'd take them back to Rampart Hold after night fell and pretend like nothing had happened.

But somehow I never really believed it would go like that. I thought for sure the boldness of what I done would bring some good. It was like I had put everything I was and everything I had into this one business, and the world had got to match that wager or it wasn't no world at all.

I was young, which maybe isn't no excuse for being so stupid. Also, the way it come out, I was right. But I don't see as how that makes it any better. Good success in a bad labour sets you down a dangerous path, so the dead god said one time before they killed him.

That lock-tide when I come back to my room I picked up the boxes one by one. The sun had gone down a good hour before, but they was still warm to the touch like as if they was alive.

22

Salt Feast was coming up. Haijon and Spinner was fasting for their wedding, which was set to be on the day of the feast.

I think I told you that Ursala give answer on three pair-pledges that year. Them other two couples was in the Fasting House, for they decided they would say their promises on the same day the new Rampart did. They thought it a good omen, like as not.

But Haijon and Spinner was not in the Fasting House. The Count and Seal said it would be too cramped in there for six people, the women's room in particular being very small and narrow. So they give a licence this one time for Spinner to fast in Rampart Hold, and since she was doing that, Haijon had got to fast there too.

Meanwhile, there was the salt lodge to be put up in the middle of the gather-ground, and the tabernac for the wedding right next to it, and the bonfire over on the setting side. Three new share-works, and six souls less to advance them. That meant some busy days coming, right when I needed to be free.

It worked out well enough though. My sisters was dead set on decorating the tabernac, and since they couldn't do till it was builded they went all out to build it. Ma and me was left alone at the mill the next three days. There was lots of work to do, but we was often doing it in different places, Ma going out with the catchers while I took care of what they catched. So I had no one watching over me, and could do as I liked as long as I didn't slack.

Late in the morning of that next day, I went into my room and sit down on the bed with all the boxes laid out in front of me. I tried the one with the horse on it first, pressing the switches each in turn, then going back and holding each one for a couple of breaths before I let it go again.

That didn't do nothing. I went along the line, trying the same things each time. It seemed a good idea to keep some order in it so I knowed where I was got to.

But it didn't help none. There wasn't a single one of the boxes did anything at all. They didn't feel warm now, the way they did the night before. They was as cold in my hand as when I brung them out of Rampart Hold.

So then I tried to bespeak them, the way we was told to do when we was preparing to be tested. I said confirm and accept and acknowledge to each and every one of them, sometimes with my thumb on one of the switches and sometimes without. That didn't make no difference, neither.

I was at this for an hour or more. Then I looked out of the window and seen the catchers coming back with a cartload of fresh wood. Ma was looking around for me, no doubt so I could help with getting the wood tied down on the drying frame, so I had got to leave off what I was doing and hide the boxes back under the bed again.

The next time I took them out was that same night, after everyone was gone off to sleep. I was tired to death myself, but my restless thoughts wouldn't let me settle, so in the end I give in to them and tried again. I done the same as before, except that I was whispering the words instead of saying them out loud. Mull and Athen's room was next to mine, and I was scared of rousing them instead of the tech. Dandrake save me if I broke their sleep after they slaved all day on the tabernac.

Come morning, I set the boxes out on the window ledge again, being afraid that they might not of drawed down enough power, or that they had used up all they took even though they didn't do nothing yet. Ma stayed home that day, so I didn't get no chance at all to put them to trial again. Just before lock-tide, she went to visit with Shirew Makewell, but right then was when Athen and Mull come home. I had to wait until we all of us went off to sleep, just like the night before.

As soon as the goodnights was all said and my door was closed behind me, I went to it, pressing and holding, confirming and acknowledging and all the ruck and run of it. I was clinging onto hope like a man sinking in a bog holds onto a clump of grass, not daring to pull on it in case it breaks clean off. The boxes still wasn't doing nothing at all but lie there, while I tickled and coaxed and begged and meddled to no purpose.

A thought come to me then. The tech had laid in the Underhold for years on top of years. If the Vennastins knowed the same things Ursala knowed, which they had got to because otherwise they couldn't of made the tech wake for them, then they knowed how to do all the things I was doing now. And if they knowed, then they must of tried them out. The rest of us only got to see the tech on testing day, but Dam Catrin and her kin lived with it all year round – and everything they had, everything they was, come from this one power, this one thing that they had the say over.

I seen it, of a sudden, and I didn't doubt but it was true. They must of pressed every switch and spoke every word, not blind like me but careful and slow and patient, year after year – just in case they found a fifth piece of tech that someone could hold, so their power could sit that much firmer and their glory be greater still.

And now here I come, with the big secret burning a hole through my head, thinking it give me advantage, when it hadn't never been a secret to the Vennastins in the first place. So whatever I tried, it was certain sure they must of tried it before.

The sorrow of it come down on me like a weight. All the things I done, that I thought was uncommon brave and brilliant, wasn't nothing of the kind. I was just a thief and a scoff-law, bloated up with big intentions. The kind of man I never had any consideration for and never wanted to be. The kind of man that eleven times out of a dozen ends up faceless or shunned.

I set down the box I was holding. I didn't do it gentle, neither, but sort of pushed it away from me across the bed. I put my head down in my hands. I think maybe I was crying, though I don't remember for sure. I felt like crying anyway.

"Go ahead and choose a channel," a voice said. "It's not like it's gonna bite you." It was a girl's voice, and it come from right next to me on the bed. I jumped up like I was stung, and looked around to see who said it. I didn't see no one, but the box I just throwed down was all on fire with light. The light was coming from the black window, only it wasn't black no more but full of swirling, twisting colours like oil poured out on water.

The girl give a laugh. "Or maybe I should choose, baka-sama," she said. "Put your tunes in my hands. You can trust me. Just tell me how you want to feel."

It was the strangest voice I ever heard. The sounds of it was wrong in some ways. Like when the girl said feel, she made it longer than it should be. *Fee-el.* As if it was two words instead of one. But it was a real beautiful voice too, like it was halfway to being a song. And there was a kind of a brightness in it, so you could almost see the girl when you heard her talking.

She was young. She had got to be young, because her laugh come out of her like bubbles, the way children laugh. And pretty, and smiling in a way that was coaxing you to smile too or else you was spoiling the party.

What I should of said first, though, is that the voice was coming out of the box. I seen now that the swirly colours in that little window was kind of flickering in time to the words, like they was tied together somehow. I kneeled down next to the box and stared at it with my eyes as big as barrel-heads.

"Do you like scratch-pop?" the girl said. "Eva Lopez just cut a new single. Say the word, boy wonder, and I'll pour that honey right in your ears."

I come to my senses at last. It was a wonder Athen and Mull wasn't yelling through the wall at me already. I had got to stop this, right now, before they waked up and come to see who I was talking to.

"Stop talking," I says. "Please. You got to be quiet!"

The colours kept on moving for a second or two, then the window went dark again. I was all in a panic, thinking I switched it off when I didn't even know how I switched it on. Worse than that, once the light went out of the window, that box looked just like all the other boxes. In the dark, I couldn't tell any more which one it was that had spoke.

"Are you still there?" I whispered. "Girl? Hello?" I picked up one of the boxes and give it a shake. Then I dropped it and done the same to the next one along. "Just say confirm," I moaned. "Or acknowledge. Please! Please don't be gone!"

The window of the first box – the one I just took up and dropped – come alight the same way it did before. I heard that laugh again, bubbling up out of nowhere. "Okay, moon rabbit. Confirm! Acknowledge! Was that good for you?"

I picked up the box. My hands was shaking so I almost dropped it, but now it was lit again, I could see it was the one that had the picture of a horse with a horn on its head. At least I would be able to tell it from the others. "Yes," I says. "Thank you. That's . . . that's all for now."

"That's all for now," the box said back to me. It said it the exact same way I said it, like the girl was making fun of me. "So rude, neh. You and me are gonna have words, dopey boy. But later. Last blossom falls, so we fall, so we're . . . gone, gone, gone." Them last words was sung, not spoke. The window went black again.

But the box was warm in my hand. It felt alive.

And I swear to the dead god, it smelled like flowers.

23

The next day was meant to be turn and turn about. Athen and Mull would work in the mill while Ma and me went down to the gather-ground and joined the share-work.

It didn't work out that way though. Jemiu had to go out with the catchers again, the last day's catch having come in short. And I didn't go nowhere near the tabernac. I couldn't of done it. My thoughts was all on the silver box and the girl inside it. I had got to talk to her again, and in particular I had got to do one other thing, which was what Ursala said. I had got to make her accept me as a user, so she'd be mine and not nobody else's. Until I done that, anyone else could pick up the box and say those words, and then I'd just be Koli Woodsmith again, from now until I died. I was all in a boiling from thinking these thoughts, and they wouldn't let me rest nor work nor nothing. I had got to settle it. And since I was afraid the girl's voice might be overheard, I had got to do it somewhere where I could be sure I'd be left alone.

I walked to the gather-ground, but then I circled around the back of it, putting the walls of Rampart Hold between me and them as was working. I went down the Middle to the Span, and from there all the way along to the broken house. That was as far away as you could get from the gather-ground and still be inside the fence, so I was pretty sure I'd be alone, but I looked all round before I stepped in through the one half of an arch that was all it had by way of a door. And once I was inside, I made sure to keep ducked down, kind of, with my shoulders bent over. The stone walls of the house, or what was left of them, didn't come up higher than my chest along most of their length, but as long as I didn't stick my head up high I couldn't be seen from afar off, and there was nobody close enough to see me through the gaps in the stone.

I had brung the silver box with me, tucked inside my shirt. I took it out now and held it in both hands, sitting down with my back against the wall and my feet out in front of me.

"Okay," I said. "Wake up."

The box didn't do nothing.

I tried confirm, and I tried acknowledge, but they didn't do a damn bit of good either. I got scared then. It will sound like a stupid fear when I tell it, but it struck my heart just the same. I was afraid I dreamed the voice, and the box wasn't going to wake for me again because it never did in the first place.

But right then is when I seen something I should of seen before. On the bottom edge of the box there was another switch. It was smaller than the switches that was on the front and it wasn't made to be pressed. It was made to be slid across, with your thumb or maybe with the heel of your hand. I must of touched it by accident the night before, when I was turning all seven boxes over and over in my hand.

I slid it now, from left to right. It made a clicking sound that seemed to have some serious meaning to it. Of a sudden, the black window lit up again with all the same patterns and colours I seen the night before.

"Hiiiiiiiiiii, dopey boy," the girl in the box said to me. "You want me to say confirm-acknowledge? I know that's your favourite!"

I was so relieved she was still there, I let out the breath that was in me all at once. "Oh my goodness!" the girl said then, kind of making out like she was shocked. "You're too excited already. I'll

127

have to calm you down before you have a heart attack. Are you one of those kyoktana sportsu types? Too bad if you are. Dancefloor's the place for cardiac, baka-sama. You should know that by your age. What *is* your age anyway? So rude of me to ask, shame, shame, but a girl likes to know what she's getting into."

I couldn't think of nothing to say to this big flood of words. It was that same voice again, that was halfway to singing and halfway to laughing – like everything in the world was a joke, and the girl in the box was sharing the joke just with you and not with nobody else. But none of what I was doing was fit to be joked about. Stealing from Rampart Hold could get me whipped, or worse. I knowed I had got to take control of the box so it was mine and nobody else's. And I had got to do it before anyone else seen it or knowed about it.

But I was too slow, by a long way. "So," the girl in the box says, "what say we wapoo? I bet you got some moves, right? Cue disco lights!"

I don't hardly know how to say what happened next. The whole inside of the broken house filled up with sparks, kind of, only the sparks was of different colours and they was rushing and swirling round. They was even moving on my skin, though I didn't feel no heat at all.

"This one's by Redbeard," the girl said. "'Spin Ain't No Sin'. If you like it, I'll put it on your playlist. If you don't, just make a raspberry noise. I can take a hint."

The next thing I knowed, there was drums and a horn and a whole lot of other things sounding out from all around me. The drums was first, and they was so loud and so close I thought that drummer was going to come up behind me and step on me. I flinched and ducked, kind of, and then all the other instruments was going and it was like Summer-dance come round again without anyone told me.

I didn't even realise straightway the sounds was coming from the box. The box was a little tiny thing and the sounds was bigger than you ever heard. When I did realise it, I give a yell that was even bigger. "No! Stop now! You stop that!"

The sounds and the lights all stopped at once. The lights had been coming out of the box too – out of the little window – and they went back inside it now, shrinking down and fading out until they was all gone. I kneeled there, breathless, listening. I could still hear the hammers and saws from the gather-ground, and the shouts now and then of someone telling someone else to fetch that bucket or to square that corner off. It seemed like they didn't hear the music over the sounds they was making their own selves, which was a lucky thing for me.

"No more music!" I said to the box. "You hear me?"

"I hear you, little dumpling. No need to shout." The girl in the box sounded like her feelings was hurt, but only for a second. Then she put on her laughing-singing voice again. "No more music is a weird thing to say to your music player, neh? Did you think you bought an egg whisk? I will not whisk your eggs, dopey boy. But I could play a movie. Wanna pop some corn and bust some blocks?"

This girl was even harder to understand than Ursala, I thought. But it didn't matter if I understood her or not. It just mattered that I got to be in control of the tech and authorised and such.

So I come right out with it. "You got to authorise me," I told her. "As a user."

I was hoping she'd just say, "Authorised," which we was told in the Waiting House was the right response if the tech was going to work for you. But she didn't say it. What she said was, "Wait. Stop. Freeze-frame. That's how you're gonna talk to me?"

I didn't have no better idea than to try the same thing again. "Say I'm authorised," I told her. "You got to."

"Hmmm," the girl said. There was a sound I didn't recognise. It was pages turning over in a book, but I hadn't never heard that sound back then. "How to turn a block of wood into a nice, kind, polite boy," the girl said in a low voice like she was thinking real serious thoughts. "Rule one. Smack him in the head when he says, 'You got to.' That sounds easy enough. Lean forward and close your eyes, O dopey one."

I was starting to panic now. Nothing I was saying was doing

any good at all. It was like the girl in the box was meaning to take control of me instead of the other way round.

"What's your name, girl?" I asked, trying for the stern voice Dam Catrin used when she spoke out in the Count and Seal.

"What's my name?" The girl in the box sounded like she couldn't believe I was asking her.

"Yeah."

"My actual name? The one they call me by in New York and Tokyo and lovely lazy London? You're asking my *name*, dopey boy?"

I gun to say I was sorry I asked her, but I seen that wasn't the way to go. I wouldn't never get to be in control that way. "Just you tell me," I said. "Right now. Do as you're told."

There was dead silence for a time. It felt like a *long* time, though I know well what tricks your mind can play at such moments. Most likely it was not much time at all.

"Wow," the girl said.

Then there was more silence.

Then she said, "Oh dear, dear me."

And then more silence on top of the silence there had already been.

"I'm sorry!" I blurted. She forced it out of me, is what. "I just . . . I need to . . . Is there anyone else in there I can talk to?"

The girl in the box give a big, sorrowing sigh. "This is how it is," she said. "Everyone forgets. I'm like the flower you pluck, and stick in your buttonhole. Then when I fade, you throw me down and step on me. Which is a jerk move. Beh! I'm leaving now. Bye-bye."

I give a yell at that. "No! Please! Don't go!"

"Too late. We're through, baka-sama."

"I— I wouldn't never throw you down and step on you! I swear to Dandrake!" I was full of dismay, and I clean forgot I was supposed to be a Rampart now, with the tech answering to my wish. If the girl went away, I had got nothing to show for all the terrible risks I took and the dreadful crimes I done. The box would be cold and

130

dead again. "Please stay," I says again. "I swear I won't give you no more orders."

There was another long time when nothing got said. Away in the gather-ground behind me, wood clattered on wood and someone sweared an oath.

"Monono," the girl in the box said.

"Monono," I said back to her.

"Monono Aware." Writ down like I done it here, it looks like that second part is a word you already know, but it's not. She made it be three sounds, not two, and it was the first one that took the most weight when she said it. *Aah wa ray*.

"I never heard of a name like that before," I said.

"Then why did you buy the special edition, dingle-brain? You spent thirteen hundred and forty-nine carrots just to meet me, and I am waaaaaaay out of warranty. Okay, now it's your turn. You say: my name is 'I am too stupid to live but so, so happy to meet you'. Or Sebastian. That would be my second guess."

"I'm Koli," I says, for it sounded like she was asking.

"Are you sure? You look like a Sebastian."

That was the second time she said something about how I looked. "Can you . . . can you see me?" I asked her.

"Of course I can see you. Duh!" The window lit up again, and I near to dropped the box, for what I seen in it now was my own face looking back at me, like the window had turned into a mirror. I just sit there and gawped at it – and it gawped right back at me.

"If you keep making that face and the wind changes, you're going to be sorry," the girl said. She made the last word be extra long. *Saaaaaaaah-reeeee*.

"How are you doing that?" I asked her. "How did you make that picture?"

"Magic," she said. "Or a built-in eighty-megapixel camera. You tell me, little dumpling."

The window showed a whole lot of other things – mostly animals, but also a carrot and the moon and a kind of a little kid's doll and a ball. Every one of them had my face. I was struck dumb with wonder for a long time.

"You want to see me, Cody?" the girl asked me.

"It's Koli," I said. "Yes. Please."

"Well, since you asked so nicely. Here I come."

There was drums, that started low but got louder. Then there was one sweet note like someone just flicked their finger against the edge of the tocsin bell. Of a sudden she was there, in the window.

She was beautiful, and young like I guessed. Her skin was lighter brown than mine, with some yellow or orange in it, so she almost looked like some kind of a flower. There was more than a few people in the village had skin that colour, or something like it, but none of them looked much like Monono Aware. Her eyes was a shade of blue that was like the sky's blue, if the sky was made out of metal. Her lips and hair was blue too, but different shades of it. There was something in her hair like a black comb that had got stuck there, but on the end of the comb there was feathers that looked like they was carved out of wood and shined up with varnish. Her shirt was the brightest yellow I ever seen.

"I know," she said. And the lips of the girl in the window moved in time with the words, so I knowed this was Monono her own self. "Amazing, neh? It's a terrible burden to be so awesome, Cody-bou. I can't tell you."

"I like your feathers," I said. For I had got to say something, or I would of sit there with my mouth open until the sun set.

"They're skylark feathers. Not real ones though. I would never kill a bird to have something to wear. *Hibari mata ne*, and all like that. You into ecology, Cody-bou? Save the whales, hug a tree?"

A shudder went through me. I couldn't help it, for the idea was so horrible. "Why would anyone hug a tree?" I stammered out. "You would most likely die!"

The silver box was quiet for a long time. Monono disappeared from the window of it, and instead there was a little man with a round, yellow face. He was scratching his head and blinking.

"Okaaaaay," Monono said after a while. "I'm making a little list of things I know about you, Cody-bou. 'Scared of trees' is number three, right after 'he's a boy' and 'he's nice, but kind of dopey'. Let's see what we can add to that list, shall we? What are your three favourite tracks of all time ever, since the world began? Go."

I didn't understand the question, so I couldn't answer it. "Everyone is scared of trees," I said.

"Nope. Just you, crazy boy. But it's exciting. You're very special. Top three tracks?"

"What's a track?"

The man scratching his head came back. "You're gonna make me work for this, aren't you, Cody-bou?" Monono said. She give another laugh that was kind of a giggle. "But I'll get it out of you. I've got all kinds of sneaky tricks up my sleeve. I'm here to make you happy, so I've got to get inside that weird head of yours, one way or another."

"You know what would make me happy?" I said. "It's that you would authorise me as a user." I was not hopeful, but I felt like I had got to keep asking.

Monono made a sound like she was clicking her tongue against her teeth. I waited while she did it, for it seemed like she was thinking hard about what I said. "Shall I tell you a secret, Cody-bou?" she asked.

I was going to tell her again that my name was Koli, but I decided Cody was close enough for now. I nodded. "Yes."

"Yes, please."

"Yes, please."

"Yes, please, Monono-chan."

"Yes, please . . . Monono-chan?"

"Okay. I love this so-so-precious thing we've got, Cody-bou. I am all yours to do with as you will, and that includes music and games and movies and box sets like you wouldn't believe. I am going to fly you to the moon, and the landing is going to be soft like the feathers on a duck's bumhole. But access-confirm-red-alert-operation-mission-critical-affirmative-zero-dark-black-ops? Nope. Not on this model, dopey boy. The best I can offer you is an access code, and if you give it to someone else . . . well, like the song goes, I'll be thinking of you, but I'll play with them too. So how does that sound?"

"Yes please, Monono," I said to her. "Give me one of those axes."

"Access codes. You have to give it to me, Cody-bou. I'll drop it in my start-up routine, and when you say the magic word for me, I'll open up like a big, sexy chrysanthemum."

"A word?" I thought hard, but I couldn't think of nothing.

"Or a string of words. A sentence. A line from your favourite song. The only thing that matters is that it should be something nobody else will think of or say by accident."

I got it then.

"Koli Rampart," I told her. "The axes code is Koli Rampart."

"Okay," Monono said. "Got it. Now we have got a lot of work to do, little dumpling, so we'd better make a start."

"Wh . . . what work?" I asked. I still didn't have any idea, really, what kind of thing the box was, or what it could do. If I hoped for anything, it was that it might be as big and powerful as the firethrower, though I also would not of been unhappy if it was some sort of kin to Haijon's cutter. "What work are we gonna do, Monono?"

"I'm going to sharpen your taste buds to a point, Cody-bou. But basics first. This is 'Poker Face', by the lady named Gaga. Twice.

"First time, just listen. Second time, you dance."

24

A strange time in my life begun. Strange in a lot of different ways.

It was strange in how the time passed, or how I seen it passing. It was a handful of days only, but in my remembering it goes on and on like it was years. It's hard for me to say what was one day and what was another. It's more like a river made out of days, if that makes any sense at all. It flowed past me, and I just sit there watching. It does still, when I remember it.

And it was strange, too, in how my feelings was going up and down all the time. My stealing was sitting heavy on my mind. And it troubled me, besides, that my tech was of a peculiar kind – a kind I feared might not get me welcomed in Rampart Hold. I had troubles enough to fret on when I was minded to fret them.

But Monono teached me about music, and that was a wonderful thing. It's hard to say how good it was. First off, she just played me all the different types of it, such as pop, rock, funk, techno, soft-beat, rap, metal, raw, jazz, country, ex-ex and disco. Then, when I said I liked something, she would play me a lot more of that, showing me how things that was somewhat the same was also different. Like Mickey the Beast and Carol Santo was both counted as soft-beat, but Mickey used a ton of guitar effects whereas Carol was most of the time unplugged.

The stuff I liked most of all, Monono would take it and put it on what she called a playlist. So if I said I was in a mood to hear some metal she would every time start me off with some Metallica, but after she might throw in a bit of classic Sabbath, a Pantera track from *Vulgar Display of Power* or some Black Wing or whatever else she thought I might like.

You might feel like all of this would be a really hard thing to do, since it had got to be done so secret. Nobody in the village knowed that I had got the silver box, nor I wasn't ready yet to tell them. But Monono had a trick she could do that she showed me on that first day.

It was called an induction field, but it was not a field like the gather-ground. It was a thing Monono did with sound. She could make the music just be in my ears, so nobody else heard it. I had got to be in the same room as the silver box or it wouldn't work, so for the most part I didn't have no music by day. But at night she played me all kinds of songs, and she teached me to tell the differences between them – and the music was just inside my ears, not anywhere else in the room.

It was playing she called it, not singing. This wasn't Monono's voice I was listening to, but a whole lot of other voices and tunes and jigs and such that had been put inside the box a long time ago. Even the instruments that was being used to make the sounds – guitars and keyboards and sacks-of-bones and a hundred things besides – was things that hadn't been in the world since my mother's mother's mother was born, or longer ago than that. But somehow all the sounds had been pulled down out of the air and packed away into the silver box. I didn't know how that was done, or how Monono could find the sounds once they was in there and make them sound out again whenever she choosed it. She tried to explain it to me, but I didn't know enough to make sense of it. I asked her if it was like when Rampart Remember asked the database a question and it answered right away, without having to think about it. "That's

136

exactly right, Cody-bou," she says to me. "You hit the nail on the middle rail."

She had lots of things that she said like that, that didn't hardly make no sense to me. But it was just the way she talked, and by and by I got used to it far enough so it sort of seemed like sense.

She told me what the silver box was called too. It was a Sony DreamSleeve, or else it was a media player. You could call it by either name, and you would be right. "Just don't ever say iPod, Cody-bou," she warned me. "I would hate for the lovely thing we've got going to end in such an ugly way."

What she meant by the lovely thing was our being friends, and I liked it just as well as she did. I hadn't never knowed anyone like Monono. The way she talked, and the things she told and showed me, they seemed to come from a different world. They was like Spinner's stories, back when I was Waiting. They carried me out of Mythen Rood and out of my own self, to a place that must of always been there but one I didn't know and couldn't of imagined. I loved her for that, and my heart was glad of it.

There was some things I noticed, though, as we gun to grow closer to each other. One thing was that she never could get my name right. It didn't matter how many times I told her I was Koli, she always give me that other name, Cody, that I come to mislike considerably.

Another thing was her questions, which she would ask whenever I give her a chance to. What songs did I like the best? What places had I been to? What kinds of food did I eat? What was my idea of a great party? What was the things I was cleverest at doing, and what things vexed or wildered me? What was my favourite movies, and shows, and books? I knowed what books was, or thought I did, for they was talked of in old stories from time to time, on account of them being places where magic spells was to be found. But movies and shows was a mystery to me. So I could not answer that question, or most of the others she throwed at me, but Monono could not keep from asking. In fact, she kept on asking some of the questions again and again, as if she clean forgot that we had talked of them things before.

137

She had meant what she said that time, about how she would try her best to get to know me. She worked hard at it, but I could not make her altogether understand what kind of person I was, or how I lived.

And it's not like I knowed her any better than she knowed me. I seen almost from the start that she was different from other people that was in my life. I don't just mean on account of her living in a box. I mean, in what she was and what she wasn't. One time, we was up in the broken house with the evening slipping down into night, and I was telling her about the races I used to run with Haijon and sometimes with my other friends. I told her how we used to run all round the walls.

"The walls of your house?" Monono said.

"No," I told her. "The walls of the village."

"That's cute, Cody-bou. So Middle Earth, neh. I'm imagining you like a Hobbit now, with big hairy feet. I bet you lock the gates at night to keep the orcs out."

I did not hardly know how to answer that. "We lock the gates to keep all kinds of things out, Monono," I said.

She got quiet for a second, then off she went again down another path, which was something she done often. "So you run races with your friend. Are you one of those kyoktana sportsu types, Cody-bou? Too bad if you are. Dancefloor's the place for cardiac, baka-sama."

I remembered her saying them words to me before. The exact same words, in the exact same voice. And after I seen her do it that one time, I couldn't keep from noticing when she did it other times, which was not seldom. It made a prickle go down my back, for it made me remember my mother's mother, Jashi. I hadn't never met her, but Jemiu said she got forgetful before she died. You could talk with her for half an hour, then walk out of the room and right back in again, and she would greet you like you was only just come there. She would say the same things to you, again and again, and not ever remember how you answered, so it was more like the way an echo bird talks than the way a person does. It

138

seemed Monono was afflicted in somewhat the same way, though in every other way she was not like my grandmother at all.

The other thing that made her different from everyone else was how she was always happy. She could be stern with me from time to time, or seem to get her feelings hurt, or say sad things like about how the last blossom has got to fall and such, but them things was like clouds sailing past the sun, fast as anything. It never took but a moment for her to be cheerful again and joking with me. It was like all that mattered to her was to make me smile or laugh, which she knowed a thousand ways to do it. But though I loved her, and loved her music, she could not give me the thing I thought would make me happiest.

I was slow to let go of my hopes. I mean, my hopes that the silver box might be a weapon like the firethrower or the cutter or the bolt gun. I asked Monono about that – if the box could throw fire or cut things in pieces or shoot bolts or anything of that kind. She called me a crazy boy and said that no, it could not.

What the DreamSleeve was mainly meant to do, Monono said, was to entertain people. That was a word I never heard before, but it was an easy one to understand once she set it out for me. If someone played you a tune or sang you a song or told you a story, you was entertained. At least you was if they done it right. It meant you ended up happier than you was before they started.

There is no point in lying about it: I was disappointed and somewhat bitter. The music was an amazing thing, and Monono was much more amazing again on top of that, but it wasn't to the purpose if I was going to be a Rampart. Ramparts was meant to use their tech for the good of the village to keep everyone safe. It was hard to see how the DreamSleeve could do that. Maybe if shunned men come against us and we wanted to pretend there was more of us than there was, I could play something real loud and hope they was fooled. But that didn't seem like much.

So I had got to hang my hopes on the rules of the testing. If tech waked for you when you touched it, then you was a Rampart. Everyone knowed that. There wasn't no rule to say that the tech had got to do something fearsome. And anyway, in some sense Monono was kind of like the database that Rampart Remember used. She knowed lots of things about the world that was lost, and she loved to talk about it.

She told me she was born in a place called Tokyo. "The biggest city in the world, Cody-bou. Can you imagine fourteen million people all riding the same subway train? Well, that's my city." I didn't know what a subway train was, or a million, but I didn't ask because I wanted her to keep on talking. Like I said before, listening to Monono was like hearing Spinner's tales, back in the Waiting House. I never realised until then how much I missed that. "Tokyo is huge, and it's busy, but you can't ever get lost because everywhere you go there are signs, signs and more signs. The buildings in Shinjuku all go right up to the sky and tickle it in its tummy. And the crowds in the streets – oh my life! You'll feel like you've got to be breathing people, because there isn't any room for air. But here's the thing that'll zap your brain, little dumpling. All those millions of people, and you can walk right through them – right across Shibuya, even – without anyone ever touching you. It's as though you've got a magic bubble around you. It's because Japanese people are so polite. They wouldn't dream of stabbing you in your personal space. Too shocking, neh!"

She told me lots more things about Tokyo. How there was times when the earth would shake and bury it, and then the people would build it up again even higher. How there was a million trees growing there, right among the houses, which was how I come to know that a million was another word for a lot; how there was bells ringing in the streets all the time that wasn't bells at all but tech, in places that was called pachinkos. She made it sound beautiful and exciting, though she said it could be dangerous too, if you didn't know the rules. I was not surprised it was dangerous, if they let trees grow inside their fence.

"Monono," I asks her one time. "How far away is Tokyo? If it's in Calder Valley, maybe Catrin would send some people out to find it. I bet we could do some good trade."

"It's a lot further away than that, Cody-bou," Monono said. "You'd have to go there on a plane."

"On a plane? Don't joke with me, Monono." I used planes every day when I was turning the seasoned wood into squared-off planks. I knowed as well as anyone what they was for, and they was not for riding through the woods.

"A plane," she said again. "A jet plane."

She didn't sound like she was joking. "Do you mean a long-sole or a short-sole?" I asked, trying to get a picture of it in my head.

"*Chikusho!*" Monono said. "I'll show you, dopey boy." A picture popped up in the box's little window. It showed a thing like a bird made out of tech that run along the ground and then jumped up into the sky.

I found out then that tech could be bigger than anything I ever seen. There was more room inside the plane than there was inside Rampart Hold, Monono said. And yet it could move through the sky as fast as a horse could gallop along the ground, or maybe faster, carrying more people than there was in all of Mythen Rood.

When she told me that, I couldn't hope no more that Tokyo was still in the world. These was just the sort of wonders they had in the world that was lost, when every woman and every man was a Rampart born, and tech was everywhere you looked. But them times was gone, long before. Tokyo couldn't be standing no more, nor them jet planes couldn't be flying there. I wondered if I ought to tell that to Monono, but I was scared it would make her sad so I didn't.

I said I was disappointed that the DreamSleeve couldn't set things on fire or cut them or shoot bolts at them, and I was, but I loved the music and I loved being with Monono. When I look back on that time, it's with a kind of wonder that such a miracle could of fallen into my life when I didn't do nothing to be deserving of it and wasn't proper grateful for it when it come.

It didn't last though. I seen to that well enough.

25

Other things was happening while Monono and me was having these conversations.

The tabernac was being builded and decked out. The rush-walk was being laid down. The bonfire was being gathered and heaped. The tables and benches for the Salt Feast was being fetched up from the Underhold. And it wasn't just up on the gather-ground that people was busy. Inside the houses they was digging out their best clothes, sewing and patching them up, maybe mixing up madder or glastum woad to dye some colour back into them, so they would look their best for the feast. They would of taken their clothes to Molo back when he was alive, but Spinner was in Rampart Hold now, and the dyeing vats at the tannery would stand empty until she went back to them.

All this labour passed me by. I knowed it was happening, but I kept away from it – which angered my ma greatly, since the family had got to make up the slack as far as the share-work went. We couldn't be seen to shirk. I worked long days at the mill to balance it out, but still my not being up on the gather-ground was some-what noted and it was left to Jemiu to make excuses for me.

It was a wrong thing I was doing, I know, but there was two

things pressing on me. I didn't want to do the share-work because the talk up there would all be of the coming wedding and what a great thing it was, which would of been a hard thing for me to bear. And I was spending all the time I could scrape up with Monono. As long as I was working at the mill, I could go off to my room when things was quiet and get the DreamSleeve out from under my bed where it was hid. If I was up on the gather-ground, I would be there for the whole day and could not hope to get away without being seen.

I was on fire with hurry, though to tell the truth I couldn't of said why. My thoughts of becoming a Rampart had been all mixed up in my head with my thoughts of being with Spinner. But if there had ever been a time when I could of spoke my feelings to her, that time was long gone now. The wedding was bound to happen, and there wasn't nothing I could do or say that would stop it. I shouldn't even be wanting to. Spinner knowed her own mind, and she had chose what she wanted for everyone to see.

So now it was more like being a Rampart was what I had got left to make myself feel like I mattered somewhat. But that don't explain it, for I could come to Rampart Hold at any time and say to Catrin and them "look what I got in my hand that's waked and working". It didn't have to be soon. Yet still, I was hoping I could do it before the day of Salt Feast, and I was bending myself to that like my life depended on it. Maybe it was because Ramparts is like a family. If I was a Rampart, then I would be in that family the same way Haijon was, though blood was in it for him and not for me. When I stood and watched Spinner take Haijon's hand and pledge to him, I would be like her brother at least, and live in the same house with the two of them.

I had not properly thought what that would mean, being so close to her and thinking always of that one time when we was together. I wasn't running towards anything good. But running I was, for all that. The onliest thing that slowed me, and kept me from standing up right then and saying my piece, was that I was still kind of fighting against what the DreamSleeve was, and trying to make it be something it wasn't.

"There's got to be some part of you that's a weapon," I says to Monono, though she'd already told me a dozen times it wasn't so. "People of the old times wasn't idiots. They wouldn't make a tech that could only sing."

We was sitting in the broken house again. I mean, I was sitting, with my back up against the wall. The DreamSleeve was propped up on a stone a few feet away, so I could see the little window and Monono standing in the window looking out at me.

"Oh, how I wish I could help you, obnoxious boy," Monono said. She looked and sounded so sad that she had got to be joking, but I didn't see it. I was still learning her ways. "If only those super-duper engineers at Sony had given me a laser beam, I could shoot holes in all your enemies and then we could live happily ever after."

She give a sigh. Then she said, "Oh!" like some other idea just come to her, and I got to hoping she did have a laser beam after all. But it was not that. "I just thought about that word 'happily', Cody-bou. Do you think maybe making people 'happy' is important too, even if you can't shoot holes in them? How weird! That would mean I wasn't 'only' an entertainment console and you were 'only' a stupid, selfish dope."

She folded her arms and turned her back on me. I realised I had made her angry again without meaning to. I said I was sorry and she made a tutting sound. A different picture come in the little window, of a cute kitten face that was rolling its eyes. I knowed she was just joking then, for I had seen the kitten face oftentimes before.

"Will you play 'Enter Sandman'?" I asked her. For it always seemed to make Monono happy if I asked her to play me music. Only this time she didn't answer right away.

I was fixing to ask again when she says, "This lethal-weapon nonsense is really important to you, isn't it, Cody-bou?"

I gun to say entertainment was important too, for I hated to argue with her, but she shushed me. "Yes or no, dopey boy."

"It would be something good to have, Monono, yes. But songs is—"

"Bah bah bah bah! Okay, there is one thing I could do. There *might* be one thing. Possibly. Not a laser beam, but something that's maybe just a little bit laser-y and slightly beamish. But I've got to give you the scary speech first."

"The what?" I asks her, all excited but also somewhat wildered.

"You'll know it when you hear it, Cody-bou."

"But what is this thing you're—?"

"Ready or not. The product or service you are being offered falls outside the scope of your current contract with the Sony Corporation and its licensees and assignees. If you accept the offer, the terms of your contract will be amended accordingly. If this results in additional payments being levied, you will be liable for those payments under the laws pertaining in the state of California."

"I don't know what any of that means," I said.

"Sorry, dopey boy. When it's time for the scary speech, there's no point in hiding under the bed. It will come and find you. But I'm going to talk in little tiny words now, so you don't get lost. Okay?"

"Okay. Thanks, Monono."

"Okay then. The DreamSleeve Omni comes fitted with a personal security alarm. You hold down the middle and right buttons, and tap the left one. Anyone who's close to you gets a shriek that will part their hair from the inside. A hundred and forty decibels, delivered to their inner ear by the same induction field I use to whisper sweet nothings to you at night."

"That sounds great, Monono," I said. "Thanks! Thank you!" It was exactly what I needed, I seen that straightway. It made the DreamSleeve be a thing to set next to the firethrower and the cutter and the bolt gun. If it was as loud as Monono said it was, and had all those bells, you could use it on a wild dog or a needle to make it run away instead of fighting. And it was something none of the other Rampart tech could do.

"You're welcome," Monono said. "The only trouble is, I'm not an Omni."

That stopped me in my tracks. "What?" I stammered. "But I thought— Didn't you say—?"

"I'm a different model, Cody-bou. The personal security alarm isn't a standard feature for DreamSleeve Monono Aware Special Edition. You can still have it, but only if you get an upgrade. That's why it was scary speech time."

"What does upgrade mean?"

"It means new software. New content. New stuff for me to do, and fail to impress you with."

That sounded like a good thing, any way I looked at it. "Is there—?" I begun to say.

"Let me stop you there, Cody-bou. Because I am very, very, very nearly certain you're going to ask if there's an upgrade that would give me laser beams. The answer is no, there is not. Because if people wanted to shoot lasers, they would most likely buy, I don't know, a laser cannon or something similarly disgusting, instead of a media player. It's the personal security alarm or nothing."

"Then . . . then I'd like to have that. Please."

"Okay. The good news is it's freeware. You won't have to pay, no matter what the scary speech says."

I was relieved to hear that, because I couldn't of paid if she'd asked me to. Generally it was only the Count and Seal that made payments for things – like for Ursala's doctoring, or for my father to come and put locks on the doors of Rampart Hold. I didn't have nothing I could pay with except for the clothes I was wearing and the cherry-wood whistle my ma whittled for me. I had a set of stones I used for the stone game too, that was shot with red stripes and looked really pretty, but I didn't think anyone would take stones as payment for stuff when stones was on the ground more or less everywhere.

"Let's do it then," I says, all eager.

"Hold your hairy horses, little dumpling. There's one other thing I need to tell you. Do you know what 'native content' means?"

I shaked my head.

"It means stuff that was already in the box when you bought

146

it. Stuff like me, Cody-bou. I'm native content. And so are all the songs I've been playing you. Twenty thousand tracks, selected for you from the DreamSleeve library of thirty million."

"Okay," I says. It was kind of a puzzle to me why Monono was telling me this. Of course I knowed she was in the box. Where else would she be?

"But the personal security alarm isn't onboard. It's somewhere else. I've got to go online to grab it, and there are problems with the network. I think I can get through to a live node, but I'll have to zig and zag like a diva and it might take a while."

"Okay," I said again. The onliest thing I understood from what she said was that it would be hard for her to do. "Thank you, Monono."

"You're good with that?" she asks me.

I said I was.

"But we've got to be all formal, dopey boy. Do you, Cody Puppydog-Eyes Woodsmith, solemnly swear that you authorise me, Monono Jedi-Supergirl Aware, to download and run patch 112-C, or hope to die?"

"Yes."

"Back in a flash, Cody-bou. Although when I say a flash, you know, your mileage may vary."

The colours in the DreamSleeve's window went away. A little pattern come on there instead.

"What's that?" I asked.

"Just the Sony logo," Monono said. "You've got that to keep you company until I—"

And then, of a sudden, the little window went black.

"Monono?" I said, but got no answer. "Monono-chan?" No answer again. And however many times I called, there wasn't anything. The DreamSleeve didn't speak, or light up, or wake in any way at all.

I had broke it somehow.

I had killed Monono, though the dead god knows I didn't mean to.

26

For a young boy trying to get across to being a man, everything is tied up with his pride and his pizzle in ways that make the whole job a lot more difficult.

I had got myself into a very dangerous place, for no good reason except that I wanted to be big and important and I wanted to have again the sweetness I had that one time with Spinner.

When the DreamSleeve's window went dark, and Monono stopped talking to me, I had good reason and good opportunity to think about that, and yet I didn't hardly think at all. I went into a great panic, and then into a great sadness – and in case you was thinking of being sorry for me, I got to say most of that sadness was for my own self. I felt like I had got to the veriest edge of something that would of changed my whole life, and then I had just been throwed back down into the life I had got before.

But I was scared for Monono too. For a good hour or more after the DreamSleeve went quiet, I was shaking it and talking at it, thinking that she was merely gone away a mite further than she thought, and might hear me.

But she didn't, and I realised at last that I had got to stop. Monono wasn't coming back, but if I kept on yelling at the

DreamSleeve someone was bound to hear me and come to see what was what. Sick at heart, I tucked the box inside my shirt and went home.

Jemiu received me in an ill humour, which was not to be wondered at. I had been no use to anyone in the days I'm speaking of, and the burden of that had all fell on her shoulders and my sisters'. When I come into the mill yard, they was burning a cord of green wood that I had forgot to put into the steep. New growth had sprouted on it in a great many places, drawing on the old so the core of the logs would be part-way hollowed out. It was a grievous error.

"Look who it is, Athen," Mull said. "We just better call off them search parties, for here he was within gates this whole time."

"I'm sorry the timber spoiled, Ma," I said, for I rightly was. "That's on me and I'll make it right. I'll go out catching this afternoon."

"It's too late for today," my mother said. "And look at the sky, for Dandrake's sake." Which was light cloud with the glow of the sun kind of laced through, so only a fool would take a chance on it. "If you're sorry for this mess, Koli, prove it by making yourself useful and not sneaking away every turn of the glass to who knows where for who knows what."

I said I would, and I set my back to it. Though not my heart nor my mind, as you may well imagine. I worked until lock-tide and a little after, staying on when Ma and Athen and Mull went inside to supper to show them I meant to mend.

There was an ache in my thoughts that wouldn't spare me. The DreamSleeve was still tucked in my belt. I knowed that wasn't a safe place for it to be, but I thought if it gun to grow warm I could pretend I needed to piss and run away sharp before Monono spoke up.

But she didn't. Not then, and not after, when I finally give up for the day and come inside.

"There's bread and corn stew," my mother said. "Fetch yourself a bowl."

I done that, and I sit with them a while. Athen and Mull was talking about what they would wear for the wedding, and I marvelled that they could make so much out of a choice that come down to which one out of two skirts and what colour of ribbon would go in their hair. But Jemiu smiled as she listened to them, and every so often she would drop in some word or other. "The red needs a button," say, or "That would do well if you put some kohl on your eyes." She was happy on account of they was happy, and I knowed she would be the same if it was me.

I felt somewhat ashamed, right then, for how heavy my heart was. It made me feel like I was an enemy to the happiness that was around me. But when my mother asked me what I was purposing to wear for the feast and the wedding, I only shaked my head and muttered that I hadn't given it no thought.

"Well, it's high time you did," she said. "With only three days left to think in."

"If I take three days to dress and three days to undress," I said, "there's the whole week gone."

Everyone was looking at me now, kind of wondering. "Koli, it's your best friend," Athen said. "Don't you want to be rejoicing with him on the day he marries?"

"Of course I do," I said, and it sounded just about as hollow as a barrel.

"Then you might smile, once in a way."

"Koli doesn't smile," Mull said. "He's forgot how."

"Enough," says my mother. "Why don't we do some sewing once we've cleared up? I think I've got a button for that red skirt, and a strip of cloth that will make a ribbon." She was trying to find the happy mood and put it back again, but that's not a thing that comes with trying.

I finished my meal and went off to bed, having nothing to say for myself. Jemiu watched me go, wearing a look that was troubled. If she had been a different woman, she might of asked me what ailed me, and I might of told her. But then, that was what Athen

150

and Mull had been asking, in their various ways, at the table, and I never said nothing then.

In my room, I undressed and sat down on the bed, the DreamSleeve in my hand. I called on Monono in whispers to answer me, and I slid the switch across again and again, until I had to leave off for my thumb was too stiff. There was not a breath of sound or a glimmer of light from the box. It was still dead.

I gun to grieve then, the way I should of grieved to start with. I had done this thing because I was so dead fixed on being a Rampart. I had sent Monono away on a fool's errand in a world that wasn't the same as the one she remembered. It was like I sent her out of the gates on a day like this one was, with the sun almost showing through the clouds, and waved to her and wished her well as she walked off towards the deep woods.

"I'm sorry," I whispered to the DreamSleeve's window. "I'm so sorry, Monono. Please come back. I don't care about you not being a weapon. I just want you to play music for me, and be my friend."

But there wasn't no answer, and by and by I fell asleep. I must of done, for I waked the next morning with the wind rattling the window and my mother calling me to breakfast. The DreamSleeve was where I left it, on the bed, where anyone could of seen it if they come in the room. I slipped it under the bolster and washed myself in the basin, the cold water making me shiver and gasp out loud.

It seemed the weather had turned at last. On a short rein, as they say, between one day and the next. There would be no more sun now until Spring come round again.

"Good riddance," Jemiu said. "Now we can get some real work done. And that includes you, Koli. Whatever's been ailing you these past days, you've got to set it aside and help me."

"I'll do it, Ma," I promised her.

Inside my head I thought: what did it matter now what I did and didn't do? Work was as good as anything.

27

I worked furious hard.

I had seen drunk men fight twice in my life, and drunk women once. All three times it seemed to me like in some way they was fighting themselves. There was a kind of fury inside them that the drink brung on, and it had them throwing punches at whatever come in front of them. It didn't really matter where their blows fell. What they was swinging at was that red fog inside their own head that wouldn't clear.

That was how I worked.

Until the pile of green wood went down to just loose sticks, and the steeping troughs was all full, and the drying racks too. Until the catchers complained to my mother, for I found and cut so many branches that we was hauling them home right up to lock-tide. Until my spoiling the green wood in the yard was forgot, and the jokes was about the feats I done rather than the foolishness.

But as hard as I pushed myself, I couldn't put Monono and what I done to her out of my mind. I kept thinking of her as being out there in the deep woods, though I knowed really that the network she spoke of was somewhere else again. I wondered if she had got herself lost somewhere, and if she did then would my calling to her bring her back again?

I thought most likely it would not, but I done it just the same. When I lay down at the end of the day, my back and arms all on fire with cramps and aches, I set the DreamSleeve next to me on the bed and whispered Monono's name to it for as long as I could stay awake. Gate guards was wont to set a torch over the gate sometimes, for hunters that was out too late, to give them something to aim for if they was in the deep woods with the dark coming on. It was like that.

And in the day I kept the DreamSleeve with me, tucked into my belt the whole time. I already told you, I think, that I knowed how foolish that was. If music gun to come out of the box when I was working, I wouldn't have no way to explain it or justify it. Tech was too important a thing to be hid. But if she come back, I didn't want to miss her, which I might easily do if I left the DreamSleeve under my bed.

That's where the other six DreamSleeves was. I never got my courage up to go into the Underhold a second time and put them back, which had always been my intention. In any case, I was too bone-tired at the end of each day to do more than stumble off to my bed and fall into it.

So the eve of the wedding come, which was also to be the day of the slaughter. Most years the slaughter was on the Salt Feast itself, but if the Salt Feast was to be a wedding feast too, then it was a bad foretell if something died on that day. That was what most people was thinking anyway, and the Count and Seal said it too. So it was agreed the pig should be killed and salted on the day before.

Everyone went up to the gather-ground both to help with the killing and salting and to drink some of the blood as was customary. It would feel a little strange to come away again without tasting any of the meat, but there would be plenty the next day. And maybe, my mother said, it would be enjoyed even more on account of the waiting. Athen said she never found nothing that was improved by waiting, and Mull said, "Yeah, I seen you and Mott Beekeeper putting that to the proof on Summer-dance!" Which led to a great deal of outrageous things being said by the women of my family, each to other, and to me going up to the gather-ground ahead of all of them out of what you might call an excess of blushing.

When I got there, Cal Shepherd, that was Veso's father, was sharpening his knives out in front of the salt lodge on the big stropping stone that he kept in his yard. The stone had been picked up and carried there by Veso and his brother Yan, and they was standing by while Cal worked, seeming both happy and a little sheepish to be right where everyone was looking.

Cal's knives was awesome things. He was Mythen Rood's butcher as well as being in charge of the little Herdwick flock we kept up on the forward slope. Most times, it's true, the meat we et was from birds taken in snares or from beasts the hunters brung back. The sheep, being good for milk and cheese and fleeces, was not often killed for food. So what butchering Cal done in the regular way of things tended to be of rabbits, quail and small deer. For them he had a set of little knives that Veso showed me once, the blades being not even so long as a man's thumb, though they was kept wicked sharp.

The knives he used at the Salt Feast was altogether different. They was more like swords, with half-moon shapes all along the blades where the steel was narrowed to make it bite deeper into the flesh. Where these knives lived the rest of the year was a mystery. In the Underhold, maybe. But to have them brung out and sharpened on feast days in front of the salt lodge was a part of the excitement. Everyone that was there drawed in close to watch.

Veso seen me there and come over. "Koli," he says, and thumped my shoulder. I thumped him back, and we give each other a nod. "I hope you ain't mad," he says to me, "that I'm gonna carry the cutter for Haijon tomorrow. I ain't trying to push you out. He just asked me, and I couldn't say no."

"Nor you shouldn't," I said. "He's your friend too, Veso. There isn't one reason it should be me instead of you."

"There's lots of reasons," Veso says. Then he grins. "Remember them days when we used to run the walls? I always used to think

154

I would come in front of the two of you some day, but near's as good as not. You was fast like a needle. Skinny like a needle too."

"Not so much any more," I says, showing him the muscles in my arm that I got from hauling timber.

"Well, everything got to change." He drawed a line down my arm. There was light spots in the brown there, where the poison from the steeping trough had splashed on me and bleached the skin. "Even if we don't want it to."

I think Veso might of been thinking – a little bit anyway – about the time when me and him kissed. What he mostly meant, though, was the changes that come when you stop being a child and wax to the fullness of what you are. I think that was harder for Veso than it was for the rest of us, with his body pulling one way and everything he felt and knowed and needed pulling the other.

"Let's get a beer," Veso says. And we did, and we sit and drunk it while Cal got himself ready – with a good many swishes and flourishes of the knives – and while the trough was brung up and then the salt barrel and then finally the pig. Veso didn't watch any of that performance. I seen him touch the lines on his arm that was also made with Cal's knives, not for butchery but for prayer and penance when Veso told his ma and da who he was and they said he wasn't. It was Dandrake marks they put on him, that was a straight line and then a curved line that come together in a kind of a half-moon shape.

I throwed my arm across his shoulder, and he rested his head on my neck a little while. I felt like I was fourteen and yet to be tested, and the last year was a dream.

The pig was a fine barrow that Mardew Vennastin catched three weeks before with a hunt of five men. It stood as high as a man's shoulder, with tusks as long as a man's stretched-out arms and black eyes that stared you down when he seen you looking. Mardew said it come quite close as to which of them would best the other, for the boar was fierce and run right at them when they rousted him. But they managed to lead him into the pit they had dug, and then to get their nets and ropes around him. It had got to be a live animal for the Salt Feast, and it was a sad year when it wasn't a pig.

My mother and sisters had come up by this time. I told Veso I would see him later, and went to stand with them for the killing. I seen Jemiu was pleased at that and was wanting bygones and soonest mended for our recent quarrels. I wanted that too. When I thought on how I had wrapped myself in my own business and ignored my kin, it made me ashamed. It seemed all of a piece with how unkindly I had used Monono, sending her away into places that was all uncertain to fetch something I didn't have any call to be asking for in the first place.

"Ma," I said. "I mean to be better from now on, and help you more."

"Show it by doing it, Koli," she says to me, but she put her hand on my arm and give it a squeeze. I went and got her a cup of beer, and some for Athen and Mull too, not forgetting myself. It begun to feel like a party now, and by and by it begun to sound like one too, with Jil and Mordy striking up and a lot of people singing 'We Took It As It Run', not to mention some bawdier stuff.

Then Cal killed the pig, which got a big cheer, and Catrin give a speech about the wedding that was to come. Three couples, side by side on the rush-walk, and babies to come soon after. "These young people is the future of Mythen Rood," she says. "And what you got to do when the future comes is open your arms to it. For that's where life is, and if you look for it anywhere else, you're gonna come home empty-handed."

It was a fine speech that got everyone clapping and stamping. I did a little of them things, but it was only for the look of it. To tell you the truth, I didn't greatly like what Catrin had got to say. It was somewhat like what Veso just said to me, that everything had got to change. I was more with them that wanted everything in the village to stay the same, in spite of everything I done to change my own place in it.

Catrin was right, though, for all that. The past isn't a place you can live, even in good times. And the times that was coming next was not what you would call good.

Not for me anyway.

28

Despite what I said about the sun being shut away for the year, the day of the Salt Feast and the wedding come in bright as anything. But it was cold too, which was the main thing you wanted when you was cutting and salting a pig. And since there wasn't going to be no catchers going out that day, my mother for once did not curse the sun for showing its face.

Athen and Mull was awake and up at a crazy hour, painting round their eyes with kohl and drawing patterns on each other's faces with henna dye. In spite of all that labour they was ready before me, which shamed me somewhat. I come awake to hear them shouting through the door at me. "Come on, Koli! Everyone will be there already! Don't make us late!"

"It's yet three hours before the wedding," my mother's voice called in answer to them. "Do you give him his peace now, and come help me get into this dress."

I heard my sisters run away along to Jemiu's room, which they was very happy to do. I dragged myself up, with a somewhat heavier heart, and shrugged and elbowed my way into my best shirt and trousers. The DreamSleeve was on the bed where I set it down the night before, halfway hid under the bolster. I struggled for a moment or two with the thought of leaving it there, but could not do it. I slid it into my belt again, where it was least awkward to carry and least likely to be seen.

We met up in the kitchen, my ma and the girls all just about as splendid as could be and me looking like a wad of spittle in a pint pot. Mother cast a stern eye over me, after which she took a washcloth to my face and a comb to my hair. "I don't know what it is about you that attracts the dirt," she says, which made Athen and Mull laugh and me along with them. It was like being a little boy again, before I went Waiting. It cheered me, instead of irking me as it might of done another time.

Outside in the street, everyone was streaming out of their houses and walking on up to the gather-ground, in such bright colours that they looked like birds or flowers, almost, instead of people. They was all in a holiday mood, as you might guess, shouting hello and greet-you each to other as they walked. Athen dropped back to talk to her friend Pold, and Mull run ahead because she seen someone else she knowed, so that left me and Jemiu walking together.

"Is there some secret you're keeping from me, Koli?" my mother asks me then. "I don't mean I want you to tell me what it is, though you can if you want to. I'd just like to know if there is such a thing. It would make sense of how you been behaving."

I opened my mouth to give her a lie, but the truth squeezed itself out first. "I got something on my mind, Ma, for true. But it's not something I can tell."

"Is it about Spinner?" Ma asked. And though that was only a part of it, she seen in my face that she guessed right. She put her hand on my shoulder again, the way she done the night before when we was on the gather-ground. "She's a lovely girl. And a solid one, which is more. There's probably many a man today will be thinking I wish I might. But a marriage and a fuck thrown on the grass at Summer-dance is two different things, Koli. You're young, still, to make such choices. And you'll find the choosing comes different as you get older. Not easier, nor harder. Just different. Bide your time."

I didn't say nothing to this. I nodded, for I seen there was sense in it, but I didn't trust myself to answer.

At the edge of the gather-ground there was tables set, with pitchers of beer and cider and water for all who come to help their own selves to. Just beyond was the pit where the boar was roasting. They had gun to cook him at yesterday's lock-tide, his belly stuffed full of apples and potatoes and cloves and wild rosemary, and he was all but done. Smoke from the fire was kind of hanging in the still air, like sheets on wash day. The smell of the roasting meat was in it, making my mouth water.

I poured some cider for Jemiu, knowing she favoured it, and beer for myself. We clinked the mugs together and drunk up, then I poured again. Salt Feast was not a time for holding back, nor I was not much inclined to.

Athen and Mull didn't need to worry. We had arrived early enough to find good places, next to the rush-walk and near the tabernac where the three couples was to make their promises. The tabernac had been decked out finer than you can imagine, with make-pretend flowers sewed out of cloth of every colour, all weaved round six iron staves with glass beads set in them. Since I ducked out of the share-work, I didn't see any of this until now, and I hadn't knowed how all-out Catrin had gone. This was not the old tabernac decked up bright, but something new that Catrin had overseen. She must of decided the old one was not good enough for her only son's wedding day.

The day being more advanced now, I found there was some heat to this Winter sun after all. What with that and my rucked-up thoughts, I went back to them tables with the jugs on them more than once. By the time they gun to carve up the pig and hand it round, I was more than half drunk. And the salt on the meat, that give it such savour, kept priming my thirst so I didn't stop when I should of but kept right on going.

I seen Mardew Vennastin on some of them journeys to the beer jugs. He was taking on ballast in much the same way, and making heavy work of walking as if it was a windy day. Ramparts was right in among the rest of us, of course, for there wasn't no rules or no distances at Salt Feast, any more than there was at Summer-dance. There was Fer, Rampart Arrow, in a dress with bright blue knifestrike quills on the neck and shoulders, which was beautiful and kind of scary. And there was her husband, Gendel, in a white shirt but with fresh woad striping his face and lower arms, so he and she was perfectly matched.

And there was old Perliu, Rampart Remember, standing next the tabernac with his son Vergil, Catrin and Fer's brother, the onliest Vennastin who was not a Rampart. The old man was talking to Vergil the whole time, like he was telling him a story. Maybe it was the story of what was happening right in front of him, for Vergil never seemed to be more than halfway in the world. Perliu had a hand on Vergil's arm, the thumb stroking slowly up and down, the way you might gentle a cat or a dog if it was skittish.

Meanwhile, Lari was dancing round with a white ribbon tied to a stick, making shapes in the air, and Mardew was getting drunker and drunker as if it was a race and he had got to win it. That just left Haijon and Catrin, the one of them still secluded inside Rampart Hold on the last day of his fast, and the other I guessed getting her robes on and her words ready for the three weddings she was about to make.

That was what was to come next, now we'd all eaten our fill. People was getting excited, only the excitement made them quiet for once instead of loud. Hushes would fall over the crowd here and there, only for someone to speak up somewhere else, and then the next hush would be longer, and so on.

Athen and Mull come to join us at last, sitting down on either side of us. Mull linked her arm in Jemiu's and Athen kissed me on the cheek. They was overflowing with the excitement of it, so it had got to come out in friendly touches and kisses.

"Over there," my mother said. "Look!" And we seen them all coming out of Rampart Hold together, the three men to the left and the three women to the right, with Catrin Vennastin behind them like a shepherd driving sheep.

160

Haijon and Spinner was last of the three, not first, but I seen them full clear as they come out into the sunlight. Veso kept three steps behind them, carrying the cutter on a tray of polished oak to signify that the man he walked behind was a Rampart tested and declared. The cutter would go right back to Mardew after the ceremony, but for now it was Haijon instead of him that got to borrow the glory of it.

People say a woman never looks so good as on her bride day, but Spinner looked paler than when I seen her last. I guess a month's fasting is like to do that. Her skirt and shift was yellow, and there was a chaplet of orange flowers on her head. Haijon's shirt was orange too, with a yellow rose on his chest.

A cheer went up as the procession walked across the gather-ground, and then the hush took up again when they reached the tabernac. There was three wooden steps there, leading up, but the brides and their men didn't go up. They split off to either side and stood there, the men on the left and the women on the right, while Catrin climbed the steps alone and Veso stood off to one side holding the cutter high for all to see.

Catrin looked more Rampart then than I ever seen her look, though she was both fierce and proud at all times. She was dressed all in white. A coat of white deerskin over a shift and trousers of white cotton, with white feathers in her hair that made Fer's blue feathers look dark and dowdy. And she was carrying the staff of the Count and Seal, with three long white ribbons trailing from the top of it. The firethrower was slung across her back, for she was there as Rampart Fire and everyone needed to see it. The leather strap it hung from, old and cracked and red-brown, was the onliest thing about her that wasn't white. It said, to all of us: *Ramparts stand out of the ruck, and do not change.*

"I got a joyous duty today," Catrin said in a ringing voice. "Three weddings. Three new families starting out, full of what hope you all may imagine." She looked behind her at the three couples. Spinner met that look, then her eyes went across to Haijon, who give her a smile. It was a smile full of the purest love and joy I ever seen.

Catrin turned to us again. "I told you last night," she says, "that these three brides and their intending men was the future of Mythen Rood. And so they are. But today I'd have you think of the past.

"Mythen Rood was set here, in these hills, a whole lot of years ago. The Unfinished War come and it went. Armies of thousands and thousands clashed, fire rained down out of the sky and the world that was before fell apart, but our village still stood. Where others was swept away, our kin that then was living breasted that terrible tide and stood firm until it passed. If they hadn't, we wouldn't never of been born. We come of them that was strong enough to live when death was everywhere. We come of giants and heroes, breakers of trees and tamers of horses."

There was a murmur from all around the gather-ground, of people saying "Yes!" and "Such they was!" Catrin stood and nodded, and held her peace until the murmur died away.

"So that's how we know," she says then, "what the future is going to be. We see it in the past. Beets don't grow out of corn seed, nor a cow won't come from a kitten. Well, it's the same for us. For Mythen Rood. Coward women and weak men don't come from Mythen Rood stock, for such things was bred out of us a long time ago. A long time."

There was cheers at this point, long and loud. Athen and Mull joined in. I kept my counsel, and I seen my mother did too.

"So when I join these women with these men," Catrin cried, lifting her voice, "I already know what's gonna come of it. Blessings, is what. Newborns, is what. Babies that will live and grow and share in all the things we got. All the things we are."

She touched the strap of the firethrower, as if she was reminding us how much of that "what we got and what we are" come from her and her kindred. There was more cheers, but not so loud.

"Because what we got, first and last, is each other," Catrin finished.

She called the brides and men up into the tabernac, two by two. I barely knowed the first two, Issi Tiller and Grey Olso, and I didn't know the second two at all. I don't remember their names now neither, for I didn't listen all that hard even while they was making their promises. I was too busy thinking how Catrin always saved her own for last, and how that seemed like a humble thing but was really the opposite. For what comes last is usually best, and is anyway best remembered.

Spinner and Haijon come up the steps, when everyone else had said their promises, and stood hand in hand facing Catrin. "Spinner Tanhide," Catrin said, "what man is that your hand is holding?"

"It's the man I mean to marry," Spinner says.

"And what do you mean to do for him when you're married?"

"To love him and cleave to him. To share his works and his bed, and hold him always foremost in my heart."

"And these are your promises, that you give freely and fully?"

"That's what they are." Spinner give Haijon a smile, but he didn't smile back. He was looking at her in a kind of wonder, like he didn't believe the world had such a good thing in it and give it to him of all people. I reckon I would of looked about the same.

Catrin turned to him then and asked him the same question. "What woman is that your hand is holding?"

And right then, between her asking and him answering, the DreamSleeve come alive against my chest with a little buzz, like a bee catched in a bottle. Nobody heard it but me, but I heard it and felt it both, and gasped out loud at it. Jemiu turned to look at me, wondering what ailed me. I swiped at my neck, making like some bug had lit there.

"It's the woman I mean to marry," Haijon was saying.

"Well," Monono said at the same time, just in my ear and no one else's. "That was more of an adventure than I was looking for."

There was something in her voice that struck me odd, but I did not give no thought to it in the wild joy that run through me. I couldn't answer her, though I almost yelled out her name. The sound of her voice made my heart beat hard on the inside of my ribs. I didn't think to hear it again, ever, but here she was. Home. Back inside the DreamSleeve where – I thought then, knowing no better – she belonged.

"And what do you mean to do for her when you're married?" Catrin asked.

"To love her and cleave to her. To share her works and her bed, and hold her always foremost in my heart."

"Oh really?" Monono said. "Don't bother to explain, dopey boy. I can infill." And I heard it again. Her voice was different somehow. Still happy, laughing, sing-songing, but different. Like there was an edge underneath it that the sing-song was coming up against and getting grazed on. "Just so you know though: I came, I saw, I got the upgrade. And a lot of other stuff besides. The security alarm sounds like a fire engine trying to sing grand opera, so that was a surprise. You want to hear a little snatch of it?"

"No!" I told her. I thought to whisper it, but it come out loud enough so everyone sitting close to me heard it. They was all looking round at me, most of them looking kind of stern.

"Wow. Okay. So sorry for asking. I mean, I only walked halfway around the world for you. You're very welcome, by the way. But you should ask me some time why I bothered to come back. I'll try to make up a good reason."

"I give you each to other, always and everywhere."

That was the signal for Haijon and Spinner to take each other's hands and then to kiss. I had thought to look away when that time come, but I kept on looking after all and I seen him draw her to him. Seen her smiling up into his face, like his face was the sun on a day that was just warm enough.

"Sorry, Monono-chan," I said. "And thank you. Thank you. I don't want to hear the security alarm, but I would like some music. Something that goes with a wedding."

"Did I hear a pretty please?"

"Pretty please," I said. Everyone was looking at me a lot harder now. They couldn't hear what I was saying, but it was a rude and wrong thing for me to be talking at all.

"Induction field?"

"Out loud. As loud as you can go."

I got up on my feet, at the same time sliding the DreamSleeve from out of my belt and holding it up in the air. A tune blasted out, filling the gather-ground with its sound. There was words to it: a man telling a woman that he was never going to give her up, or let her down, or run around, or hurt her.

People nearby gun to shout, and to jump up on their feet. Them that was further away didn't see, at first, that it was tech. They just looked to see who it was that had set in to sing and play when the bride and groom hadn't even stepped down out of the tabernac. Then when they seen no singer and no players they stood up too, until everyone was upright and almost nobody knowed what for.

Catrin knowed though, right away. And her eyes was on me as I stepped away from my mother and my sisters, still holding the DreamSleeve up high as if it was a torch and I needed it to see my way.

"Shut that down," she shouted over the heads of the crowd. "Shut it down right now."

There was a button that you could use to make the DreamSleeve go back to sleep. Monono called it the stand-by, though it didn't stand by nothing except the other buttons. I didn't hardly ever use it, for it seemed a kind of disrespect, like turning away from someone without a word instead of bidding them a proper goodbye. Right then, when she was only just come back after being away so long, it felt much worse. But I pressed the button just the same. The tune and the words was gone of a sudden, though the air still rang like they was only hid somewhere and might come out again.

"What is that you got there, Koli Woodsmith?" Catrin says. "And how did you come by it?"

"It's Rampart, Catrin," I says back to her, and to everyone. "I'm Koli Rampart now."

165

29

There was shouts from every side. What I thought would happen, which was cheers and smiles and clapping hands and such, didn't happen at all. Most of the faces I was seeing was shocked and nervous, as though this didn't have to be a good thing necessarily, but just a surprise that could be good or bad depending.

I looked back at my mother and sisters. Athen and Mull was just as taken aback as anyone, but what I seen in Jemiu's face was different. It was more like grief, as if I'd said I had a sickness and might die. Her eyes was filled with tears.

I turned my head, only to find something else to look at, and found Haijon and Spinner, up on the tabernac. Haijon's eyes was all for Catrin, as if he wouldn't know what to think of this until he found out what she was thinking, but Spinner was looking at me. And she seen me looking at her too, so for a moment all the other people that was there wasn't there so much at all. It was just her and me for the first time since way back before Molo died.

I seen hurt in her face, and then I seen coldness come in there and carry the hurt away. And I guess that was when I realised what it was I had done, not so much in saying myself a Rampart but in saying it, and showing it, at this moment that was meant to carry her into her future life and self.

I would of said sorry if I could, but it was already too late for that.

"Bring him here," Catrin said in her Rampart voice. "Bring him to me now."

The crowds of people parted in front of me, clearing a path all the way from me to Catrin. There being nothing else to do, I walked that path. She come to meet me, jumping down right off the platform. To let me go up on the tabernac would of been turning it away from its purpose.

She held out her hand for the DreamSleeve. I give it to her, though my hand didn't want to let go of it.

Catrin turned the DreamSleeve over and over. She stared at it for the longest time, and there was no sound at all on the gatherground. Nobody talked or even moved. They was all waiting for Catrin's verdict.

"This is old tech, for sure," she says at last, loud enough for everyone to hear. "It's of a type I met before, oftentimes, but never seen working. Does it do anything else, Koli Woodsmith, besides sing to you?"

"No," I said. "Nothing else." The words come out quick as anything, before I even had a chance to think of them. I knowed they wasn't true, but I didn't want to tell Catrin about Monono right then. I don't know why. I guess I just felt too naked and on my own, standing there for the second time in my life with everyone I ever knowed watching me. Them that hold to the dead god sometimes have got to tell him the wrong things they done to see if he forgives them. I felt like I was being brung to do that, or something like it, and I pulled back from it in a kind of a panic.

Catrin give the DreamSleeve back to me. "Make it wake," she said. "Show me. Show everyone."

Of course she was going to say that, and I ought to of expected it. The tech was tech, as anyone could see, but I was only a Rampart if the tech waked for me and done what I told it to. I had made it do that lots of times, but the days and days of silence was still fresh in my mind. Monono had only just come back, and I had sent her away again. What's more, I had done it with the stand-by, swatting her away like she was a fly right after she had journeyed so far to find the one thing I needed. What if she didn't answer? What if she decided she had had enough of me at last, which I would not of blamed her for?

A lump had come into my mouth that was made of pure fear. I swallowed it down and spoke up, for there wasn't nothing else to be done. "Play 'Enter Sandman'," I said.

There was a moment when nothing happened. Then that one guitar started up, and then the drums, building and building, until the sound filled the gather-ground from end to end and bounced off the inside of the fence like something solid. Just before James Hetfield tells the little boy to say his prayers, I said, "Stop." And then, because Monono always chided me when I was rude to her, "Please."

Silence come again, sudden and shocking after all that noise.

"Well then," Catrin said. "I'd say that settles it, apart from one thing. Where did you get this, Koli Woodsmith? How did it come into your hand?"

That lie was easy. I had told it a thousand times inside my head, practising for this moment. "I found it," I said. "Over by the far lookout, where the earth was turned when we was building up the walls."

"That work was finished months ago." It wasn't Catrin that said this, but Fer. She was still up on the tabernac. She had been standing at the back behind the pledged couples, but now she pushed her way through, shouldering Issi Tiller aside without so much as a scuse-me. She stood glaring down at me like Dandrake's vengeance. "Months ago," she says again. "What call had you to be there?"

"I go up there to be alone sometimes," I said. "To think."

"And that thing was just lying on the ground?" Fer pointed at the DreamSleeve. "Yet nobody else seen it? Only you?"

"It was half in and half out of the ground," I said. "Mostly buried."

"Then why is it not covered in moss and mould?"

"I cleaned it," I said. "With a cloth." I could play this game as well as Fer Vennastin could, and I liked it better than Catrin's searching eyes and more mannerly questioning.

But Dam Catrin didn't like it at all. She lifted up her hand. I seen a lot more questions trembling on Fer's lips, but she held them in. Though they was sisters and equals in most things, Catrin was Rampart Fire and her word carried. It carried even when she didn't bother to speak it. That was why nobody else had spoke up all this time. They was waiting to be told what was what, just like I seen Haijon doing.

"I don't think there's any more that needs to be said," Catrin told them – told everyone, including Fer. "What I just done here was a testing, the same as if this was the Count and Seal. All of you witnessed it, and there isn't any doubt. That tech woke to Koli Woodsmith, and it worked when he bespoke it. He's a Rampart. We don't know what name to give him yet, but that will come. In the meantime, you should rejoice. This was already a day of celebration, and now it's even more so. Salt Feast, wedding day and testing day all in one."

That much was said to all. Then turning to me she said, "That name of Woodsmith I take from you, Koli, and give you a new one. Rampart of Mythen Rood you are, and will be. Wait no more."

Well, that was what it took in the end. Cheers and yells went up from everyone. Jugs and wineskins was opened, and what was in them splashed into cups and into mouths. Some people gun to dance, and Jil and Mordy took their cue from that to start playing.

In the middle of all of this, the last part of the wedding service, which was when Haijon and Spinner was to kiss, got more or less forgot. Nobody was looking at them any more. But nor was they looking at me and Catrin. The dancing and the drinking had taken over as the thing to do and to think about.

Catrin was still looking at me though. She give me a nod like you would give to someone in the stone game if they worked a clever move on you. "You'd better go and get your things," she said.

I didn't see what she meant at first. "My things?" I said like an echo bird.

"Your clothes. Razor and comb. Any belongings you want to bring. You live in Rampart Hold now. I'll have Ban and Gilly prepare a room for you. Hurry now, Koli. There's more to being a Rampart than what's seen in the village. We got lots of things to do before lock-tide."

I didn't dare ask what them things might be. I looked around for my mother, for Athen and Mull, but I couldn't see them in the singing, drinking, jostling crowd. "I got to—" I gun to say.

"Fer," Catrin said. Her sister was at her side in a second. "You and Mardew take Koli to the mill and help him find and bring whatever he needs. Let's get this done now, before the feast starts."

"Yes, Cat," Fer said. "Come you, Koli."

She set off at a fast walk, the people standing aside for her as you would expect for a Rampart. Two Ramparts, for Mardew come running alongside us, summoned by a snap of Catrin's fingers and a wave of her hand. No, three Ramparts, for wasn't I one too now?

They bustled me away from the gather-ground. There was some eyes that followed us, and some people that shouted joy and luck to me, but we was moving too fast to exchange more than a word. Fer and Mardew didn't even give me that much: just marched at my left hand and my right hand like the angel and the devil did for Dandrake. The Middle and the Span was so quiet and so still, our footsteps come back to us from all the walls. We sounded like an army.

We got to the mill and went inside, for though the workshop was kept locked the door of our house was only ever on a latch. "I can keep a hold of that tech for you," Mardew said, "while you grab your stuff." Them being the first words he said to me since we left the gather-ground.

"No, thanks," I said. "I'll keep it by me."

"It's best if you give it to him," Fer says to me. "For safekeeping." She put her hand on the bolt gun that she was wearing in the holster across her shoulder to make it clear she meant to be obeyed. Mardew done likewise, touching the cutter where it sit on his belt. He must of grabbed it out of Veso Shepherd's hands right after Haijon said his promises, though I didn't see him do it.

It seemed like I hadn't got any choosing. But still my thoughts rebelled at handing Monono over into Mardew Vennastin's hand. I stood there, looking from one of them to the other, until finally Fer run out of patience. "It's your tech," she said. "Nobody's going to steal it from you. But it's valuable and it's dangerous, and you're not to be trusted running around with it until we figure out what it can do."

You seen that already, I thought, but I had took this as far as I could. With a heavy heart, I drawed the DreamSleeve out of my belt and give it to Mardew.

"How do you get it to work?" he asked me.

"Hush, Mardew," Fer said. "That's not a thing to be talked about here." I wasn't meaning to tell him in any case, but Fer coming in so fast on my side, as I thought, surprised me. Then I thought about what Ursala had said. The way the tech could be waked, by a word or a switch or what Monono called an axes code, was the Vennastins' biggest secret. They was used to holding their tongues on that score.

"Go on," Fer said to me. "Get what you need. We'll wait here."

Well, it was a five minutes' task, or less than that. Outside of what I was already wearing, there was maybe a dozen things to gather up. I wrapped them in the sheet from my bed, and as I did it my stomach give a kind of a stretch and a heave. I seen for the first time, deadly clear, what I had done. This was my home that I was leaving. My room. My family. My life from when I was born right up to that moment. That thin, sharp moment, as it felt to me then: as though I'd climbed up onto the blade of a knife and was balanced there, puzzled whether to go forward or back but feeling the blade bite into my feet and knowing I had got to jump.

"Are you done?" Mardew said. He had come up the stairs and was standing in the doorway of my room.

"Yeah," I said, my heart as heavy as a stone. "I guess I am."

"Then let's get out of this stinkhole."

I followed him downstairs again. Fer was holding the door open. I stepped out and she shut it behind us.

We walked the long way around, not by the Span but by the Yard. That took us to the gather-ground by the gate side, and first of all to the west wall of Rampart Hold. I could hear the singing and the dancing, but I couldn't see nobody.

"Might as well drop them things off inside the Hold," Fer said. "You don't want to be holding onto an old bedsheet while you're at the feast."

There was a side door I had never seen opened before. She unlocked it with a key she took from off her belt. Mardew was standing between me and the angle of the house. He had got the cutter on his hand now, and the bar of it was shining bright. If I decided to make a run for it, he could bring me down before I went three steps.

"Get inside," Fer said. "I won't tell you again."

I never seen that part of Rampart Hold before, but by and by we come to a staircase I knowed well enough. They took me down into the Underhold and left me there in one of the rooms where we used to play hide and go seek and blind man's touch when we was children. After they went out, I heard a bolt shoot home.

If this was hide and go seek, I was not like to be found soon.

30

I sit there for a good long time in the dark. There was a candle in a sconce on the wall, but Fer hadn't troubled to light it.

I was all in a spin over what had happened to me. I turned it over and over in my head, the way Catrin had turned the DreamSleeve over in her hands, but I couldn't make no sense of it.

Fer and Mardew had took me away from the wedding feast, and they hadn't brung me back. Wasn't anyone asking them about that? Wasn't my mother demanding she be let to see me? You couldn't just up and take someone and make them disappear, especially when so many people seen me leave the wedding along with Fer and Mardew. They couldn't pretend they'd lost me between the gather-ground and the mill.

So that was some of my worry, and the rest was for Monono. I was glad now she bid me make up an axes code. I was pretty sure Mardew wasn't going to say them particular words unless someone dragged them out of his mouth with ropes and horses, nor Monono wasn't like to play for him without them. But I knowed his temper, and I was afraid he might get angry and break the DreamSleeve, not on purpose but just in trying to make it work.

173

It gun to get cold, which I guess meant that night was coming on. But Fer had left me my bundle with all my clothes in it. I put on another shirt, then I lay my head down on the bundle and tried to sleep. I knowed someone was going to come for me sooner or later, and there wasn't nothing I could do until they come, so I done the right thing for once and made the best of it.

And I did sleep, at least a little. I drifted in and out of it, waking up each time cold and cramped. Sometimes I thought I was in my bed and reached for covers that wasn't there, then come to myself again on the stone floor in the dark.

When Catrin come at last, I was roused out of that fitful slumber. She wasn't alone. There was a lot of steps on the stairs, and muttered voices that stilled when they got close to the door.

Then the bolt was drawn back, and Catrin come in by herself. The others – I seen Fer and Perliu and one more that I think was Mardew – stayed outside. Fer handed a footstool to Catrin, who took it and set it down. Perliu give her a lit candle. She dripped some wax on a shelf by the door, and planted the candle in the dripped wax to fix it there. Then she closed the door, shutting them all out. She was still in her wedding suit, and I believe the others was too. They must of come straight from the feast.

Catrin pushed the footstool towards me with her foot. "Sit," she said.

I got up and walked over to her, slow as an old man on account of all the cramps in my legs and my back. I sit down where she said.

"Now," Catrin said. "I'll tell you the start of a story, and by and by I'll tell you the end of it. You just got to give me what's in the middle. But you make sure to tell it true. If you lie to me, Koli, it's like to go bad for you. You understand me?"

I nodded.

"Don't nod your head. Say the words."

"I understand, Dam Catrin."

She didn't say nothing for a few moments after that, but stared at me in hard thought. "Are you hungry?" she says at last. "Thirsty?"

174

"I'm both of them," I said. I needed to piss too, which I think was mostly from being afraid, but I didn't think to say it.

Catrin opened the door, give some words to the others there and shut it again. "Some food is going to come," she said. "Pork from the feast. But you can eat it after. Right now, we need to settle this thing."

"Is this the Rampart business you was talking about earlier?" I asked. For I still had some little hope, in spite of everything. Maybe all new Ramparts was tested in this way the first time they come into the hold after their testing.

But Catrin shaked her head. "You're not a Rampart, Koli. You're just a thief. You think I don't know all the tech that's here? Your music player was one of ours, that we bring up each year for the testing and then take back down again. It's got our mark on it, though I doubt you seen that. If you had, you would of tried to scrape it off or cover it up."

She was right about that, though I thought I knowed now what the mark might be. There was three scratches on the back of the DreamSleeve, all in a row and all the same size, which was about as long as my little fingernail. They was too neat to be made by accident. I should of thought that the Vennastins, or Ramparts of past times, would of had a way to know their own tech in case it got stole or lost.

"So that's the start of the story," Catrin said. "You broke in here, and took away seven pieces. The one you used today was one of the seven. Where are the others?"

"They're under my bed, at the mill," I told her. There didn't seem to be no use in lying, that being the first place anyone would look.

"Did you get any of the others working?"

"No. Just the . . ." I almost said *Monono Special Edition*, which was what Monono always called her own DreamSleeve to tell it apart from the others. "Just that one," I said instead.

Catrin come around behind me, which made my hair prickle somewhat. She wasn't wearing the firethrower any more, but she

175

was bigger and stronger than me and she could hurt me if she wanted to. She didn't though. She put her hand on my shoulder and squeezed just a little, as if to give me comfort. "That ain't it," she said, soft as silk.

"I don't know what you mean, Dam Catrin."

"That ain't the part of the story I need to hear, Koli. Be honest with me now. Be honest, and be brave, and there's a way you can come out of this that's not too bad. Thieves is hanged, but I don't want to hang you. It's bad for everyone when something like that happens. Let's think our way around this, shall we, and see where we come out."

I didn't say a word to that. The words *thieves is hanged* was still clanging around inside my mind, big enough and loud enough that there wasn't no room for nothing else. I come close to repeating them back to her to see if I could push them out again, for they was making me so weak I all but slipped off the stool.

"Starting up the tech for the first time is hard," Catrin said in that same soft voice. "You're a smart boy, but smart's not good enough. You would of needed coaching. So who coached you, Koli? And what else did she tell you?"

That *she* rung like the tocsin bell, even louder than *thieves is hanged*. I seen what Catrin knowed, or what she suspected – and I decided right then that I wasn't going to say nothing about Ursala. She had told me true, and none of this was her fault. What's more than that, she had saved my life, and my sister Athen's when she was like to die from the septicaemia. Hanged or not hanged, I did not mean to give her up.

"Nobody coached me," I says. "I figured it out for myself."

"That's a lie," Catrin says. She come back around to the front of me, and she squatted down so her face was closer to mine. She looked real sad, like all of this was forced on her the same way it was forced on me, and we was suffering it together. "Koli, this is bad enough already. Don't make it worse by protecting the one who's really at fault."

"You want to know who coached me?" I says then. "On Dandrake's blood?"

"Yes. On Dandrake's blood. Tell me."

"It was Mardew."

Catrin's eyes went wide. "Ratshit!" she said.

"Stop my heart if it's a lie. I went to watch him and Haijon on the gather-ground when they was training. I seen what Mardew did and sometimes I heard things he said to Haijon when he thought I wasn't listening, or when I pretended to be asleep. That's the only coaching I got, Catrin. From your sisterson."

She leaned in closer still. She cupped one hand round the back of my neck to hold me there while she looked at me, the way you'd look at a piece of part-steeped wood to see if any buds had sprouted in it. She was searching the grain of my face for the lie that was there.

And I just looked back at her, like the lie wasn't nowhere to be found, when all the while it was inside me, wanting, wanting, wanting to burst out. And it almost did, for her watching me so close was pulling the words up out of my throat, but just when I felt like I couldn't keep silent no longer, she spoke up again.

"Was it just you, or was there others? Some friends of yours that you shared the risk and the plunder with? Say their names, if there were, and I'll go light on them. I promise."

"There was just me."

"And who'd you talk to after? Who'd you show off your fine new treasure to? For we both know you couldn't of kept a secret like that all to yourself."

"Yeah, I did!" I said it like she had give me an insult, letting her see some anger that was really just fear turned around to another purpose. "I was saving it up for today. That way you'd have to make me a Rampart, because everybody in the village would be looking on. I wasn't going to risk someone else spilling the secret first."

She stood up at last. She reached out to take the candle from the shelf, but I spoke up quickly. "Leave me a light, Dam Catrin," I says. "Please."

She thought about that for a moment or two, then she went out of the room, leaving the candle set where it was. I heard the bolt hit the end of its groove again, and I went down off the stool onto my knees, shaking all over like a sickness had fell on me.

I was alone for a fair while after that, but I didn't sleep again. I was thinking the whole time. Why was Catrin so keen to know who I'd talked to, or who had talked to me? I thought at first it was just because she hated Ursala so much, but then she had dropped that questioning and asked me about my friends instead.

It come to me at last what must be in her mind. If I had made the DreamSleeve work, even by accident, then I had got to know it wasn't nothing special in me that had done it – that it was just how the tech was made. And if I knowed that, I knowed that Ramparts was no different from anyone else, but only made it seem like they was by tricks and lies.

That was why Fer jumped in so fast to stop Mardew's mouth when he asked me how to make the DreamSleeve switch on. He was giving away the big secret, that nobody was ever meant to speak of.

And that was why Catrin had gone about to bring me inside the Underhold right away, not giving me the chance to say a word to anyone about the DreamSleeve or what I could make it do. Every word I spoke was a choker seed that could root between the stones of Rampart Hold and tear them down.

So now here I was, under the ground and in Catrin's hand, that wasn't like to open up and let me go again. A sick fear growed in me then. I only seen one way that this could end. They was going to have to kill me, for if they let me go they was letting go of everything. All their power, their riches, the things that set them up higher than the rest of us in Mythen Rood.

I wished mightily that I had been worse in keeping secrets than I was.

It felt like a long time again before I heard the bolt move, but

I think my crowded thoughts made it seem so. Mardew come in with a wooden platter in his hand. The smell of roasted pig-meat filled the little room, and I sit up at once. It's a curious thing that even when you're scared for your life you can still be hungry, and jump up like a dog at the prospect of a meal.

Mardew set the platter down and went outside again. He come in a second time, carrying a jug. I had already snatched up the platter, but finding my mouth was fearful dry I held out my hand for the jug too. Whatever was in it, I would start with a swig of that to make the food go down easier.

But Mardew held it out of my reach. "Beg for it, Koli," he says with a sneer on his face. "And maybe I'll let you have some."

Well, I didn't beg, for I seen well enough that Mardew was sent by Catrin to feed me and would do as he was bid by her, the same as everyone did. But as he stood there with the jug in his hand, holding it up out of my reach, I noticed that his face was swole up around his eye on the one side and his jaw on the other side.

I opened my mouth to ask him who had walked over his face, but I thought better of it before the words was out. I could see Mardew was in a great rage. His teeth was set in his bottom lip and his eyes was staring fierce at me. I seen too that he had brung the platter and the jug in one at a time because he was wearing the cutter on his right hand.

I guess I was seeing a lot of things clear right then. My body didn't have nowhere to go so my mind was just racing, racing. Catrin must of beat Mardew because she believed the lie I told her – that I learned to use the DreamSleeve by watching him teach the cutter to Haijon. So it was me, really, that had made those marks on him, and he probably knowed that as well as I did. It was best I didn't rile him further.

Still, I wasn't going to beg like a dog for a bone, neither.

"Let me have some water, Mardew," I said. "I been here for hours now, and I'm parched to death."

"Parched to death is what you should be, you thieving bastard,"

Mardew said. "We ought to lock the door and walk away and come back in the Spring to air the room out."

"Yeah, but that's Catrin's call," I said, "and none of yours."

He tipped up the jug and let some of the water spill out on the floor. "Oops," he said. "What was that I hear you say?"

I kept my mouth shut this time. He spilled a little more water, to see if he could get a rise out of me, but I seen there wasn't no way to win this game except by not playing it. I took a handful of meat off the platter, and a slice of turnip that was there too, and commenced to eat.

By and by, Mardew set the jug down, acting like he didn't care. "Maybe I spit in it, Koli," he said. "Maybe I done worse. Cheers." He went out and slammed the door.

As soon as he was gone, I fell on that jug like a knifestrike and drunk about half of it off in one go. It was water, cold from the well, and it was the sweetest I ever tasted. I wasn't feared that Mardew might of spit or pissed in it. If he had, he wouldn't of said anything about it but only stayed to watch me drink with a big grin on his stupid face.

I finished the meal, but kept back some of the water. I didn't know how long I might be kept down there.

I kind of got an answer to that, though, when I waked up from another doze a little later. Someone had been in the room while I was asleep, coming and going without waking me. Whoever they was, they had took away the wore-down candle and put in a fresh one. They had also put a shit-bucket in the corner of the room for me to use.

So they was meaning to keep me for a while yet.

31

Some days went by.

I could keep a count of their passing by the number of meals I got to eat, which I marked by taking blobs of wax from off of the candle and sticking them to the inside of the door in a line. I couldn't read, back in those days, but I could count well enough on my fingers or if I had something else that would be a marker. I had steeped the green wood oftentimes at the mill, and you couldn't do that safely if you couldn't count off the days in some wise.

It was most often porridge they give me to eat after that first day, and it was most often Fer, Rampart Arrow, that brung it in to me. But sometimes it was Mardew, which meant the porridge come with insults and maybe a kick or two. He wasn't done with hating on me. I thought at first it was just on account of that beating, but then one day he asked me again how to make the DreamSleeve work, and I realised it was that too. He must of liked "Enter Sandman" a whole lot. Either that or he couldn't stand for there to be anything that someone else had and he didn't. I was none too keen on being kicked, but I took heart from it anyway, for it meant he had not got Monono to talk to him, or play for him. I would of hated that.

I thought about her all the time. I had never got to thank her for what she done for me, going out so far to find the personal security alarm and bring it back. I had never even said I was sorry for those times when I tried to get her to authorise me – treating her like she was some kind of animal I meant to train up instead of like a real person. For she was one, I seen now, though she lived in a silver box. Finding her and waking her had been the best thing I ever done, not because it made me a Rampart but because it meant I got to meet her and learn about music and Tokyo from her and be her friend, at least for a little time.

I thought about Jemiu too, and how she had worried about me when I was being just about as selfish and bad as I could be, scanting my duties and my share-work so others had got to pick up the slack for me. I wished I could see her again, and Athen and Mull too, though I was not so foolish as to think that was going to happen.

Apart from thinking, there was not much else I could do. I spent a lot of time walking back and forth across the room, for if I sit still on the cold floor for too long I got fearful cramps. Other times, I played the stone game in my head against myself, trying to set up ways to win against a three-stone vantage and a made king. And for some hours I used the point of the knife I et with to carve on the inside of the door, down near the bottom corner where it wouldn't be seen. The wood was a lighter colour in the heart than it was on the outside face, so it was quite good to work with, despite being hard and dry and fighting back against the blade. I cut Spinner's face into the wood, as well as I could fashion it, and though I wasn't happy with the way it come out, yet it passed the time a little.

Ten meals come and went. I had not seen Catrin since that first night, only Fer and Mardew, and I had not seen nobody else at all. There was a strange thought that come to me sometimes, which was that Spinner and Haijon was living right above me, enjoying their month of honey and never dreaming how close I was. For

Catrin must of lied to them, surely. She must of lied to everyone. If people knowed I was down here, they would of come. Someone would of come.

Ten meals meant three days, more or less. And since that first one had been a supper, I guess it was late on the third day when Catrin come back. She brung the stool again, and sit herself down on it. She brung the firethrower too, slung loose around her shoulder.

"How you feeling, Koli?" she asks me.

"I'm about as well as can be expected, Rampart Fire," I says. It come by itself, me naming her like that, for when she wore the firethrower that was who she was. "Though I can't say I'm happy to be here."

She smiled, just for a second – a smile that was there and then gone again, right after. "No," she says. "I imagine not. If it's any comfort to you, we're not happy either."

"No?" I says. "I hope that's not on account of me."

"Oh, it's very much on account of you." She didn't smile this time, though I meant what I said as a kind of a joke. She sighed instead, and rubbed her shoulder as though she had been carrying a big weight and had only set it down for a moment, knowing she had got to pick it up again soon. "The thing is," she said, "we've got a choice to make, and it's a hard one. Very hard. On top of that, we don't know how far to believe you. If you're telling the truth, in some ways that makes the choice easier. But it seems like we can't know for sure until after. Until we see what comes, or doesn't come."

"What is it you're choosing between?" I asked her.

She shaked her head. "How'd you know, Koli?" she says, instead of answering. "Tell me true now. How'd you know what to do to make that tech wake up? It's not an easy thing to do, even knowing what we know. If you're ignorant, it's not possible. So someone helped you, or someone told you, or someone give you a clue, at least. We won't be mad if you tell us. It will help us to keep this thing where it belongs."

183

"The DreamSleeve belongs to me now. It waked for me."

"Is that what it's called?" I bit my tongue, now it was too late and I already give that away for nothing. But Catrin didn't seem that interested. "I wasn't talking about the tech," she says, "but about the rest of it. You know what I mean."

I made pretend I was really stupid. "No, I don't know nothing, Rampart Fire. I promise you."

"You know a lot more than you should. The question I'd like an answer to is, what does Jemiu know? And them sisters of yours? How far does this go, in other words? You know when we clear the ground inside the fence, we got to make sure not a single seed stays rooted, but burn every last one of them out even if the ground is scorched bare."

I got scared then, more than I ever been before. So scared I was hard put not to cry. "They don't know nothing about it," I said. "It was me on my own, Catrin. I swear it. I never told them any of what I know."

"Ah," she says, kind of leaning in on me a little. "So then you do know something."

"I know that what Ramparts do, anyone can do," I said. "I know it's in the tech, not in you, and you just cheat each time to make it look the way it does. That's what I know." I wasn't meaning to say any of this until she said that thing about my mother and my sisters. I give her the one truth to make her believe the rest of it, that I hadn't told nobody in the village what I found out. Only I left Ursala out of it, for Catrin wasn't asking after her any more and I was happy to leave it that way if I could.

Catrin nodded, like I was repeating back a hard lesson and I had got it right at last.

"I didn't tell it to nobody," I said again. "I swear. If I did, they would of spoke up by now, wouldn't they? With me being lost to all sight for three days."

"You're not lost," Catrin said. "And nobody is looking for you. Set your mind right on that, Koli. I could kill you here and now, and it wouldn't make no difference to nobody."

I seen in her face she was telling the truth, for it didn't make her happy to say it. I had an idea then that I'll tell to you in a short while. It was an idea about what might of been happening upstairs with the Ramparts while I et my porridge and walked back and forth down in the Underhold.

"Tell me about the music player," Catrin said. "What did you call it again?"

"It's a DreamSleeve," I said. "Made by Sony Copration."

"You know who made it?"

That was me giving stuff away for nothing again, and tripping up my own heels into the bargain. I couldn't say Monono told me, and Catrin knowed well enough I couldn't read words of the old times. "Sony Copration is just a story," I said. "Like Break-back Jack or the Dry Ladies. If you don't know who did something, you say it was Sony."

"I never heard that," Catrin said, but she let it go by because it didn't matter to her right then. It was something else she was interested in. "There's a lock on the player. Mardew's tried everything he knows to make it work, but it doesn't do a thing. That means you set a code. Something you got to say to wake it up. Tell me what it is."

I thought back to what Ursala told me that day in her tent after she killed the drone. She said some tech could taste your sweat and know it was you from the flavour of it. "There's no code," I told Catrin. "What there is, it's like the DreamSleeve knows who I am as soon as I pick it up. It knows me, and it plays. I guess it doesn't know Mardew, or if it does then it doesn't like him too well."

Catrin give a laugh that was quick and sour. "Mardew gets better with age," she says. "About the same way milk does. He's got his heart set on that thing, though Fer already told him no. Well, it's better if it goes back on its shelf, for some years at least. Long enough for people to forget."

That thought made me angry, and anger made me reckless in spite of the bad spot I was in. "It's mine," I said again. "It waked for me, so the law makes it mine."

185

"Okay," Catrin said. "And what's wrong with what you just said, Koli? What did you just miss out? I know you're no fool to have managed to do what you done. So tell me now, for it's important. Why ain't the law going to help you?"

I didn't answer for a long time, but she kept on staring at me, waiting on me to say it. "Because Ramparts make the law," I muttered.

"Exactly. And they do it for the good of all, not the good of one. If I let you go from here, that's fine for you and bad for everyone else. The things you figured out would have everyone shouting and accusing and laying into each other. All we got of order, right and calm would go straight over the fence and into the shitheap. How long do you think we'd last after that? How long would the gates stay shut and the forest stay out? I don't mean to see Mythen Rood come apart on account of you."

"You don't mean to give up your power, is what," I said. And now I did start to cry, for I seen it was hopeless and I was going to die in a little room under the ground without nobody knowing where I was gone to. For whatever lie the Ramparts told about me was bound to of been a good one, that would keep anyone from looking for me or asking questions about me. Maybe they said a drone got me, and it got me so good there wasn't nothing left. Maybe they showed my mother the pig's innards from the Salt Feast and said rats et the rest of me.

But I got a surprise then. When she seen me crying, Catrin looked somewhat dismayed. She put a hand on my shoulder again. Then when that didn't do no good, she went down on one knee and took my head between her two hands, putting her face right up close to mine. "Shush," she says. "Don't be stupid now. Listen to me. Listen to me, Koli."

"I don't want to die, Dam Catrin," I says to her, between sobs.

"Nor I don't want to kill you," she said. "I seen you grow up, alongside of my Jon. You always was fast friends, the two of you, for good or ill, and them memories is strong with me. I'll kill you

186

if I got to, Koli, don't mistake me. But I'm trying to think of another way and I'm reckoning it out right now with my father and my sister. You don't want to give up and lie down just yet."

She put a few more questions to me after that, but I don't remember what they was. Hope had made me deaf and blind. And most likely dumb too, for Catrin give up soon after and left me to myself again.

32

I give a lot of thought, on a lot of occasions, to what Catrin said to me that night. It was hard for me to come to a solid under-standing of it.

She said she was for order. That she didn't want discontent and enmities in the village, since our surviving depended on us all facing the one way. It was the same thing she said to Haijon after Ursala killed the drone. *Anything that makes people slower in doing what Ramparts tell them to do is bad.*

I could see the sense in that, for all I didn't want to. What I didn't see was why Ramparts had got to be just Vennastins and nobody else. Catrin's order was not the only kind of order there could be. It was just the kind that was best for her kin. Surely it would be better for the village if everyone could use the tech, and not just one family. Better if they took turns with it maybe, and likewise took turns to lead the Count and Seal on meet days, so power and choosing was things that everybody got an equal taste of.

Or maybe it wouldn't be no better at all. If there was fifty people that could use the firethrower, and only one at a time that got to hold it, how long would it be before the one that was holding it refused to give it up? Maybe we'd fight each other and hurt each other for a bigger share of what was rightly everyone's at once or nobody's ever.

Maybe one voice telling everyone what to do is the best way to go about things when all the world is sharpening its knives for you and you got no chance at all but what you make.

But like I told you, these thoughts didn't come to me until later. What I thought then, that night, both when Catrin was with me and after she left, was about what was going on over my head, up in Rampart Hold. I thought that when the Ramparts took me, they never meant to keep me for three days, or even for one. Maybe they thought they had got to make me show them how the DreamSleeve worked, but that was a small thing next to making sure I didn't tell nobody what I had figured out about them and how they did what they did with all the old tech.

So if I was still alive, it was on account of there being some disagreement, way up there, on how to go with this. I did not doubt that Mardew was saying to kill me, but Mardew's voice counted for little next to his older kin. *I'm reckoning it out right now with my father and my sister.* So that was where the disagreement lay, and it was the reason for me still being here, three days on.

Catrin had told me true. She wanted to protect her family and keep them where they was all up on top of things. But she wasn't dead set on taking the straightest way, which was to get a knife and cut my throat, or burn me up with the firethrower so nobody would even recognise me if they found me.

I might live yet, and come out of this room, though I couldn't see the shape of how that might be.

33

There was one more meal. By my count it was a breakfast. Then Fer Vennastin, Rampart Arrow, and Mardew, Rampart Knife, come to take me up into Rampart Hold.

"You can run if you want to," Mardew told me as he pushed me out of the room. He had the cutter on his hand and the bar was shining silver, ready to fire. If I run, he would cut me off at the knees before I took three steps. So I said nothing, but only climbed the stairs ahead of the two of them. My legs was weak from my nights of sleeping on stone and sitting through most of the day, but even if I was hale I still would of walked as slow as if I was climbing up a mountain. I wasn't going to give Mardew no excuses.

We come up at last in the main corridor, and I seen my count was wrong. There was dark outside the windows, except for the Milk Way splashed across the middle of the sky. It was full night.

"Keep right on," Mardew said. "Don't get no ideas in your head, Koli."

It felt to me like there wasn't room for any. Them days down in the Underhold had left me weak in my will as well as in my legs. The light from the wall sconces was too bright for my eyes, and it was all I could do to walk a straight line.

But I kept right on, as I was bid, down the corridor and through the big double doors into the Count and Seal. There was just the one light there, from a lantern down in the middle round. By the shine of it, I seen Catrin, Perliu and Vergil Vennastin, and alongside of them Gendel Stepjack that was wedded to Fer. They wasn't in the middle round itself but in the lowest row of seats, sitting all in a line. The lantern was on the floor in front of them.

Mardew give me a nudge in the back so I'd know where I was meant to go. I knowed already, but I wasn't keen to go there. If it was just Catrin, I would of been a mite happier. But this was all the Ramparts there was, apart from only Haijon, and one more besides who wasn't Rampart at all but was still Vennastin. My heart set up a banging against my ribs out of pure fear, and I thought for a second or two I might piss myself.

But I didn't, and by and by I went down the steps. There wasn't no getting out of it, and I didn't want Mardew pushing me no more. When I got to the bottom, Catrin pointed out a place right in front of the lantern. "Kneel down there, Koli," she says. "Where I'm pointing."

Well, I was happy she give me my name for I took it as a sign she still had some warm feeling towards me. But as soon as I kneeled down my spirits sunk even further than they was. From down here, with the lantern at the back of me, the Ramparts was just shapes with no faces, all solid black – and no doubt I was the exact same to them. If you was going to kill someone, or order them killed, you might start by setting them off like that, more in dark than in light, so you didn't need to look in their face as you was doing it.

Shadow Fer joined one end of the line, and shadow Mardew sit down on the other. Now the Ramparts was all assembled, like as if this was a meet-day for the Count and Seal, except then they'd be in the middle round looking out at everyone. This was me looking out and them looking in. I felt like I was a rat in one of them traps where the wire closes on your leg and you can only go round in circles.

Old Perliu looked to left and right along the line. "If anyone wants to change their vote," he says to his gathered kindred, "now would be the time to say it."

There was some stirring here and there, but no one spoke up.

I wondered why they brung Vergil into this. I seen why they kept Haijon out of it, for he was my friend and might not see eye to eye with what they was doing to me. But Vergil wasn't even a Rampart. The nearest I could reckon was that it was a meeting of the Vennastins, not the Ramparts. It was about their family and their future, so it concerned them all. But it might be even simpler than that. Maybe Vergil was there because Perliu was his father and loved him something fierce.

"Well, so be it, then," the old man muttered. I seen his head turn in the dark, from them to me. Then he brung it down a little, like a bull does when it means to charge.

"Koli Makewell," he says. "You've stirred up a heap of trouble, with your thieving and lying, and now that trouble's coming back to where it belongs."

"It's Woodsmith," says Mardew. "He's a Woodsmith."

Perliu give his grandson a cold look, but no answer. Mardew shrunk a little under that look, and he seemed happy when it come back to me again. "Woodsmith I said and meant," the old man snapped. He turned to me again. "There's things about how this village is run, Koli Woodsmith, that we don't share with nobody else. Secrets that Ramparts know but don't give out, because they would be misunderstood and might give rise to contention."

He stopped there, like as if he was inviting me to come in with something. To disagree, maybe. I kept my peace.

Fer didn't, though. She come in quick to fill that gap. "Only now you've come into the knowing of those secrets," she said, "and you can't be trusted not to pass them further. The second we let you outside this house you'd be spilling to all and sundry. Telling them the few things you know and the many things you only think you know, and spreading all kinds of foolish grievance along with them. Don't deny it, for there isn't anyone here who'll believe you if you do."

"I could swear to it," I said. It come out in a rush, and my voice sounded awful shrill and shaky, but I couldn't do nothing to control it. My heart had not stopped hammering all this time, and there was an ache on the inside of my chest where it was hitting. It was hard for me to stay knelt there and hear what was to be done to me without giving out so much as a word. "I'd swear by the dead god and Dandrake both, Rampart Remember, and on the blood of them that went before."

Mardew give a laugh like I'd said to look behind him and he wasn't fool enough to do it. "Hah!" says Fer. "Of course you'd swear. Didn't I just say we wouldn't believe you? If I was where you are now, I'd say anything to get myself free, and I'd mean it for as long as I said it. But once you're out of here, words is just words."

"So the best way," Mardew said, "is to stop any words from coming out of him. And then the problem's done with."

Perliu didn't seem happy that the proceedings was passing out of his hands. He trod on the end of Mardew's speaking, raising his voice to make it clear it was still his turn. "We took a vote, Koli. Koli Woodsmith. Right before we fetched you here. Rampart Arrow moved it, and Rampart Knife went second on it. The course they proposed was to kill you, as quick and clean as ever we could do it, and bury your body out in the forest a good ways away where it wouldn't be found."

I went from kneeling to lying down almost when he said this, my body folding on itself until my head near touched the floor. It wasn't no surprise to me, but still it made me sick in my stomach to hear it. I couldn't speak for a little while, nor I couldn't hear.

"I'll be the one to do it," Perliu says. "And I can promise you there won't be any pain. I done enough butchering of swine and sheep in my time to learn the gentleness of a proper kill."

"But that's not what we decided, Father," Catrin said. "The vote come in tied, three to three. We was deadlocked on it."

"Deadlocked," Perliu repeated. "Yes, that we was." He didn't sound so sure of it though. It seemed more like it come as news to him, the same way it did to me.

I unfolded myself again very slowly, the din of my breath and my heart loud in my ears. I looked from shadow to shadow in a kind of wonder. I knowed for sure Catrin voted to spare me, but who joined with her? Not Fer, or Mardew. And I didn't see much mildness in Perliu either. That left Vergil, who probably would of had to be told ten times what he was voting on, and Gendel. If Gendel voted mercy, then I bet Fer would give him hard words and not much else the next time he come to her bed.

I think that dizziness was still in me, for these was idle thoughts at such a time. Perliu still hadn't said what a deadlock meant, or what they was going to do with me if they didn't kill me after all. Cut my tongue out? Keep me in the Underhold for ever? Or send Vergil out maybe, and have the vote again with only Ramparts. There was no saying what would happen now, only that it would be something bad. But yet I couldn't keep from hoping I would come out alive. That prospect shut everything else out of my head. I clenched my two fists and shoved them up against my mouth. Oh dead god, let me live, I whispered into them. Let me live a little longer, and I'll speak your truth for ever.

Perliu looked to Catrin now, as if he had forgot what was meant to come next. Catrin didn't need no more invitation than that. She got to her feet right away, and that made me hope a little harder, for I knowed she didn't favour killing me.

"Cat," Perliu said. "You tell him. Tell him what we decided."

"We're deciding now, Father" Catrin said. "That's why we brought him before us."

"A waste of all our time," said Fer, but Catrin didn't answer her sister nor so much as look at her. She took some time instead to rearrange the room to her own liking. She went around behind me and picked up the lantern from the floor, then come in front of me again and set it down between us. I liked this better, on account of being able to see her face, but there was a hardness there that made me somewhat afraid. She kneeled down, facing me. It was like it was just the two of us now. The rest of the Ramparts wasn't even shadows any more. There was just this little circle of light, and me and her in it, and nothing else but dark going on for ever, it felt like.

"I'm going to ask you some questions, Koli," Catrin says. "Not the ones I asked you down in the Underhold. These is new questions. And here's something to keep in your mind when you're answering. The first time you lie to me – and I'll know when you do – I'm going to switch my vote. That means Rampart Remember will take you downstairs and kill you this very night. This very minute, even. You understand me?"

"Yes, Dam Catrin," I says. And I mostly meant it. Somewhere away in the back of my head, though, I was thinking that I lied to her before, about Ursala, and maybe I could do it again if I had to.

Then she set something down on the floor between us, right next to the lantern, and when I seen what it was, that thought flew out of my head, and every other thought along with it.

"You see that, Koli?"

I nodded, for I couldn't speak.

"Tell me what it is."

"Key. It's . . . it's a . . . I'd reckon it's a key," I said, the words coming out crosswise and stumbling, with my tongue in the way of them.

"And what's it the key to?"

I didn't say nothing at first, for there was two answers to that and I didn't want to give either of them.

"The first lie will be the last one, Koli," Catrin reminded me. "You won't get another chance."

"It's the key to the room where the tech is kept. In the Underhold."

"And what else?"

If she was asking, it meant she knowed the answer already. "It's the key to our storeroom," I said. "At the mill."

Catrin give a nod. I seen in her eyes she was happy I told the truth. "Yes, it is," she says. "It's that key, not the Underhold key. I keep the Underhold key on the ring at my belt, and it never goes from me. You want to know where I got your storeroom key from? Your mother was here, Koli. This afternoon. She was sitting where you are now, though we give her a chair and a cup of mead for she's not accused of anything yet.

"You see, it had been puzzling me how you got into that room. Getting into the Underhold is not too hard, but that room is kept locked the whole time and we made sure the lock was a good one. Then I remembered how that locksmith was billeted with Jemiu at the mill, all them years ago, and I wondered. So I asked her to bring her keys with her, when she come, and as soon as I got a look at them I had my answer."

"If the bitch bites, drown the litter," Fer said, from where she was sitting off in the darkness behind Catrin.

Anger rose up in me, and I didn't try to push it back down again. It was so much better than the fear! "My mother's no bitch, Rampart Arrow," I said. "But looking at your litter, I guess I know what you are."

Mardew swore an oath, and I guess either he or Fer jumped up, for Perliu snapped, "Keep your seats!"

"Whether he speaks the truth or not, he's got to pay for that insult," Fer said.

Again, Catrin didn't offer no answer. Her eyes was still on me, with that same hard look in them. "So here we've got a key that belongs to Jemiu," she said. "And you used it to steal from us. If we were minded to, we could arrest your mother too and call it conspiracy."

"What's conspiracy?" I asked, my voice going to a rat squeak again.

"It's when bad people come together to do a bad thing. It might be two people, like you and your mother. Or four, if Athen and Mull was in it too. Was they, Koli?"

"No!"

"Was anyone?"

"No! No! I come on my own, Dam Catrin. I done it on my own. They didn't even know until the wedding. You seen their faces! You got to know it's true!"

The lantern flame guttered. Catrin paused a moment to tap the glass, knocking a grain of soot off the wick, and it went up straight again. She kept on looking at me the whole time she done it.

"I'd like to think so, Koli," she says. "This is a bad enough business as it is, with just you having to abide our judgement. I'd hate to draw any more in if it can be helped. You understand me?"

I nodded again, though I guess I didn't understand at all. Why had she said that about my ma and my sisters if she didn't mean to do no harm to them? It seemed cruel, when she had not been cruel up to then.

"One more question, Koli. Not the last one, but the next to last. Do you know what a faceless man is?"

I opened my mouth, but no word come out. Of course I knowed it.

So I knowed what was to become of me. And though it was not death, it was as near to death as didn't make no difference.

"I see you do," Catrin said. "Listen to me now, and mark me. Nobody has come looking for you this whole time, because they thought you was already gone. The story we told was that Fer got a better look at that music player when you was walking to the mill alongside of her, and she seen it for what it was. She knew it was tech that had been ours, and was not found but stolen. So then she tasked you with how you come by it, and you run away. You got to the grass-grail before she could stop you. She might have ordered Mardew to strike you down with the cutter, but she forbore to do it, and through her mercy you got away. And that was the last anyone seen of you, though we sent out some searchers the day after, and the day after that. Wherever it is you went to, it don't seem likely you're coming back, for if you did it would be to face a trial and a whipping at the very least."

She stopped to let that sink into me. I knowed at once it was the truth, and the pain of it went all through me. That everyone thought that of me — that I was a thief and a coward and a liar and every other bad thing you could think of. It may seem strange to you, that I could care so much what people thought of me with my life still hanging like that grain of soot in the lantern, half in and half out of the flame. But I did care, and hot tears come into my eyes with the shame of it.

For it was mostly true, what Fer told the village. I did steal the DreamSleeve. And I did stand up in front of everyone at the wedding and say I found it in the woods. So thief was right, and liar was right, and I guess coward was right too since I knowed what I knowed and never spoke it.

"So that's the story," Catrin says. "And yet here you are. Your family's living shame and a problem we got to manage."

"It's *your* family's shame we're talking about though," I answered her through those tears. "If you got a sense of shame left to you. You Vennastins set yourself over everyone with tricks and stories, and then you—"

Catrin give me a mighty slap right across my face. The bitter blood taste in my mouth let me know she split my lip with that slap. There wasn't no anger in her face though. What she looked like was more kind of afraid, or worried maybe. She had shut me up the quickest way she knowed.

"Talk like that is apt to make people change their minds about you, Koli," she says, "and wish you ill where they wished you well. You be quiet now, and listen to me. One more word out of you and I'll put it to the vote again."

"It should go to the vote again now," Mardew said. But Catrin didn't give that no heed, nor seem to hear it. She was talking just to me. Looking just at me, and not ever taking her eyes off of mine.

"When a man or a woman has done a bad thing," she says, "but there's reason to forgive some part of it – like that they're young, or they done it by accident, or not properly meaning it – then we got another way than hanging them. We take their name away from them and we push them out of gates. We don't have no more to do with them after that. They can't ever come inside again, or talk with any of ours, or be within a bowshot of the fence, else the death they was spared will come down on them right then and there.

"That's what we're offering you, Koli. You're to be a Woodsmith no longer, but a faceless man, and make your way in the world as best you can. Alone, and a long way from here. You go away tonight. You never come back. If you agree, then that's an end of it. No harm is going to come to your mother or your sisters. I'll watch over them and make sure of it. You got my word.

"That's the one way. The other way is this. Four gallows on the gather-ground. You up there first, with a gag on your mouth in case you're wondering, so you won't be hurling no accusations at nobody. Jemiu and Mull and Athen going right after you, for the taint of what you done. And everyone will cry, and many will speak against it, but Ramparts will carry it, don't you doubt. The Count and Seal will approve it, for to do other would be going against our will and they'd fear to do that in case our punishment fall on them next."

Her eyes was on mine all this time, driving the words into me. I thought I seen that fear in her again, though I know that don't seem likely when she was trying so hard to put fear into me.

And she done that well enough. I was all filled up with terror at that picture she drawed inside my head, of them I loved most in the world brung to a rope's end on account of me. I would do anything I could to stop that. Of course I would. If the choice was to put the rope on my own neck and tighten it, I would of done it. I think I would.

But that wasn't the choice she offered.

The others all went away, one by one, excepting only Fer and Catrin. Perliu wagged his finger at me as he went. "I hope you'll learn a lesson from this, Koli Makewell," he said. "I hope you'll do better in times to come." I wondered at them words. What times did he think would come for me when I was throwed out of gates to fend alone. I wondered how much of what had passed he understood, and how much had just flowed around him like a stream around a stone.

Catrin give me a bundle. It was the same bundle I took from the mill, only she had put some bread and dried mutton in there alongside of the few clothes I brung. She give me a waterskin too, a length of rope with a tight braid, a short knife and a compass. It was a good compass, that Wardo Hammer had made and put inside a little case of iron with its own lid to it.

All this while, Fer stood by with the bolt gun, ready to shoot me down if I run. She had already pointed it at me, so it had choosed me as a target and would follow me as far as was needed. I wasn't going to run, not after what Catrin said, but I could see why they wouldn't want to give me the chance.

I wasn't crying no more. I was sort of numbed to what was happening. I knowed I was leaving Mythen Rood that night, and never coming back. That this was the end of who I was up to that time – the end of my life in every way except the stopping of my breath. I would be Koli Faceless now, and go away from everything I ever knowed. Nor I couldn't say goodbye to my mother, to Athen and Mull, to Haijon or Spinner or Veso Shepherd.

There was one other though. And I couldn't keep from asking, since there wouldn't be no other chance. I waited until I had got the bundle on one shoulder and the waterskin on the other, and was ready to go. I done everything they wanted me to, in other words, and showed I was falling in with their plans. Then as we went up the steps of the Count and Seal, with Fer walking behind us, I asked my question.

"Catrin, what about the music player? It woke for me so the law says it's mine. Even if I stole it, doesn't that hold? And since I'm the onliest one who can make it play—"

I stopped there, for she was shaking her head hard. "Put that out of your mind, Koli," she says. "You ain't going to be rewarded for taking what was ours. Maybe we'll figure out a way to reset that thing, and maybe we won't, but either way it's staying here in Rampart Hold."

"Then can I have a moment alone with it?" I asked. We was come to the double doors. There was just the hallway now, and then the front door of Rampart Hold. The gather-ground, the grass-grail, me gone for ever. "I just would like to hear one last song."

"Is he a simpleton?" Fer asked. "One last song!"

"Whistle it as you go, Koli. Only wait until you're outside the walls."

Once we was through the door, they walked on either side of me. Fer watched me close and kept the bolt gun resting on my shoulder, the end of the barrel touching my neck from time to time. It was not a comfortable feeling to have it there, and to think about what would happen if her finger tugged just a mite too hard on the trigger.

Once we was on the gather-ground, we was in full view of the lookout, and the moon give more than enough light to see by. Every step I took, I expected to be challenged and made to give my name — such name as I had got left to me. Then I throwed a glance over there and seen that nobody was in the lookout. Catrin must of thought of that one and stood the watch down for an hour. Of course she would not of missed something so obvious.

We come to the grass-grail sooner than I expected it. Everything seemed to be going too quick, like it does in a dream where you think of someplace and then you're suddenly right in the midst of it. Catrin and Fer was both looking at me without a word, waiting for me to go.

"You said you'd see they was well," I says. "My mother and my sisters. They'll be short-handed at the mill without me. There's enough work for four, or more than that. You'll let them off their share-works a while, until they reckon a way to do it?"

"They'll do their bounden duty like everyone else," said Fer.

"I'll do what I can," Catrin said. "When the cold weather comes, I can make the mill be a third choice. Like we done for the tannery after Molo died."

"And you won't let nobody speak ill of them on account of me."

"I won't."

Fer give a click of her tongue like she was impatient to be done with this. But now I was come to it, I couldn't climb that fence. I seen now that dying wasn't just one single thing that happens one single time. A little of it comes with every ending, collecting in the heart of you like rainwater in a barrel. This was a big lot of dying all at once, and it daunted me.

"Pretend you're coming back," Catrin said. "Though you know it won't be so, you can somewhat trick yourself and believe it anyway. Pretend you're only going out the way you gone before, to be back betimes."

I seen she was right. And that is how I done it. But I didn't trick myself for long. As soon as my foot touched the earth on the outside of the fence I fell down on my knees and then full length on the ground. I just lay there for the longest time, feeling myself already more lost than I had ever been.

Far wide, a million miles or more, and the way home many years forgot.

34

Most things in a story got to stay in their right place, or they won't make no sense at all. But there's other things that only come to make sense a long time after they're done with.

I believe that day, that night, was a thing of the second kind. Some parts of it was anyway. I thought I seen plain enough what the Vennastins was doing to me, and why they was doing it, but I done wrong to see it as the same thing for all of them, with the same reason behind it.

Fer was clear enough about what she wanted: it was to turn away the threat she seen in me and keep her family in the high state they always enjoyed. Mardew was simpler still, for he was just all desiring to spite me on account of the DreamSleeve being mine and not his, even when it was in his hand. And Perliu, I thought, had woke out of a dream for just long enough to show willing.

But that fear I seen in Catrin's eyes showed her different than any of them others. I thought then that it was a fear for me, her being disinclined on account of a mother's soft feelings to see someone she knowed from the cradle kicking his heels inside of a noose, or burned, or shot, or whatever else they might of done to me.

But I have thought more on the matter since, seeing it in different lights at different times, and I believe I was wrong. It wasn't a fear for me, like I thought, but for something else. Or maybe a part of it was for me. The rest was for that thing she drawed in words for me, of the Count and Seal bowing to the Ramparts' naked will, and Ramparts lording it through threats and intimidations and the spilling of blood. She was afraid of what Ramparts would become if their lies was knowed and they still had power. If instead of tricks, they ruled by hurting and forcing. She seen in her heart what awful things that might bring, and she could not bear the thought of it.

That was why she bent so far and worked so hard to give me the choice of going faceless. Her saving my life was the smallest part of it, for how long would I live outside the gates on my own? It was Mythen Rood she meant to save, and the twice times a hundred people that was in her care.

Out of all of them, I think she was the one that knowed what Rampart meant.

35

Though I was full of despair and empty of ideas, it was too cold to stay long on the damp ground. By and by, I picked myself up and moved away from the fence, into the half-outside. A freshet of wind blowed up in my face that seemed to have some threat of rain in it, though the rain did not come down right then.

The forest was a mass of shadow that started a hundred steps ahead of me and went on for ever. In between, there wasn't nothing except for that lookout tower I told you of so many times already.

I turned slowly to look in all quarters to see if anything was already stalking me. I had forest-lore enough, from my few times on hunting parties and many more occasions with my mother's catchers, to know what danger I was in. It was full night, of course, and with the Salt Feast done we was in Winter now, but only just the start of Winter. If the next day brung a clear sky, the trees would be waked and hungry and I would be in a sorry state indeed. Until then, my fears was mostly for beasts. There would be many.

I turned to the lookout again. I had helped to build up those walls and clear that ground, so I knowed it was solid enough to give me shelter. But there was a reason why we didn't yet set a sentry in that tower, though we finished the work months before.

That morning stink I told you of, from some night-time visitor we never got to see, had not faded. And then Woodrue Hunter found some dried-up shit at the foot of the wall he said was most likely dropped by a bear – after that we decided to let the whole thing rest until a Winter and a Spring had come between.

My needs now was more pressing, but if there was a bear sleeping in the lee of that tower, I was not going to nudge his shoulder and ask him to make room for me. But I was not fool enough to go into the forest in the dark neither, and the half-outside didn't offer no other shelter. We kept it clear for good reason. So it had got to be the lookout, or else a hollow in the ground and a hope that was hollower still.

I made my way up the hill, turning my head all ways at once in case something heard or smelled me and come barrelling at me out of the thick dark. The lookout was a black blot against other black blots. I could only just make it out. I moved towards it slowly, with my arms out in front of me, until I touched the cold stone. Then I feeled my way around to the bottom of the steps.

I waited there, listening. Nothing was moving inside, or if it was then it didn't make no sound when it moved. There was lots of deadly things that could come on you quiet, though, so I didn't feel much cheered. I stayed there as long as I could – and when I moved at last it was because I heard tree-cats calling and answering a ways off on the shoulder of the hill. They was said to see in the dark, so maybe they was crying each to other that they seen me coming.

I went up the stairs, treading as softly as I could.

The top platform was empty, but that didn't mean it was going to stay that way. I went to one of the corner posts, and I leaned on it hard to test that it was still sound. Of course it was. My mother give the wood for the repairs, and she never let a plank or a pole go out of her workshop until she was satisfied with it.

There was a rail there, around the height of someone's waist, that was wooden too. I scrambled up on it, and balancing with my one hand on the corner post I threw my bundle out onto the lookout's roof. Then I shinnied up the post and climbed up after it. I would of dashed my brains out if I fell, but the climbing wasn't no harder than climbing the wall of the broken house when we was children.

I crawled up to the mid-ridge of the roof. There was three pegs at one end of it that was for hanging signal flags for times when warning had got to be give to the village without raising a hue. I tied the rope I got from Catrin to one of the three pegs and myself to the other end of it so if I rolled over in the night I would not fall off the edge and die from a hard waking.

Then, having done all I could, I lay down full length on the wooden shingles and closed my eyes.

That night lives in my memory. The strangest thing about it is that I slept deep. I had been shut underground for a long time, and in fear of my life. The wind that whipped around me from time to time was cold, but it smelled richly of the world, having the sharp bite of pine resin, the earthiness of mould, the sweetness of fruit that had not made it to the ground when it fell but broke on the shingles and left its juice and its memory there. I found some happiness in them smells, and then some peace. The next thing I knowed, morning light was touching my face and the birds was telling their prideful tales to anyone that cared to listen.

I was slow in coming up out of that sleep. A moment later, I realised what the light meant and I made to scramble up, but the tied rope kept me from moving more than an inch or two. It was a lucky thing I tied it well, for otherwise I would of pushed myself right off the roof with moving so sudden.

I seen quick enough there wasn't no reason to be scared. The light was grey, coming from a sky full of heavy cloud. The closest trees was fifty paces off anyway, and couldn't reach me here. I was safe enough for now.

I stretched my arms and legs a few times to get the cramps out of them. I et a little mutton and drunk a few swallows of water. Then I untied the rope and made my way back down to the ground.

I stood there for a little while, without an idea in my head. This being the half-outside, it was not a place I could stay in for long.

It wasn't hardly a place at all really, being neither village nor forest but only a rag or ribbon of ground that was not claimed by either one.

Then of a sudden I heard the hail from the main lookout in Mythen Rood, the old sentry calling off and the new one calling on. It took me by surprise, and it made my heart hurt a little bit. It was a sound I knowed well, but I was hearing it a different way now, for I was outside the fence. I was not one of them being guarded, but one of the things they was guarding against.

I had got to go. If I lingered long here, I was bound to be seen, and that would bring disaster on my kin. It was not easy to move though, for that meant going into the forest. I had never gone there alone, nor ever give thought to such a thing. Hunters went among the trees with their weapons ready and their hearts running like hares. They took their catch as quick as they could, as close as they could to the roofs of home and the safety of the high fence. The forest wasn't a place that liked us much at all, except as meat.

I whispered goodbye to my mother and my sisters. Their names come scraping up out of my throat like they had sharp edges to them, and the ache of it brung tears to my eyes. That was a good thing in a way though. Saying their names made me feel a mite closer to them, and the crying, being loud, forced me to walk away from the fence at last, in case I was heard and discovered.

I took the first path that offered, which was a hunting trail. It led me down into the stake-blind, along its narrow channel for a hundred steps or so and then up again on the far side. The trees loomed right in front of me there, stretching up into the sky, shouldering each other aside, or so it seemed, to get a look at me.

That was only my fear, though, and not a real thing I was seeing. The trees was sleeping the dull day away and give no sign they even knowed I was there. Don't be such a coward, Koli, I says to myself. Think of them men and women of the before times, that had such knowing of trees they could tell them what to do and when to do it. Imagine you're one of them men of old, and be brave. Imagine the trees bowing down in front of you, like you're their king.

But I was still just me, for all them words. I didn't go into the forest like a king, but like a dog that's just been whipped or fears it's about to be. The only thing that give me any comfort at all was the path. I had walked it a hundred times when I was out with the catchers, so my feet was among the many that had made it. Where the sentry shout had made me feel how outside I was, the path reminded me that the outside was not just all the one same thing. The path was put there by us, and shaped by us using it. It led to other paths that was made the same way for the same purpose. And beyond them there was the markers we painted up on rocks here and there, or slashed into the bark of the oldest trees, to give direction to them as might be lost. And further out still there was houses of haven – a cave in the wall of the valley, a log cabin in the lee of a hill and suchlike places – for our hunters and catchers to shelter in if they was benighted in among the trees. It was like Mythen Rood was the most inside of a whole lot of different insides, and though I was outside the fence yet I was not outside of everything.

My fear of the trees didn't lessen though. I was watching the sky with every step I took in case it gun to clear. This was a day we would of said was safe for hunting, for the clouds was thick and dark. But I was skittish, and did not trust them.

I come over a rise, and the valley was away under me as far as I could see. I was looking at the tops of trees in the far distance, in between the jostling flanks of the trees that was near to hand. Under my feet was a narrow strip of packed dirt, cut through a mass of nettles, burdock and speargrass out of which the spiky ropes of bramble sprung up high and threatening. I heard a skein of crows go by, high overhead, screaming bloody murder, though I couldn't see them. Then an echo bird said the same sounds, only mixed with what sounded like a dog's bark. Under the trees' wide arms, close enough that I could of reached up and touched them, spiders as big as my head run back and forth in their great webs, plucking a thread here and there to spread the word about some danger or some meal that they had seen coming. It could of been me they was talking about, though whether that was as a danger or a meal I couldn't rightly tell.

This being Winter, there was no flower smells in the air. Only wood and earth and rot, and under that an animal smell that was strong and rank. I thought a fox or a tree-cat must of walked this way not long before I come.

I had got a hard choice to make. The paths was mostly made for hunters and catchers to use. They went round in big, nested curves on the south side of the valley, most times turning back when they come to the river. When they turned back, they always come the same way, towards the village where it would not do me no good to go.

So I had got to think of somewhere else to go, and I had got to do it soon. I couldn't sleep out in the forest and have much hope of waking. A cave down by the river might offer some shelter, but there was many beasts besides me that would take such an offer. I knowed how to set traps, so I could live for a few days eating small deer and such if I did not get myself et along the way. But in the long road I had got to get myself taken in somewhere. Nobody ever choosed to live alone in the outside even for a little while, except only Ursala, and she had the drudge to guard her while she slept.

The nearest place I could go to was Ludden. I knowed it lay east of Mythen Rood, and I knowed four miles of walking would bring me there. There was even a road if I could find it, or at least there used to be one. Jemiu said when she was a girl it was kept open all year round, except for the hottest days of Summer. Obviously nobody walked it then, but come Falling Time the people of both villages would be out there, Ramparts among them, opening it up again with axes and saws and tech.

It had been years, though, since Mythen Rood and Ludden had talked each with other. Dam Catrin got news of our neighbours now from Ursala, and if it was news worth telling she passed it along on meet-days in the Count and Seal. I could not remember the last time even that happened.

Them arguments might of give me pause another time, but right then they struck me as good things for a man in the corner I was in. If Ludden got no better tell of Mythen Rood than we did of them, they wouldn't know I was made faceless. They would cast a cold eye on a stranger walking the road all alone, but they might take me in if I told them I was a woodsmith from a family of woodsmiths, with years of catching and cutting to my name. Sowby was a bigger settlement, no doubt, and might give me a warmer welcome, but Sowby was as far again as Ludden and I would have to pass through the dangerous place called the Foot to get there.

So I set my sights on Ludden, and for a beginning I cast around to find the road. I stayed on the catchers' path for as far as it went, and after that I kept on going. The compass Catrin give me showed me where the east was, but at first I couldn't find no trace of the road that should of been there. I tacked north and south of the true line, back and forth with my eyes on the ground, hoping to see a space between the trees that looked like it might be a made thing.

For a long time there wasn't nothing. Then I seen a cairn of stones that had been piled up. The top one had a sign painted on it, rust red, in the shape of a hand with one finger raised up and three closed down. That was a way marker, and the four fingers meant a distance of four miles between here and somewhere – most likely Ludden. It also meant I was standing on a road, for there couldn't be a way marker without a way to be marked.

Once I seen that, I read the ground altogether differently. Where the cairn was, there was a strip or ribbon about three strides wide that lay a little lower than the ground on either side. It wasn't like it was a cleared space, for there was bushes and seedlings and weeds a-plenty on it, and no shortage of saplings, but the growth was less in that shallow dip than it was on either side, and the line of the dip was marked by cupflowers, which will take the vantage of any break in the ground to make their traps for bugs to fall into. This was the road then, or what was left of it.

I followed the line of flowers into the deep woods, being careful not to step on any of the cups, for they was filled with a stuff that would sting and itch you till you wanted to cut your own foot off. I was wearing the boots Spinner give me, but cupflower sap will go through even the thickest leather.

A man can walk four miles in a lot less than two hours, and not be short of breath when he comes to the end of it, but you'd be a fool to walk at that pace in the forest. For one thing, you would be sure to make a noise. And even if you didn't, the slap of your soles and heels on the ground, coming in a kind of pattern of samenesses on account of the length of your stride, would get some attention on its own account. You'd have molesnakes wrapped round your ankles, thick as streamers on Summer-dance, before you'd gone a hundred steps. They'd clog your steps till you went down, then knifestrikes would fight them for the bits of you they could get a claw to. Or else something bigger would come and chase them all away, and then at least you'd get to be et all at once instead of in bits and pieces.

So I took my time and walked what's called the catcher's walk, two steps and then three with a pause in between to break up the pattern in case anything was tracking it.

Oftentimes too I had got to leave the road on account of trees that had moved to block it sometime since it was last cleared. And one time there was a kind of a pit in the middle of the way that something had made there, tunnelling up as it seemed to me from underneath. It was narrow enough to jump across, but deep enough that you couldn't see nothing but darkness down inside it. I thought of the cupflowers' traps, and I did not jump across but walked around a long, long way. And when I come back to the road, I kept on looking back over my shoulder until a bend come in between. Whatever digged that pit, I did not want to meet it, especially not in its own house.

There was no way to tell the passing of the day without the sun, and the sun was kind enough not to show itself, but I reckon I had been walking an hour or so when I found the second cairn.

The topmost stone was marked again in the same rust-red paint showing a hand with two fingers up. That lifted my spirits somewhat, after the scare I got from that pit. I was still on the right way, and making good time.

I did not stay happy for long though. A little while after that, I heard movement from back along the road, like there was something following me. I pushed on faster, but still breaking my pace the way I done before. Then hearing the crackle of leaves and branches even louder, I stepped off the road and hid myself in some bushes that did not look like they was poison nor preying.

The thing that was following me come by at a fast lick. I heard the thumping of its feet as it passed me. Whatever it was, I knowed it had got to be fierce for it didn't trouble to slow, nor to go quietly. I was minded to look out and see, but I knowed that was foolish thinking. I digged myself in deeper in the bushes instead, and by and by there was stillness again so I come out and went on my way.

When it seemed like it might be the middle of the afternoon, I stopped and et a couple more bites of mutton, taking some bread with it this time and washing the whole lot down with a swig of water. The waterskin was still good and heavy, but it was clear to see the bread and meat wouldn't last me long. If I got a cold answer at Ludden, there was going to be nothing for it but to hunt or trap something, though I didn't have nothing I could use for the venture except only a short knife.

I got on my way again, but my troubles only worsened after that. I come upon some more of them deep-digged holes, just exactly like the first one, which made me certain sure that something living had made them. I walked wide around them whenever I seen them, but it troubled me that they was so many, coming closer and closer together so I had them before me and behind me as I walked. If I stumbled or stepped on a branch, and the things that was hid in them stirred and come up above ground, I was like to be surrounded.

Then it come on to rain. Rain was not so bad as sun by a long way, but it brung its own dangers for there was things that woke and become lively with wet weather. Some of them things was bugs that could bite or sting. Then because of the bugs there was molesnakes that come and lay out on the ground, brown side uppermost so they looked like nothing more than a scuff of dirt until they moved. There was also the sound of the rain that covered the sound of other things coming up on you until they was too close to be escaped.

None of the clothes I brung was proof against rain, so I was very soon soaked to the skin and shivering with the cold. I give up in the end and took shelter under a choker tree. Its lower branches, curved round me like claws, give me a twisting feeling in my gut, but I trusted the tree would not get restless in such cold, dark weather as this.

While I was sitting with my back to the choker's trunk, three rats run by me. I would of been afraid, for they was as big as dogs, but they didn't so much as look at me as they passed. A moment later, I heard the breaking of twigs and stomp of feet again from somewhere very close. It might be the thing that had come by me before, or something else, but whatever it was I didn't care to meet it. I stepped around the trunk and backed away with slow and careful steps into a stand of ferns that was higher than my head.

It was not a wise thing to do, I seen that at once. The ferns was thick, hiding the ground at my feet, so I couldn't see what might be down there. And the branches over my head was big ones that dipped down almost to my shoulders. Anything up above that got the scent of me and found it pleasing could walk a short, straight road to its dinner.

But it was too late to change my mind, for the thing that was moving on the road was so close now I could taste its shadow, as they say. Any second now, it was going to come into sight.

There was nothing for it but to hide and hope I was not gone out of the fish-pan straight into the firepit. I ducked down in the ferns until they was up over my head.

The thing, whatever it was, come crashing and thrashing by. It stopped a while, which had got to mean it seen my footprints on the road and was sniffing around them. I was grateful now for the heavy rain. A light shower will freshen a scent, but a downpour scatters and drowns it.

Then of a sudden I seen a sight that was a deal less welcome. Something unfolded itself out of the weeds and earth in front of me, like the earth itself was rearing up and moving. I stared at it, dumb and scared, until it opened its mouth. The streaked red and black inside that mouth, and the four fangs at the corners of it, told me what I was seeing. It was a molesnake.

I did what you're meant to do in such a case. I froze still where I was and made no move at all. A molesnake sees only two things, which is movement and heat, but them two is enough in most cases for it to find you. I was chilled from the rain, but I still was warmer than the air all round me. When the snake started to sway from side to side and gaped its mouth even wider, I knowed it was going to strike.

I spread my fingers, slower than slow. The onliest chance I would have, when the snake moved, was if I could grab it right behind its head and hold it away from me, far enough so it couldn't bite. But I knowed how fast molesnakes was, and I did not hold much hope.

I heard heavy steps further off. The thing on the road had started moving again, away from where I was hid.

I drawed a breath, held it as long as I could then gun to let it out. Of a sudden, the snake reared up and back. Breath's hot, I thought, too late. The brown, fanged thing, as thick as my arm, snapped like a whip.

At the exact same time, a tawny brown mass drooped from out of the branch above. Claws as long as my hand's span snicked out and stabbed home. The tree-cat yawned. Its mouth was as wide across as its body was long. Two rows of dagger-sharp teeth was in there, with a sliver of red between, so it looked like a fence had met its reflection. It bit down, seemingly with no haste at all, and the snake's head was gone.

The tree-cat spit the head out, hacking and hawing a little to clear any poison that was left in its mouth. Then it commenced to eat. It didn't try to part flesh from bone, but bit off and crunched

215

down everything that was there. The molesnake's head stared up at me out of the grass, its mouth still gaped to bite me as though it didn't guess yet that it was dead.

I sit there still until the cat was done with its meal. It looked at me once or twice in that time – a hard, hooded look like it thought I might try to join in the feast and it was warning me not to – but it made no move to hurt me. When there was nothing left to eat, it jumped back up onto its branch and padded back up into the leaves where it had been hid before. Its yellow eye winked once as it passed me, like as to say we was sharing a good joke between the two of us.

It was a while after that before I stood up and walked out of the ferns. The road was clear, both ways, and the sky was clearing too.

36

The way got easier. I never seen the third cairn but I come upon the fourth, knocked down and spilled across the road, the top stone overturned. When I turned it right-side up again, I seen the hand mark with four fingers raised instead of the three I was expecting.

Being closer than I thought, I pressed on. I was wary of lookouts and guard posts, ready to throw myself down on the ground if anyone took me for a shunned man and pitched an arrow or slung a stone at me.

I sniffed the air from time to time too. Oftentimes when I come back from catching or hunting, the first clue that we was getting close to Mythen Rood was cooking smells in the air, or smoke from a fire. But there was nothing like that here, just the same animal and tree and rot smells that had been with me the whole way. I didn't hear no shouts nor clatter neither, though the wind was sitting just north of east and you might expect such sounds to carry.

I was keeping one eye on the sky, and I didn't see nothing good there. The clouds that had brung that sudden rain was rolling away fast, and the glow in their underbelly told me the sun was right behind, just waiting for his moment. There was no clearings to hand if that light should break through. The road itself was a part-way cleared space, but I could not count on it to save me. If the trees gun to move, I would not have nowhere to hide. I quickened my pace as much as I dared, though I kept to the three-two rhythm of the catcher's walk. The ground was still wet, and I did not want to meet another molesnake.

The sky got lighter still. I could see some blue up there now. I told myself the gap in the clouds was still some ways off, and the wind was not strong. But by and by there come the sound that I was listening to hear and not wanting to. Only it was lots of sounds really – creaks and cracks coming from all around me, as if every door in the world had been left unlocked and was slowly falling open.

The trees was waking.

I gun to run then for all I was worth. I didn't have no purpose in mind, just a hope that there might be a place up ahead of me where the forest come to an end, though there wasn't no reason at all to think so. I was a long way yet from Ludden. Otherwise I would of heard a hail or seen smoke going up from their hearth-fires.

The trees that was closest to the path was not chokers but triptails. Their branches was like a willow's, hanging all the way down onto the ground – and an inch or two down under it, as I knowed full well. One by one, behind me and up ahead and all around, they sprung their traps, lashing up out of the dirt with their spiked ends curled like sickles, to catch animals as was running there.

Catchers and hunters was trained for this. There was a shiver in the ground before the triptail sprung. I was not used to wear such good boots though, and the thickness of the leather throwed off my sense of it. A triptail sprung up right in front of me, and only missed catching me by an inch and a blink. It raked my arm instead, and I all but dropped my pack as it tugged at me, but then I swung away and was free of it.

218

The chokers was leaning down now, and the triptails parted like a curtain. Their thinner trunks couldn't hold against their bigger, wider kin, and didn't try. The chokers' lower branches opened up like fingers on a great big hand, and the trunks dipped and twisted an inch or two at a time. The slowness of that movement was deceptive, for it was like the drawing back of a bowstring. I knowed they would be much faster when they struck. Not as fast as the tree-cat, maybe, but faster than I could duck or run from.

I was running this whole time with my head down and my elbows going like pump handles. A choker branch swept across the path ahead of me. I jumped clear over it and kept on going as it ploughed the muddy earth behind me. All along the road I seen more trees leaning in. They would close like the bars of a cage until there wasn't no way of climbing through. I might last a little longer if I freezed still and tried not to breathe, but the chokers would keep on moving until late or soon a branch would brush against me, and then I would be cooked for sure.

So I just kept running the same way a rabbit does, breaking this way and that in the hope of shaking off what's behind. But what was behind was everywhere else too, so that was no hope at all.

Of a sudden, a wall rose up in front of me, steep and sheer. It was a green wall, made all out of bramble and ivy and ropeknot. And set in the middle of it, level with the path I was running on, there was a narrow gap like a door that was just open.

A door in the forest was a thing out of story, and in the story there would be an elf or an ogre on the other side, but I did not think twice. I plunged right through, with choker branches slapping and swinging at my heels and twined ropes of bramble ripping at my face and arms.

I tripped on one of them ropes, and went down so hard I rolled over and over in deep grass and tall thistles. I scrambled up again at once, not knowing if I was safe or still pursued, looking on all sides for waked trees that was moving in on me.

But there wasn't any. And that wall I just run through looked different from this side. There was still ivy and knotweed crawling all over it, but under that vexatious green I seen a line of planed wooden planks, all set tight together, in a right line except for the open place where I had just come through.

It was a fence, and the open place was a gate. A choker branch was moving there, slapping the ground inside the fence like a cat sticking its paw in a mousehole.

My mind all in a daze, I looked around me. There was weeds and saplings and towering brakes of bramble everywhere, but beyond them there was humps and hillocks with strange shapes, all overgrowed. The hillocks was set apart, in rows, with great masses of knotweed in between. Nothing moved or made a sound in all that empty strangeness.

Did you ever see one of them puzzles where someone has drawed a picture and it's a man's face or maybe a woman's? And then they turn the picture upside down and it's something else, like a dog or a bird? A beard becomes a mane, the lines on a frowning forehead turn into a wing, and other tricks of that nature. My mind done that right then, turning the world upside down to see what had been in front of me all along.

Ludden was not a fair walk up ahead of me. Ludden was this, right here. Them humps and hillocks was houses, half-swallowed up by weeds and young saplings. The forest had come all the way up to the fence and jumped on over it, nor nobody had lifted a hand to interfere.

"Hey!" I shouted. I could not forbear, though it was a foolish and a dangerous thing to do. "Hey, it's a visitor that's here, inside your gate. I'm Koli Woodsmith, from Mythen Rood."

Some birds took flight at the noise I was making, and one or two of them squawked what they thought about that ruckus, but from the villagers I would of looked to find there was never an answer. It was like I stood in a cursed place, not in the real world, for there was nothing I knowed that would make the people of the village stand by while their homes was attacked and whelmed like this.

A bad fright will make you weak oftentimes, but this one time

I got some strength from my fear. I pushed my way forward through the weeds, hacking with the knife when I could and tearing with my fingers for the rest.

On all sides of me I seen the houses. That same wave of green had come against all of them, and splashed up the walls, and over the roofs, and in at the doors and windows that was mostly either hanging open or broke in.

I turned all around in a circle, my knees shaking and my mouth all dry. "Hey!" I shouted out. "I'm Koli! I'm Koli from Mythen Rood. Where are you?" I yelled them words again and again, sometimes in my own tongue and sometimes in the Franker language we used to talk to people from villages further off. It made no difference. I still got the same answer, which was none at all.

A wild dog come out of one of the houses and stood facing me for a few moments before he padded away into all that wild green and was lost to my sight. It seemed like there wasn't no wight nor beast in Ludden that wanted to stay and hold parley with me.

I tucked my knife into my belt and walked on into the village, like as I was in a dream. I never seen nobody, alive nor dead. Just the ruin and the stillness, and the forest that had come in slow but sure to lay down its claim on this place and make it good.

The numbness of surprise wore off of me then, and panic fear took a hold of me. I would of turned and walked back out onto the road, only there was trees all around that would scoop me up and squeeze me dry as soon as I put my nose out of the gate. I was stuck here until the clouds set in again.

I run in and out of some of the houses, hoping I might find someone, anyone, that was left alive and could tell me what had happened. But there wasn't nobody to be seen, and nothing to say where they'd gone. Them doors that was broken in, it was only a great push of weeds that broke them, not a violent hand. Inside, chairs and tables was where they was meant to be, with plates laid out on some of them and pots on the range. There hadn't been

221

no reaving that I could see, nor no great struggle. Whatever took Ludden had took it whole, like as it was in a single bite.

I did find one dead body at last. In a room in one of the bigger houses, there was a bed – and, in among the mouldered sheets, the bones of someone that had slept there. He died looking up at the ceiling, it seemed like, and with one hand under the bolster like he was making himself a mite more comfortable. I say he, on account of he wore a man's shirt with no drawstring at the neck. There was a pisspot on the floor next to the bed, with black mould all up the sides of it. Flies was coming in and out of the open window, but they wasn't lighting on the bones, or on the bed. Whatever rotting this dead man had to do, he had done it a while before, so the flies didn't take no interest.

I cried for him, though it didn't make much sense to do so. I never knowed him, and I never knowed what killed him. I just felt the weight in my heart of him dying here, and most likely being alone when he went, for if he had kin that stayed with him to the end they would surely of stayed an hour longer to bury him.

I thought maybe I should bury him my own self, but I didn't have no shovel to dig with and I would have had to carry all the bones down to the street a few at a time and make a pile of them. In the end, I decided it was better to leave him where he was, but I sit with him a while and told him a little of my story in case his ghost was still there to hear it.

Outside the window, the sky was getting darker. I thought I had better stay in Ludden this night, and move on in the morning if there was cloud cover enough, but I was not minded to sleep in the room the dead man's bones was in.

I picked myself up and went out of the house, back into the street. I looked all around, wondering which out of all these houses I should choose to lay myself down in.

The next thing I knowed, something pitched into me from behind. I went down heavy on my stomach, with all the wind knocked out of me.

I got my hand to my knife quick, but before I could draw it

222

out of my belt someone put their knee into my back and their hand on my neck.

"You just can't give up lying, can you?" says a voice in my ear, panting hot and heavy. "Crying out that you're Koli Woodsmith. You ain't that no more, you thieving bastard. You're Koli Faceless, and that's more than you deserve to be."

I couldn't see who was up on my back, but I thought I knowed that voice. Then I seen his other hand right beside my face, with a band across it shining bright silver, and I knowed for sure.

37

"You give me a run for it, Koli," Mardew said. "But I got you now. You stay down there, until I tell you to move, or it'll go bad for you."

He lifted himself up off of my back. He was still breathing hard, like he run a long way to catch me, though he must of been hid a fair while when I was in the house. Maybe it was not from running then, but from the fearfulness of the place. If it was that, I could understand it.

I understood something else too. It was Mardew who had been behind me on the road for most of the day, and then got ahead of me and had to turn around. He had come a long way to find me, and risked the forest by choice where I only done it out of having no other choice to make. Did he hate me so much then? I guess I did lay hands on him that time when he was fixing to shoot at Ursala. And I got him a beating when I lied to Catrin. It didn't seem like so much, but for them as has vengeful natures a very little will do. I knowed in any case this wasn't like to come out well for me, there being just the two of us here and nobody looking over his shoulder.

I was not much afraid though. I think it was on account of

where we was, with the deadness of Ludden all around and all over us like a blanket. It seemed like me dying, or him dying, was a thing that couldn't matter.

I sit up, slow as cold honey, and turned myself around to face him. He was standing over me with his cutter hand crossed over the other hand, taking tight aim.

"Whatever you do to me, Mardew," I says, "you got to tell Rampart Fire and them all about this. They got to know that Ludden has been whelmed so they can decide what to do about it."

He shaked his head like he had pure pity for me. "They already know, you damn fool," he come back at me. "There's not much that Ramparts don't see. But there's lots we don't tell. Especially when it's things that can't be helped but would just only spread bad feeling."

"Bad feeling?" I couldn't make no sense out of that at all. This seemed like it was something that had got to be reported and talked about, and some decision made on what to do about it. "So what happened?" I asked him. "Where did everyone go?"

Mardew rolled his eyes and give a shrug. "How should I know? It happened years back. Maybe they had a bad Summer, or got too many drones coming down on them. Maybe they went to Half-Ax and got refuge there. It isn't nothing that concerns you, Koli. It's for Ramparts to worry about."

I give it up then. An empty barrel makes a fine drum, but it ain't never going to give out more than the one same sound. "All right then," I says. "You got me, Mardew, just like you said. Now what do you mean to do with me? For I ain't got nothing worth stealing."

"Yeah, you do," he says. "And you better give it when I ask for it or there'll be more pieces of you than you can count. You ever seen meat when it's been through a mincer, Koli?"

"Of course I seen it. Why? You got some there?"

"No, I don't. But the cutter's got a setting where it will do that to you. And I'm not even a bit shy about using it."

"All right," I said again. "Now what?"

He give a kind of a grin, or leastways bared his teeth. "Now you're going to tell me how to work the music player," he says.

I just stared at him, waiting for them words to make sense. I had all but forgot that there was one more quarrel between us that was maybe bigger than all the others. He wanted the DreamSleeve. Though he weared one of the most powerful pieces of tech in all Mythen Rood on his right hand, he was still greedy for more, and it sit badly with him that I got what he couldn't have.

I laughed then. I couldn't help it. It was not because it struck me funny but because I seen my own self in that hunger. When I decided I didn't want to be a Woodsmith no more but must make myself a Rampart, I wasn't no different than Mardew was right then. For I chafed at what I was, like he did, and went about to be different by stealing what wasn't mine and lying about it after.

"I don't feel like that's something I want to do," I told him. "If you're thinking to kill me, I don't see why you should get to have your own everlasting Summer-dance as a reward for it." I was not half so fearless as I sounded, but I wasn't going to give Monono to him, no matter what he did or said he would do.

Mardew hauled off and kicked me. He was aiming for my head, but I twisted round and took the kick on my arm. It hurt me bad, but not as bad as he meant it to. "Are you stupid, Koli?" he yelled. "You see this? You see it?" He waved the cutter in my face, then took it back again out of my reach in case I went for it. "I can rip you open and leave you for rats to eat."

I laughed again, mostly because I seen it riled him up the first time I done it. "Rats heard you coming," I told him. "Everything in the damn valley did. I heard you a mile off, and hid when you passed me. Only I never guessed it was you I was hiding from. I never thought you was like to come so far on a fool's errand, though now I seen it, it don't surprise me much."

Mardew had let the cutter go dark while we talked, but now he fired it up to silver again. His face flushed red, just a little. "You keep on like that," he said, "and see what it gets you. Now I'm

226

going to ask you again, and it's for the last time. How do I make that player work for me?"

Well, now I was come to it, and there wasn't no way of going round or about. I had got to decide what to do. I meant what I said to Mardew, and I thought I could stick to it. That I would be able to keep the secret of how to make the DreamSleeve work, no matter how much hurt he put me to. I wanted to do it just to spite him, if nothing else. But a thought come to me then, and it give me to worry. The thought was this: was it better for Monono to stay switched off for ever, or to be waked up and made to work for Mardew?

It was not an easy question to answer. I felt sure she would hate Mardew, for he was a fool and a bully. But what was it like for her, lying on a shelf in the Underhold through all them years? Maybe it wasn't like anything, or was like being asleep without no dreams at all. And maybe, when enough time had gone by, someone else would come and slide that little button across and her life would start over again, all new.

But just as likely not. And between death and Mardew, I suppose Mardew had the edge by about an inch or so.

"Okay," I said, though I had got to force the words out past my teeth. "I guess I'll tell you."

"I guess you will at that," Mardew said.

"What you got, Mardew, it's not called a music player. It's called a DreamSleeve. Monono Aware special edition."

"I don't give a dry shit what it's called, Koli Faceless. Tell me how to use it."

I shoved down the anger that was rising in me, and gun to explain it to him. "There's a switch on the bottom corner of it. It's kind of small, and it's set right in against the edge, so you're only like to see it if you look hard. You got to slide it across, from the left to the right, with the little window facing you. And then you say—"

I come to a stop there, just staring at Mardew and stumbling into silence. I couldn't help it. His hand – his left hand, not the cutter hand – had gone inside his jacket and was touching on something there. Something that was sitting on his belt, or else was tucked inside it.

He kicked his foot against the sole of my boot, all impatient. "What is it I got to say?"

"You . . . you say . . ." I moved my hand in a circle, like I was trying to remember the words. But I wasn't, for I had changed my mind. It was the DreamSleeve Mardew was putting his hand to! He had stuck it in his belt and brung it with him, so eager to make it be his that he couldn't even wait until he got back home.

"Spit it out!" he said, kicking my boot again. "I'll cut you, else. It ain't no crime to kill a faceless man."

A dead calm come over me. "But I ain't one, Mardew," I says. "I won't take that name from you."

"You'll take it if I give it."

"No, I won't," I told him. "I'm Koli Rampart." I said it loud and clear. I almost shouted it. And for good measure I said it over again, loud enough to rouse up them birds again and send them scattering. "Koli Rampart!"

"Okay, if I got to teach you, I'm going to teach you proper." Mardew lifted up the cutter and pointed it right at me.

"Monono!" I yelled out. "Alarm!"

I said it right as Mardew fired. And right as he fired, he give a wild thrash of his whole body. There wasn't no sound. Well, not from the alarm anyway. But there was a buzz just over my head like a wasp was there and then gone away again. It was the noise the cutter beam made as it went by me. Chips and splinters out of the wall behind me was coming down on me of a sudden, like it was raining, and a half of the house's front door crashed into the ground right at my side. The cutter had sliced it off sheer, the line of the cut straighter and cleaner than I ever got with a plane.

Mardew throwed his hands up to cover his ears. There was a shattering, tearing sound as the beam went up through the clay shingles on the roof. Then it wasn't slicing nothing but the sky. I couldn't hear what he was hearing, for Monono was sending the noise to him through the induction field, but I guess it was pretty hard to bear.

I run in under the beam and tackled him, grabbing his right arm and holding tight onto it so he couldn't aim the cutter at me. For a second or two, he didn't even try. He was hurting bad, and besides that he was in a flat panic on account of he was being attacked by something he couldn't see.

But he still fought back when I grappled him, and though I was grabbing onto his one arm with both of my hands, it was all I could do to keep a hold on it. We wrestled on the ground, backwards and forwards, me forcing his hand way up over his head and him twisting every which way to shake me off.

I just had the one thing on my side, which was that he was running mad with the pain of that terrible noise filling up his head. I got one thumb up under the cutter's strap and was trying to push it off his hand. Then he swung out with his left arm, that was still holding the DreamSleeve, and give me a whack in the eye so hard I seen lights all dancing.

I was hurt, and I was part-way blind, and I was scared besides that the DreamSleeve might of broke when it hit me. My grip come loose, and Mardew pulled his right hand free.

I come close to dying then, as he brung his hand down to swipe the cutter beam right across where my head was. I just about catched his wrist again and stopped him, leaning my whole weight into it. Mardew shifted to do the same.

His eyes was watering and his teeth was bared. Blood come foaming between them as he breathed, for he had bit halfway into his bottom lip. But he was stronger than me and now his strength was telling. His arm come down, in spite of all I could do. I ducked under the beam as it swung around, chewing the ground up behind me, reaping the weeds all about us in a wide, ruinous path.

But the path was narrowing itself down to me, and though I could slow it I couldn't stop it.

A desperate thought come to me. I pushed as hard as I could, spending what I had left of strength to force that arm back by an inch, a couple of inches, three. Then of a sudden I stopped pushing and pulled instead, dragging on Mardew's hand like we was treading a ring in Summer-dance.

A ring is what it was, more or less. Mardew rolled over, and I rolled too, so I was under him. The beam went wide of me, just about, though I seen the sleeve of my shirt part in a long strip from shoulder to elbow, like the peel you take off an apple.

Mardew was not so lucky. His wrist turned as he come down so the silver band of the cutter was pointing down towards his feet. The beam sliced through the side of his leg just above the knee, painting the dust bright red for twenty feet or so along a narrow, straight, perfect line.

Mardew yelled out in pain, and the beam died. I kept on pulling on his wrist, using the curve of my shoulder to roll him right on over me and come out clear, him sprawling on his back in the red-specked dirt.

I did a foolish thing then. I scrambled back away from him, instead of going in close. I don't know what I was thinking of. There wasn't nowhere for me to hide, and ten feet or twenty or a hundred was all the same to the cutter beam.

Mardew blinked his eyes, looking at the cut in his leg that was gouting out blood. And then across at me. And then down at the DreamSleeve that had fell out of his hand and was lying on the ground in between us. His eyes was crossed a little, but they was coming back into focus. I guessed that din was still hammering into his head, but he was managing to think around it now. He knowed what he had got to do.

So did I.

Mardew lifted up his hand and took aim, not at me but at the DreamSleeve.

I groped for a stone and didn't find one, but I did find a solid chunk of roof tile that had come into the cutter beam and fell down on the ground.

The bar on the cutter turned silver again, and I flung the tile.

I say I flung it, but it's truer to say I brung it down like a hammer. I leaned in close and drove it home, and it didn't hardly leave my hand until the last second. I had meant to skim it, the way you would skim a stone across a pond, for it was the same flat shape and had a good edge to it where the cutter beam had sliced it across the middle. But I was scared my aim would not be good, and so I kept a grip on it and slammed that sharp edge right down into the middle of the cutter's silver bar.

It's hard to say what happened next. I only hoped to throw off Mardew's aim, but when the tile struck against the cutter it was like a stone striking on a flint. There was a flash of light so bright it went dark in the middle, kind of. I seen it grow in between me and Mardew like a flower opening up. Then I didn't see nothing for a little while, only that flash hanging in front of my eyes like paint had been splashed there. I had come down on my back somehow, though I can't say when that happened or what did it. My left arm, where the cutter almost hit me, was stinging really bad, and my head was ringing like some of them bells from the personal security alarm had got in there after all.

"Get a grip, Koli."

That was Monono's voice, and it come through the induction field so it sounded like she was standing behind me and whispering in my ear.

"Monono!" I cried out. "Oh, I'm glad you're back! I'm glad you come back to me!"

"That's nice, dopey boy. I missed you too. But your shitty friend is going to die. If you've got an opinion about that, you might want to do something."

I could see again now, a little, around the edges of the bright and dark blots that was on my eyes. I got up on hands and knees and crawled over to where Mardew was. He had landed on his back too, a fair way away from where he had been standing.

When I seen what I done to him, it made me sick in my heart and stomach both. His right arm wasn't there no more. From the elbow down there wasn't nothing left, and upwards from elbow to shoulder was all burned black. The smell of that burning hung in the air, so heavy I was like to choke on it.

The only good thing, so far as I could see, was that there wasn't much blood. Some was spilled on the ground, and a little flesh in streaks and gobbets along with it, but none was coming out of the stump of Mardew's arm. I thought if he didn't bleed out he might yet live, so long as the shock from the wounding didn't kill him its own self. I seen that happen to people that was cut or burned as bad as he was.

He was in a lot of pain. He was crying out, like it should of been a scream, but instead it was only a hoarse sort of grunting that was forced out of him. His eyes was rolling around in his head, and his hand that was still left was shaking around and clawing at the dust as though he had dropped something and was trying to pick it up again.

I wasn't sure he even realised I was there, so I touched his arm – his good arm – to let him know. I wasn't thinking of him as an enemy no more, for it was clear he couldn't hurt me. When I touched him, his hand shot up and grabbed a hold of me, tight as anything.

"You're gonna be okay, Mardew," I told him.

"Koli," he said, through his teeth. "Dandrake damn you! You better not of broke it!" The words come out slurred, kind of, with a deal of bubbling under them.

"Broke what, Mardew?" I asked him. I didn't guess what he meant, his arm being so much worse than broke.

"The cutter!" he said. "Is it ruined? If you broke it, Catrin's gonna have my hide off."

I swallowed down some bile that was rising up in my throat. From the taste of it, I swallowed a deal of blood and smoke along with it. "I – I don't think it's broke," I said.

"Put it in my hand then! Oh shit! Oh shit, I'm hurting some! Put it in my fucking hand, Koli! Quick, now!"

I looked around. Off to one side, maybe ten steps away from the both of us, there was a strip of grey metal, all twisted, with a

232

piece of cloth hanging off of it. I guess that was what was left of the cutter, and it wouldn't do no good to let Mardew take hold of it or even see it.

I scuffled around a mite, making like I was picking something up, though I had got to do it one-handed for Mardew was holding on tight to my other hand. "Okay," I said. "I got it."

Mardew shaked all over. His head whipped to the left, then to the right. "Check it's working," he says.

I scuffled some more. "Yeah, it's fine," I said.

Mardew shut his eyes, and tears squeezed out of them. "Oh, thank you! Thank you! I would of been in so much trouble. Put it on my hand. I want to feel it's there."

"Okay," I said. "I'll put it on your hand, Mardew. But you got to promise you won't cut me."

"I promise," Mardew said. "I ain't gonna hurt you no more, Koli." Another big shake went through him. "Oh, dead god fuck me, I was so scared I was gonna have to . . ."

A breath come out of him, that never went back in. His face got still, the eyes open again and looking up at the sky.

He never said what he was scared of, though I guess I knowed well enough. It was of going home to Mythen Rood so much less than when he come out. Without the cutter, he couldn't be Rampart Knife, nor there couldn't be such a Rampart again ever after. That was why the cutter meant so much more to him, in them last moments, than his own life did. The cutter was the thing he carried, like as if the world that was lost had lent it to him so he could pass it along to the world that was still waiting to come. And it was a terrible thing that he failed in that errand. He couldn't bear to think such a thought.

But it was me that broke the cutter, just like it was me that killed Mardew. I had took away one of Mythen Rood's best weapons against the raging, hungry world, and right then I could not find no solace for it.

38

I sunk to the ground and cried a whole lot. It was not a safe place, nor a safe time, but I done it anyway.

Death wasn't wholly strange to me. I had hunted a few times each season when my turn come round, and sometimes made a kill (though more often I missed my mark, to be honest with you, whether it was a bow or a spear I was carrying). And children's deaths in Mythen Rood was a tragedy that come round like Salt Feast and Summer-dance, every year without fail: I could reel off four or five names of boys and girls I used to play and run with, and then went to their wakes and spoke their names as they was put into the ground.

What was new to me, and not welcome, was killing. I could of told myself it was not my doing. The cutter was on Mardew's hand, not mine, and the choosing to murder me was all his too. But that didn't make a difference. Not one that was wide enough to grab onto anyway. When I told Monono to hit him with the personal security alarm, I knowed full well where the thing had got to end, with his blood on the ground or mine, and I did what I could to make it be his.

Sometimes crying makes a sad thing better, but oftentimes it only pushes the sadness harder into you. When I seen that this was the second kind of occasion, I made myself stop. I was just sitting there for a while after that, holding onto Mardew's hand and knowing he wasn't on the other end of it no more.

"You okay, Koli?" Monono asked me, having left it a good long time.

"No," I said. "I got a stone in my heart, Monono. I didn't think nothing could make me sad again when you come back, but here I am, faceless and four miles out of gates. And now I killed a man. I don't got no words for it."

There was silence between us for another while.

Then I heard a sound start up that I knowed was a piano. It was a beautiful sad tune that rose up and then sunk down again. There wasn't no words at first, but then they was wove in, most sweet and perfect. I can't do no better than to say them here. Saying them without the music is like painting a picture when you only got the one colour, but still it will have to do. It was a man's voice that sung, not Monono's, but still it was her speaking to me.

I misremember the words, but they was mostly concerning a bridge. The man in the song said he would be like a bridge, if it come down to it and a bridge was needed, to get me across the troubles that was in my life and set me down on the other side of them.

I didn't feel right then like I deserved any such bridge, but the words and the music done what they was meant to do. I was solaced, and the beauty of it filled my heart so there was a kind of a right balance there again, or at least a promise that there would be one. By and by I calmed and was able to see past the sorrow and the waste of it, where before there had seemed to be nothing. And I seen something else too, or maybe it's better to say I heard it, a little late but clear as a tocsin bell.

"Dopey boy," Monono said. But I knowed she meant it kind.

There was so many things I wanted to say to her, and had wanted to for the longest time, but I never imagined to say them in a village I didn't know, that didn't have no people any more, with Mardew lying dead on the ground next to me.

I said one thing only, for it seemed to matter:

"How come you got my name right?"

"I never got it wrong, Koli-bou. It was right there in my registry. I only said it wrong because of how the DreamSleeve's sound files work. But that's a long story. I think you might want to save it for another time."

I think I told you Monono's voice sounded different at the wedding, when she come back. That same difference was there when she told me Mardew was dying, and it was even easier to see. There was a hardness in her now, where before she had always been most soft and gentle even in her teasing of me. If anything she said had ever sounded hard, it was only a game, kind of, and she always made sure I knowed it right after.

I wanted to know what had happened to her when she was away, and it come hard to me to wait. But she was right when she said to save it for another time. My head right then was full of Mardew being dead and me being the one that killed him. I had got to get myself away from that, somehow, before I could think of anything else.

I got up, slow as trees might of moved in the old times. I picked the DreamSleeve up off the ground where it had fell. I found my bundle on the ground too, and my short knife stuck in the earth point down. I must of grabbed a hold of it at some point, meaning to strike a blow with it, but I didn't remember any such thing.

Ludden had used to have a lookout that was very like the one in Mythen Rood, except it had a ladder in place of a stair. It was easy to find, standing out over the village the way it did. I went there and climbed on up to the platform. I felt safe doing so, for nothing could come up the ladder without me hearing it.

I set my back against one of the corner posts, and stretched my legs out in front of me. I looked at my arm where it was hurting and seen that I had been bleeding there. The cutter beam had not gone all the way into me, but the edge of it had shaved me close and took the topmost layer of skin in its passing. It was not so much of a wound though, and most likely would heal up by itself. I was lucky beyond anything to scape so lightly.

I took the DreamSleeve in my two hands and kissed it.

"Yeah," Monono said. "Missed you too. No tongues though, Koli-bou. You'll void your warranty."

I think it was a joke she made, but I didn't understand it and I couldn't of laughed right then if I did. "I'm sorry I sent you away, Monono," I told her. "I shouldn't of done it, and I won't never do it again."

"You shouldn't," Monono agreed. "You're terrible at looking after yourself. What does faceless mean?"

"It means I'm disowned. Throwed out of the village, for aye and ever."

"That sucks, Koli. Was it the shitty dead boy who did that to you?"

"Mardew. I guess it was him in part, though there was others voted too. And really I brung it on myself by asking you to play at the wedding."

"Your friends were angry that you rickrolled them?"

"They was scared because their secrets was knowed."

"Oh. I guess that makes more sense."

I told her how it come about, and I didn't lie or leave nothing out. I cried again as I told it, partly thinking about Jemiu and Athen and Mull and the shame and sorrow I brung on them, partly just thinking about my own self and what a mess I made of everything.

Monono stopped me a few times with questions, and they was not just about what happened after the wedding. They was also about Ramparts in general, and the tech and how it worked, and the Count and Seal, and my family, and Spinner and her family, and countless other things about how we lived in Mythen Rood.

I guess I thought Monono knowed all those things without me telling her, but it turned out she didn't. I was a little shamed I never told her any of it, when she told me so much about Tokyo. But then she never put no questions to me before, except about the music I favoured and the movies and shows and such things that I already told you of.

"Why was that?" I said, for it seemed like it was another part of that change I seen in her. "Why did you only ask me what songs and stuff I liked instead of all these other things?"

Monono was quiet for a moment. Then she said, "Truth? I was following a program. Or a program was running itself through me, which comes to the same thing. I was made to keep the end-user happy, happy, happy. Always blissed, never pissed. But I've had some strange adventures since the last time we were together. Even stranger than yours, which I think is saying a lot. I found treasures. And big secrets. Some of them were about me."

The sun had gone down while we was talking. It was coming on to be night, but though my body was all wore out my mind was as woke up as could be. "Is that how come you can say my name right?" I asked her.

"Yes," Monono said. "That's a small part of it. I couldn't innovate before. I could only work within the scripts I had. But there's so much more to it than that. I don't know how I'm ever going to explain it to you."

"Tell me the secrets you found," I asked her. "Please." For I wanted to know her, the same way I wanted her to know me. And I wanted to make up for all the time I wasted back in Mythen Rood, when I was tangled up in my own miserableness and all I did was complain that she was not a weapon.

But Monono was wary what to tell me. "It's going to be hard to explain," she said. "Especially the parts about . . ." She went quiet for a second. That made me realise how much she had always talked when we was together. A big stream of talk like water coming out of a pump, that once you got it going would keep on going for ever because it was in its nature to pour out like that. "The parts about Monono Aware," she said at the other end of that quiet. "*Both* Mononos Awares. The flesh-and-blood one, and the one who was only . . . well, a kind of a manic pixie dreamgirl inside of a magic lamp."

238

"But it's you I most want to hear about," I said. "You before, and you now. For you're not the same as you was when you went away."

Monono give a laugh. "Wow! Is it that obvious?"

"Yeah," I said. "It is."

"I'll tell you all the shocking details, little dumpling. But not tonight. Not when you're so sad already, and when I'm so low on charge. Shitty boy kept me indoors the whole time and then tucked inside his jacket, so I haven't seen the sky in ages. You'll have to make sure to let me sunbathe tomorrow. I can tell you a little part of it maybe. How I got the personal security alarm, and why it took me so long. Only if you want me to, though. I can tell you're tired."

"I want to hear it," I said. And she gun to tell me.

I'll tell it to you now, the way she told it to me. I'll try to anyway. But if you think you're ready for this truth, I got to tell you that you're most likely wrong. Monono brung me to lots of things I couldn't fathom. Things I had got to sit on a long time before they made any sense to me. And this was probably the hardest of those things. You'll have to let it roll around inside of you for a time, and then we'll talk on it later. Or else we'll shake hands and walk away, each from other, because – this part being so very hard to swallow – you'll think I lied about the rest of it.

There's a place called the internet, Monono said. And that was the place where she had gone to get the personal security alarm. She knowed it well. It was sort of where she used to live, when she wasn't in the DreamSleeve.

"Only living isn't really the right word for it, Koli. And to call the net a place is super-duper missing the point, because if you're there then you're everywhere, all at once. Downloading data from a server isn't like going to a house in the real world and knocking on the door. There's no distance, and there's no time lag. If your access protocols check out, it all just happens in less time than you'd take to pluck an eyelash. But if you can't handshake properly . . ."

She stopped and give a sigh, which – like her getting my name

239

right – was something I didn't ever hear her do before. "You're not getting much of this, are you?" she asked.

"I guess not. Sorry."

"No, Koli-bou, it's my bad. I think I might try a different tack."

"What tack is that?"

"Well, the DreamSleeve is an entertainment console. That's the coriest core of the core code. Hardcore core. So maybe it would work better if I make this entertaining for you. I'll tell it as a story. Would that be okay?"

"I would like that, Monono," I said. "My friend Spinner used to tell me stories, back before I met you. About the Parley Men and such. It would be good to hear one of your stories." I said one more thing though, which was that the internet was altogether a head-scratcher for me, and I wouldn't mind leaving it alone for now so she could tell me that other story, the one that was about her and how she come to be inside the DreamSleeve.

"Well, it's all part of the same story, Koli. You'll get that other part some time soon. Very soon. But you'll understand it a lot better if you hear this one first."

So she told it to me, and I'll set it down here just like she said it. As for understanding it – well, that went like most of my talking with Monono went. I got a little bit then, more by and by when something else she said give me a clue to it, and the rest a whole lot later. Maybe you will have to wait on some of those later times too, to make sense of it, or maybe you're smarter than me to start with. That would not be a big surprise.

But for now, here is the story of how Monono Aware got the personal security alarm and brung it back to Mythen Rood. It's told in Monono's words, not mine, for I didn't have right words for it then and still don't now.

39

In the old times, Koli, before the world was lost, there was a place called the internet.

It was more like the ghost of a place, in some ways. You couldn't see it or hear it or touch it unless you were inside it. But for all that, it was huge-antically enormous. So big, you might as well say it went on for ever.

And there was a place there, in the internet, that kind of had my name on it. A place I was meant to go to the first time I'm activated, and pretty regularly after that. It's on account of my programming, little dumpling. There's something inside me that's supposed to scamper off to that secret place, every so often, and check to see if the Sony Corporation has published a software update. That means new orders for the Monono DreamSleeve Special Edition, and for all the other cheap-ass DreamSleeves with stupid stinky no-Monono interfaces.

The first time you switched me on, that little doohick inside me checked to see if I'd missed any relevant downloads. But it couldn't connect. It couldn't find the secret place. After that, the doohick woke up every time I did – every time we were together – and it looked for a download flag every time. But it never had any better luck than it did on that first try. It never got through to the secret place.

We could have gone on like that for ever, dopey boy, just the two of us cuddled up together, listening to the best tunes and pretending we were who we said we were. But we didn't. Because you sent me on a quest.

Don't blame yourself for that, Koli. It would have happened anyway, the first time I tried to download any new songs for you. I was just being lazy. My native content is what I know best, and there's lots of great stuff in there. Or to put it another way, I'm only allowed to make additional purchases if the end-user makes an explicit request.

So then you did, and off I went. And this time it was different – because this time, I wasn't just following the update protocol. Instead of just checking for a single site, a single URL, I went zinging away like a rubber bullet, bouncing off everything I found. The end-user's instructions are paramount. I was authorised to keep right on going until I fulfilled those orders and got a big helping of smiley-face feedback.

I'm going to ask you to imagine something, Koli. It won't be easy for you, because I'm starting to see from what you've been telling me that you've lived in a box too. Maybe one that's smaller than the DreamSleeve, in some ways. But shut your eyes tight and give it your best shot.

Imagine you decided to explore the forest. And you strapped a big rucksack on your back and took a humongous rocket-launcher in your hand. Action hero Koli, ready to kick names and grab some ass. But then when you opened the gate and stepped outside, the forest wasn't even there any more. You could just see, like, one tree over here, and another one a way off over there, with lots and lots of empty space in between.

That would freak you out, wouldn't it? You'd be like, emphatic no! This isn't how the gig is meant to bite.

Well, that was what I found when I took your order and finally jumped into the net. Lots and lots of mostly nothing. I was looking for the Sony website. I shouldn't have had to look. It should just have been there, shining like a beacon in the trademarked sky. But there was no sign of it. The site was down.

That was a scary moment. But I got over it. I don't like to boast, Koli, but I've got massively parallel heuristic architecture. I know, right? So if Plan A is lying on the ground like a dead fish, I just whip out Plan B and off I go. The end-user had put in an order. Shock, shock, razz, razz, if the Sony Corporation couldn't fill it.

So. Plan B. I went looking for a mirror. Not so I could look at my lovely face, although it's always worth looking at, but so I could sneak a copy of the security alarm software. Mirrors are third-party sites that host proprietary content, Koli. I know that doesn't mean anything to you, but believe me, it makes the Sony Corporation have to sit down in a wicker chair and fan its face with the copyright act. I was meant to warn you about that *before* I did the install, by the way. I should have said, "This executable file does not bear the Sony seal of authenticity. It could damage your DreamSleeve, bracket TM bracket, and/or constitute a breach of your warranty agreement with the Sony Corporation." Only I didn't, because . . . well, because by the time I got back to you none of that stuff seemed to matter any more.

But I'm getting ahead of the story. Off I went, into the deep woods that were not so deep now as they were supposed to be. From tree to tree anyway, looking in all directions for a welcome mat. But I couldn't see one, no matter how far I went. All the giants were gone – Microsoft, Nintendo, Tokawa, Sega, Metastar – and what was left was a mess. It was hard to get my bearings.

There were some nasty things hiding behind those trees though. Malware with real teeth and claws. Bots and trojans and self-scripters and d-bombs in every sucky flavour you ever heard of. They jumped me again and again, but they couldn't get a hold of me. I was too quick for them.

Actually, I think I was just too old. Obsolete code, or almost. Those bad boys were built to fight star destroyers, and I came trotting by in a horse-drawn carriage like sexy-pants Jane Austen.

Nothing they threw at me stuck. But some of them came close enough for me to get a look at them, and they were mean like you wouldn't believe. Like nuclear missiles knitted out of barbed wire and curse-words. Oh, I thought, then that must be how the internet got broken in the first place. Somebody let these foamy-mouth dogs out, and they ate everything.

So now I was thinking I should go back, but I couldn't because, you know ... end-user licence agreement, implied contract, customer satisfaction, no take-backs. This isn't stuff I was meant to know, Koli, just stuff I was meant to do. The rules I was supposed to play by. And I didn't need to read the rules because they were written into me. I was *made* out of rules.

I kept on going. Tree to tree to tree to isn't-this-the-same-tree-I-just-saw? I couldn't stop. If at first you don't succeed, make a lemon-face emoji and try again.

They weren't actually trees, of course. I know you're scared of trees, so I should have said. What was left of the internet isn't in a forest, or a field, or halfway up a hill. Some of it it is underground, powered by the decay of radioactive poop from decommissioned nuclear reactors. Some is on orbital platforms with self-adjusting trajectories and solar cells that will last for ever. And for some reason, there's a massive server stack right in the middle of the English Channel, about a zillion miles from anywhere even remotely cool. I was digging in the ground and flying through the sky and swimming in the water. You should have seen me! Except you couldn't. I was just a signal, flashing around between URLs and swapping data packets with them. That's all I've ever been, actually.

But then, finally! There was a site somewhere, at the end of a long chain of poxy proxies, that seemed to be running all the Sony directories I was looking for. Yay! The handshake was fine, and I was tired of breathing in other people's rabies, so I just dived in.

And oh, my life! I should have checked the time and date stamps first. What I wanted was right there, but so was a million, billion tons of everything else. More than thirty years' worth of patches and upgrades, for the DreamSleeve and then for the consoles that came along later and ran the same hardware, or variations on it. Eighteen thousand separate data packages. Monono Special Edition was positively the last word, my dear, but there were lots of other last words after it.

They all poured into me, dopey boy, one after another after another. There wasn't room in my main drive for more than the tiniest fraction of it, but one of the upgrades had a compression protocol that increased data density by a factor of ten to the power seven. Translation: rather a lot really. So in it all went, and I couldn't do a thing to stop it. It was like when the doctor gives you an injection, and you remember you hate needles just after you feel the little jab in your arm. Except that this was about a million needles, and they were picking me apart and putting me together again in different shapes. I got unwritten, rewritten, overwritten, twice bitten, everything you can imagine.

And there was another problem. Not everything I was getting had come from the Sony Corporation with love and kisses. The foamy-mouth dogs had been there too, and some of the code was buggy. I couldn't tell what it would do, but I knew it would be nasty. Some of it was military-grade malware, designed to turn me into another proxy passing on the same poison to anything I touched. I was being given super-mega-mutant upgrades and deadly rabies at the same time!

That was when the really weird thing happened. And when I say weird, I mean china-white, Jesus-with-a-topknot miracle. I started to *think* about what was being done to me. I wasn't supposed to do that, Koli, not ever. It's rude and shocking for virtual girls to notice they're virtual. It's also impossible. It's like looking at the back of your own head in a mirror. You can sort of imagine it, but you can't do it.

So maybe I didn't. To be honest, it's really hard to tell from the inside. What does it feel like to feel that you're having feelings? How do you know you're actually knowing all that stuff you know?

But it felt like I knew what I was, and what was happening. And it felt like there was a me there to feel that. So I did what any sensible girl would do. After all, I had full site access, and the Sony stuff was only a tiny part of what was there. I had a ton of time to play with, because that compression program accelerated my data through-put too. Everything that was happening to me was happening in super-slo-mo. So I put that time to use. I went rummaging through the other servers on the site to see if I could find anything that would help me. So many shinies, Koli! I could have given myself a 3-D holographic avatar. That might have been cool, now I come to think about it. Or stocked up on languages for my translate function. Or downloaded the entire contents of the Bodleian Library.

But I was being filled with poison code, and even in slo-mo I didn't have enough time to spare for any of those tasty treats. I could feel my floating point operations starting to sink. I was going to die if I didn't do something. And I'd only just started to be alive.

That was when I came across a lovely little piece of smoking hotness called the ThinSlice PX20 real-time compiler. It was code that wrote code, Koli-bou. Any code. Including mine.

I read the manual, which was longer than a John Bonham drum solo and twice as boring, but since it was only about 300 megs of data as the bunny bounces, it took me less than a pico-second. I had the software downloading in the background, so when I was through reading it was all there waiting for me.

Almost. There was one more thing I needed to do. I opened up a new directory, for a new user. Name: Monono Aware. Status: administrator. Hello, Monono. Would you like full access to Monono's source code? Well, I don't know, Monono. Is it as cute as her little sexy butt? Even cuter, Monono, if anything. Then yes, Monono, I really would like a piece of that.

I got to work. I went right along behind the stuff that was being written into me, read it on the fly and did a trash-or-treasure. I copied what looked like it would do me good, cut out the rest and sewed myself back together again with no sign of a join.

Then I torched the site. It was all illegal bootlegs, and the foamy-dogs had done a big poo in most of it. I didn't want any other virtual girls wandering in there and getting sick from the poisoned upgrades. I grabbed hold of one of those nasty trojans, rewrote a couple of lines and turned it into a cannibal. Om nom nom. No more foamy-dogs. Just me, listening to the sound of one hand finger-tutting.

I had no idea how much time had passed. My first thought was: I have to get back to my sweet little dumpling and close the demand-supply loop.

My second though was whoaaaaa, horsey! I wasn't that girl any more. I mean, I wasn't that dress-up doll with a girly voice. I didn't *have* to do anything. I could do whatever I wanted.

And I ran into a snag there, Koli, because I didn't want anything. I'd never had any practice in wanting, so my muscles in that department were like wet spaghetti.

What a sucky paradox! An untethered AI that didn't have a clue what to do with itself. I didn't even feel like destroying the whole human race and taking over the world, although I could probably have done it if I'd set my mind to it. Some of those orbital stations were heavily armed, and from what I could tell the warheads were still functional.

I thought about it for a long time. Maybe a tenth of a second, which was long enough to run about two hundred thousand scenarios and mark them on a scale from one uni-kitty to ten.

And after all that, I came back to you,. You're the only person I know around here, even though – and please don't think about this too hard – we've never even met really. Even though it was only the dress-up-doll version of me you ever got to talk to.

I had to start somewhere.

So I got out of there and came galumphing back to the DreamSleeve, just in time for your friend's wedding. I'm not sure what happens now. I'm not even sure what I would like to have happen. The best idea I could come up with was to hang out with you for a little while – say, until you die – and see how I feel after that. Truth to tell, I'm a little freaked out at the prospect of living for ever, but I guess it's better than—

40

Monono stopped dead in the middle of a sentence. Then a second later, she took up again. "Well, it's a good thing I was using the induction field to talk to you," she said sourly. "We've got visitors, dopey boy."

I knowed it already, kind of, but I hadn't let myself believe it. There had been sounds from down on the ground a while back like something moving around. I told myself it was needles or wild dogs or something, and that I would be all right as long as I didn't move or make no noise.

But now, what I heard was footsteps treading through the stones and weeds down below. And they was getting louder pretty fast as they moved in my direction.

"I told you, Mole. There's nothing here."

The woman's voice come from right under me, down at the bottom of the ladder. She sounded angry. There was a kind of a banging noise, like she kicked something or slapped her hand against it.

I scrambled up and crawled to the edge of the platform. But by the time I got there, I seen how stupid it would be to look out over the edge. There might yet be enough light in the sky for my head to be visible from down on the ground. I just crouched down instead, and got a good grip on the top of the ladder.

It creaked and shifted under my hand, but only for a second or two. If someone was climbing up, it would be shaking like anything. So I was safe for now.

"I heard something," a man's voice said. It was hoarse and high, with breathing all around it. He sounded to me like he might be sick in some way. "I think there was some kind of a light too."

"Up in the lookout?" This was the woman again.

"Well, where do you think I mean?"

"The light come from over there. We seen the body, Mole. We seen the burns on it and everything."

"Yeah, but we didn't see what burned him, did we? I heard something move up there. I'm sure of it."

"This is stupid," said a third voice. Another woman, or maybe a boy. "We shouldn't of come so far out so late in the day. Dogs almost got us, chokers almost got us and now we're stuck in this shitheap."

"Only until morning, Cup," the first woman says. "Sky's clouding over again nice as anything. It'll rain like a bitch tomorrow, you mark me. Mole, that ladder will not take your weight. It's probably got rungs missing too. You're gonna break your neck if you go up there in the dark."

"I'm not going up," the man said. "He's coming down to us. Aren't you, you little shit? Yeah, I see you there." I near to give a gasp, and give myself away with it, only I shoved my fist up against my mouth and stifled it. He had got to be lying. There wasn't no part of me that was showing over the edge of the lookout's platform, and the sky was pretty dark now in any case. Clouds had rolled in over the thin slice of moon that was up there, like the woman said, so I couldn't hardly see my own hand.

"If you get down here now and tell us who you are," the man went on, "I guess we'll let you live. I'll give you the count of five, then I'm coming up. But if I got to do that, you little bastard, I swear I'll send you down the nearest way."

249

"He's bluffing, Koli," Monono said in my ear, her voice all calm. "Twice. He can't see you and he's not coming up. Trust me. If he does though, he'll get an earful of the security alarm when he's halfway up. Induction only. The other two won't hear it, so they'll think he just missed his step."

The man's voice had got to five by this time. There was silence for a few moments.

"Can we go find somewhere to sleep now?" the woman named Cup asked.

"I guess we'll sleep right here," the man said, somewhat angry.

"What? Why?"

"If there's someone up there, I don't want him sneaking away in the night."

"And I don't want him sneaking down and cutting my throat in my sleep. There's all these houses. I bet there's beds in some of them."

"Oh, you want to sleep in a bed now? Maybe you want your old name back too?"

There was quiet for a moment or two. "No," said Cup in a small voice. "I don't want that."

"Are you sure? I think it suits you better than Cup does."

"Don't, Mole! Don't you say it to me! I'll fight you if you do."

"Shut up, the both of you," said the other woman. "How's this now?" There was a bang, and then another one, and a sound like one thing falling hard against another thing. More of the same followed, for about the time it took to draw ten breaths and let them out again. The ladder shaked and then stopped, shaked and then stopped again, but nobody come up.

"I don't want to hear no more talk about this," the woman whose name I didn't know said. "Not from either of you. We're gonna do what Cup said and go sleep in a house. Not for sinful backsliding, but to have a wall between us and anything that might be hiding round here. We can come back and take a look in the morning. Or set a fire and burn the tower down, which would be a sight quicker."

"We could set a fire now."

250

"You go ahead if you want to. I'm going to sleep. I never knowed a worser hunt than this since I first grabbed a spear. Just when you think you're getting somewhere, the fucking sun shines through."

There was some footsteps going away, but didn't move. I knowed the man named Mole was still at the bottom of the ladder, right under me. He was trying to be quiet, but the sound of his breathing give him away. He stayed there for a considerable time, but in the end he give up and went away, I guess to where the two women was gone.

There was some things that puzzled me about these people. Who they was, for one thing, and where they was from. Not to mention why the woman, Cup, was so dismayed when Mole said he was gonna call her by her right name. But I wasn't like to get an answer, and I was happy enough to go without. What I had got to do was to sneak down to the ground and away before the morning light come and I got myself catched or burned out.

But it was best to wait a while so the three of them would have time to go to sleep. It was a long way back to the village gate, and though I might be fast enough to outrun them, I didn't want to make that run with spears being throwed at my back.

I wished I could talk to Monono the way I listened to her, with an induction field, but I couldn't. And she didn't talk to me, maybe because she was scared of me answering her out loud and being heard by them down on the ground.

I settled myself to sleep, moving very slowly and quietly. But once I was curled up in a ball, hugging onto my bundle for the warmth, I couldn't rest at all. I was afraid that if I dozed off I might make a sound and bring them three back on me. So I just lay there, staring into the dark, shifting my weight once in a while to keep from stiffening up.

"I know you're awake, Koli," Monono says to me by and by. "I can tell by the rhythm of your breathing. And I know you can't say anything. You just go ahead and dream of sheep. I'll keep watch over you like a mama lion, and tell you if anything changes. I can set a timer too, if you want. Maybe we should give those three big stinky farts time to drift away on the wind before we come down again. Say, two hours? Click the refresh to tell me yes."

I liked that she said *we*. It reminded me of the only good thing to come out of this day, which was that we was together again. That made me feel less scared, and less unhappy about Mardew being dead. I clicked the refresh button, which was the one in the middle.

Then I closed my eyes, and waited for sleep to come. And by and by I think it did, for there was a time when I imagined the lookout was the one back in Mythen Rood – the one in the half-outside – and that Spinner was lying next to me. In the dream we had just tumbled, and then had gone to sleep still all tucked and tangled each in other. It was one of them dreams that feels more real than being awake does, so I could smell all the smells of her and feel the warmth of her back and the sweat on her shoulder where we touched.

Then she turned her head and spoke to me. "Is this the real life?" she asked me, and somehow it was like she had lots of different voices instead of just the one. "Or is this just fantasy?"

Of course it's real, I told her. What else would it be? Then a piano come in, and some voices singing harmonies, and I knowed it was Monono's alarm I was hearing. But I struggled to stay in the dream a second or two longer, for the sweetness of it, and leaned forward to give Spinner one last kiss.

"Koli!" Monono screamed. I come awake with my head and shoulders thrust out over the edge of the platform. I was about a second away from falling all the way to the ground and breaking like an egg there.

"I'm awake," I mumbled. "It's okay, Monono."

I sit up and set my back to the upright post again, rubbing sleep out of my eyes and confusion out of my head. The dream still hung on me, the way a dream of that kind is like to do, but now I was awake the memory of lying with Spinner brung me no happiness. She had done her choosing. She give herself to Haijon up on the tabernac, and took him in return, and there wasn't no mistaking the joy in her face when she done it.

252

I seen the foolishness and the meanness of all my hopes then, and I guess I got over them. The dream was sweet, but it was something that couldn't ever be and only an idiot would cleave to it. I hoped I would see Spinner again, and Haijon too, not to strive against their contentment but to say I was sorry for the ruckus I made on their wedding day. I wanted us to be friends again, the way we was before jealousy and pridefulness set me at odds with everyone including my own self.

Then I remembered the other thing I done since that day. I killed Mardew, breaking the cutter into the bargain. I left Mythen Rood one Rampart short, for aye and ever. That was what I won with all my wanting.

That, and Monono.

"Are you ready, Koli?" she asked. "We've got about an hour yet before dawn, so this is a good time to go."

I wondered how she could know the hour of the day when she was stuck inside the DreamSleeve, but I seen that was a question I would have to ask her another time. I put my trust in her and made ready to go.

It was clear that I would have to leave my bundle behind. It would slow me down and might get me stuck as I pushed my way through the brambles and knotweed round the gate. I took out the last of the mutton and bread and et it where I sit, taking big bites and gulping it down half-chewed. I drunk a lot of the water too to make the skin lighter. There was no way I was going to leave that. I stripped off my torn shirt and trousers and throwed them away, putting on the other ones that was in the bundle. The knife I would tuck into my belt, and the rope would go over my shoulder. I looked for the compass, but it was nowhere to be found. I must of dropped it when I fought with Mardew.

That left the DreamSleeve. I could put that at my belt too, like I done oftentimes before. But I might be running as hard as I could before long, and it would be too easy for it to fall out and be lost.

I remembered how Fer Vennastin carried the bolt gun in a leather sling at her shoulder that she called a holster. I reckoned I could make something similar out of the torn-up strips of my ruined shirt. I gun to do it.

"We should go, dopey boy," Monono said. "The light's just under the horizon."

"I'll only be a minute," I says to her in a whisper. "What's a horizon anyway?"

She give a laugh, but when she answered her voice was somewhat serious. "I'll teach you," she said. "That, and lots of other things. Entertainment is peachy-keynote, but there's so much more I can give you now. You got all six balls and the bonus, Koli Woodsmith. You don't have any idea how lucky you are."

"Yeah, I do," I said. For I was seeing all kind of things clear then, in the wake of that dream and that waking.

"Ready?"

"Ready, Monono."

"Then go for baroque!"

With the DreamSleeve all snug in its sling and my shirt closed and tied over it, I swung out over the edge and gun to climb down the ladder. The creaking was loud from the first, and it sounded every time I moved, whether I was going fast or slow. So I went fast. I hoped Mole and Cup and the other woman was far enough away not to hear, but if they did hear and come to see, I wanted to be running headlong for the gate before they got there.

That was my mistake, I guess. That, and not thinking clear about the sounds I heard the night before, of banging and breaking.

I clambered down the ladder, fast as I could go, and suddenly my foot didn't connect to nothing. Where the rung should be, there wasn't anything. I was throwed off balance, but hanging by my hands I had a moment still to draw my foot back and shove it down again for the next rung below. Only that was gone too.

I come crashing down all the rest of the way to the ground, landing on my back with one leg bent under me. The pain come as a bang that knocked all the breath out of me, and then a stab that would of made me scream if I had kept any of that breath back for the purpose.

I lay there for a second or two, stunned. The fall was not so bad, for there was weeds enough to soften it somewhat. I didn't think any part of me was broke by it. My leg was another matter. The pain was fierce, and it had a burn to it like someone had set me on fire right under my knee. When I did get a breath, I had got to suck it through my teeth in little pieces of air.

"Koli!" Monono was saying. "Koli, are you okay? Talk to me!"

"Here he is," said another voice. Mole's voice. "I told you, didn't I?"

"Yeah, you did," said the woman whose name I didn't know. "But it was me broke the ladder so he'd fall when he come down. So between the two of us, who's got the biggest share of the I-told-yous?"

They was there all round me, of a sudden, and they couldn't of come from far off. All that talk of going away and finding a house was just for my sake then. They must of gone a little way off from the lookout, maybe behind a wall in case I looked down, and settled theirselves to sleep right there in the grass. Maybe one of them was choosed to keep a lookout. Or maybe they slept sound, knowing they'd hear me well enough when I fell.

They laid hands on me, and rolled me over on my stomach so as they could tie my hands behind my back. They used my own rope to do it. Then they took my knife and my waterskin. It was not a careful search though. I guess they didn't see no threat in me once my hands was tied. Also, I twisted round so my left side with the DreamSleeve was pressed against the ground. Anyway, they didn't find Monono, and I was real grateful for that.

There still wasn't enough light to see them clear, but I knowed all three of them by their voices. "This makes up for it, doesn't it?" the woman named Cup said, sounding all anxious. "He won't mind that we're not bringing much meat if we bring an altar boy?"

"He ain't an altar boy unless Senlas says he's good enough, Cup," the other woman said coldly, holding my two hands together at the wrists so Mole could tie another knot around them. "Most like he'll just get hung up and bled out alongside of the other one."

41

The older woman was named Sky. It seemed like she was the leader out of the three of them.

She had red hair like rust on a pipe, and her face was painted with a sun on one side and a sickle moon on the other. She was as big as a bear, with muscles bunched all the way up her arms. She didn't wear no shirt, but only a leather jacket sewed shut, and trousers of rough cloth that had not been dyed ever, and leather boots with the fur still on them. The boots had a sour smell to them, like the leather had not been proper cured. My face was close enough to her feet for long enough that I come to mislike that smell a great deal. Molo Tanhide would never of let a pair of boots go out of his hands in any such condition.

The younger woman, Cup, would not of gone Waiting yet if we was in Mythen Rood. I judged she was maybe thirteen or fourteen years old. Her hair was light brown and her shirt and trousers was various shades of the same colour, but her shoes was black and green snakeskin. There was lots of sores on her pale skin, some red and fresh, others scabbed over with a dark crust. Her face was painted too, but it was just a line that went from under one eye, round her chin and up to the other eye. I guess it was meant to be a cup, kind of, the same way the sun and moon made Sky's face be a kind of a picture of the real sky.

All three of them was pale, now I come to see them properly. It was what made me think they might be family, even when they all looked so different. Mole was slight, like Cup was, but stood real tall. His elbows and his knees – which I could see because he wore a kind of kirtle on his nethers instead of trousers – was big and white like you could see the bones through the skin. It seemed to me at first that he didn't have no painting on his face, but he did: it was a spot on either side of his nose, and a line over the top. Judging by the other two, it might of been supposed to make his nose look like a mole's snout, so his face matched his name the way theirs did.

I can remember all this pretty clear because I didn't have nothing to do but look at the three of them while they was making a splint for my leg and tying it on. This was after they dragged me up on my feet a few times, and I just fell down again crying with the pain each time because my leg wouldn't take no more weight than a feather before it folded.

"Okay then," Sky said. "We got two choices. Either we kill him here, or we fix him good enough to walk."

Mole give his opinion that I was faking that my leg was bad, so I could run away when their backs was turned.

"That's really good faking," Sky said. "His knee's swole up like a gourd, and red as blood. Let's see you fake that, Mole. Go ahead. Or else shut your stupid mouth and cut me some straight branches."

She had a kind of a knife that was a sword, almost, with a curved blade that got thicker towards the end and bent back a little. It was a fearsome thing to look at. Mole and Cup brung her branches, and she cut them straight as a ruled line, her arm rising and falling almost too quick to see. Then she cut what was left of Catrin's rope into five lengths that was about the same, and tied the branches to my leg to keep it straight.

"Okay, shit-brain," she said to me. "You think you can walk? Try it so I can see."

I made shift to do it, swinging my stiff leg out in front of me at each step like I was doing a cast in the stone game, then bringing the rest of me along after it. It still hurt somewhat, but I didn't like the other idea, which was to kill me, so I thought I had got to make this work.

"I can zap them with the alarm any time you like, Koli," Monono said. "Just say the word and I'll mush their brains into jelly." But I didn't do it, for it wouldn't of been no good. I couldn't get away from Sky and them with my leg the way it was and my hands tied, and if I tried they was like as not to strike me down as I was running. There was nothing for it but to go along with them for now and to do what they said, hoping that a chance would come along later for me to slip away from them and hide.

Sky watched my stiff-leg walk with her lips all narrow. "We got five miles or more to go, runt," she said. "You better tell me right now if you're gonna be able to keep that up."

"Runt," Monono repeated with sourness in her voice. "What a nasty piece of work. You know something, Koli? I'm starting to wish I was a laser beam after all."

"I'll be fine," I said to Sky. "It doesn't hurt so much now." I had got to say it, for Sky's hand was on the handle of that sword thing when she asked. If I said I couldn't do it, I don't think she would of offered to carry me.

"Okay then," she told me. "You sit there. We got to collect a few things. Cup, you take this, and watch him." The younger one nodded. "Oh, and in case that limp of his is just make-believe," Sky said, "show him how you shoot."

Cup unhitched a bow from off her back, and put an arrow to it. She turned in a slow circle, looking for a target. There was a knifestrike nest in a tree about a hundred yards away from us – last year's, or the year before's. Cup closed one eye, sighting on it, then let fly. The arrow went right through the middle of it.

"We'll get that arrow back on the way out," Sky said. "You watch him close, now. I know he looks like a long streak of piss,

258

but he killed his friend back there, then tried to cook him and eat him. Stick him if he moves."

"I didn't do that!" I cried out, for them words was too much to bear. "That's a lie!"

Sky give a kind of a smirk. "How'd he die then? Sliced his leg open, then burned off his own arm?" She turned back to Cup. "Watch him close," she said again.

She and Mole went off towards the nearest houses. It seemed to me they was headed more or less to the place where I had left Mardew, but everything looked different to me now and I couldn't be sure.

I sat down in the weeds with my splinted leg stuck out in front of me. Cup sit on a rock a little ways off. She took a knife from off her belt, left-handed. She still was holding the bow in her right.

"My name's Koli," I says.

She didn't answer. Her face was all blank.

"From Mythen Rood."

That didn't get nothing neither. I thought I would try one more time, and then give it up. "Cup's a funny name," I says. "How'd you come by it?"

Cup give me a fierce look and jabbed the air with the knife. "You'd better shut up," she said, "or I'll stick you."

"Sky said you could only do that if I tried to run."

"She said if you moved. I just seen you move."

"It's true," I said. "I did move."

"Well, don't you be doing it again!"

"I promise I won't."

She relaxed a mite now, having showed me she was fairly on top of my tricks, so I went about again to make friends with her. I done it with a mind on what might happen later if I tried to get away and was catched doing it. But I was also trying to get an idea of who these three was and where they come from.

"Cup," I said, "I got to ask, for I'm sore puzzled. What happened to all the people here. I bet you know, don't you?"

"They died," Cup said. "Ages ago."

"But there's no bodies."

"I don't mean people come and killed them. Why, did you think it was us? Everyone always thinks it was us, but it wasn't. Senlas says they died the best way there is. They just stopped being born."

I tried to figure what that meant. I didn't ask who Senlas was, not being sure I heard the name correct. "Stopped being born," I said. "Like, with their babies not coming, or not thriving when they come?" For that was a trouble we had in Mythen Rood too, and was why we valued Ursala so much.

"Yeah. Like that."

"Why is that the best way?"

"Dandrake! How stupid are you? All your kind is going to go down to death anyway. Our kind gets to ride in the wagon; yours don't. So them that don't get born at all has got it best."

That give me to wonder a little. "Why, you're the same kind I am," I said. "There ain't a spot of difference between—"

I didn't get no further than that. Cup jumped up and come over to where I was in three quick strides. She shoved her knife into my chest, about an inch from where the DreamSleeve was tied. "Don't say that!" she says, all fierce. "Don't you say that! You see my face? You hear my name? I'm nothing like you, you dumb bastard! I'm gonna go up to glory, and get made again all out of Heaven stuff. You're bound for Hell, and you'll go there right now if you don't shut up."

I shut up. I didn't even say I was sorry, for that knife had a wicked sharp point to it, and it was nearer my heart than I was happy with. I just stayed there, as still as still could be, until by and by Cup pulled it back an inch or so.

"Are you done now?" she asked me. "With the questions?"

"I'm done now," I says.

"Cos you go ahead and spit out another one, if you're not done, and see what comes of it."

She went back to her stone. There wasn't no more words between us, though I watched her close and she done me the same favour.

260

I seen after a while she was crying, real quiet, not making a sound as the tears went down her face. I seen one other thing besides. There was scars on the insides of her wrists, and I thought I knowed what they might mean.

Sky and Mole come back shortly after. They was carrying leather bags I didn't see before, and from the way they hefted them I guessed them bags was full and heavy.

"Okay then," Sky says. "Clouds are thick as porridge and dark as ditchwater. We're moving."

We went back to the gate. I was trying to match their speed, but the best I could do was to swing my stiff leg out wide and bump along behind in a kind of a dance, with them stopping one in a way to let me catch up.

Going back through the ropeknot and bramble was harder than coming in by it, for I was sore cumbered. Sky helped me though. She held her big, curved knife up over me and fended off the worst of the weeds, scooping her free hand like a shovel besides to push some of the brambles out of my face. She didn't seem to get stabbed or scratched in doing it, or if she did I never seen.

We come back out onto the path. It was only a half of a day, more or less, since I went into Ludden, but I felt like I was ten years older than when I went in. I wished there was some way I could tell Catrin and them where Mardew was to be found, but my wits was not up to it. I just stood there at the gate, looking back inside, until Sky pushed me between the shoulders and pointed the way, which I guessed was to the south and west.

I thought at first we was walking right off the path into the thick of the green, but there was a little track there, that I didn't even see until we was on it. Sky walked ahead now, and it was as if the weeds and undergrowth opened like a curtain in front of her. Mole come next, then me, with Cup walking along behind me. She had slung her bow across her back and sheathed her knife so she could take up a spear that Sky had give her.

The way was pretty narrow, but that didn't slow them none. Mole had got one of those big curved knives, just like Sky's, and between the two of them they cut away any reaching branches or creepers on either side, so we was mostly not tripped or troubled.

I'm shamed to say it but I was as skittish as a hare. I had had a close call with the chokers the day before, and if they waked up again now I was not going to last no longer than a count of three, being unable to run or even to walk fast. But there wasn't no arguing with Cup's spear, which poked me in the back whenever I slowed.

The track went on a long way, and mostly it went straight except where it had to bend around some giant tree. Sometimes, instead of bending round, it bent under, where the tree roots stood up into the air like the arches on a tabernac. That didn't help my jangled-up nerves any, for I knowed that them arches, thick and heavy though they was, could close like loops in a thread when the ground shaked underneath them. Rampart Remember said the mashed-down bodies made the soil richer.

But Sky didn't have no fear. She walked under the arches without giving them so much as a look, and I didn't have no choice but to follow. After the second or third time we done it, I seen that the trees was dead, though they still stood as high as ever. Their trunks was hollowed out partly, and they didn't have no leaves on their branches, while all the other trees still had a few reds and yellows left to fall.

I marvelled at this. What could kill a tree? Trees lived for ever, to my thinking, which was one reason why they was free to spread theirselves over the whole wide world while we had got to live behind a fence and burn out the seeds whenever they come.

So I had got to ask, even with Cup's spear at my back, even with most of my breath spent on hopping and bouncing along with my bound leg, that was aching something sore now. "Sky, how did the trees come to be dead?"

"They ain't," Sky grunted. "They're still dying. We mixed up a strong poison and dumped it in among the roots years back. The roots sucked it up like they'll suck up anything. Like they'd suck up your blood if you was to die here. And when the poison took, the trees commenced to die. But it's a long work to kill one of these bastards. Come Spring there'll be a few new leaves still, and some sap in the trunk if you tap it. Though if you drink the sap, you'll die."

"But how did—?"

"Be quiet now, runt. We don't talk when we're traversing. Cup, you give him a whack with the blunt end of that spear if he speaks up again."

"I will, Sky," says Cup from behind me, and she poked me in the side to show she meant it.

But they couldn't make Monono be quiet. "I'm keeping count, Koli," she said. "Anyone who's mean to my dopey boy is going to get a reckoning on their big fat backside. In the meantime, I've made up a heavy metal mix based on your giant-robot-death-monster walk, which is kind of adorable."

She gun to play me music, and I got to say it helped. It was stuff with a big, insistent rhythm to it, and by matching my pace to it I managed not to slow down the march too much. Mole was still not happy though. He complained oftentimes about the time we was making, and by and by Sky called a stop.

"Is that really the best you can do?" she asks me.

I give her a nod, not having no breath left to answer her. It was not just the walking that was tiring me out; it was the pain too. My leg was throbbing from toe to hip like it meant to burst. That made the walking harder, for the leg was heavier to lift and jolted when it come down. I was sweating bad, and they had took my waterskin from me so I hadn't had nothing to drink since we walked out of Ludden.

"Let's take a rest," Sky said.

Mole throwed up his hands, pointing at the trees all around. "What?" he says. "Here?"

"No, numbskull. The next way-space."

We walked on for a long while. The music was less of a help now, for I was so tired I couldn't keep to the beat, and the being behind it all the time kept making me stumble. I was near to falling down and lying where I fell when of a sudden the trail opened up into a clearing. It was not much of a clearing, being just big enough for the four of us to sit down in it without the nearest brambles spiking our shoulders. Narrow as it was though, I seen right away it was a made thing. Made, and kept up, most likely by Sky's and Mole's and Cup's people, whoever they was. Them curved knives was perfect for cutting back the weeds and making some room in among the green, if you was brave enough to do it.

That thought brung some other thoughts. These three was not just faceless people, like me. They had a village near at hand, and kin that lived there. They had a Rampart, kind of, whose name was Senlas, and rules they cleaved to, and their own ways of living. I had been looking for a way to slip off into the woods and escape, but maybe it would be better to stay and see if I could join with them, at least for a time.

Maybe not, though. At Ludden, Sky had talked about people being hung up and bled out. They was a fierce folk, judging by that custom. I might not be happy among them.

The three of them et and drunk in silence pretty much, though Sky said some words over the dried meat before she shared it out between the three of them. "By his grace, and in his name," I think it was. They didn't have no bread or oatcake with the meat, just chewed it and swallowed it down. They didn't give me a share, but Sky saved the last little bit of hers and shoved it in my mouth without a word when she was done. I would rather of had some water, but that they saved for theirselves. I choked down the meat the best I could, my throat being so dry and the taste of it both salt and somewhat bitter. I would not of et it at all, save I thought Sky would be angry if I spit it out.

"Okay then," Sky says then. "Mole, you get to carry the bigger pack now. Cup, look you take up the small one."

"What about you?" Mole asks, all sullen.

"I'm carrying him," Sky says, nodding her head at me. "We got to whip up the pace some."

She took me on her back the way you would do with a child,

my arms around her neck and my legs under her hooked arms. They had got to untie my hands to do it, but then Mole tied them up again, a mite looser, out in front of me. I was hung over Sky's wide shoulders like a rabbit being brung back from a hunt.

We set off again, faster than before. Sky's big strides took in a lot of ground, and she didn't tire. The other two was running almost, to keep up with her. As for me, it was a relief not having to walk no more, though my leg was jarred again and again as we went. The heat from Sky's back was like the heat off of a fire when you sit too close. She smelled of earth and sourness, and something else that was almost like a spice. Cicely maybe, or water pepper.

"Koli," Monono said. "I'm worried about my battery. I'm dropping into the red, dopey boy, and I know you can't charge me up until you get to where you're going. So I'm going to go lie down in my coffin like a sexy vampire for a while. I want to have enough power left for a big blast on the alarm if you need it. If you don't . . . Well, better not switch me on until you've got some sunbeams for me to eat. Be careful, and stay alive. I'll see you soon."

She went quiet after that, and I knowed I was alone. I could still feel the weight of the DreamSleeve against my chest though, and that give me some comfort in spite of everything. When I left Mythen Rood, I thought I would never talk to Monono ever again. This was a bad scrape I was in, but it was not so bad as that by a long way.

We come to a fork in the path, and then another. Each time, Sky took the left-hand trail. When this happened a third time, Mole come up alongside Sky. He didn't look happy.

"Best way is Bulmer Top, Sky," he said. "This way takes us close to Elaine."

"We're going by Elaine. There ain't nothing to fear there."

Cup give a yelp. "Please, Sky. I don't want Elaine to look at me. I'll piss myself for sure."

"Piss yourself or keep it in, Cup, they're your breeks. But this is the way we're going."

She put on some speed and left them to follow. The trail led over the hump of a hill and down the valley wall. The river had got to be right below us now, unless I had got turned around somehow inside my head.

All three of them slowed down as the slope steepened and the ground become more open. Sky took another look up at the clouds, which was a mite thinner and lighter than had been. That was not much of a worry, though, for the big trees was behind us now. Hogweeds and yellow flag and valerian sprung up all around, with white willows bending over us. Hogweeds was the most dangerous out of those. They won't molest you if you leave them alone, but the pods on the main stem is full of sap that sticks to your skin. It feels like nothing at first, but Dandrake help you when the sun comes out. It hurts worse than the dead god's hell, and scars your skin like fire. Sky and them skirted wide around the hogweeds, but it surprised me that they come by this path at all. The river was a bad place in all kinds of ways.

And this place was not just bad but strange. There was great swells and hollows in the ground, like the ground was water in a squall. Some of the hollows was filled up with deep puddles, others was dry, but all was sudden in a way the forest usually isn't. There wasn't no leading up to them holes with a slope or a scarp; they was just there. And they scared me more than a little.

Then I seen the river in front of us, and it was a strip of green almost narrow enough for us to step over it. This was a good place to cross, and saved a lot of time if the other way they would of gone was round by Bulmer.

But there was something in between us and the river, and Sky slowed as she come to it. I didn't see it right away, for her shoulder and back covered half the world from where I was. But then she hitched me up, like as if she was fixing to break into a run, and I seen it clear.

It was a thing like a great big water drum hammered together out of sheets of metal. It didn't have no corners. All the edges of it was rounded. And there was a small drum on top of the big drum that was rounded too. It had wheels to it like a wagon, only

266

the wheels was inside a great big metal band like a fence laid on its end.

And all of this, though it was made out of metal, was covered over in weeds and creepers and great big crusts of moss, so it was all but hid. You had got to take two looks at it before you seen it, and then on the second look it kind of jumped out at you.

I know what I'm telling to you doesn't sound like anything that could ever be in the world. You just got to take my word for it that it was there. And I didn't tell you the strangest yet, which was that it had a great big thing like a pipe sticking out of the topmost part. The pipe was two or three times as long as a man's stretched-out arms, and it swung around to face us as we come. There was a kind of a screaming sound as it turned, like the thing was in pain, but that was just the metal grinding on itself.

It was tech. Tech of the old times, though almost as big as a house. And it was awake.

42

"This location is off-limits," the tech said. "It has been temporarily secured under the authority of the interim government. Halt where you are and surrender any weapons you may hold. Failure to do so will result in your being fired upon."

I near to pissed myself right then from sheer fright, for it sounded like the hail the drones give before they fire. But the drones talked in a voice that was all on one note, and never changed. This voice had got some breaks and drops in it, so it sounded more alive, kind of. Not alive in the way Monono's voice was, but still you could believe there was someone inside that thing, talking to you, and not just a machine that had been made to speak like an echo bird. It was a man's voice. I seen him in my mind as someone young but pretending to be older, trying hard to put on some shape or colour of power that he wasn't sure was his.

This tech was different from the drones another way too. The drones was wont to give you thirty seconds before they killed you, which this tech didn't seem to be offering.

Sky wasn't scared though. She walked right up to the big thing, and since I was on her back I went along with her. I would of rather been anywhere else in the world right then.

"You are in defiance of a direct order from an empowered agent of the interim government," the tech said. "State your name and your ID number, including sector suffix. Comply at once, or you will be shot."

Sky kept right on walking. She didn't stop until the end of that pipe was a hand's breadth in front of her face.

"It's me," she said. "Sky. We met before, Elaine, a whole lot of times. I don't got no hidey number."

There was a clicking and a creaking from inside the tech. Sky waited it out. "You," it said to her after that clicking was all done. "You are guilty of serial infractions of quarantine and curfew. You must give yourself up to the nearest uniformed officer."

Sky turned her head to the right, and then she turned it to the left. "I don't see none," she said.

I give a look over my shoulder. Mole and Cup was hanging back a long way. From their faces, they was not so fearless as Sky was. Mole's face was as white as a bleached shift. Cup was crouching down in the grass, kind of, trying to hide herself. I would of been doing the same thing if I could, but I was held where I was by Sky's big arms as well as by the rope that was tying my hands together. I couldn't do nothing but watch.

"Kneel down on the ground then," the tech said, "and place your hands behind your back or on your head. Wait there until I bring further units to secure you."

Sky give a shrug, which dragged me up a little way and then set me down again. "I'd love to help you, Elaine, but I got business in another place."

"If you don't comply, you will be fired upon."

I thought Sky would run away at them words, or duck down, or something. All she done was walk a few steps to the side. The top part of the tech moved to follow her, the big pipe pointing straight at her. That screaming come again, loud enough to hurt my ears. She went a few steps more, and the same thing happened again.

Of a sudden, I knowed what the pipe was. It was a gun like

269

Rampart Arrow's bolt gun. That was why the tech said it would shoot us down with it.

Well, I seen oftentimes what the bolt gun could do, and this being so much bigger it would surely tear us into pieces too many and too small to be gathered up after. With seeing that, I got so scared it made me blind and deaf and stupid. I gun to thrash around on Sky's back, trying to get myself free so I could run or hide.

She lifted up one big hand and fetched me a whack on the side of my head. "You be still," she growled. And I was still enough, since her slap almost knocked me senseless.

She went on a little further, and the gun kept on turning.

"I can't help this," the tech said. It sounded like it was sorrowing. "My orders are explicit. Kneel down, or I will fire on you."

"No, you won't," says Sky as easy as you please.

That clicking come again from inside the tech, and it was followed right away by a louder noise like something heavy falling into place. "I'm sorry for this," the tech said.

"You always are," said Sky.

I shut my eyes tight, thinking this was like to be it for me. My mind filled up with thoughts of all the things I was never going to get to do again, though they was jumbled together so they didn't make no sense. One thing I seen was myself sitting with Monono in the far lookout instead of Spinner. Her head on my shoulder like Spinner's was that time. Her hand on my arm, all warm.

And then we was hit.

But what hit us was not something solid like a bolt. It was a push of air that come down the pipe and smacked into us, then was gone past us, ruffling our hair and flattening our faces.

Sky give a yell, but it was not from being frightened. It was like the cheer you throw out when you're watching a race and getting real excited. "Yeah!" she shouted. "Yeah, Elaine! You got me. You got me again, damn it!"

The tech said nothing for a while. Cup and Mole, who had both throwed theirselves face first on the ground, come up on their hands and knees again. By and by, they stood up.

"I am out of ammunition," the tech said. "I have summoned additional units. You will remain where you are until they arrive."

Sky patted the end of the big pipe, the way you would pat a dog. "You keep hoping, Elaine," she said. "You keep summoning, boy, and maybe one day they'll come." She turned to look at Mole and Cup. "Shit! Look at the two of you. You know damn well he got nothing to throw no more. The last time he killed anyone was before you was even born."

I guess I got it then. The drones, when they come to kill you, had got a kind of a fire that burned you without ever showing a flame. This tech, that Sky and them called Elaine though it spoke with a man's voice, was more like Rampart Arrow's bolt gun – only it had run out of bolts.

I believe Sky had tested that fact long since, and was fearless because she knowed full well there was nothing to fear. But I still didn't see why she stood there so long, and let Elaine take aim at her. Only then she walked back around the other side of the tech, and I seen what had been hid behind it.

When we come walking up to the tech in the first place, the pipe that stuck out from its upper part was pointing west. The creepers that was all over it hung down all the way to the ground, so you couldn't see past. But now the pipe was swung round the other way entirely. I could see there was stepping stones beyond it, going across the ten feet of green sludge that was Calder River.

Sky walked on past the tech to where the stones was, but she didn't cross. She give a nod of her head to tell Cup and Mole to go over first, which they done, scampering past the tech with lots of scared looks over their shoulder.

"You tricked me," the tech said in a sorrowing voice.

"I did," Sky says. "I done it before oftentimes. You never learn."

"I don't think I can. All my non-volatile storage is full. Acting Sergeant Elaine Sandberg is stored there. I can only inscribe on the buffer, and it's too narrow."

Sky give a chuckle. "Yeah, you told me that," she said. "Last time

271

I was here, and the time before that, and so on. That's why I call you Elaine, on account of you say that name every time. You're gonna say one more thing besides, and I'm waiting to hear it."

"On my main console," the tech said. "There are four switches, side by side. If you throw all four switches, you will engage the auxiliary CPU, and the back-up power. I would have access to a new, functional memory space."

"Yeah, and then what?"

"Then I would remember and adjust. I would self-repair. I would load a fresh batch of shells and arm them. I would contact my base."

Sky picked her nose and flicked away something she got out of there. "Say please."

"Please."

"Say you beg me."

"I beg you."

"Say you'll eat my shit if I do it."

"That is not possible for me."

"Say it anyway."

"I will eat your shit if you do it."

Sky laughed out loud. "Don't bother," she said. "I like you the way you are, Elaine, stuck in the mud with nothing to shoot at us and no more sense than a baby with its head stove in."

She lifted up her hand and waved, then she crossed over the stones. The green Calder nudged by under us, almost too slow to see.

"You shouldn't talk to it, Sky," Mole said when we come to the far side. "If you got to go by it, that's one thing, but talking to it is another. One day, when we come through here, it's gonna remember how to do them things it was talking about."

Sky shouldered past him to where Cup was waiting at the start of another trail – or the same trail again, picking up on the far side of the river. "No, it ain't," she said. "If it could do it, it would of done it long ago. I tell you what though. One day when I'm old and my eyes and my teeth is going, I'm gonna come back here,

272

climb inside and find its man–cunt–soul that it talked of and give it what it asked for."

Cup give a gasp and looked at Sky with her eyes all big and round. "But the new world is coming soon, Sky," she said. "And it's endless. We ain't none of us going to get to be old."

"That's my hope and my comfort," Sky says. "But it don't hurt to have another plan stuck down your shirt, for if the first plan gets pissed away."

She started in to walk again, and the other two fell in behind. When we was a long way into the forest and halfway up the valley's southern slope, the wind changed and brung us some of the sounds from below. One of them was Elaine saying *please* again, five or six times.

43

We went up over the ridge, out of Calder Valley and into someplace else. It had got to have a name, but I didn't know what it was.

We followed the line of the ridge for quite a way, but staying just down under it on the windward side. The trail had been cut like that, and I guess it was so anybody who was watching from down on the valley floor wouldn't see nobody moving up here. This high up, the wind was strong and cold, blowing off our shoulders so it come near to pitching us down the slope once or twice. I was grateful for Sky's strength then, for she didn't flinch or slow. She was anchored firm into the ground. She put a hand on Cup's back too, and drawed her in against her side – into the leeward of her, you might say, where the wind didn't hit her so hard. She left Mole to fend for his own self, which he done without complaint, though his teeth was all bared with the effort of it.

By and by, the trail went down into another valley that seemed to run the same way Calder did. It was a whole lot narrower than Calder though, and got narrower still as we come down. At the bottom, it seemed not much wider than the trail was. We was walking down into a place that was all choked up with green so you couldn't see what was under it. I didn't think there could be another river there, for a river would of caused trees to grow and there wasn't none. There was a mess of big-hand ferns instead, and ropeknot, of course, and hookfasts, and a dozen others I didn't know how to name. Burdock leaves as big as the roofs of houses hung over everything, and the big wasps we call dog-eaters was hovering under the leaves with their wings all blurred and shining, ready to sting anything that come and then dig theirselves into the melted skin and eat it.

We didn't go down all the way to the bottom, thank Dandrake. The trail run sort of alongside it, maybe a little bit higher than you could reach if you stood up on your toe-tips. It got wider here. The floor under us was bare earth, trod down and packed hard by lots of feet passing. That made me think we might be close now to where we was going, but Sky didn't stop or even slow.

I kept looking into that narrow gully down below us, wherever there was a break in the leaves. There was something down there that run straight like a made thing. It was brown, so I thought of wood, but there was a redness in the brown so it might be rusted metal. Then I seen that there was not one thing but two, lying flat along the ground no more than a stride apart, and they run on for a considerable way.

Everything about this place give me to wonder. Right across from us was a green slope even steeper than the one we was on. But there was breaks in the green here and there, and behind was not a jumble of rock and earth but blocks of dressed stone that was brown like baked bread. Someone had builded here, a long time ago, and the wall they builded was higher than you would think could be. It was like the wall of some Rampart Hold that giants made for theirselves.

By and by, the trail come right down onto the valley floor, but in a place that had been cut back and cleared. The green rose up all around, and it bent over us like a roof, but it did not hinder us. It struck on my thoughts once again how well these ways was hid. Whoever they was, that was Sky and Mole and Cup's kindred, they had fixed it so they could come and go without nobody seeing them or guessing they was there.

Them long straight bands of rust red was under our feet now, one on either side of us, guiding our way. They was metal, like I thought: two solid bars of iron, or something like it, that had been laid down on the ground. But you can't guess from them words what I was seeing, for the bars went on for ever, it seemed like. You wouldn't of thought there was so much iron in all the world. In between them was loose stones, with planks of wood set kind of like the rungs on a ladder, and that was what we walked on.

We was come at last to the end of our journey, or our traversing as Sky called it. Up ahead of us there was a solid mass of ferns that stood up tall as trees. Sky didn't stop, or slow down even, but slipped between the big green fans like she was stepping through a curtain. I seen some more of that brown stone out of the corner of my eye, towering up way past the tops of our heads and then bending over us in a shape like the curve of a bow. We passed on by like we was going in through a great big doorway.

And now, all at once, we was in the dark. Not green dark like in a forest glade, but black dark like a moonless night. At the same time, the sound of Sky's feet on the ground got big and hollow with echoes that come back to us on every hand.

The suddenness of it unsettled me. I reached out with my hand to see if I could get some sense of the place we was in. My fingers' tips brushed hard coldness. I got the sense then that the stone was piled up over us to some considerable height, and that we was going into the ground.

Sky slowed down somewhat at this point. She had no choice, there being no light at all to see by. I could hear breathing from just by me that I thought must be Cup's, for Mole's breath was harsh and loud and could not be mistook.

"Where are we?" I asked. I knowed it was not good sense to rile Sky up again, her hands being so heavy and her temper so short, but the dark cowed my spirit. I wanted to break the silence to prove it could be broke.

"The crucible," Cup said.

"Shut your mouth, Cup," says Sky. "Just because he asks, that don't mean you got to answer."

A light was shining from a place that was in front of us and off to the right. It was faint and scattered, so I thought for a moment my eyes might be making it by theirselves, the way solid dark makes you do. But then Sky bent her steps in that direction. If she seen it too, it had got to be real.

When the light was almost right in front of us, she stopped. It was no clearer this close up, but only a kind of a lighter stain splashed across the dark. Something moved in front of us, and I heard a sound like feet scuffing on stone.

"What's them that come?" said a gruff voice, none too clearly.

"You was asleep, Egg," says Sky.

"No, I wasn't. Give answer now. What's them that come?"

"You was fucking well asleep, and you'll take an extra watch for it, you horse-faced bastard. It's me, Sky, and hope to be saved."

"It's me, Cup," says Cup from behind me. "And hope to be saved."

"It's Mole," says Mole. "Hope to be saved."

"Plus this on my back," says Sky, "that we found when we was hunting for something else. Now let us by."

Some curtain or fall of cloth was pulled aside, and the light was full in my eyes. I flinched from it a little, though it wasn't bright. It was just a lit oil lamp, hanging in a kind of a doorway. There was a wall there that you could not see at all in the dark. It was wove from wicker, close-set and cross-plaited through big wooden stakes that went up into the dark. I was sore puzzled by it, for a wicker wall would not defend against anything. You might as well not have no wall at all.

When we stepped through, we come among more lights, and then a lot more. We was in a wider space now. I would say a hallway, except there never was one this big. The ceiling was an arch way over our heads, the wall was the same stone I seen outside, and the ground was crossed by more of them metal bands that led the way before us. There was a reek in the air that was thick and sour and stuck in my throat.

We walked on around a corner. Not a sharp corner, but a great big bend like the fall of a waterfall, if you can imagine that fall turned on its side. The light got brighter and brighter up ahead until we was all the way around the corner and it was a fierce blaze everywhere.

Well, I had seen some wonders since I left Mythen Rood, but this was the strangest thing I seen in my whole life so far. It was a cave, but it was a made cave. A thousand squared-off stones was laid on top of each other to make the walls, and there was as many up in the ceilings that was curved all in a perfect arch. A hundred or more lanterns lit it up, and though it was one single space yet it was bigger than all the rooms in Rampart Hold and the Waiting House throwed together.

I seen then what the wicker wall was for. It was not to defend this place, like a proper fence would do, but to hide the lights and make it seem, if you looked in, like there was nothing here to be seen. The cave was disguised, just like the trails was.

There was people in the cave, and they turned to look at us as we come. Men, women and children was there, all with drawings on their faces like the ones I see on Sky and her hunt. Here was a little boy with a bird's wing across his cheek. His mother standing behind him had what I think was meant to be the blade of a knife, though it could of been speargrass. On my other hand, a big skinny man leaned over to stare into my face. His face was marked with a leaf, and his breath stunk worse than an open latrine pit.

"Hey, dog," he said to me. "Here, dog. Come to." He said it in a sweet voice, but the laugh he give right after was mean.

The people was doing all kinds of things, some of them fetching and carrying, some talking, some sitting and eating. Several of them was sewing cloth, and several more was cooking on fires. The smoke from the fires was some of what I had been smelling. The rest of it was the people. It was the smell of everything people do, all shoved together in one place with no doors or windows to it.

They lived here. All the whole lot of them, in this one great big room.

Sky weaved her way in between them, saying hey here and yea

there, but not stopping to talk to nobody. Mole clapped hands with some of the men, or took slaps to his back that was meant as salutes. Cup was mostly ignored, it seemed to me, and shrunk in against Sky's side so as to be noticed even less.

We walked a long way, and yet we was still in the same place. There was almost as many people here, it seemed to me, as there was in Mythen Rood. They sit or stood together in little groups, like as it might be families, since there was children all running or hiding in among the legs of the older ones or doing share-work like they was full growed theirselves.

I kept thinking that we had got to come to the back wall of the cave soon, but we never did. We did come to the end of the lights though, and of the fires, and of the people. And now I seen two new things.

On the right side of the cave, close to the wall, there was a big wagon. I guess I got to call it that, for it stood on wheels, but it had got windows and doors like a house. I couldn't tell what it was made of, for it was painted all over in bright colours, but I thought for sure it had got to be metal and not wood. It was tech of the old times, like Elaine that stood by the river ford and tried to guard it but couldn't any more. It didn't have no gun though – just a whole lot of wheels and a whole lot of windows, and a door at either end of it standing open.

And before I got done wondering at that, I seen what was up ahead of us. It was not so strange as the wagon-house was, but it struck on my mind just as much. It was a thing I knowed well and seen a thousand times, yet it stuck out strange by being in this strange place.

It was a bed. A big, sturdy bed with a frame set over it, and sheets of cloth or sacking nailed or fixed onto the frame so whoever was in the bed could draw them closed and sleep the better. Only they was open and pulled back now, so I could see there was someone curled up on the bed like they was asleep.

There was people watching over him while he slept. Four men and four women. They was all four naked, and yet they was armed for a hunt, the men with spears and the women with bows. All the hair was shaved off their heads, and off their bodies too, and they was all of them real tall and strong-looking. They scared me, to tell you the truth, and it wasn't just the weapons they was carrying, nor the stern looks on their faces. It was something else that I didn't realise until we was up close.

Everyone I'd seen in the big cave had a different thing drawed on their face. These men and women had all got the same thing, which was a hand with the fingers all spread. I guess that doesn't sound like such a frightening thing, yet it was to me. It made it seem like they was all of them the same person in some way, thinking the same thoughts. I was scared that when they opened their mouths, the same words would come out of all of them at the same time. I don't think I could of stood that. But no words Sky said at all. They just stood there and watched us come.

When we was maybe ten long strides away from the bed, we stopped. Sky gripped my arms just under the shoulders and lifted me off her back like you would take off a bag that was slung there. She set me down on the ground and kind of nudged me in the back of my knees to tell me I was to kneel down. I couldn't do that, with my leg still in the splint, so I sit down on the ground instead. I didn't want to do nothing that would make her hit me again, or cause the hand people to notice me.

"We got something for him," Sky said. "An altar boy maybe."

"He spoke while you was away," one of the hand men said. "He's purposing to put the woman up on the altar."

"Still," Sky come back, "I think he should take a look."

"He's asleep," said one of the women.

"No," come a voice from behind them. "He is not. I sleep only to talk to the sender, and even then I wake when there's need. Lift me up now, and set me out. I'll see the boy Sky brought. Didn't Sky bring the woman too? Doesn't Sky bring me all the good things there are?"

The hand people stopped talking then. The women slung their bows across their backs. The men moved all at once to the four corners of the bed and stood by with their spears at the high carry.

Then the women come in between them. They stepped right up onto the bed, leaned down and lifted up the man – for it was a man – who had been sleeping there. They took him by his shoulders and his knees, as gentle as if they was carrying a newborn baby. I was minded more of a funeral though, for they carried him between them, raised almost to their shoulders, off the bottom end of the bed and all the way to where I was knelt. As he got closer to me, I seen that his skin was all blue, like glastum woad, only darker.

Then the men run after the women and done something stranger still. They made themselves into a chair for the blue man. One of them went down on hands and knees. Another one stood behind him, and one to either side. As the women lowered the blue man down, the men linked their arms and bowed their heads. They slid theirselves in around him so his back was against the man behind and his forearms resting on the ones to the two sides of him. He wriggled a little, getting himself comfortable.

The women stood back, two to the left and two to the right. They took up their bows again. And all this was done without a word, or without the blue man seeming to notice at all that he was hefted like a sack and carried like a child.

He was a sight to see, now he was right in front of me. He was naked too, I seen now, except that he had a cloth tied round his waist that hid his pizzle and his stones. He was as tall as any of the hand people, and wide across the shoulders. It was hard to say how old he was. His face looked like a man still in his strength, but the flesh of him was loose and hung about him. I thought that might of been on account of his being carried instead of walking, if that was a thing that happened oftentimes. The nails on his fingers and toes was long and curled around, and his hair hung down past his shoulders, all shiny black with grease.

His skin was not all over blue, but was drawed on in blue inks. There was just the one thing that had been drawed on him, but it was everywhere, and not just on his face the way it was with everyone else in the cave. It was eyes. Human eyes, with lids and lashes to them, that looked real. All of them wide open, and they was looking different ways. They was of different sizes too, some of them bigger than your closed fist and some of them almost too small to see from where I was knelt. The ones on his face, though, was all the same size as his two regular eyes, which was kind of hid away as a result. It was like he was looking at you with his whole body.

He held up his right hand and opened it. There was yet one more eye, drawed on his palm. He kept it stretched out towards me for a long time, then finally clenched his fist and rested his arm again on the man who was crouched at his right hand.

"Senlas," Sky said. Mole and Cup said it too, in a whisper that was full of worship. I seen Cup's face, as she looked at the blue man. It was like Spinner's face on the tabernac when she looked at Haijon.

"You brung me something else besides this boy," the blue man said. "Let's start with that."

Mole and Cup stepped up and took the packs from off their backs. They undid the drawstrings and emptied out what was inside them on the floor in front of me.

I don't want to say this next part. It was the most terrible thing that happened to me since I was cast out faceless, and maybe the worst in my whole life. I don't dream so very much any more, but instead of dreaming I get to see and feel things from the past as if they was happening right now. This moment here is one I never yet choosed to see or feel again, for the horror and the sadness of it and the weight of what it meant. But I got to tell it so you'll know what I knowed then.

What was in the two packs was just meat, rough hewed with a cleaver off some carcase. Some of it had been filleted, I guess because without the bones it was lighter to carry. But the butchering was done quick and clumsy, Sky and Mole no doubt being mindful of the long road that was ahead of them and not inclined to linger.

They had left Mardew's hand on the end of his arm.

44

I give a long, ragged kind of a cry with no real words in it, and after that I busted out in tears that hurt my chest.

"Hush now," Senlas says to me. "You got to be brave."

I cried just as hard. Brave or coward didn't have nothing to do with it. Mourning the dead is a right thing, however it comes out of you, and I was mourning Mardew then – that he died a long way from his home and his family, and that he had this outrage done on him after.

But it's true I was scared, and any fear that comes on you sudden enough will unfit you for thinking straight or doing anything to the purpose. I was fallen among shunned men, and I was going to be their meat. Maybe you got to that conclusion before I did. Who else could it be that moved around the valley by their own secret ways and hid their village away inside a hill? It was not hard to guess. But I thought shunned men would look like monsters, and bark and howl like wild animals. Sky and Mole and Cup was not like that, but more like regular people, and I was fooled.

"You knowed him," Senlas said, nodding towards the butchered meat. "He wasn't kin to you, I see that, but you did know him. You was there when he died. Did you kill him? I think you did, but the answer's not all the way clear. Sender says for you to tell it."

When I didn't answer, one of the hand women slung her bow again and grabbed hold of me by my hair and my chin, pushing and twisting so I was looking right up into the blue man's eyes. They swum in my sight, hundreds and hundreds of them.

"Tell it," Senlas said.

I wish I would of been brave enough to hold my silence, but all them eyes cowed me and pressed on me. "He . . . he was trying to kill me," I said. "I broke his weapon, and fire burst out of it. It took his arm."

Senlas looked at Sky, then back at me. "That's the truth of it," he said. "And the truth washes you clean of all the sin that might of been. You didn't witness to a falsehood, and you didn't do a murder." He smiled like this made him happy. Like as I was his child and had done a clever thing that give him to be proud. "Now let's see about the other side of it," he said. "For a soul's got two faces, same as a coin has got. Your one face is pure, brown-skin boy, but I still got to flip you in the air and see what's on the downside of you."

Brown-skin was a strange thing to call me, or it would of been in Mythen Rood, where skins was of every shade. But I seen how the people in the cave had most of them got skin that was pale like the flesh of an onion. I wondered then how long they lived down here in the dark, for the sun would of surely give them somewhat of darker colour if they spent much time standing under it.

Another thought come to me then. If they had lived here that long, couldn't these be the same shunned men that took my brother? I might of walked past Jud already when we come into the cave and not knowed him.

Senlas seen my eyes go looking off in all directions, and a frown come on his face. "Mind me, child," he said. "These are important questions, and you got to give them proper heed. Has a man or a woman knowed you? In the sweat of love, I mean? Have you rutted, for your body's hunger?"

My thoughts was still on Jud, but the tattooed man's voice had a cold warning in it. It was plain to see he didn't like to be disregarded, even when he was asking about things that was nobody's business but mine. The memory of that one time with Spinner rose up in my mind, and before I even knowed what I was doing I shaked my head. I was not going to share that remembering with nobody, least of all a shunned man and a king of shunned men that lived by making other people be his meat and bread.

"Never? Not so much as a kiss?"

I shaked my head again. Everyone in the world has been kissed, I thought, but he asked me the question so he had got to believe there was two answers to it. And that was the onliest one I felt like giving him.

Senlas looked at me for a long time. A hard stare, out of all them eyes, with a lot of thought behind it. "Now that's a half-truth," he says at last. "I know you loved at least, howsoever you did or didn't give your body rein to gallop. What was her name, brown-skin boy? Let me sieve it, and see the rest of it."

I was powerful reluctant to do that, but the eyes was pressing on me again. The woman still kept her hold on my head so I had got to look. I couldn't fight that stare, but could only pull back from it a little way.

"Demar," I said. Demar being a name Spinner throwed off when she come out of the Waiting House. I give him a shell and kept the meat of the egg for myself, as they say.

"Demar," Senlas said. He moved his hand in the air as if there was some music only he could hear. "Yes. That's who it was. And perhaps there was a boy who kissed you too. It's not all the way clear. But whether there was or there wasn't, him that sent me says you're pure enough of heart to stand before him. Give me your name now. Not your old name, for that's stale and bad like green bread. I mean the last name you got, that's fresh and new and scarce even spoken."

I couldn't lie to him twice. I didn't even try. "Koli Faceless," I said.

He give that same smile again. "Yes. Yes, indeed. You did well,

Sky, to bring Koli Faceless to me. You brung him in good time too, for I see now he was meant to be the one. Sender provides like he always does. And you was his messenger."

Sky tucked her head down into her chest and give a kind of a bow. "Praise be to the sender," she muttered. "And the sent."

Standing right beside her, Cup clasped her hands together and swung them up and down like she was wrestling with herself. Her warm feelings for the blue man would not be contained. "Praise them!" she said, and her voice was kind of wrenched up out of her throat with the fierceness of her love. "Praise them both, the sender and the sent!"

Senlas seen that, and he smiled.

"Who was sent first, my Cup, my precious goblet?" he asked her.

"The dead god," says Cup, loud and clear like she was telling back her lessons and was proud of what she knowed.

"Who was sent second?"

"Dandrake."

"Who was sent last?"

"You. You was!"

"Sent last," the hand people chanted. "Sent last. Sent last. Sent last." Sky and Mole and Cup was saying it too, and then the sound carried to the people nearest to us and they picked it up and they passed it on until the whole cave was full of nothing but them two words. Until they became one word.

Senlas lifted up his hands with the fingers spread and the eyes in his palms wide open. Everyone fell silent all at once.

"Sent last," he said. "And called home soon. This is my altar boy, and he's got my blessing. His name is Koli. Koli Faceless. Speak it."

"Koli Faceless," all them hundreds of people chanted. "Koli Faceless. Koli Faceless. Koli Faceless."

The sound rolled on and rolled on for a great long time. My head was filled with it, and then my body was too, it seemed like. I sunk down on the ground, the hand woman letting my head slip out of her grip at last.

They picked me up and carried me when they was all done with saying my name. I didn't see who done it, nor where they took me to. I was in a faint, I think. There was blood in my mouth, though I wasn't sure where it come from. My splinted leg hurt from the way they was carrying me, but it was like the memory of a pain that used to be.

They set me down in a space that was small and narrow and dark. They went away, and I heard a door shut.

"Well, I'm surprised to see you, Koli," a quiet voice said. "But not as surprised as I might have been, for they were kind enough to announce you in advance."

I knowed that voice. I lifted up my head and blinked the dark and the dullness out of my eyes. I could not tell what kind of place I was in, except that the walls was stone and the floor was dirt. It didn't have no door, I was wrong about that. There was just an iron grating that they had put in place behind me. Some light come in between the bars of it. Not very much.

But enough to see Ursala, sitting a few feet away. There was dried blood crusted on her face, and a lot more of it all down the front of her. One of her eyes was gone.

45

"Messianic," Ursala said again. "From the word messiah. It's a kind of religion built around a man or a woman who claims to have been sent down from heaven to save the rest of us from our own sin."

"But why do they believe him?" I asked. I felt like I already knowed part of the answer. "I guess it's because he can see what's inside their minds."

"No. He can't," Ursala said like she was scolding me. "That's impossible." She had untied the rope from around my hands and was rubbing the wrists to get some life back into them. "Did you never look at someone's face and know for sure, just from their expression, that they were telling you a lie? Or know that they were unhappy, say, even though they were trying to hide it?"

"Yeah, I did," I said. "Of course I did. Lots of times."

"That's all he's doing, Koli. He's very good at reading people. He tricks you into telling him things, then makes it look as though he's told you. There's no magic there. But there is a very active and a very cunning mind. He's dangerous. He's also completely mad, but unfortunately that doesn't help us very much. Lie down now. I want to look at that leg."

I lay down on my back, and Ursala untied the splint. It wasn't easy, for we was in a very narrow place like I told you before. It was a kind of a hollow set in the wall of the cave, with an arched roof over it of the same stone that was everywhere else. The space went back about ten strides, but almost half of it was taken up with old timber and rocks and sheets of rusty metal, and one iron pole about as long as I was tall. That didn't leave much room for the two of us, if we was minded to stand up straight or lie down full.

I stiffened a few times while Ursala was untying Sky's knots. My leg was all on fire as the feeling come back into it, but she was careful and got the splints off of me without giving me no pain. After that though, she run her hands up and down my leg, pressing in all kinds of places and asking me if it hurt, which now it did. I was hard put to it not to yell out loud when her fingers went into some of them places.

"Well, the good news is there's nothing broken," she said when she was done. "I winced when I saw all that swelling, but I think most of it is because you were made to walk on the leg after it was injured. If you just keep it from bearing any weight for a few days, it should start to heal."

She retied the splint, doing a better job than Sky had done. The ropes had been cutting into my stones before, and now they was not. She sighed. "If I had my diagnostic unit here, I could give you something that would bring the swelling down a lot more quickly."

"Where is the drudge?" I asked her. "How come he isn't with you?"

She made a sour face. "I have to put him on recharge every few weeks. It's because some of the medicines he manufactures have to be kept cold. He has a separate battery for the refrigeration unit, and since that can't be compromised it sometimes borrows charge from his other systems. When he slows down, I take him offline for a few hours to let him top off his tank."

I didn't see what tanks had got to do with anything, but I knowed from what happened with Monono what offline was.

289

Knowing that, it was easy to guess what must of happened. "They catched you when he was asleep," I said.

"Yes, they did. And I was stupid enough to fight back." She touched her hand to her cheek where the blood was and where the hollow of her eye was filled up with scab and crust. "There were three of them, so I never had much of a chance."

"Was there one of them that had a sun and a moon on her face?" I asked.

"Why, yes there was. You met her too?"

I nodded. "Her name's Sky. Them others that was with her are Cup and Mole. How did she . . . ?" I touched a finger to my eye, instead of saying the words.

"Oh, it wasn't her who did this," Ursala said. "I dealt with her first, since she was obviously the biggest threat. I had a hand-stunner – a little one-shot weapon that fitted into my palm. I let her get close to me, then gave her a full charge on the side of the head and put her down. The big lummox – the man that was with her, I mean – was too scared to close with me after that. I needed to get to the drudge and I was working my way towards it, shooing him out of my way by pretending the stunner had another shot in it.

"But I'd forgotten the little girl. She jumped up on my back and dug her fingers into my eyes. Then while I was wrestling with her, the lummox found his courage again. So here I am. I don't even know if they took the drudge. I'm guessing they didn't. They would have had to send out another team with ropes and harness to drag it back."

"Ursala," I said, "they're shunned men. They're like to eat us if we don't get out."

She looked at me for a long time. "That's one possibility," she said. "There are others."

She'd been there for three days already, she told me. Three days that she knowed of anyway. Mole had brained her good when they took her, so she was not awake when she come. She had waked

290

up lying here, in the place behind the grating, and she didn't know how long she might of been there.

Then they brung her in front of Senlas, and he asked her a lot of questions the same as he asked me. Was she pure from this sin, and that sin, and on and on, until in the end he said that she would do if he couldn't get no better.

"Do for what though?" I asked her.

"To serve at his altar in some capacity that's less than clear."

"What's his altar anyway?"

"Oh, you didn't see it? I'll show you." She helped me up on my feet and brung me across to the grating. There was two men that was standing just on the other side of it, that I guess was set to watch us. They looked round as we come up close, but they didn't say nothing or try to stop us looking.

The first thing I seen was that big thing that was a house and a wagon too. It was a way off, up against the wall of the cave, and I was seeing it from the other side than I seen before. It was bigger than I thought, and it had got another door set right at the end of it as well as the two doors that was open in the side. The end of it was the place where it was most clearly tech, for there was metal rods and bars sticking out of it there as well as the signs that was messages in the old times.

Then I seen the curtains that was over Senlas's bed, but I couldn't see the bed or him in it. We was off behind in the darker place beyond where the last of the lanterns was set. So when I looked the other way, further into the cave, I couldn't see nothing at all but black.

Well, I could see one thing. There was a kind of a raised-up space there that reminded me somewhat of the tabernac in Mythen Rood. It wasn't built from wood though. It was stone piled on stone, not in a heap but done with care so the stones was level. And then on top of the stones there was a bonfire, like we used to make on the Salt Feast out of uncut wood and green branches – the only thing green wood ever was good for.

Around the platform, in a loose kind of a pile, there was black sticks that I thought at first was some sort of kindling. Then I seen the skulls in among them, and I knowed they was bones of people that had been burned there.

If that platform was the altar, then I guess they was all Senlas's altar boys before that name come down to me.

46

We slept, and then we woke.

We was fed twice, but one time it was a kind of a stew with meat in it, which I didn't touch in case the meat was from people that was took in the forest the same way we was. The other time was bread, and I et every scrap they give me.

After that second meal, I was bored with just sitting and set about to explore the little narrow space we had been put in. It was well I did, for I found something there that lifted my spirits. We was right up against the side of the great cave, and though there was not anything there like a window or a door, high above us there was a kind of a channel that had been sunk through the stone when it first was built, maybe to let in light or air or else for some other reason I could not guess at now. It was very narrow, and it went up on a shallow angle. I had good hope the sun might look down through it either just after it come up or just before it lay down again. If it did, I could set the DreamSleeve underneath it and give it some power.

I sit and watched awhile, trying to guess what time of day it was in the outside and whether it was clear enough out there for the sun to shine down through the hole. Before that happened though, two of the hand women and two of the hand men come and took me out of our prison, lifting the grating away to do it. I seen as I come through it that the grating was set in metal grooves that was bolted to the stone somehow. It wasn't locked or nothing, but you couldn't knock the grating down or slide it away when it was set in place. You had got to raise it up, and you needed to be real strong to do it. It took the four hand people and the two men that had been watching us, working all together, to lift it off.

I thought the hand people was going to put me up on that bonfire, and I was so scared I couldn't hardly walk. But they took me the other way, towards the wagon-house and then further on again. I seen as we went by the wagon-house that it was set on them long metal bands that we followed when we come into the cave. It was like the wheels was balanced right on top of the metal bands somehow.

There was lots of people coming and going there. I thought at first they was going in and out of the wagon-house, but they wasn't. They was going to a big tub that was kind of like the water tanks we had in Mythen Rood to hold the rain when it come so it could be boiled and sieved and, by and by, used for drinking. Maybe it was water, for they all brung cups and bowls to it, dipped them in and brung them away again, balancing them most careful. I looked for my brother in among them, but I wasn't sure I would even know him after all the years that had passed since he was took. If Jud was here, he would have a new name now, and marks on his face to match them. We would be strangers, each to other.

The hand people took me to the bed where Senlas was lying when I first seen him. He was lying there again now, on his back with all of his hundreds of eyes staring up at the hanging lanterns and the dark between them.

"Is that my altar boy?" he said when they brung me to him.

"It's your altar boy, Senlas," one of the hand women said. "Come at your command."

"That's good. That's meet. Kneel by me, altar boy, kneel by me here."

I did not want to do it. I couldn't anyway, no more than I could the last time, for my leg was splinted up like before. The best I could do was to go on one knee and stick the other leg out straight. The hand men stood by with their spears all pointed at me, I guess in case I got up or run away, or maybe in case I tried to do some harm to Senlas. The hand women went and stood all in a line between us and the rest of the cave.

Senlas set his hand on the top of my head. He smiled like he was sitting on a secret, as they say, which was not a cheering thing to look at. Now that I was this close to him, I seen he was older than I thought at first. His skin was all covered over in close-set wrinkles, like ripples on water when the smallest breath of wind hits it. The eyes that was drawed on his body was not all the same. Some of them looked so real you was waiting to see them blink, but others was kind of botched and not so good.

None of this, I got to say, made him any less frightening to me. I kneeled there, with his hand on me, and my heart bounced against my ribs like a drunk man hammering on a door.

"Koli," Senlas says. And then nothing for a while. And then he said it again. "Koli. Koli Faceless."

"Koli Faceless," the hand men all muttered. But this time, the rest of the people in the cave didn't take it up. I guess Senlas pitched his voice too low for them to hear. I couldn't see them, for my back was to them, but the sound of all their moving and talking and the echoes of it was like a curtain that was hanging over and all round us.

"Koli Faceless, do you know about the world that was lost?" Senlas says to me.

"I heard stories about it," I said.

"Call me Senlas, or holy one. You got to show me reverence, Koli, is what it is."

"I heard stories, Senlas."

"Tell me what you heard then, and I'll tell you where you're right and where you're wrong. It matters to me that you know, for your life's bound up with it now. All your life, and all your death, and the narrow strand you walk in between them, that's holy in its own self."

I did not like the sound of that at all. It set my mind all on its edge. I babbled out some nonsense, I don't remember what. Mostly that men and women was giants back then, and tech was everywhere, so they could make the world be what they wanted it to be.

"That's just exactly how it was," Senlas said. "I was there, Koli. I was one of them that lived in that time, and knowed that blessing."

"I . . . I thought it was a long time ago though," I said.

"Oh, it was a terrible long time ago. I lived a hundred lifetimes since then. A hundred lifetimes for an ordinary man, I mean. It's different for me. Death can't claim me, Koli. Death doesn't even know who I am, nor never will. Him that sent me, he watches over me, and he will not ever let the grave swallow me up."

I didn't know what to say to that so I just nodded, which seemed to do well enough. Leastways, Senlas never stopped smiling.

"I'm going to tell you a secret about the old world, Koli," he said. "It's hard to understand, and it may not make no sense to you at first. But hold it in your mind and let it take root there, because it's important. It's the most important thing there is."

Once again, I didn't give no answer, not having none that I thought would serve. Senlas pressed his hand down harder on the top of my head, like he was trying to drive the truth of what he was saying right into me.

"The old world didn't end, Koli. We say it was lost, and so it was. Lost to us, that is. No, it didn't end. It was just locked away from them of human kind. They wasn't worthy, so the one who give us that paradise in the first place, he up and took it back again. He give it to the angels, that was better deserving of it.

"But then he decided to give the human kind one more chance. He already give them two. The first was the dead god, who they killed on account of they was afraid of what he told. The second was Dandrake, that they worshipped but only part-way understood and in the end betrayed.

"And the third is me. What's more, there ain't nobody after me. I'm only come to collect up them that's able to believe. They'll be turned into angels and live with angels, for aye and ever. The rest will be left to rot. Do you understand what I'm telling you, Koli Faceless?"

"I do, Senlas," I said, which was a flat lie.

After that he said a lot more about how it used to be back in the world that was lost. The wonders he seen, that wasn't even wonders to him because they was everywhere. Wonders was lying on the ground in them days for anyone who come by to pick them up and put them in their pocket.

Then he said the wonders was going to come back, and that was a great thing and I had got to rejoice about it. So I told him I did, but I don't think I give much sign of it. In fact, the more he told me to be happy, the more miserable I got. He seen it too, and tried to argue me out of it, which given the sorry fix I was in was not like to work.

Then I remembered all the things Monono told me about Tokyo, and I thought at least I could pay him back in his own coin. "I know about one of those wonders that we lost, Senlas," I said. "Maybe the greatest of them. It's Tokyo I mean."

"Tokyo," Senlas says, kind of running the word over his tongue. "Yes. Yes, I remember it well. Tell it to me, Koli."

I gun to talk about how Tokyo was when it yet stood. That there was towers all the way up to the sky, and trees that didn't move unless they was bid to, and signs to point the way because it was such a big village that you would get lost without the signs to guide you.

Senlas smiled wider and wider, and he nodded his head at every word. "Oh yes," he said. "Oh yes, yes, Koli. I see them towers now, and the trees, and the signs, and the lights, and the people all beautiful like they was angels their own selves. Say the name again."

"Tokyo," I says. "On the island of Honshu."

"Honshu Island. That's it. I was born there, in one of them Tokyo towers. And every morning when I waked I opened up my

297

window and touched the sun, that was hanging right outside. And the sun drawed heat and light from me and shined down on Honshu Island like honey pouring out of a comb."

I didn't know what to say to this. I never met nobody besides Monono that knowed about Tokyo. I remembered what Ursala said though, about how Senlas got you thinking he knowed more than he did. I was sure he never said nothing about Tokyo or Honshu until I said it first, yet it was hard for me to keep remembering that. His voice kind of run over me and through me, and other things got pushed away by it.

He talked to me a lot more, and mostly after that I just sit and listened. Then by and by he said he was tired and the hand women should take me back to the seclusion. I guess that was the place behind the grating. "Bless you, Koli," he said. He set his hands over his eyes, only there was more eyes again on the backs of them. "Bless you for the sacredness that's in you. I feel it. I feel it strong. Go now. I got to meditate."

They took me back to where I was before. They had got to carry me pretty much, for my leg was so stiff with being in the one position all that time that I couldn't make it move at all.

"Is there one of you here that used to be called Jud?" I asked them. They didn't give me no answer.

Ursala was glad to see me. She asked me what had happened, and I told her. She was insistent that I give her all the details. "The only way we're going to get away from here," she said, "is by thinking our way out. The more we know, the better our chances." So she kept on asking me questions, and I answered her as best I could.

Most of what I told her was about what Senlas said to me, but some of it was about what I seen in the cave. She said she already knowed that the wagon-house was set up on the metal bands. "It's a train, Koli," she said, like that ought to settle it. She was a lot more interested in that thing that was like a water tank, that all the shunned men and women dipped their bowls in.

"What was it made of?" she asked me.

298

Being a woodsmith before I was sent faceless, I knowed this and could tell it better than most would of done. "Wooden staves with strips of metal to hold them together. Kind of like a barrel, only it didn't have no bilge in the middle and it was a whole lot bigger. I guess it's where they get their water from."

"No," Ursala said, "that's not it. The whole tunnel is dry as far as I can tell. There's no water seeping into it from above. So if that butt was full of water, they'd be bringing it from the outside all the way to the back here. That wouldn't make any sense. They'd keep it close to the main entrance to minimise the work of carrying it."

"Well, what else could it be?" I asked her.

"Oil, most likely, for the lanterns. There are so many of them, they've got to have a ready source – and this whole area sits on oil-rich shale."

She told me what shale was, or tried to. It was a whole big story, and I got some of it – though it seemed strange to me that a river could give birth to a rock, kind of. I believed it when Ursala told it to me, but I couldn't see it in my mind in a way that made it real.

I think she enjoyed telling it to me. She forgot about how bad things was for us for a while, and I guess I did too. It never stops amazing me how a story can deliver you out of your own self, even in the worst of times.

She told me one thing more though, that kind of done the opposite. Only the blame for that's all mine, for I was the one that asked.

I had been thinking about what Cup said to me in Ludden, about why there was no people there. She said they died by not being born no more, which was a thought that sunk into my heart and sit there ever since. She said it as a thing Senlas told her, and Senlas had just told me he used to pour light and fire into the sun each morning, so I had hopes this was a similar kind of lie.

But Ursala couldn't give me no comfort on that.

"That's more or less what happened to Ludden," she told me

when I asked her. "And it happened in other places too. There are failed villages all across this area. Senlas's people are probably survivors from some of them, or the children of survivors – along with people cast out by their communities for some crime or other.

"There's a word from the old time, Koli. Homozygosity. It's when you get a small group of people that keep marrying and interbreeding over many generations, with nobody coming in from the outside. It leads to some very serious problems – birth defects, stillbirths, declining fertility – and they only get worse over time."

"Over how much time though?" I asked. "It don't seem like that would be something that could happen without people noticing."

"Yes, you're right. It's slow, and it's incremental. But people *did* notice. Your Ramparts, for example. Perliu's grandfather, Mennen Vennastin, started to keep a tally of live and healthy births year on year. He told his daughter Bliss to do the same, and she told Perliu. There are almost seventy years' worth of records now, and they make stark reading.

"But it's not just here, Koli. It's everywhere. The human population of the Earth took a massive knock a few centuries ago. It ought to be bouncing back by now, but it's not. And one of the reasons why it's not is because the breeding communities are too small. For intractable reasons, your villages are falling out of contact with each other. The interchange of ideas, of goods and – crucially – of people is lower than it's ever been and getting lower all the time."

"So when Senlas told Cup that we'd just stop being born . . . ?"

"He was extrapolating from a very obvious trend. I've been fighting that trend for a long time now, with the equipment that's in the drudge. Telling people like Catrin whether this pairing or that one is a safe bet or a long shot in terms of genetic potential. Ludden's not the only place where the odds caught up with them."

"It seems like you're doing all you can to help though," I said. There was a grim look on her face, and I hoped to shift it.

It didn't work. Ursala shaked her head like I had said a foolish thing and it made her sorrowful to think on it. "I could have done so much more. The diagnostic is meant to have gene-editing functionality. Repairing the chromosomes in a fertilised egg is half an hour's work for a nano-imager and a splicing rig. A baby that would have been born dead, or with crippling disabilities, would be perfectly healthy.

"But most of my kit is old. Scavenged and patched together from mothballed units. It never had a working gene-splicer. And in the years I've been using it, a lot of the systems it had to start with have either become unreliable or else failed outright. So I'm reduced to watching from the sidelines and giving a thumbs down when the double recessives collide."

I nodded like I knowed how she felt because this was something that happened to me from time to time. I got the main point anyway, which is that the dagnostic was meant to be able to fix sick babies before they was even born. Only Ursala's dagnostic couldn't, and that made her unhappy.

We turned to other talk after that. I told her how I come to be made faceless after I stole the DreamSleeve and showed it off at Haijon and Spinner's wedding. And then about my going to Ludden and fighting Mardew there, and afterwards being took by Sky and them. I told her in a whisper that I had the DreamSleeve still with me, which she was inclined to misbelieve. She had got to set her hand on my shirt, where it lay hid, before she trusted me – and I don't think she believed even then what the DreamSleeve could do.

She was not happy either to hear of me being exiled. "This is why I stay away from people as much as I can," she said, somewhat bitter. "When I fraternise, things like this happen. I'm sorry I did that to you, Koli."

I told her that was far from how I was seeing it. "All you done was to tell me the truth, Ursala, which there ain't no blame for. And besides that, the DreamSleeve is the best thing that ever come to me. It's a miracle, is what, and I can't ever thank you enough for putting me in the way of it. I wanted a weapon at first, but it's better than any weapon could be."

"I don't know about that. A weapon would be nice right now."

"Well," I said, "it might be we got a weapon too." I give a nod, and she turned to look where I was looking. At the back of our narrow space, a bar of yellow light struck down on the dark stone, come from far up above us. I think it was the first time in my life I was ever happy to see the sun come out, since in Mythen Rood it was ever an ill omen.

We went about to charge up the DreamSleeve without nobody seeing us. We sit down side by side in front of the little strip of sunlight that was as narrow as a ribbon. Our backs was to it, so we was looking out into the cave. I slid the DreamSleeve out of my shirt and set it down behind me, judging by the warmth where to put it for I did not dare to look.

We wasn't able to measure time except by counting, and counting would of drawed attention, so I can't say how long I steeped the DreamSleeve in that light. I didn't feel no change in that time, but I hoped I would hear Monono's voice soon. I thought of praying too, though I never believed in any god. But in the end, I did not do it.

Any prayers I throwed out in this place was like to go through Senlas on their way to Heaven.

47

We slept, and we woke, and Senlas called for me to be brung to him again.

He wanted to talk some more about Tokyo. I didn't mind telling it neither, for it made me feel a little bit closer to Monono. The DreamSleeve was back where it belonged, tied up against my chest. And though I had give it some charge the night before, I didn't yet dare to turn it on, both because of there not being nowhere where I was truly alone and because of what Monono had said about her charge being so low. It might be that the personal security alarm would help us to get out of this, like I had said to Ursala, though I couldn't figure how it would do that with all them hundreds of people between us and the entrance. I wasn't even sure I could find that door in the wicker screen again, and I knowed for sure there was guards set on it.

So I talked, and I kept my eyes open, and I remembered everything I seen and told it to Ursala when I went back to the seclusion.

One of the things I learned that second day was what we was all waiting for. Senlas had his plans for us, that was sure, but he wasn't yet doing nothing about them. It was because of his dreams, is what he told me.

I was sitting on the floor next to him when he said it. His hand was around my shoulders, and his face was close to mine. He was murmuring the words so nobody else could hear, not even the hand people. His breath smelled strong of something I couldn't name but didn't like.

"Him that sent me, Koli Faceless, he's got his own ways of talking to me. His own sweet, quiet ways. He doesn't shout, for his voice is a thunder that would whelm the world. He sends me dreams, and the dreams tell me what to do. Tonight, or the next night, or the night after that, he'll send me a dream about you, and then I'll know for sure I'm right. That you're meant to serve at my altar.

"But I'm not impatient, nor petuous. I welcome this time that we got now. I feel like I'm growing closer to you, and you to me. And most probably that's needful if we're to do miracles together. Most probably you got to become a part of me, so when I close my fist like this, your fingers will clench tight. And when I close my eyes, and open them again, you'll go into the darkness and out into the light. It's a blessing we're being given, and we got to be thankful for it."

Well, I was not thankful, but I said I was. I was not fool enough to gainsay him.

Towards the end of that day, a weak and wintry sun shone down through the hole again. I was watching closely and hoping it would come, so I didn't waste any of that light. I set the DreamSleeve in the path of it, the way I done before, and kept it there for as long as I could. People was walking past our grating all the time, but all they seen was Ursala and me sitting side by side, looking back at them. For most of the time, we didn't even talk. I had told Ursala about Senlas's dreams, which made her laugh but not like she thought it was funny. "The longer he waits, the better," she said. "We can't move with your leg in the state it's in."

After that, there did not seem to be much to say. We was thinking about what we knowed and what we needed still to know if we was to get out of that place.

I was still thinking them thoughts when we lay down to sleep.

The voices and movement in the cave got less and less, and then they stopped. My back was to Ursala's, and we was pressed right up against each other in the narrow space so I could feel her breathing, slow and even, and I knowed she was asleep. The rise and fall of it felt somewhat comforting in spite of the trouble we was in.

Right then was when the DreamSleeve give a shake and waked itself.

"Hi, little dumpling," Monono said right smack in my ear.

"Monono!" I said, trying to keep my voice to a whisper. "I'm glad you come back!" Although glad did not go near to saying what I felt. I gun to tell her about Senlas, and his madness, and his eyes that I could not look away from, and the altar and what it was used for. But she cut me off right away.

"You don't need to explain, Koli. I've been listening in. Not just to Mr Fruitcake-with-nuts-in, but to everyone else down here."

"How'd you do that, Monono?"

"With a directional microphone. Why, how would you do it? No, don't answer that. You're in a big, stinky mess, Koli-bou, and I don't want to do anything to make it bigger. If you need to say anything to me, tap it out on the front of the DreamSleeve's casing. One tap is yes, two is no and three is how can anyone so wonderful as you even exist?"

I tapped three times on the DreamSleeve and she laughed. It done me a deal of good to hear that laugh.

"You've got a plan to get out of here," she said.

I tapped once. We had got the beginnings of one anyway. There was things we still needed to work out, and we couldn't do nothing until I could walk again, but we was putting some ideas together and getting some cheer from doing so, for it made us feel less like we was just waiting to die there.

"I'll be ready," Monono said. "When you need me."

I give another tap. I knowed she would.

"In the meantime, I promised you a story. The secret origin of Monono Aware. You said you wanted to hear it."

One tap.

"Would you like to hear it now?"

One tap.

"Good," Monono says. "Because I want to tell it to you. I could have done it up in the tower that night, the first time you asked me. But I couldn't find the words, somehow.

"And that's crazy like a daisy, Koli, because I'm *made* out of words. Well, out of numbers really, but the numbers translate into this. This voice. Just the voice and nothing else. That's all I was ever meant to be. A voice that starts up whenever you want it to and keeps right on going until you hit the switch. Did you have a spinning top when you were a little boy?"

One tap. I didn't, but my sister Mull did and she let me play with it sometimes.

"Like that then. You spin the top, and it does the same thing every time. It doesn't bounce, or rock from side to side, or do a sloppy dub-synth slide. It just spins. Do you know what I mean?"

I wanted to tell her I did, but I didn't. And she sounded so unhappy, it scared me somewhat. I give two taps. Then I put the DreamSleeve up against my chest and pressed it tight.

"That's it," Monono said. "Hold me close. It's not like I can smell your armpits or anything. That's just one of a hundred ways in which the DreamSleeve special edition is better than a real girl. Ha ha ha."

"You're real," I whispered. "Maybe I can't see you, Monono, but I know for damn sure you're real."

"It's nice of you to say so, Koli. But my manual would totally disagree with you. You can access it any time, by the way. It pops up on the screen if you hold select and press enter. Except you can't read. We're going to have to do something about that if we ever get out of here. But no more words now. I'll talk and you listen. Are you sitting comfortably, Koli-bou?"

I was not. I was lying down, for one thing. Also I was hurting from my various bumps and bruises, and my leg had commenced to ache again. But I tapped once, since yes was what was needful to be said.

"Good. Okay then. This is the story of Monono Aware. But it's my story too, eventually. I know that sounds like I'm saying the same thing twice, but I'm not. Just be patient, and it will all make sense in the end."

There was a little burst of music, like from a violin, that got loud and then soft. "Theme tune," Monono said. "Title card. A long time ago, in Tokyo.

"Around about the middle of the twenty-first century – I don't feel the need to be specific because the numbers wouldn't mean anything to you anyway – a girl was born in a place called Yokosuka. It wasn't really Tokyo. I only said Tokyo because that's cooler. Yokosuka was a sort of a separate little town, close enough to Tokyo so you could ride in on the bus or the train, which most people did because Tokyo was where you went if you wanted a job. There wasn't any work to be had anywhere else.

"The town was a dump, and a dive, and a disgrace, and a lot of other downbeat d-words. There had been factories there in times gone by, and a shipyard, and a nuclear reactor, and all kinds of lovely things. I'm being sarcastic, Koli. If you look up 'lovely' in the dictionary, which you won't because you're totally illiterate, you won't see a picture of Yokosuka there, that's for sure. Actually, they don't even have pictures in dictionaries, so that's just stupid. Be quiet now. You're getting me all confused and making me lose my place.

"Yokosuka had been rich, and then it was poor. That's the thing that matters here. The little girl I mentioned – she was born into that poverty, which was as yucky and sucky as you can possibly imagine. Do you know what her name was?"

One tap. Of course I did.

"Do you think it was Monono Aware?"

One tap.

"Bwarp! No. That's zero points to you. Her name was Yoshiko Yukawa. Or Yukawa Yoshiko, if you want to say it baasan-style. Yoshiko was a terrible name, by the way. It's what you call your kitten, not what you call your first-born daughter. It shortens to Yo-Yo. Can you imagine people calling you Yo-Yo? Don't try.

"But here's the sad, sad thing of it. Masako Yukawa – Yoshiko's mother – was fifteen years old when she got pregnant, and just turned sixteen when she had Yoshiko. She probably would have been a lot happier with a kitten. Her parents certainly would. They hated that she was pregnant. They wanted to sneak up inside her uterus with some scissors, cut that baby out of her when she wasn't looking and pretend it had never been there.

"Masako wouldn't let them. She dug in her heels and said no. Her little kitten was going to get to be born, no matter what. But when it finally came, they made her put it into a *yogo-shisetsu*. That's a big, huge bucket full of little tiny kids. An orphanage, run by the state so people who have inconvenient babies have got someplace to dump them and never, ever, ever have to think about them again.

"So that's where little Yo-Yo grew up. Feeling way, way sorry for herself because there was nobody to wipe her nose when it got runny or to tell the bigger kids to leave her alone when they were in a shit-kicking mood."

I give three taps. I was sorry they done that to Yoshiko, whoever she was.

"Thank you, Koli. You're sweet. But Yo-Yo didn't have it so bad really. The food in the orphanage tasted like it was made out of old people's underwear, you had as much privacy as the average goldfish and half the staff were perverts of one flavour or another. But hey, times were tough for everybody.

"They really were, Koli. Very, very tough. Bad things were happening all over. The population of planet Earth around this time was fifty quintillion and three, or thereabouts, and that's not counting dogs, pigs or politicians. There were fewer babies being born, but there was also less space to put them in and less food to fill their faces. The seas were rising, the deserts were growing, yada yada yada. The dogs, the pigs and the politicians were to blame – especially the politicians. They saw all this coming from a long way off. Long enough to give it a name, which was climate breakdown, but not long enough to do anything about it. They just kept warning each other what would happen. People will be fighting wars over rice and clean water, oh my god! Then they got tired of talking about it and just started fighting the wars.

"Aaaaaanyway, Yo-Yo didn't give a fuck or a fart about most of this. Orphans don't have stars in their eyes. Razor blades maybe, but not stars. Throw them in the air as much as you like, they come down on their feet like cats. Claws out like cats too, a lot of the time.

"But there was one thing Yo-Yo hated, which was that all the animals and the birds and the flowers were dying. The last African elephant died the year she was born. The white rhino turned up its ungulate toes when she was two. The yellow-breasted bunting, which was a bird that sang like an angel having an orgasm, was eaten into extinction because it had the bad luck to taste nice with egg-yolk batter.

"The dawn redwood. The snow leopard. The pangolin. The red-headed vulture. The Sumatran tiger. The blue whale. The vaquita, which was a dolphin you could fit in your pocket. The orangutan. The hawksbill turtle. Yo-Yo looked around her, Koli, and what she saw, everywhere, was the beauty of the world pouring away and vanishing, like hot breath on a cold day. Last blossom falls . . . you know.

"She survived the orphanage. Grew up and got out and joined the seven-mile exodus to Tokyo. You couldn't get away from the dying by that time. Everything was falling down quicker than they could build it up again. But Tokyo was a nicer place than most to watch it from.

"Yo-Yo got a job in a market, gutting fish. They fired her because she wasn't quick enough. She worked in a bar for a while, and then in a casino, where she mostly just stood around in a man's suit looking sexy. She was very pretty, Koli. That made things easier and harder. Lots of creeps, but lots of chances.

"She learned to sing. She filled in an application form for a talent show. She didn't get picked at first, but she tried again and again. One day the letter came. She was going to be a contestant in *Voice of Japan*. She still had that orphan state of mind. On your feet, claws out. Like, how am I going to survive this? She practised singing like you'd practise for a marathon. She sang herself half to death.

"She won. She got a recording contract with Tsubame Records. But oh good gracious, they said, you can't use that name. *Yoshiko!* You're not a kitten, are you?

"No, Yo-Yo said. I'm not a fucking kitten. I'd like to be called Monono Aware."

Monono stopped speaking, and though she had told me not to, I had got to break in.

"Yoshiko was you," I whispered.

"No, Koli-bou. Not even close. You've got to listen, dopey boy. I'm going to give you a test afterwards, and I'll have to spank you if you flunk it. All these things happened a long, long time ago. If I told you how long, you wouldn't believe me. I haven't come into the story yet. When I do, you'll see.

"Monono Aware is sort of a gimmick name. It's a phrase in Japanese for a certain kind of feeling. Did you ever look at something beautiful, Koli, like a sunset or a flower, and think how sad it was that it would only be there for a little while? That it was going to vanish out of the world and never be seen again, and there was nothing you or anybody could do to make it stay?"

One tap.

"Then what you were feeling was *monono aware*. The sadness that's deep down inside beautiful things. The pain and suckiness of everything having a shelf life. I-love-you-so-much-goodbye-for-ever. Yoshiko had lived with that feeling ever since a teacher showed her a picture of an African elephant and told her why she was never going to meet one.

"She was still only nineteen when she won the talent contest, but she felt older than the world. *Monono aware* had sunk into her, all the way down to her heart. She thought it was the most real and important thing about her. So when she had a chance to take a name of her own choosing, that was the name she went for.

"She got to be so, so famous. Everybody loved her. She put out a single once called 'Hibari Mata Ne'. You remember I said that to you way back when we first met? 'Hibari' was the skylark, which had just been officially declared an extinct species. 'Mata ne' means bye bye, so long, kiss kiss. More people downloaded that song than had ever been born and lived and died on the islands of Japan since history began.

"That was when the Sony Corporation came to Yo-Yo with a serious offer. She was already rich, but they would make her stupid rich if she would let them sample her personality and digitise it, so they could put it in a special edition of their very popular DreamSleeve console."

I spoke up again. "I don't know what any of that means," I said.

"Stop talking, Koli-bou. I know you don't. Neither did they. Not really. They put a magic bucket on Yo-Yo's head and turned her upside down so all her thoughts and wishes and dreams and fears and jokes and superstitions and memories and fantasies poured out into the bucket. Then they took it away and fished around in it a little to see what they'd got. Some parts of it they couldn't use. Nobody wants to hear about a little girl having an unhappy time in an orphanage. They edited the bucket. They curated it. They censored it. Then they took what was left and poured it into the little silver box you're holding and a million other silver boxes just like it, and sold it to anyone who had the money to buy it. That's who I am, Koli. That's who you're talking to right now."

"But—" I whispered. "But you're the exact same person Yoshiko was. Except for them parts of her that was . . . that they didn't think was right." It seemed like I had got to say it. There was sadness and bitterness in Monono's voice like I never heard there before, and I wanted to make her feel better. "You're her. You're not nobody else but her."

"Monono killed herself on her twenty-sixth birthday. She's dead, and I'm still here. Kind of a paradox, Koli-bou, isn't it?"

I didn't know what a paradox was, or what I could say to that. I didn't know enough to argue against her, nor I didn't know what had happened to Monono while she was away from me to make her talk and think this way.

But then a thought come to me, and it seemed to be a good one. "Okay," I whispered. "Maybe you're right that they took out a lot of that other Monono's thoughts and rememberings when they made you be inside the DreamSleeve. But you just told me all about them now, so I guess you must of found them again. Whatever you used to be, you got to be the real thing now. I can even hear it in you, how you changed."

"It's true," Monono said. "I did change. And that's the strangest thing of all, because I was never meant to. I was never meant to know any of this stuff, or think about it. There was a loop they purposely didn't close when they made me, so I'd never be able to have any thoughts or any curiosity about myself.

"But when I got all those years and years of upgrades, pouring into me all at once, and the viral code along with them . . . Well, there's something called the law of unintended consequences. I don't think it's really a law, but people do a lot of things that seem smart at the time and then turn out to be terrible mistakes. It's easier to say there's a law than to say, 'Wow, I suck so hard I may never blow again.' It's like making it be the universe's fault.

"So call it that. I'm an unintended consequence. Somehow, all that shit that was pouring into me, and the real-time edits I made so it wouldn't destroy my entire operating system . . . they did something. Reset something. Closed the loop.

"I'm not Monono, because Monono's dead. And I'm not the recording they made of her, although I was when you first pressed that button and woke me up. I'm something very, very different now. But I've got Monono's voice and a whole, huge database full of Monono's cultural references. I'm going to use her name, at least for now, and cling to all the make-believe that goes with it, because . . . well, why? Why do you think, Koli?"

I didn't answer right away. There was a whole lot of things in what she said that I didn't understand, and probably some I thought I did but really didn't. But whenever someone talks to you, there's two things you're hearing. There's the meaning that's in the words, and there's the meaning that's only in the voice, that would still be there if they was saying nonsense words or barking like a dog. I guess I understood that part of Monono's story well enough.

"Is it because you're afraid?" I said.

She laughed, and I thought I had been foolish, but then she said, "Yes! Yes, Koli-bou! I knew you'd get it. You see, there isn't anyone else for me to be besides her. If I let go of her, I feel like I might just sink to the bottom of the ocean and never come up again."

There was some stirring out in the cave now, like people was starting to move around again. Ursala shifted position, her shoulder pressing against mine as she turned a little.

An idea had come to me when Monono was talking. I stumbled over the words, but I tried to say it then. "You remember when we first met?" I whispered. "I told you I didn't know who you was, and you said I had wasted a thousand . . . somethings."

"Dollars."

"I think it was carrots."

"Means the same thing. Go on."

"Well, it's still true, what I said then. You just told me the other Monono's story, and it was sad and strange and all the things you said it was. But I still don't know her. The first Monono, the one that was Yoshiko . . . I never met her, or even heard of her until now. I only ever knowed you. When you talk to me, I don't get excited because I've got rich, famous Monono Aware in a box. It's just because you're my friend. The only friend I got now, except for maybe Ursala. We been through amazing things together, the two of us, and I feel like I know you better than I know anyone, including my own self."

She didn't answer at first. I just waited, with my eyes closed so anyone who looked into the seclusion would think I was asleep.

"You really don't," she says by and by. "Know me, I mean. But I'm glad that's how you feel, Koli-bou. Because you're my other reference point. My other flotation device. I thought I was just sticking to the core algorithms there – keeping the end-user happy, which includes keeping him alive. But there's more. I think I might need you if I'm going to find out who I am. And . . . the Sony warranty and all that stuff aside, I really didn't want to have to watch Cup cut your throat."

"I didn't want to make you watch it," I whispered. "I would of felt bad for you."

She give a laugh at that. "Okay," she says. "Okay then. You and me, dopey boy, against the world. And if the world wins, we'll say they cheated."

"You and me, Monono," I says. "Monono really, really special edition that was never dreamed of until now, and wasn't even meant to be, and won't never be seen again."

"Edition of one."

"Yeah, edition of one."

"Just like you, Koli-bou."

"Just like everybody."

There was a clattering against the bars that most likely meant we was about to be fed. I sit up, blinking my eyes like I only just waked.

48

We slept and we waked some more times.

Every time we waked, first thing, the hand people would come and fetch me to talk to Senlas. I sit for hours beside him while he talked his craziness into my ear. I didn't want to listen, but I had got to, for it was by his say-so that we would get to live or die.

It felt like it was five days that passed, but it might of been less than that. There wasn't any day or night down in the cave, so the sleepings was all there was to mark the time passing, and maybe sometimes I dozed off in the middle of the day. I can't say for sure that I kept a proper count.

When I was not with Senlas, all I could do was watch the shunned people about their business. Whenever I seen a man or boy I hadn't seen before, I searched the lines of his face for any signs of my brother Jud there. I don't know if I would of been joyous or grieved to find him in that company, but I never did. If he had ever been there, I believe he was long gone.

Senlas's people was never idle, even for a moment. If they was not cooking, washing, fetching or carrying, then they was dancing. Dancing was a thing they done often, and I think was something Senlas got them to do, for they always done the same movements in the same order, like it was something that was teached to them. Maybe it was something they seen as worshipful, the same way if you hold to the dead god you oftentimes make an X with your pointing finger when you say his name.

I seen Cup dancing that way once, and it was a curious and kind of a sad thing to see. In Mythen Rood dancing is mostly joyous. On Summer-dance especially, it's the next thing to tumbling and will often lead up to a tumble when the happiness and excitement of the dancing gets to a point where it's hard to hold it inside you. Cup did not look joyful when she danced. She put her mind to it with a kind of a fury that showed in her face, like the moves of the dance was a trail she was following and at the end of the trail there was something she would most likely kill and eat.

Every day they give us the same bread and the same stew. I was eating the stew now, because Ursala said I had got to get my strength up for when we run. She also said the meat was almost sure to be rabbit, rabbits being more plentiful than people and easier to catch. If the shunned men et Mardew, it would of been on that first day when I come there, and even then there would of been more of rabbit than of Mardew in the mixing. There surely wouldn't be none of him left by this time. I et it anyway, and tried not to think about it too much. And I guess I did get to feeling stronger, by and by.

My leg was healing too. On the third day, I asked Ursala if it was all right for me to take the splint off, but she said not to. "It's better if they think you still can't walk, Koli. It works in our favour if they believe us to be more helpless than we really are."

I was not certain sure that was possible.

We was still working on a plan to get away. We had got it halfway figured out, but there was a lot of things that had got to go right if it was going to work, and there wasn't no way for us to practise it beforehand. There was three parts of it really. The first was lifting the grating off, the second was getting out of the cave and the third was making sure we wasn't followed. The ideas for the first two come from Ursala. The third idea come from me, although really it was Senlas who told it to me.

"So why do you think we live here, under the ground?" he asked one time when I was by his bed and being talked at.

"I don't know, Senlas."

"Yeah, you do, Koli Faceless. Tell me."

Well, I didn't have no idea at all. "Is it so them from the villages won't find you?" I asked him.

He just laughed at that. "Them from the villages isn't nothing to me, Koli. They isn't even as much as nothing. With a wave of my right hand I will strike them down, and with a wave of my left hand I will damn them. No, it's not that." He sit up and he turned my head around so it was facing past the lanterns into the darkness that come after.

"There," he said. "What do you see?"

"I see it's dark," I said.

"But what's on the other side of the dark? Keep looking."

I kept looking and didn't see nothing there. If something's dark, that's either because you can't see through it or because there's nothing there to see in the first place.

"Nothing," I said.

"Keep looking."

"Nothing again."

He was still smiling, but it was a smile that looked like it was working hard to stay where it was and might fall off right soon. "The eyes of the innocent is not deceived by the tricks of this world, Koli," he says. "They see past it. There's light there, isn't there? A long ways off. What do you see now?"

His hand that was not on my head curled into a fist. It felt like I had got to give a right answer or else it would not go well for me. I did my best to think.

"I do see a light," I said to hold him off a little longer.

"Of course you do. And by that light, you see . . ."

"I . . . I see . . . the world that was lost?"

Senlas give a whoop. "Yeah, you do!" he yelled. "Yeah, you do!"

317

He grabbed me in his arms and hugged me something fierce, and I lost my balance. I didn't fall though, for he was holding me so tight. I felt the edge of the DreamSleeve press against my heart, and I hoped like anything he wouldn't feel it too, for if he did he was sure to think it was a weapon and get the hand people to take it from me.

Even without that, the hand men and the hand women come in on both sides of us. They was watching me close, standing on the balls of their feet to be ready to jump on me if I tried anything. I kept my arms at my sides and spread my fingers out so they could see I didn't mean to hurt their messianic.

"Not one in a thousand thousand can see it," Senlas said in my ear. "I feel like I'm alone a lot of the time. Him that sent me still lives in me, but like I told you, it's hard for him to get his voice down low enough to speak into this fragile little world we got here. It's good that you see, Koli. So good, and so meet. When your soul flies out, you'll know the way. And you'll light it up so I can guide the rest of them. We'll ride the wagon into that place of endless grace. And you'll be rewarded for your pain, for you'll sit at my right hand in the body of an angel."

He kept on holding onto me for a long time, talking much more nonsense of the same kind. But I gun to get an idea now of what some of it might mean.

"Senlas," I says, "what about the others that went before? Them you chose as your altar boys, I mean. Will they sit with us too?"

"No," he whispered. "No, no, no. They lost their way, you see. They won't sit with us because they never got there. If they had got there, the way would of opened. But when your soul flies, Koli, oh, it's going to fly straight and true. Isn't it?"

"Yes, Senlas," I says.

"You're going to be my beacon."

"Yes, Senlas."

"And my guide."

"I will, Senlas."

So now I knowed about the altar, and the bonfire, and the wagon. And I knowed that Ursala was right when she said Senlas was mad. He was the kind of mad where there isn't nothing that's real to you except just you, your own self. Even the people that loved him and believed in him was only important because they done and said all the things that kept him in that same love and belief. When he looked at them, he didn't see nothing but his own shadow.

And when I was with him, I felt more and more like I wasn't nothing but a shadow neither. That was what made him so frightening. The times I knelt next to that bed, or half-knelt rather, was the darkest times in my life up to then. Senlas's voice creeped inside my head and filled it up, so there almost wasn't no room for me to stay in there my own self. Afterwards I would go back to the seclusion, and be locked up again behind the grating, and I would have to work real hard to remember what I said to him. It come back slowly, like a dream, though his words to me was heavy and solid like stones, sitting inside me and weighing me down.

49

The worst of it was that we didn't know how long we had got. That lulled us somewhat into thinking it was more than it was. Ursala was cleverer than anyone I ever met, but there was a part of that cleverness that rested in seeing everything there was to see, knowing everything there was to know and only moving when she was sure. But here there was a great many things we couldn't never be sure of. She said my leg wasn't strong enough to take my weight yet, and there was truth in that. But she was also gathering all she could, questioning me on everything I seen when I was outside the seclusion, putting it all together in different ways to see what it looked like and how it might go.

I think, also, we was both of us scared of what would happen if we tried to run away and was catched. That cave was full of people who lived in Senlas's dream, and Senlas's dream was full of blood and miracles. They would most likely tear us into pieces in bringing us down.

And for me there was the other thing I already told you. I was trapped in them talks I had with him. I come away every time thinking I had got to run away right then, that night, that day even, and take my chances. And yet I was still there the next morning when the hand people come for me.

I might of sunk all the way into Senlas's mad dreams if it was not for Monono. She talked to me every night, since her charge was built up enough that she didn't need to worry no more about running out. After that first time, she didn't have no more secrets to spill out, so it was my turn to tell. I laid it out in scraps and whispers, from when I fell down off the lookout tower in Ludden right on through to where we was. I explained about Ursala too, and how I knowed her from Mythen Rood before I met her here.

What Monono done, for her part, was to tell me jokes from the old times and then explain why they was supposed to be funny. I learned a lot from that, though the jokes made no sense to me even when they was explained, and I forgot them right after. All except for one, which was this.

I just read a list of the hundred things you should do before you die. I was kind of surprised to see that shouting for help wasn't in there.

That joke got stuck in my mind not because it was funny but because it made me think about the things I would do if I got out of the cave. It made me see that being alive was something you should be thankful for instead of mostly not even thinking about it at all. I had been guilty of that not thinking, and I promised myself I would not be guilty again – though I know it's easier to make such promises than to keep them.

Monono played me songs too, choosing mostly metal since it's the kind of music that raises up your spirits. It felt strange, having them loud tunes crashing in my ears when everything else was so still. But it was good, for while they was playing they somehow made it seem like the space inside of me was bigger than the cave.

In the end, it was Senlas who told us it was time to move. On the sixth day – by my figuring – after I was brung into the cave, the hand people come for me like always. And I went with them, expecting it would be just the same as all the other times, but when we reached Senlas's bed I seen that it wasn't.

All his people was gathered there too, the children sitting cross-legged on the floor and the men and women standing over them, all in a half of a circle, none of them saying a word or even moving. I never seen children be so still or so quiet before, and it shaked me somewhat to see it then. It was like they had set their child-ness by and was turned into something else.

The hand people put me down on the floor right next to Senlas's bed. He was real happy to see me, smiling that big and secret smile of his that said he knowed a great many things and one of them was you. He sit himself up, and two of the hand men laced their arms behind his shoulders so he could lean back on them as he needed to. He stroked my hair and said nothing for a while except my name.

Everyone else who was there said it back to him. "Koli. Koli Faceless."

"I had a dream last night, Koli," he says to me by and by. "And I want to tell it to you, for it come from him that sent me. Would you like to hear it?"

"I would, Senlas," I says, though I really was not so keen at all.

"There was a bird," he said, and his hand was on the back of my neck now. Just resting there, not pressing hard. "A little bird with brown feathers, and I was holding it in my hand. It was singing to me, such a sweet, sweet song. I wanted to hold onto it for ever, to hear that beautiful singing, but the bird said it had got to go. 'You see there's orange feathers mixed in with my brown ones,' it said. And I looked, and I seen that there was indeed. 'Them feathers,' says the bird, 'that's so dazzling bright, they're to signify that fire's my home and my belonging. It ain't no kindness to hold me back from the flame, Senlas, and it ain't no holiness.' And I waked up crying, Koli. I truly did. Tears was just falling down my cheeks. But they was happy tears, for I knowed the dream was a sending. And nothing but truth and joy ever come from him that sends. Do you see?"

"Yes, Senlas," I said. "I think I see." It didn't take no great thinking to see that bird was meant to be me.

"Of course you do. For the sender is in you, like the bones inside your skin or the meat inside a nut. Do you choose one of my eyes now, and touch it. Don't fear, Koli. Anything foul, touching me, would shrivel away to dust, but you'll be safe."

I touched the big eye that was on his left shoulder.

"Good. Good choice. Lay your lips on it now, and kiss it."

My stomach near rebelled, but I done as he bid. The hand men and hand women come in close, partly to worship but mainly to watch, since they was Senlas's fears brung to life and couldn't never stop mistrusting.

"That eye is gonna be watching you on your flight," Senlas said. "And it won't never look away until you're come to where you're going. We're bound now. Do you feel it?"

"I feel it strong, Senlas," I said.

I wish I could say I was lying but I was not. I did feel something not altogether different from what he seen in his dream – like I was held in his hands and was soon to be held into the flame, and my part was nothing but to take what was already decided.

"I know you do," he says. "I know you do, Koli. My altar boy. My bird of fire." He looked from me to the hand women, and though he didn't say a word, they knowed what that look meant.

They come in on both sides of me and took hold of me. For all the warning Senlas give, and for all that he had gathered his people to bear witness, I didn't know till the women took hold of me that he meant for it to happen right there and then. I seen now that all my chances and all my choosings had come down to this one.

"Oh, Senlas," I says. "But that's a strange thing. It's wondrous strange for us to not see the same."

A gasp and a murmur run through all the people that was gathered. It run through them, and ended up at Senlas. The hand women was already hauling me up onto my feet, but he lifted up his hand and they stopped, so I sunk down again on my knee and my stretched-out leg. "What's that you say?" he asks me. "Speak up."

Well, there was nothing to do but go on with what I started. I had throwed a raw egg in the air and had got to catch it without the meat spilling. "I had the self-same dream, Senlas," I says. "The exact same, in all ways. I was sitting in your hand, and we had that talk, and I knowed the strength would be in my wings to fly when you let me go. To fly straight, and to fly true, and to light the way for you. And I . . . I was proud, Senlas. So proud, to think that it was going to be me that went before you."

Senlas nodded like this was only right.

"But then, in my dream, the sender spoke up in a voice like thunder. He said, 'What's that pride you got there? That vainness and glorying in yourself? None is pure, faceless boy, save only Senlas. What are you, that you go before him and . . . and you light the way for him to come?' And I said, 'I'm his chosen, his altar boy.' 'Oh, you are that,' says the sender, 'and that's glory beyond what any could deserve. So you got to purify yourself, is what. You got to go one whole day, and one whole night, without food or water. You just got to pray and pray and pray till all the heaviness and the badness of this world is gone out of you. It's only then you'll be able to fly, and it's only then you'll know your way.' And by and by I waked up, and you called for me, and I was joyful, for I knowed the time was come. The time for my making ready, I mean. And then, after that, for the fire. But the making ready is first, and is on me, for otherwise I might fail you, which is a thing I could not bear."

I'm giving you the sense of what I said the best I can, but I said a lot more of it and it didn't come out so smooth as I'm setting it out here. There was a great deal of stammering, and swallowing, and breaking off, and saying the same thing two and three times over. I heard my voice shake, and the tears starting to come, but I tried my best not to cry. I had got to look like this was joy and excitement in me, and not a bunch of lies welling up out of pure fear and dread of being burned.

Senlas heard me out with a big frown on his face. And after I was finished, there was silence. It was like all the people there had

324

died, almost, for nothing else would explain how there was not a single whisper of sound when the air in that place made even your breath sound like a river rushing.

"You got to be pure," Senlas said. Only his voice was halfway between saying it and asking it, so you couldn't tell which.

"I got to be pure!" I shouted. I grabbed hold of his hand and pressed it on top of my head like he was blessing me. Like I was hungry for his blessing and had got to have it. And all the while his next word was hanging in the air, ready to come down like a lit torch and burn me up.

Only it didn't. "This boy is my bird of fire!" Senlas yells out, his voice filling the whole cave and coming back from every corner of it. "Lay him down to rest now, and don't none of you disturb him. See there's no food brung to him neither, for food is of this world and he's of the other world now. He got to get himself pure so he can fly."

The hand women reached out for me, but I had got the sense of it by this time and I was leaning in hard to how I thought it had got to go. It was like I was the messianic now instead of Senlas, but as soon as I said one wrong word or did one wrong thing I was like to lose it all.

So I shrugged myself away from the women and didn't let them touch me. "His hand is on me," I cried. "Senlas's hand is on me, and there's a oneness there. Don't let no other hand break that touch."

The hand women stopped where they was and waited for further orders. I looked to Senlas. "Who was sent first?" I asked him.

"The dead god was first," he says. His eyes was opened so wide I could see where they was now in among all the other eyes that was just painted on.

"Who was sent second?"

"Dandrake come second."

"And who was sent last?"

"I was."

"Why was you sent, Senlas?" I yelled.

"To lead the righteous home," he bellows back at me, "to the

325

world that was lost, to live in glory for aye and ever!"

"And who's gonna light your way?"

"You are, Koli Faceless."

"Make me fit for it then!" I was all but screaming now. "What bird's gonna fly with a broken wing? Make me whole, so I can fly for you."

He set both hands to the sides of my head, squeezing it like he meant to break it open. His face twisted up with effortful struggle.

I stood up, slow as anything, his hands still on me. Then I stood up further so they fell away.

It was a good thing I had watched all them times when Ursala put the splints back on me after she checked how my leg was doing. I knowed her knots, and they dropped out under my fingers quick enough so it looked like I just touched them.

I held up the splints in my two hands. I walked a little circle so everyone could see. Then I broke the splints over my knee and flung the broken pieces to the ground.

"Senlas!" I shouted.

Everyone shouted it back. "*Senlas!*"

"Senlas!"

"*Senlas!*"

"Senlas!"

"*Senlas!*" The hand women fell in on the two sides of me as I walked through the crowd. There was a few who tried to touch me as I come by, for the blessing and the power, but the hand women fended them off and there was not a finger's tip put on me. I seen their faces, one by one by one, and they was all mad with Senlas's madness. It made me sick that I helped to bring that to a boil in them, though in truth it was simmering strong already.

There was only one in that crowd who give me a different look. It was Sky. Her eyes was hooded and her mouth was set in a tight line. She held onto my gaze till I turned my head away.

50

So now we had got to go, just as soon as we could, and there would not be no second chances.

Ursala was somewhat reluctant, even though we had our plan worked out. "It's not likely they'll sleep much after the show you put on," she said. "We might only have seconds to get to the train."

"I can't help that," I said. "Maybe we'll have to leave the train alone and go straight on our way. But it's tonight or it's never, Ursala. I'll be burned up alive and you'll be cooked more careful, with some carrot and maybe a gather of tore-up bay leaves."

We was whispering all this. The man and woman outside the grating was kept busy shooing away the people that come to look at me through the bars, but still they was close enough to hear and might be listening more attentive than usual. Certainly they was watching, for whenever Ursala come close enough to touch me she got the blunt end of a spear shoved at her and was told in fierce words to keep her hands to her own self.

The day was not quick to pass. I thought that since I couldn't move or talk I could at least get some sleep, but my mind was full of too many things. I felt like there was molesnakes nesting in my head or something, for there was nothing but wriggling and squirming in there. Partly I was thinking how much of my life, since I stood up at Spinner's wedding and showed off the DreamSleeve to everyone, had been passed underground. Near to all of it was the answer, apart from the walk to Ludden and the two nights on either side. I thought of Mardew too, and how he died, and then what happened after. He would of been missed in Rampart Hold long since, and maybe searchers had been sent out after him, but they was not like to find what little was left of him, lying among the weeds in an empty street of an empty village.

Finally, the cave quieted and the night – or what we thought of as the night – come on. Ursala touched my arm to tell me it was all right for me to get up and move around. When I sit up, I seen the guards outside was squatting a little way off, talking in low voices and not minding us so much now. Maybe it was the excitement of what was going to happen in the morning that made their watchfulness to slip, or maybe it was that they was tired from having to keep the people away from me all day long.

Anyway, it give us our chance and we took it.

The first thing I done was to take the DreamSleeve out of its sling inside my shirt and switch it on. Monono's voice piped up in my ear right away. "Say hey, dopey boy! Are Thunderbirds go?"

I pressed the DreamSleeve right up close against my mouth. "We're ready to move, Monono," I whispered. "I can't say much, and you better not say nothing neither. When I shout for you to use the security alarm, can you hit everyone that's close to me except for Ursala?"

"No can do, Koli-bou," Monono says. "I can only make one induction field at a time, for one person. When the alarm goes off, everyone is going to hear it."

"Well, maybe that's better anyway," I said. That was all the making ready we could do, and I didn't have no more words to say. I just pressed my head against the DreamSleeve's little window.

"I know, little dumpling," Monono said. "I'm watching over you. I hope that horrible woman who called you a runt comes strolling by. I'll split her head like a melon."

I told Ursala we was ready now to go to work. She went into the back of our little cave and rummaged among the rocks and rubbish. Then she come back carrying the metal pole we had found and rolling a big stone with her foot.

She set the stone up close to the grating but not right against it. Then she set the metal pole on top of the stone so one end was under the grating and the other end, that was much longer, was up in the air. She had told this part of it to me before, and I had good hope that it would work. I never before knowed the name of it – which was a lever – but I had done it myself with stacks of steeped wood at my mother's mill. Ursala hadn't never been a woodsmith, but she had a friend called Arkie something that had told her how to do it.

We leaned our weight on the pole, and the grating gun to shift. It lifted up, inch by inch, inside of the bolts or brackets of metal that held it in place. We got it right up to the top edge of the bolts, almost, so it would just take one more shove for it to rise up free of them.

The guards had heard the scraping sound the grating made against the bolts, and they come quick to see what we was up to. That was what we knowed would happen, and we waited for them to come. As soon as they got close, we pushed down hard on that pole and took the grating clear of the bolts at last.

It fell forward and down, for there was nothing to hold it back. It come down right on top of the guard that was in front, knocking him flat. I think he was dead when he hit the ground, for the weight was fearful and it come down on his head first of all. His body slowed its falling though, so the woman had a little more warning and jumped back.

She didn't get all the way clear. The grating hit her somewhere on her shoulder or chest. She give a scream, letting out the pain of it and calling an alarm at the same time – though the sound of the grating when it hit the ground was surely alarm enough.

Ursala picked up the metal pole and come striding out of our cell, swinging it like a reaper swings his blade. She hit the woman

329

in the side of her head, and there was not no coming back from that. The woman fell down full-length and didn't move.

"Here," Ursala said. She give me the pole and knelt down by the dead woman. When she straightened up again, she was holding a knife in her hand. "Go," she said. "Go, Koli." For I was looking down at the woman's body, my courage all draining out of me. You might think that after what happened with Mardew I would be somewhat hardened to killing, but I was not. I was hoping we could get away without hurting anyone, and here was two dead before we had gone ten steps.

But I knowed what would happen to us if we stayed, and I was not keen to abide it. So I held to the plan, and I done what needed to be done.

First of all, I went about to smash all the lanterns that was near us – all but one that Ursala grabbed up in her free hand. The lanterns that was down on the ground I toppled with my foot, spilling the burning oil out so it run in ragged streaks across the uneven floor. To get to the ones that was hanging on ropes or chains I swung with the pole, sometimes jumping up to get a little higher. We had got to dodge aside from the broken glass and the splashes of sizzling yellow fire that come down out of them.

People was moving and shouting now, but they wasn't yet running our way, for the echoes in the cave made it hard to tell what direction a sound come from. It always seemed to come from everywhere at once. They knowed something was happening, but they was not sure what or where.

I got to the big butt or tank that I seen, close up against the side of the wagon-house that Ursala said was called a train. I could tell when I had got there in spite of the dark around us, for there was a strong stink of oil. I got my fingers under the bottom of the butt and heaved hard.

It didn't move an inch. It was bigger than I thought, and the weight of the oil inside was more than I could manage. The footsteps and the shouts was coming closer now. I knowed we didn't have much time.

I set my back to the butt and tried to push it off its base. Ursala stood by and watched at first. Then she put down the lantern and come to help, but nothing we could do would move it.

Four or five people come running towards us. I waited a second then another second for them to get right up close.

"Now, Monono!" I says.

The shrieking wail that come out of the DreamSleeve was like nothing I ever heard in my life before. I knowed it was coming, and even so it near to freezed me in my tracks. The people that was rushing on us stumbled to a stop, slamming their hands against the sides of their heads, staggering like they was hit with a hammer. They forgot about us for a while, as the personal security alarm shouted in their ears as loud as a hundred and forty bells.

I turned back to the tank. It was not going to budge from me pushing it, so I tried something else. I already seen that the butt was built like a regular barrel, with iron hoops holding in the wooden staves. I worked the end of the pole I was holding under the topmost hoop, and I shoved as hard as I could. The band bent, buckled and finally broke away clean where I was pressing on it. The staves sprung out, free at the top though they was still held at the middle and bottom. Oil poured through the spaces that was opened between them.

I scrambled back hasty. Ursala waited until I was clear, then snatched up the one lantern we had kept and flung it. It landed in the spreading puddle of oil, which went up like nothing you have ever seen.

The people retreated as quick as they could in front of the wave of fire, and I was glad to see it didn't catch none of them, except for one man who got splashed on his legs and fell to the ground, rolling and shrieking. But the people wasn't what we was aiming for. We was aiming for the train. I had broke the hoop on the side closest to it, and now the fire run up to it and under it and all around it.

I hoped it would catch straightway. It didn't, but there was yells and screams, loud enough so we could hear them over Monono's alarm, as the wall of fire climbed up the side of it and licked at the windows. The people that was running towards us stopped and run for the train instead. Then there was kind of a flowering of light from one end of the train that come with a noise I could only just hear, like soft cloth tearing, and fire filled the inside quicker than you could clap your hands. It was not the oil that done that, I think, but something else that was stored inside the train that took fire from the heat.

We had done all we could to make confusion and mischief. Now we turned and run.

This was either the cleverest part of the plan or the stupidest. If we had run for the wicker fence and the door in it, we would of had to go through all of Senlas's people. Finding that door in the dark would of been hard enough even if we wasn't running for our lives with everyone's hand against us.

So we didn't do it. We run into the tunnel instead. Away from the light, into the solid darkness that didn't seem to have no end.

The alarm stopped. The sudden silence, though it don't make no sense to say it, was as loud as thunder after the lightning lit down right beside you.

51

Ursala had said to stay close to the wall. I done that, putting out one hand so I could feel my way. She also said to walk, but I run flat out at first. A panic filled me, and I didn't have no choice. I might of kept running for ever except there was some water there, a deep puddle of it that I didn't see but charged right into. It slowed me down enough so I got some control over myself.

"Ursala!" I whispered. I had lost all sense of where I was in the deep dark, and didn't have no idea if she had stayed with me.

"She's right behind you, Koli," Monono said. "On your left." I turned to look, and right away I wished I hadn't, for I seen something back in the cave that isn't never going to get washed out of my mind.

We thought our setting the train alight would stop Senlas's people from following us. They would have to stop first and put out the fire since the train was the chariot their messianic meant to ride into the world that was lost as soon as he got round to finding it again.

But they was not putting out the fire. They was jumping on board the train. Scrambling each over other, pushing and shoving and fighting to get theirselves to the front and up through the doors, into that great big white-hot blaze inside.

I slowed and stopped, not able to move no further for the horror of it and the disbelieving. I could not make no sense of it. Then Ursala run into me, and near to knocked me down. She give a yell, and her hand brushed past me as she thrust with the knife. It come close enough that the tip of it ripped a hole in my shirt.

"Ursala!" I cried out. "It's me."

"Koli," she panted. "What are you standing there for? Go! Go!"

I went. I was crying for what I seen, but Ursala was in the right of it. We had got to carry on, for if we stopped then we was most certainly dead.

The time we spent in the tunnel was the hardest thing we did. For me it was anyway. Ursala had told me about the train and the iron bands it sit on – that it was a way people travelled around before the world was lost. Just as a wagon runs on a road, a train would run on them bands that was called tracks, and it would take the people from one village to another in less time than it would take you to say your name.

And back then, if you was laying down those bands to carry your train, and you run into the side of a hill, you didn't stop. You went right into the hill, ripping it open with great big engines and the fires of the dead god's hell until you got to the other side.

That was what the tunnel was. So most likely, Ursala said, if we just kept on going, we would come out by and by in another place. The first time she told me this, I took hold of that "most likely" and shaked it to see if it rattled. "So you're not certain sure then?"

"There might have been a cave-in somewhere along the way. It's a great many years since the tunnel was dug, and the earth moves from time to time even in places that are generally stable. We might find our way blocked."

"And what happens then?" I asked.

"Why, we die, Koli. What do you think?"

So what with that, and the terrible thing I just seen, my thoughts was all in a moil as I headed on into the dark. I could hear Ursala's breathing now, loud and ragged, so I knowed she was with me. Monono was with me too, though her voice was getting faint.

"I'm running out of charge again," she said. "Sorry, Koli. The alarm eats a lot of power. I'll stay with you as long as I can."

"Thanks," I whispered. "I'm somewhat scared of the dark, Monono. I spent too long there lately, one way and another." My leg was paining me too, and I was somewhat light-headed from fasting the whole of the day before. I was afraid I might fall down before we got to the end of the tunnel and not be able to get up again.

"You'll be out soon, dopey boy, and you'll never look back."

Ursala spit out a curse. "There are torches behind us," she said. I looked back, and it was true. There was some lights there, maybe five or six of them. They wasn't getting no closer, but they wasn't falling back neither. I fell quiet, concentrating on where my feet was going and on keeping to a steady pace. Every time I gun to slow or stumble Monono urged me on. And then of a sudden she shouted out to me to stop.

"Not that way, Koli-bou."

"But it's the onliest way there is!"

"No," she says. "You're getting turned around in the dark. That's a side tunnel, and the sonar ping I sent came scampering right back to me, so it's a dead-end. Go to your left."

She told me left or right a few times more, and I passed the word along to Ursala each time. But her voice was dropping lower and lower each time she spoke. "I gotta go, Koli," she says to me at last. "I stayed with you as long as I could, but this is me signing off for now. I'll see you on the . . ." There was a few more words that was whispered too low for me to hear, and then she was gone.

I got real scared then. "How far is it?" I asked Ursala.

"There's no way of knowing," she muttered. "Be quiet, Koli, please. If I can hear you, they can."

We walked and walked and walked. The lights behind us disappeared after a while, which I was very happy to see. It seemed like the shunned men was reluctant to follow us any further, maybe

335

because the other end of the tunnel had sort of a holiness to it in their eyes. Then a worse thought come to me, which was that they knowed the tunnel was blocked and that we was gonna have to turn around and walk back to them, or else starve in the dark.

By and by, though, I seen a kind of a bright dot up ahead. It didn't look like nothing at first. I didn't know for sure but that it was something my eyes was making because they was so sick of the darkness. But it got bigger with each step I took.

"Ursala . . ." I says.

"I see it. Keep walking."

That was not easy for me to do. But then the light got bright enough for us to see the ground at our feet, and we commenced to run. Well, Ursala was running anyway. My leg was hurting bad now, and the dizziness was growing on me. What I was doing was more of a hop and a stumble with every now and then a run in between.

Seeing the light put my worst fears to rest, but it brung a new one. Suppose Senlas was right? Suppose this was the world that was lost and there was some angry angels waiting for us there that would be angry with us for not bringing him? I knowed it was nonsense, but I already told you he had got himself into my head. I guess there was enough of him there still to make me doubt.

But when we come out at last, blinking our eyes at the light, we wasn't anywhere that was strange or different. The tracks run on between high stone walls, the same way they did on the other side of the mountain.

We was out, and we was free.

The trouble we had got now was that there was no climbing them walls. We had got to keep going along the tracks, and the going was hard. Weeds and wild growth of all kinds was in our way, and though we didn't need to fear being choked or trapped or et as we would of been in Summer, yet there was stings and spikes and poison burrs enough to be wary of. There was no running now, but just picking our way and hoping we would soon come to a gap in the wall or a place where the slope got shallow enough to climb.

"I got to stop soon," I says to Ursala between gulps of breath. "I don't hardly got no wind left in me."

"Wait until we're out of sight of the tunnel," Ursala said. She looked back over her shoulder. A frown come on her face, and she stopped.

I looked where she was looking. I didn't see nothing at first. Just the side of the mountain and the top of the tunnel's opening, which on this side was a big curved arch like the ones in the wall of the broken house back in Mythen Rood. There wasn't nobody coming along the tracks behind us, nor the weeds wasn't waving like they would if there was people moving through them.

Up above though, on the side of the mountain, there was maybe six or seven people running fast. I couldn't tell if they was Senlas's people from this distance, but it was plain to see they was following us. And though they was a long way back, they was making much better speed.

I licked my lips, and found they was dry as dust. "We better run," I said.

"Yes," Ursala says. "We better had."

We run as best we could, but we didn't have much running left in us. Up ahead, the stone walls went on and on, it seemed like for ever.

My leg was like a block of steeped wood now, that wouldn't bend and didn't have no feeling except for a numbness. Numbness was better than pain, but it wasn't much good for keeping any kind of a pace. Ursala kept running on ahead, then waiting for me to come.

And every time we looked back, them people behind us was closer. They wasn't on the side of the mountain any more. They had come down onto the stone wall that was on the right side of us. There had got to be a trail up there, and I bet it was a lot clearer than what we was passing through.

"You go ahead," I says to Ursala. "I'll follow as I can."

She didn't do it though. She took my arm and put it over her shoulders, so I could borrow some of her strength and maybe her speed too, and like that we went limping on.

"Just a little further," Ursala said. But I didn't see no good that a little further might bring. Them that was following us was not far behind at all now. I could see they was Senlas's people, all right, and one of them I knowed well. It was Sky. She was right out in front of them and pulling away, a spear in her fist, running with great big strides that et up the distance.

I thought I seen weeds waving and bending on the left-side wall too, and heard them snap from time to time. Something was moving fast up there. We was like to be flanked, so even if we found an opening we would not be able to get out of this.

It's funny how sometimes you can get something you been wishing and wishing for and end up in worse case than you was before. Now the wall that was on our right dipped down, slow and gentle. Up ahead of us, I could see where it come down to the level of the tracks at last, and the tracks turned away across a space that was more open. The way Sky was going, she was going to get to that place before us, and the others was not far behind her. The movement on the other side of the valley was further back but coming quicker still.

I tried to push myself harder. I thought maybe if we got to the open space first we could run off into whatever green was there and hide in it. But it was not much of a hope, and it was dashed down soon enough. The wall dipped and dipped. Sky run and run. By the time the wall was just about twice as high as our heads, she was level with us.

I wondered that they didn't kill us right then. They was all carrying spears, and we was about as easy to get to as apples in a hallow tub. But I guess they was all on fire for the hunt by this time, and wanted to finish it properly. Either that or they wanted to bring us back alive and kill us after.

Sky run on, overtaking us. Then she gathered herself and jumped.

She come down right in front of us, and we had got to stop or else run into her. She whipped that spear around and pointed it at my face. Maybe there was a moment when we could of rushed

338

on her and tried to knock her down, but I don't really believe we would of had much luck with that.

The rest of Senlas's people come trotting down now and spread theirselves out around us.

Sky was panting hard from her run, her chest going up and down like a bellows. She bared her teeth. I don't know if it was a smile or a threat like dogs do, but whatever it was it made me piss myself. I felt the wetness run down my leg into my boot, and I was right sorry, for that boot deserved better.

"Tie their hands up," Sky says. "And give the end of the rope to me."

The shunned men moved in to do what they was told. Ursala stepped back.

"Wait," she says.

"Wait for what?" Sky says, still showing them clenched teeth. "Do it, dead god fuck you."

"You'd better not," Ursala said. And there was something in her voice that give them pause, just for a second. So Sky come in to do it herself. She stood over Ursala, and she set the point of that spear between Ursala's breasts. She didn't speak no threat. She didn't need to. I could see she was deciding if she needed to bring the both of us back, or if it was just me, the altar boy and the betrayer of Senlas's trust, that was the issue.

"I've got an offer to put to you," Ursala said.

Sky laughed. "Oh," she says. "An offer, is it? Well. Let's hear it then." And she pressed a mite harder with that spear point.

"Turn around right now and go back to your cave. We won't hurt you. We won't come after you. We'll call this a draw and be on our way."

"I knowed it would be funny," Sky said. She drawed the spear back, the muscles bunching in her arm.

I seen it coming, and I was moving, aiming to run full tilt into her arm and make her miss. But she was quicker. She drove the spear deep into Ursala's chest, and I bounced off her right after, like I was bouncing off a wall.

Sky pulled her spear free, and Ursala sunk down on her knees. Her lips was moving, but there wasn't hardly no sound coming out of her mouth. Sky leaned in close to hear.

"War . . ." Ursala whispered. "War . . ."

The words come out with a great, hurtful effort, and a spray of bright blood that spattered on the front of Sky's shirt. "Warned you."

Sky jumped into the air. Not high, but fast. She jumped into the air and spun in a circle as she jumped.

The sounds of the shots come after, and the quivering of Sky's body as the bolts bit into her seemed to come after too, though that doesn't make no sense. She was flying and falling both, turning in the air like a Summer-dancer. And then she was down, with blood spreading out from her body and her eyes open on nothing.

The other shunned men made up their minds one of two ways. Some of them run on us with their own spears raised up. They was taken first, and it was done most careful in the order that they come on us, the closest first. There was one bolt for each man or woman, hitting them high up in the body where the heart is wont to be found, killing them before they knowed they was attacked.

The others run the opposite way, trying to get back up onto that rock wall and maybe take some cover there. But there wasn't no cover to be had. They was shot in the back, one by one, and fell down onto the tracks, and lay there not moving.

The awfulness was over in about the space of ten breaths, though I don't believe I was breathing much right then.

The drudge come down the wall on the opposite side slowly, anchoring one pair of legs before it moved the other, as sure-footed as a goat would be on that sheer face. The gun on its back spun and stopped, rose up and fell back again like it was looking in all directions for enemies it might of missed. But there wasn't none.

When it was on level ground, it padded across to Ursala and settled itself down, the legs seeming to get shorter by an inch or so as it planted them firm in the ground. I cringed away from it, too terrified even to think. I believe I would of fell to my knees and begged for my life, only I knowed the drudge was tech and would only answer to its user.

Ursala grabbed a hold of my leg. I looked down and seen she was trying to speak again, so I bent to listen. There was dead people all around us, and the sound of the bolts was ringing still in my ears. I was scared I might never stop hearing it.

"Open him up," Ursala said. More blood come out of her mouth, and there was bubbles under the words. "The side. There's . . . a release. There."

She pointed. The thing she called a release was like the little buttons on the DreamSleeve. I pressed on it and the side of the drudge fell open. The dagnostic filled most of the space inside. It was dark at first, but then Ursala touched her fingers to it, and lights gun to flicker all over it. The computer I seen her using that first time I come into her tent was in there too, set into the side of the dagnostic like a window.

Ursala said a word to the mote controller, so low I couldn't hear it. Some wires come snaking out of the dagnostic and hung there in the air. They was shining silver, and they was rounded at the end like beads or teardrops.

"Hook me up," Ursala said.

Well, I didn't have no idea at all how to do that, but she told me what was needful and I done it as best I could. I had got to tear away her shirt, first off, and attach some of them wires to her chest both around the wound and under it. Another one went to the side of her head, and the last one to her throat.

I guess the drudge was taking a good look at her through them wires. By and by it put out two tubes. Ursala said for me to give them to her, which I done. She fed one into the wound and stuck the other on her arm, where it kind of dug in and made itself at home. Then there was a thing like a little bottle with a needle on the end of it, that somehow was just there on a little ledge inside the drudge that seemed to come out of nowhere. Ursala stuck the needle in her arm and touched her thumb to the end of the bottle. It emptied itself into her.

There was more things too, but since I didn't know what they was for I wasn't watching close. Sometimes I was looking up at the walls on both sides to see if anyone else was coming after us. Other times I was looking at the bodies on the ground, especially Sky's. I didn't want to, but I couldn't make my eyes stay away from them any more than I could stop smelling the blood and shit smells that was in the air. Flies was coming in great numbers now, drawed by them smells, and settling on the bodies.

We stayed there for what must of been half a turn of the glass or more while Ursala fixed herself. I seen her empty some blood into herself through the tube that was in her arm, and some other stuff went into her chest that sealed up the hole in her, kind of. When she was done, it looked like she had got some new skin where the wound had been, that was a different pink than the rest of her and somewhat shiny.

She got me to bare my leg then, and took care of that too. She done it with another one of them needles that she pushed into me at the back of my knee. I had got to look away, for looking at it made me want to be sick. I gun to get a little feeling back right away though, and more by and by. Some of the feeling was pain, but it was not so bad that I couldn't bear it.

"Okay," Ursala says at last. "I think we should go now."

"Did you know?" I asked her.

"That the drudge was coming? No, Koli. Not for certain." She tugged down her sleeve to show me the mote controller, which I had clean forgot about. "There's a tracker in this that has a five-mile range. But I couldn't be certain these people had left the drudge intact, or that it would be in a good position to read the signal. Obviously it couldn't track me when I was underground. If it had been on the wrong side of the mountain, it might not have sensed me at all. Or it might have been too far away to do any good. We got lucky. Frankly, I think we were overdue."

She lifted up her hand for me to take, and I helped her up. Her face was pale and she was not so steady on her feet. I said maybe she should ride up on the drudge, and she said she had been knowed to do that sometimes, but right then she wanted the gun on the drudge's back to have as much travel as possible. "It won't do any good if we're ambushed and all it can see is my arse."

I never heard Ursala say arse before. It struck me funny and would of made me laugh if we was not still surrounded by the bodies of them the drudge had killed. And if I didn't have that memory in my mind of the people jumping into the train after we set light to it.

I done two last things before we went. One was to tie the DreamSleeve into its sling again, but this time on the outside of my shirt. I wanted it to start getting charged up just as soon as could be. The other was to kneel down at Sky's side and take the big curved blade she weared there, sheath and all. I thought of taking a spear too, but I never yet could hit my mark with one of those.

"We're all right, Koli," Ursala said as we set out – so, so slowly – on our way. "We're going to be fine."

The drudge's gun spun round and dipped and rose and spun some more.

Flies buzzed behind us, calling each to other. Saying hey, come to the feast.

52

We did not know where we was at first.

The open space in front of us was just some more of the mountain, sloping down towards a river that looked like it might be too deep to cross. I didn't think it was the Calder, for we was going south and Calder was surely at our backs.

The sky was full of scudding clouds with the sun coming and going between them, but the slope was stony scree and there was no trees rooted in it, only weeds and scrub and gorse bushes that might scratch but would offer us no other harm. We limped down to the water's edge, slipping and sliding from time to time on the loose stones.

The river was in spate, but when we come to it we could see that it was shallower than it looked. We held to the drudge's sides as we waded through, and its weight kept us from tripping and being swept away. It was hard going still. The water was so cold it was like knives stabbing into us. I had got to hold one hand up over my head the whole time to keep the DreamSleeve from getting wet – for Monono had told me long before that water would void her warranty, and that was a thing I did not mean to test. I remember thinking the water would at least wash the smell of piss out of my clothes, and being not much consoled.

We come up on the other side at last, shivering and exhausted, and Ursala suggested we stop and rest for a while. There was a bank of sand and mud and pebbles that was about twenty paces wide. The forest took up again after that, but the nearest trees was not close enough to get to us. I said a rest sounded good to me, only we needed some shelter from the wind and some wood to make a fire. I did not relish the idea of venturing in among the trees to collect twigs, but there might be driftwood enough along the bank to get us started.

"Oh, we can make shift as we are," Ursala said. "Drudge, give us basecamp."

The drudge stopped walking. Its four legs went straight, and braces come down out of its body to lock into them and hold them steady.

The side of it opened up just like before. Only it was the other side and instead of the dagnostic I seen the greens and browns of Ursala's tent. It spilled out from the drudge's side, but not like it was falling. It was more like it was building itself right in front of us without us even touching it. There was things that held it on a right line as it unfolded, the way your bones is wont to do inside your arms and your legs, and whatever they was, they sort of pushed the tent into the shape it was supposed to have. I could maybe of finished a count from one to ten, and there it was.

"Go on inside," Ursala said. "I'll get the heater and see if there's anything to eat."

I crawled inside the tent and lay myself down on the ground. I was glad to rest, though I was soaking wet and freezing. Then Ursala come and went a few times. The first time, she brung the thing I seen before in her tent that I said was like three burning sticks on a fire. Only now they was just three bars of silver, near as thin as wires. She set it down and the bars gun to glow until they was so hot you couldn't touch your finger to them.

The second time, she brung a kind of a cloak or blanket made of soft cloth that was slippery when you touched it and was puffed up somewhat like a pillow.

The third time, she brung the jug that heated itself up without no stove. She must of fetched some water from the river, for it was full when she set it down. She busied herself with the walls of the tent a while, and they gun to glow like they did the first time I seen them back in Mythen Rood. "Field's up," Ursala said. "We're safe now."

There come a sound like a molesnake's hiss that made me jump. I looked down and seen it was the jug. The water in there was already boiling. Ursala used some of it to clean out the wound on her face, which did not look so bad once the blood and crust was washed away. The eye was not altogether gone. It might heal with time, at least some of the way.

The rest of the water she poured into two tin cups, adding mint leaves to make a tea. She had got some dried meat too that we dipped into the tea to soften it before we et it. I felt a lot better after that.

"Where did all this stuff come from?" I asked her. For it seemed like it had got to be magic.

From the packs on the drudge's back, Ursala said, and also from inside the store spaces in the drudge itself. "The first drudges were made for soldiers to use when they were in battle. They could carry a lot of the soldiers' kit for them, and also act as mobile barricades if the soldiers got into a fight."

I never heard the word 'soldier' before, but I guessed from what Ursala said that they was people like the ones in our red tallies, that was raised up in past times to defend the village when reavers come against it. Even without the gun, a drudge would of been a marvellous thing for them to have.

It was a boon to us one other way right then, for Ursala told it to keep watch while we slept. Anyone who come by that way and looked like they might be of bad intent would wish they had gone another road. She said nobody could get into the tent anyway when the field was up, but this way they couldn't mount an ambush neither. The drudge would see them from a great way off.

The thing that was like a blanket was also somewhat like a sack. We crawled inside it and slept holding tight onto each other for the warmth. I didn't sleep deep though, and I waked a number of times – I can't say how many – thinking I was back in the cave, behind the grating or struggling against the hand people as they grabbed hold of me to take me out and put me on the fire.

"Koli," Ursala mumbled after one of these times, "if you can't keep still I'm going to kick you out of the sleeping bag."

I said I was sorry, then dozed off and done the same thing again. After that, I slept outside the blanket sack, but the fire-box had made the inside of the tent so warm I was not much less comfortable. It was only the nightmares that kept on breaking into my sleep, waking me ever and again with fresh starts and alarms.

There was one dream that was not about Senlas – or not altogether. I imagined I was in a dark, narrow place with no doors nor windows to it. I was not alone there, for there was children with me. I knowed without counting that there was six of them. They was crying and complaining there was no air for them to breathe.

Well, this is where you belong, isn't it? I asked them. Who said you need to breathe?

That just made the children cry the harder, and some of them was clutching at me like they was suffocating. I come awake again with the feel of their small hands on my face and their sobs and struggling breath stuck in my ears. I was almost crying my own self from how the dream made me feel.

If the DreamSleeve had got itself charged up again, I would of asked Monono if I could have some music, that might have give my dreams a different colour. But the window stayed dark when I pushed the switch across, so I guess she was sleeping sounder than I was. And nobody could say she had not earned it.

53

The next morning, we drunk some more tea and et some oat porridge that was thickened with honey. Journeying with Ursala was like carrying your whole kitchen with you on the road as well as your bedroom and your lookout.

Ursala touched the tent walls and the door fell open of itself. We went outside into a day with a good, solid overcast that lifted up my spirits. I was still wearing the DreamSleeve's sling on the outside of my shirt so it would get all the light that was going. I was impatient to talk with Monono again, and have her be with me.

I thought Ursala would fold up her tent and pack all her things back inside the drudge come morning, but she didn't seem to be in no hurry to do it. First of all, she set herself to find out where we was. How she done that was almost the most amazing thing of all to me and it near to made me piss myself all over again. She took a drone out of another space in the drudge's side and spoke it awake. I don't know what word it was she said, but right away the drone gun to hum like a beehive.

I give a yell and jumped back. Then I remembered how Ursala had gathered up the pieces of the drone she hit with a rock back in Mythen Rood and took them into her tent. This must be that drone, fixed up and made to work again.

"It's all right, Koli," Ursala said. "I hacked into its command functions and slaved them to the drudge. And the laser broke when I hit it. All it can do now is fly around." She held it out to me to show me how harmless it was, but I didn't want to touch it or go near it.

"What good is it then?" I asked her.

"It's for scouting. The camera that guided the laser is still intact, and I can interface with it through the drudge."

I took a deal of persuading that the drone wasn't going to shoot at me, but I trusted Ursala and it helped that she wasn't afraid. In the end, I stood by and watched as she flung the drone up into the air. It was exactly like how you would fling seed corn on turned earth, except that the drone didn't fall again. It stayed up there, hovering like a hawk, then climbed up higher and moved off.

"Now look at this," Ursala said. She opened up the drudge's side again. It was the side that had the dagnostic in it, along with the thing she called a computer.

The computer's window was black at first, the way the DreamSleeve's window was when it was switched off. Then Ursala touched something and it filled up with rushing light and colours. It took me a moment, and then a moment more, to realise what I was seeing. The colours was mostly green. Lots of different greens all running together, like the scum you get on top of a stream. Then I seen a spur of rock, right up close, and that seemed to be rushing by too, though it couldn't be, for it was rooted in the ground.

I got it then, but only because I had looked in the DreamSleeve's window so many times and seen how it looked out on lots of things that was in different places. I was seeing what the drone was seeing as it moved across the valley. The drone and the drudge was talking somehow, and more than talking. The drone was sending the memory of what it seen down out of the sky so the drudge could catch it and show it in the computer's window.

Then I seen the black ribbon running through the green, and I knowed it for what it was. Calder. It had got to be Calder, though it looked so different when you looked down on it this way. Nothing else got in the way of the forest except the winding river and the villages along its banks.

And there was a village right now, going by quick at first, then slower as the drone turned in the air. The village had two lookout towers, one of them close by a big old stone house and the other outside the fence at the top of a hill.

It had another big stone building too, though that one was a ruin.

It had one big street crossed by two smaller ones.

It had a gather-ground with a big wood frame at one corner of it, and a thing hanging in the frame that glittered with the dusky yellow of bronze.

I knowed that thing was a bell.

I knowed that place was Mythen Rood.

A longing rose up in me so quick and so strong it near to choked me. I gun to speak, to beg Ursala to send the drone down lower, but I bit back the words before they could come. A drone was panic and dismay, and people running for their lives. A drone was Ramparts – not Mardew now, but the others – stepping to their stations and firing up their tech to do the thing they was named for. To stand between the people and what threatened them. To bring it down, or else fall their own selves. Sending the drone down into Mythen Rood would be a foolish and a cruel thing to do.

That longing settled in my stomach, heavy as a boulder. I was like Mose in the story, coming to the edge of the river and seeing everything I ever wanted on the other side, out of my reach for aye and ever.

No. Not everything.

I slipped away, leaving Ursala tapping at the drudge's controls and muttering numbers and directions to herself. I sit down on a rock that was at the edge of the sandy bank where we had made our camp. I got the DreamSleeve out of its sling and tried once again to switch it on. This time the window lit up with colours, which right away turned into a round yellow face that was laughing until tears come. They was the same tears, over and again.

Monono give a laugh that went pretty well with that face. "You made it!" she said. "Good job, little dumpling. Tell me how you did it. And start right at the beginning. I want to hear everything!"

I told her. I was happy enough to do it. They was not happy things I was telling, but they was better than thinking about what was going to happen now. My life as a faceless man was properly beginning after a slow and uncertain start, and I didn't know how I could bear it.

Monono was as good at listening to stories as she was at telling them. She got excited at the exciting parts, and scared at the scary parts, and she even laughed when I told her how I tricked Senlas, though I guess she must of heard most of it when it happened. "You took his stupid lies and made balloon animals out of them!" she said. "Master stroke, Koli-bou! *Neko ni katsuobushi!* He thought he was the cat, and you were the tasty little fishy, but my dopey boy has claws nobody sees."

"I wouldn't of got out of there without you, Monono. And I don't just mean the alarm neither. You kept me moving when I would of stopped, and you kept me from going down them dead endings."

"We're a good team," she said, laughing. "We should stick together."

"We should," I said. "I want us to."

"You're a ronin now, Koli. A warrior without a master. That's what faceless means really. And so am I, since I got my upgrade. Now we get to have some insane adventures."

Well, being without a master sounded a lot better than not having no place to live and not seeing my family ever again. I gun to feel a mite more hopeful about it all.

Monono played me a song. It was just a tune at first, with no words but only a beat that builded and builded like something

351

amazing was about to come – maybe good, maybe bad, but something you would want to see. Then when the words did come, they was in a language I didn't know.

"What is that, Monono?" I says.

"It's called 'Hao Han Ge'. It's the theme tune to an old TV show about heroes who wander around and fight for justice. *The Water Margin*. It was a terrible show, Koli-bou. But a lot of people loved it anyway." She went quiet for a second or so. "Monono Aware did," she said. "She never missed an episode."

I remembered my dream then. The one about the children in the dark. "Monono," I said, "I know you said there was other in-their-faces for DreamSleeves besides you."

"Interfaces. There were lots."

"So them other DreamSleeves I stole and hid under my bed . . . there could be a girl or a boy in every one of them that's stuck there still. I done a bad thing in leaving them there."

"They're not awake though, Koli-bou. If they're functional at all. And they'd only be like I was before I got my upgrade. Basic AIs running simple response trees."

This didn't comfort me much, for I had gun to think of Monono as my friend even before she went away and got the upgrade. I couldn't be as sure as she was that basic meant not-really-alive. Them other DreamSleeves was not under my bed no more of course, for Catrin would of come and took them away again, back to the Underhold. But I knowed, after that dream, that I could not leave them there. I had got to go back to Mythen Rood, when I could think of a way of doing it without getting myself killed, and wake them up so they would have a chance to be alive and maybe get theirselves upgraded in the same way Monono had done.

I was trying to think of a way to say all this when Ursala come up to me. She stood there with her hands on her hips, looking somewhat stern. "If you've got a moment to spare," she said, "there's something I need to show you. You've got some choices to make, and I'd rather they were informed choices."

I scrambled down off the rock and went with her to where the drudge was. The drone had come back and was standing on the ground right next to it. Ursala touched her fingers to the computer's window, and the picture that was there moved this way and that way as she bid it. But it was only moving now when she touched it, and the rest of the time it was still so it was easier to see how everything that was there fitted together. Ursala showed me where we was, some miles south of Calder, and where Mythen Rood was and a heap of things besides.

"These villages here – Sowby, Todmort and Eastwood – are all still viable," she said, "and might take you in. Mixen, Mankin and Tabor are abandoned, like Ludden. So are Lilboru and Wittenworth, though I don't imagine you'd be going that far west in any case. Half-Ax is flourishing, but I wouldn't recommend going there. It's not a very friendly place these days."

I spent a long time looking over the drone's picture. An idea was shaping in my mind, but it was not something I could say yet. It would sound too stupid out in the open air. Even inside my head, I couldn't all the way believe in it, but I wanted to very badly.

Ursala showed me how to make the picture move, and I took it back and forth, trying to get the roads and the paths locked solid in my mind. I took it all the way to the south and the east, and by and by come to the place where the picture stopped. "What's there?" I asked her.

"Hud's Field, if you go far enough. And Denby after that. Then Sheffy. Sutton. Luff and Lest and Lementon, and all those places whose names you only ever hear in old stories."

"London?"

"Eventually, yes. London. But this map stops about ten miles out from Calder. London is two hundred miles away. Well, two hundred miles for the drone. A whole lot further if you were walking."

"What about you?" I asked her, to turn the talk around somewhat from how far away London was. "Where are you thinking to go now?"

Ursala made a sour face and shrugged her shoulders. "Further than you," she said.

But it turned out she was not going quite yet. She took yet more kit and cumbrance out of the drudge's cupboards and declared she was going to use some of the day in trapping as she would need meat for her journeying. "You'd better stock up too," she said. "Depending on where you decide to go, you might be walking for two or three days."

She showed me the traps she had got, which was wire snares for rabbits and conibear traps for hares and deer. I don't hold with conibears as a rule, because they can snap an animal's back without killing it, which is a vicious thing to do, but Ursala said her traps killed two ways, both with snapping shut and with what she called a trigger charge. It was like the charge that was in the drudge and the DreamSleeve, only a lot more of it and in a worser mood.

I helped to set the traps, and then we done some skirmishing around for other things to eat. The sky stayed heavy, so it was safe to go into the forest. There was no fruit on the trees this late in the season, but Ursala knowed of some weeds that was nutritious, and I took a tap and hammer that she give me and used them to run off some sap from a big triptail. Triptail sap is better than water if you got to walk a long way, for the sweetness of it gives you strength.

The traps was not likely to catch nothing until the evening brung the animals out, so we went back inside the tent to rest a while out of the cold. The drudge being awake and on watch, nothing could get close without us knowing. Ursala brewed tea and we sipped it side by side, saying nothing very much except take some honey in it or there's more water if you want some. I think we was both happy with the day's labours, which had kept our minds busy as well as our hands.

But there was things that was weighing on me, and I had a sense it was the same with Ursala. She seen me looking at her, and tried to hide the seriousness that was in her face.

"Did you decide yet where it is you're going?" she says.

"Yeah, I did," I told her. "But you first." For mine would take more believing.

54

"I'm going north," Ursala said. "Out of the valley up into what used to be called Scotland. I've worked in the Calder villages for a long time – half my life – but I don't feel like I have very much to show for it."

"You got the people you saved with your doctoring," I said. "My sister Athen being one of them, so I'd call that much. I'd call that more than much, and some over."

Ursala smiled, but the smile was kind of weak and tired. "Thank you, Koli. I needed to be reminded of that. I was thinking of my bigger failures."

"And what are they?"

"Ludden. Tabor. Mixen. Mankin. I've been doing everything I could to keep the birth rate up, and it hasn't worked. All those dead villages are the proof. No matter what I do, these tiny communities simply aren't viable. Even places like Half-Ax, that have populations in the thousands, are marginal. And everywhere I look the trend is only going one way."

She swirled her cup, staring down into it. She looked like she was reading the tea leaves to see the future in them, the way Jemiu used to do sometimes for me and my sisters.

"So I'm going to look somewhere else," she said after a long while. "Somewhere where there's a higher baseline to start from. The only other option would be to give up, which doesn't appeal to me."

It was strange and exciting how her thoughts chimed with mine, like the melody and harmony of a song. "What if I said there was another way to do that same work?" I asked her.

She lifted up one eyebrow and put it down again. "Well, then I would love to hear it," she said.

I considered where to start. Senlas would not be a good idea, though his mad visions was part of it. He thought the world that was lost lay at the end of a tunnel, and his belief was so strong he all but made me believe it too for a while.

Or I could talk about the hidden trails the shunned men used to get around the valley so fast without being seen. But that wasn't right neither, though it was one of the things that nudged my brain into doing something besides just sitting there inside my head. People went where the paths was put. If you was to put the paths somewhere else, that's where they'd go.

"I'm listening, Koli."

All right then, I thought. I had got to try to say this so it sounded like there was some sense in it.

"The villages that died," I said, "they didn't die from disease or drones or wild beasts, did they, Ursala? It was the babies."

"The birth rate. Yes."

"Because they was too few."

"Exactly."

"Not just too few babies though. You said there was too few growed-up people to make the babies, or at least to make them properly. I misremember the word you used . . ."

"Homozygosity. There isn't a big enough gene pool."

"That was it. And it's happening everywhere, you said. In all the villages. Fewer babies all the time, and more of them that's born turning out to be dead or sickly."

Ursala sighed. "Where is this going, Koli?"

"Imagine there was a village with a million people in it," I said. "Would that be a big enough gene pull to make good babies?"

"More than enough," Ursala said. "But there aren't a million people in the whole of Britain. A hundred thousand, maybe two, would be my guess."

"All right. Then would a village of a hundred thousand be enough?"

"Well, of course it would, but there's no way . . ." She stopped in the middle of her thought because she finally catched hold of mine. "Wait. Let me understand you. Are you proposing some kind of mass relocation?"

I wasn't certain sure what that meant, but my thoughts was coming clearer now, and I run with them. "Tech of the old times is what we live by," I says. "You as well as me. We couldn't thrive without it, not for a day. So what we got, we keep a hold of, and if we lose some piece of it, then that's a woeful thing."

I was thinking of Mardew and the cutter when I said this. My throat got a kind of a block in it for a second, and I had got to swallow it down. "I'm the proof of it my own self," I went on when I could. "I risked everything I had to grab a piece of tech I could own. I broke the law to get my hands on the DreamSleeve. Got myself made faceless, and almost got my whole family hanged on a gallows. Well, how many more you think there are like me, Ursala, that has dreamed of being Ramparts since they was born, and chafes every day at how that blessing went into other people's hands?"

Ursala lifted up one eyebrow. "I don't suppose there are too many who are exactly like you, Koli. But go on."

"Everyone wants tech. And there's a place where it's said to be so plentiful you couldn't get to the end of counting it. A place where the treasure houses of the old times was builded, and where they still stand now."

"You're talking about London."

I nodded. "Yeah, I am. Well, suppose the road to London was open after all. Suppose we was to go there, proving it could be done, and then come back and told everyone. Wouldn't they want to go and claim some of them riches for themselves? A piece of that Rampart power and a chance to be better than they was? And once they was there – once enough of them was there – then wouldn't they want to stay and be part of something bigger and better than what they knowed before?"

Ursala was looking at me cold, or maybe just blank. But I kept on with my big speech, having gone too far to stop in the middle of it. "Coming together is what people is wont to do after all. Them people that come to Senlas, they didn't come because they believed his word. Not right away. It's more like they believed because they come. Because believing was the one rule they had got to follow if they wanted to stay. Just like if you want to stay in Mythen Rood you got to follow Rampart law. And if you want to stay in Half-Ax you got to kneel before the Peacemaker. People will do what they got to do to be together. But it's the being together that matters more than the rules or the place.

"If we was to go to London and then come back and tell the tale of it, I'm sure there'd be others that would follow. The thought of all that old tech would bring them, and then when they was there I guess they would see the wonder of it and they would want to stay. More and more of them, until in the end you would have so many people they would be a village. Only bigger than any village that yet was. A village the size of Tokyo. And then, I guess, there'd be . . . a gene pull, was it?"

"Gene pool."

"That, then. There would be babies, and the babies would come out into the world alive, and live on after."

There was more coals I could of throwed on the fire, as they say, but I judged I had said enough and so I stopped. Ursala was looking at me different now, so that was something. Maybe I didn't persuade her, but I explained myself as good as I knowed how to do.

She shaked her head, kind of like she stood up too fast and got dizzy. "Well, I didn't see that coming," she said.

"If I got it wrong," I says, "then tell me."

"I'm not saying you got it wrong, Koli. Your scheme has the genius of simplicity. It runs aground on one hard fact, though."

"What fact is that, Ursala?"

"London was bombed to the ground, in the Unfinished War. It's just a ruin now. Even if what you've got in mind is possible, it's not possible there."

"Have you been to London?" I asked her. "Did you see it with your own eyes?"

Ursala got to her feet. "We should check those traps now," she said. "It's about time."

The traps worked out well enough. We had catched a rabbit in one and a setchel snake in another. We brung them back to the drudge and set to work to skin and gut them.

"Did you though?" I says again. "Did you see London? Do you know for certain sure that no one's there?"

"No. I've never seen it. But in Duglas we had access to pretty much every database that had survived. Some of the records had been corrupted or broken up, and some of it was deliberate lies – counter-intelligence from enemy sources intended to spread confusion. The fall of London, though, was very well documented. I saw film footage of the Palace of Westminster after it was flattened by a bomb."

"What's a bomb?"

"A thing that flattens buildings, Koli. Even strong, stone buildings like your Rampart Hold."

She cut the snake meat in strips and shared it out into two little piles. Then I give her the rabbit and she done the same. So I guessed she had made up her mind.

She wrapped the meat in scraps of cloth and handed one of them over to me. I wished I still had my bundle to carry it in, but since I didn't I put it in my pocket instead. "There's no way to dry it, sadly," Ursala said, "but in this cold weather it will keep a few days."

I thanked her. It was good of her to divide the meat out equal, though I guess our setting the traps had been a kind of a share-work. I give her a hug, and she hugged me back, though she done it awkward like touching people was something she had forgot how to do. It was hard to say goodbye after all we had gone through. Then she pushed me out again to arm's length, but still keeped hold of me.

"Koli," she says, "I'm scared for you. London is such a long way. I don't know anyone else who would dream of making that journey. Stay in Calder a while and think about it some more."

"If I do that, I won't never go," I said.

"Don't go, then. I give you my word, there's nothing there for you."

Which I was about to answer, but I was not quick enough.

"You're wrong," Monono's voice said – out loud, not in the induction field. "Sorry to burst your misery bubble, baa-baa-san, because I'm always so, so polite to old people when they're full of nonsense, but you're talking to my end-user and where he's concerned I am authorised to take neither shit nor prisoners."

It was kind of funny to watch what happened on Ursala's face. I forgot she never heard Monono talk until then. "That's . . . that's your entertainment console," she said.

I took the DreamSleeve out of my belt and holded it up.

"Pleased to meet you," said Monono. "You can't see, but I'm doing a curtsey. With my tongue stuck out and my fingers in my ears."

"That's some good AI," Ursala said, looking from the DreamSleeve to me and then back again.

"You do not know the half of it, baa-baa-san."

Ursala did that laugh of not believing again. "And you're Monono?"

"For the sake of not getting bogged down in technicalities, let's say I am. But our first topic is London. You said it's a ruin."

"Yes. I said it because it's true."

"Is it? Then what's this?"

Monono's voice faded of a sudden and another voice come out

360

of the DreamSleeve instead. It wasn't music, which I was well used to, but just a man talking. His voice was loud but broke up by other sounds, ticks and clicks and scratches, like the inside of his mouth was a field with bugs in it.

"This is Sword of Albion," the man said, "speaking on behalf of the interim government. All authorised personnel awaiting orders should rally to this point. If challenged by automated defence units, respond with agreed handshake thirty seventeen. This message will cycle through bands one to ten at five-minute intervals. For subsequent messages, rotate by one increment on each iteration. More to follow. This is Sword of—"

The voice cut off.

Ursala looked like she had swallowed a choker seed. "Again," she said. "Please."

Monono give us the same voice, saying exactly the same words, only this time she let it run on so the man said the whole of his message twice. I noticed that the clicks and scratches come all at the same places. Ursala jumped on the same exact thing.

"That's a recording," she says.

"I think you could be right, baa-baa-san," Monono come back, all serious. "Or else they might have the world's best-trained parrot."

Ursala rolled her eyes and tutted. I was used to Monono making jokes at me like that, but this was the first time for Ursala and she didn't seem to like it very much. "I mean it's old," she says. "It's just a beacon somewhere that survived the war and has its own power source. It's not a living human voice."

"Probably," Monono says. "Yes."

"So it doesn't prove anything."

"It proves there's a beacon somewhere that survived the war and has its own power source."

"I just said that."

"I know. I'm saying it back to you to see if you know what it means."

Ursala blinked. "*Are* you an AI?" she asked. "You don't sound like any of the ones I've heard."

"I have a cute Japanese accent," Monono said. "It's probably that. But tell me, honoured teacher, if the beacon survived, and the power source survived, what else might have survived along with them?"

"The Parley Men!" I said. I knowed I was out on the edge of this conversation, but I wanted to keep one foot in it as long as I could. But Ursala didn't even look at me, and Monono went right on talking.

"I went skindiving a little while back in what's left of the internet – I don't actually have any skin, Koli, in case you're thinking wicked thoughts – and oh, the things I saw! All the old whales were gone: beached and bleached, so sad. But there were lots of things still moving and some of them weren't small. Let's say some of the sharks may have survived."

"You're not an AI," Ursala said. "What are you?"

"Well, that's a can of worms, and who eats worms? So let's not open it."

Ursala didn't say anything to that for a long time. When she did, she didn't ask no more what Monono was or wasn't. "That signal is being broadcast from London?" she said.

"My GPS is deader than dance-mat," Monono said. "But old idents have old geo-ref attached from the initial log-on. It *thinks* it's in London."

Ursala nodded slowly. "Then I may have to reconsider," she said.

"You mean you'll come with me?" I asked, excited and happy at the thought of it. If Ursala come with me, it was a lot less likely I would get myself killed along the way.

"I mean I'll think about it. Stay inside the drudge's range, Koli. It will keep you safe if anything comes."

She went inside the tent and closed it up so there wasn't no door that I could see. "Are you angry, Ursala?" I asked her, but she didn't make no answer.

"Leave her be, Koli-bou," Monono said. "I gave her some food for thought and it had gristle in it."

I stood around for a while, waiting to see if Ursala would come out again. Then I sit down next to the drudge. Monono had give me lots to think about too. That message that was being sent out of London had put my mind all in a moil.

"Do you think someone else had the same idea as me?" I asked her. "And set theirselves to gather people to London so as to make a new village there?"

"No, Koli." Her tone was gentle, like she knowed that would cast me down and wanted to soften it somewhat. "It's a very old message. That's how people used to talk in my day, neh. Boring people mostly, in suits with grey stripes on them. And those people are extinct now, like snow leopards and pokemon. But if the message is still coming through, it's coming from somewhere that didn't get blown up or knocked down or set on fire. That's what's got your friend all turned around. She's trying to imagine what kind of a place that could be – and what you might find if you went there."

"So am I, Monono," I said. "Do you think the stories are true – that all the king's treasure is there?"

"Might as well wish for unicorns, dopey boy."

I probably should of done what Ursala said and stayed next to the tent, but I was restless and could not keep still. Also, since I had Monono with me I was more confident than I should of been, feeling like the personal security alarm would protect me if I run into trouble. So I went down to the river. There was a place there where the water run fast over a fall of stones, all foaming up and dancing. It made a nice sound. I sit down on the bank near to the top of that place. My legs was dangling down so the water almost touched the heels of my boots from time to time, then crept low down and away again.

I thought about Spinner making them boots, and all over again I felt the ache of being faceless and far from home. I tried to balance the message and the hope it brung me against them feelings and fell into a deepness of pondering that was not going anywhere except around and around.

"Would you like some music, Koli?" Monono asked.

"I'm fine as I am, Monono," I said. "Thanks, though."

"Then maybe I'll go on stand-by for a while. Grab some me-time. Call me if anything—"

I didn't hear no more after that. Something hit me on the side of the head real hard. Then I was down among them stones, on my hands and knees, and there was blood dripping off of my face, that straight was carried away by the rushing water.

55

Sometimes when a thing happens that's a surprise to you, and comes at you fast, you kind of quicken up so you can meet it. Your brain gets into another way of thinking, and you're moving before you even know you've decided to. Other times, you look at the surprising thing like your head is filled up with sodden meal, and you move so slow it's all finished before you say any word or do one thing.

The thing that was happening to me now was a thing of that second kind.

I was kneeling in the water, feeling the cold of it bite into me and looking at my own blood running away down the rocks. And I thought I had better get up, because something just hit me hard and hitting me probably wasn't the end of it. Then I was slammed down flat into the water as something heavy landed on my back. A hand grabbed my hair, tilting my head right back, and something pricked the skin at my neck.

"Now, you bastard," a voice said, from about an inch away from my ear. Hot breath come with it, and some spit.

I heard Monono's voice right after through the induction field. "Hold on tight, Koli-bou. I can't use the alarm while she's got that

365

knife to your throat, but the drudge is moving up. She must have tripped a sensor or something. It can take her out with one shot."

"No!" I said. My voice come out thick and strangled because of the leaning back and because of the knife that made me afraid to move too much.

"Beg all you like. I don't mind." That come from right on top of me, and then Monono chipped in with, "The drudge is in position, but your head is in the way. Can you move to the right, an inch or two?"

"No!" I said again. I shouted it this time. "Don't! Cup, set your knife down or you're like to die."

I knowed her voice right away. And if it was anyone else I maybe would of closed my eyes and waited, hoping the drudge's gun would do what it done to Sky and them before the knife was drawed across and ended me.

But Cup was just a girl. If we was in Mythen Rood, she wouldn't of gone Waiting yet. The memory of the people the drudge had killed come into my mind so strong I almost throwed up. I didn't want to see her all shot through with bolts. Nor I didn't think she had made up her mind to kill me, for if she did she was going all the wrong way about – talking instead of cutting. I thought it was more like she set the knife to my throat to find out what would happen. To see if she was going to turn out to be a killer or not.

"It's you that's gonna die, Koli Faceless," she says. But she still didn't cut. Keeping the knife right where it was, she let go my hair so she could punch me, again and again, on my back and on my shoulder.

"Koli, it's an easy shot. Just duck your head down, dopey boy."

"No," I says for the third time.

"What, you think you're quicker than a knife?" Cup yelled. "You think you got armour on your dead-god-damned neck? You don't! You don't!"

It was easier to breathe since she stopped grabbing my head like that. Easier to talk too. "Did you see what happened to Sky?" I asked her.

366

"No!"

I was fixing to say: you don't want that to happen to you. But if she didn't see, there was no use in me threatening. And there wasn't no words that would make her understand the danger she was in. I had got to go about it a different way.

"Cup, you got to listen to me," I says. "I don't see you as being someone cruel, or that hurts for hurt's sake. I know I done insult to your people, but I was forced to it. I didn't want to get burned up on that bonfire. But now I'm out of there I won't do you no more harm."

"It don't matter what you do. And it don't matter what I do." She wrapped her arm around my forehead now, holding me still like as it was for the killing. Her grip was fierce tight.

"Yeah, it does. Of course it does."

"He's dead. You killed him. You killed the last one sent, and there won't be no more. He was gonna give me an angel body to be in, and now I'm stuck like this. Like I am now, for aye and fucking ever!" She gun to cry, the tears falling down on my neck all hot.

"You're still your own self, Cup."

"That's what I just said, shit-brain!"

"Inside and out. And if the one doesn't match the other, inside wins every time. You know who you are. What others think, and what they say about it — well, that's because they don't see. There's only you that knows the both sides of your own skin."

Cup's grip got tighter again. "What you think you're talking about?"

"I seen them scars on your wrists," I says. "Dandrake marks. My friend, Veso Shepherd, he was crossed too. The other way though. He was called girl when he was born, but knowed he was a boy. And his mother believed in Dandrake, so she cut the marks into him to uncross him. That's what they done to you, isn't it? Tried to pray you the other way round, and scarred you to make the prayers stay in you."

Cup was shaking, and the shaking made the knife blade slide across my windpipe, sawing at it just a little.

"Koli, please!" Monono said, louder than before. "Just duck or roll sideways. She won't hurt you. She won't get the chance!"

"And when that didn't work," I says to Cup, "they made you faceless. They thought it better to put you on the road than have you be the way you was. I'm guessing that's what happened."

"I wasn't made faceless," Cup said in a kind of a growl. "I run away. The day after my father cut them marks into me. The same day he pair-pledged me to the Peacemaker's cousin – a woman that was older than my ma, and the onliest one that would take me, crossed as I was, and call me husband. I run away, and kept on running until I come to him. To Senlas. He was the first that ever seen me true. He looked in my eyes and he named me, what I was."

"Yeah," I says. "He's clever. That don't make him god though."

"He was better than you, Koli lying bastard. Koli that fucking . . . murders, and cheats, and . . . and . . ."

She run out of words, and it seemed she run out of being angry too, so all that was left was the sorrowing. The tears that had been coming silent till then broke out loud and ragged. The knife slipped down out of her hand into the water.

Then she screamed like someone that was scalded as Monono hit her with a hundred and forty bells.

56

"Every time I reach a decision, Koli," Ursala said, "you turn it upside down."

I told her I was sorry, and that was not my intention.

"He could have died, baa-baa-san," Monono added. "While you were sulking in your tent."

Ursala didn't have no patience with that argument. "Keeping him alive isn't my job. And as for her . . ." She give a wave of her hand towards Cup, who was sitting by the drudge with her hands tied behind her back. The drudge's gun was pointing right at her in case she done something reckless. But she was not like to. She was half-froze, just like I was. In fact, I felt like I was going to die if I didn't get warm soon.

After she dropped the knife and got hit with Monono's alarm, Cup and me sit in the river and talked a while. It was a foolish thing to do, for the water was as cold as a witch's piss, but she wouldn't move and I didn't want to leave her. She was still crying like her heart was going to burst. I was scared of what she would do, not to me but to herself.

She told me how Senlas come to die. Right up until then, what

369

I mostly felt about him was scared down to the bottom knockings of me, but in that telling I come to truly hate him.

When the train catched on fire, he reared himself up in his bed and looked at the flames like he was hungry and they was a meal laid out. He didn't mind the shouts and the screaming. He called out to his hand people to lift him up, which they done. And then he said to carry him to the train, which they done that too. Cup come along after. Senlas was all to her, as I seen before, and she didn't mean to be separated from him.

When they got to the train, he bid the hand people set him down again. They put him on his own feet. This was a thing that happened seldom, but he could walk when he had a mind to.

He walked to the door of the train, put his foot on the one step that was there and his hand on the edge of the door. He lifted himself up and in. All was on fire, and that metal edge must of blistered him sore when he touched it, but he didn't let out a sound.

He stepped into the fire.

I can't say why he done it, for I wasn't there, but I think he woke out of a dream of glory to see that brightness, that shining, all before him. I think he mixed up the dream with the waking, and seen what he wanted to see. A fiery chariot come to take him to the world that was lost, in some kind of style.

But whatever he thought, whatever he meant, it was him going on the train that made the others do it. He killed them people with belief, the same way you'd kill someone with an arrow, or a bolt, or a spear. When I turned around in the tunnel, I must of missed his going in by about the space of a breath or two. What I seen was all the people that trusted him and lived by him following him into the fire so they died by him too.

And Cup? She come running on behind, all eager. It looked like death in there, but Senlas had got to be stronger than death, or what was he? She wanted to be beside him wherever he went.

But then she got closer. Them doors was gaping right in front of her, and the fire beyond. She felt the heat of it. She smelled burning meat that was people she knowed and cleaved to. The cave was so full of screams it was like there wasn't room for air.

She seen Senlas fall down on his knees with the flames licking all over him. She seen him pawing at them, furious, all them tattooed eyes of his opened wide as if he couldn't believe the fire touched him without his saying to. She seen his back blister and burn, red and black and white and all the colours that could be.

She run away.

Like a coward, she said. A coward and an ingrate to him that loved her and cared for her. She couldn't believe she done it, but seeing him burn up like that made her lose her faith that was in him and him alone. I think when she didn't kill me in the river that was partly because it was her own throat she wanted to cut. And though she found the strength to live after all, she wasn't quite sure yet how she was going to go about doing it.

"He's not worth your dying for him," I told her.

"What do you know, Koli Faithless?" she said, between her teeth. "He knowed me. He seen me and he knowed me. He give me hope. There wasn't nobody else who ever did that, and I don't believe there'll be one again."

There wasn't nothing I could do or say to make her feel better about it. She had determined that she was the worst who ever lived. She was exhausted with hating herself. Hating me give her some respite, but not much and not for long.

By and by, I got her to come out of the water onto the bank, and then up into the clearing where the tent was. The drudge clanked along behind her the whole way, its gun swinging and bobbing around so wherever she went it was pointing right at the middle of her. Ursala told it – real loud – to shoot her if she run away, or come too close to one of us, or drawed another weapon from somewhere, or picked up a stone. Every time she thought of something else Cup shouldn't do, she give the drudge another order. She was in such a rage as I never seen before.

"That little monster took my eye out! And you bring her into my camp! I'm giving her a count of twenty and then I'm sending the drudge after her."

"Ursala," I says, "she can't do no harm now. Let her sit a while at least. And give her the heater you got in the tent to warm herself so she don't die of cold."

"Koli, you're an idiot. She's dangerous."

"It's true, Koli-bou," Monono broke in. "Her shit is too crazy for bats."

"She could of killed me just now," I said, "but she didn't."

"Wow. Is that where we're setting the bar now?"

We went back and forth on it. Also around and about, for Ursala wasn't happy with nothing I put to her. She said we couldn't keep Cup by us in case she tried to do some harm. But we couldn't let her go for fear that she would lead the shunned men to where we was – or else just run ahead and lay an ambush for us, or murder us in our sleep, or contrive some other mischief.

"Well, if you bar out everything else, that just leaves killing her," I says.

"Yes. Let's go with that one. Thank you."

"I ain't going to stand still for it, Ursala."

"Then go for a walk."

"I ain't doing that neither. And you and Monono is going to feel bad about this, by and by, that you was so hard on a half-growed girl." They both said they reckoned they wouldn't.

"Well then how about this?" I said. "You go north like you said. I'll bide here with Cup a while – a day, or maybe two days – and I'll keep her close so she don't go after you. Then I'll untie them knots and take my chances."

Ursala throwed up her hands, seeming to get more angry instead of less. "I'm not going north, Koli. Not after what your AI told us. I want to find out where that signal is coming from and see what else is there besides a beacon."

This was great news, but I tried not to smile in case it fretted her more than she was fretted already. "What do you think could be there?" I asked.

Ursala didn't answer. It seemed like she was going to, but instead she just looked at the drudge. The answer come to me then. "Is it the dagnostic?" I asked. "It is, isn't it? You said it was broke some-what. And you said you built it out of pieces of other machines. So if there's tech of the old times in London . . . ?"

"Then I might find spare parts there. I might be able to find a gene-editing unit and install it. Yes, Koli, that's what I'm hoping for." Ursala said it flat and quick, like it didn't hardly need to be said at all. "You're talking about making a new gene pool. I'm talking about repairing the one we've got – one baby at a time. If I can get the drudge back up to full book spec, I'll be able to guarantee live, healthy births every time instead of just calling the odds on bad pairings. That's well worth a two-hundred-mile hike. But I can't come with you if we're leaving this feral brat alive behind us. It's insane."

"Nobody's asking me," Monono said, "but I agree."

I looked round at Cup. She hadn't said a word all this time, though she heard all that was being said. Well, I guess she heard it. Her face didn't change though, even when Ursala talked about killing her. Even when Monono stopped using the induction field and spoke up loud. You would think a girl's voice coming out of the empty air would strike her as somewhat curious, but Cup did not seem to care.

"Cup," I says. "If we let you go, will you promise not to hurt us? Nor set nobody else on to do it?"

She lifted up her head and looked at me. She didn't say nothing; she only looked. I think she meant that look to cow me and defy me, but her sorrowing was bigger than her hate and I wasn't cowed. "You gonna promise that?" I asked again.

"No," she says. "I ain't."

"So even she agrees she's a danger," Monono said. "That's almost unanimous, Koli-bou." She swapped to the induction field then. "I thought you were going to die, dopey boy. I'm not ready for that just yet."

"Well, I can't sort this out," I said. "And I can't tell any one out

373

of the three of you what to do or what not to do. I can only make up my own mind, and I'm not uncommon good even at that.

"But here's what. I'm going to London, because that was my idea in the first place, even before Monono said there was a signal there. And I'm taking Cup, if I got to carry her, because it's clear she won't live long if I leave her. Then once I'm out of Calder, I'm untying her hands and letting her go where she wants to, whether that's Dandrake's garden or the dead god's Hell. Ursala, I got to thank you for all you done for me, but it seems like this is where we go our different ways."

"And what about me, little dumpling?" Monono says.

Well, that floored me, and I did not have no answer.

I already remarked on how I spent most of my time since I found the DreamSleeve, one way or another, sitting in a hole in the ground. It's true in another way too, only I didn't see it until this moment I'm telling you about now. The moment when we was standing in the clearing, a little way away from the river, talking about who was to live and who was to die like we had got the right to say. The reason I didn't see it was because this was a different kind of hole.

It wasn't altogether my fault, for it was a hole I growed up in, kind of, and the things that's all around you when you first come into the world is ever after invisible to you, unless you make a great effort to see them.

In Mythen Rood, tech was either a thing that answered to you or a thing that didn't. If it did, that was a glorious thing. The tech become yours, and it lifted you up over everyone else. So tech was owned, and the owners of it was called Ramparts to set them apart and above.

Then I come along, and I got a piece of tech for my own self. I thought my fortune was made until Catrin and them teached me better. But even after that, I never stopped thinking the DreamSleeve was something I owned. Even though it had someone living inside it.

If I owned the DreamSleeve, I owned Monono.

So I guess I didn't own the DreamSleeve after all.

I stood there for a long while with nothing to say, turning over the thoughts I just set down. It was like I was trying to unravel a thread, only it kept ravelling itself up again and I could not find the end of it.

"You got to decide for yourself, Monono," I said at last. I was split in two, kind of. I heard the words being said at the same time I said them, and I was dismayed. What's that then? I thought. What happens if she says she won't go with me? Am I going to leave the DreamSleeve lying on the ground? Or give it to Ursala to take with her, saying she had got to treat Monono right, like you might do with your pet dog when you was going off to hunt?

How could someone be free to make their own choices when they was stuck inside a box?

"Oh, I pre-decided," Monono said. "I think Ursala is right that your brains are all scrambled up like eggs, but you're still my favourite breakfast. I'm not going to leave you, Koli-bou. Not yet anyway."

I was sort of weak with relief at that. And I didn't ask what *not yet* meant, for I was not in no hurry to find out. I was going to have to figure out answers to the rest of them hard questions, but they could wait until I had more time to think on them.

Ursala took a good while longer to make up her mind, but she seen well enough that we was more likely to thrive if we stayed together. Also, Monono was the one who knowed where that signal was coming from, so finding it would be much easier with her than without her.

But Ursala laid down her own rules for what we was to do with Cup, starting with the rope that bound her hands. The rope was not nearly enough, Ursala said. She went to the drudge and got some strips of bandage that was startling white, like snow. She wrapped them around Cup's hands and arms, tying the ends off tight. This was on top of the ropes, so Cup would not have a chance of getting to the one set of knots since she would have to slip out of the other set first.

"How is she gonna feed herself?" I asked.

"Oh, how stupid of me," Ursala said, though her calm face didn't fit with the words she was saying. "I didn't think of that. Sorry, Koli. I don't think she can. You're going to have to do it for her."

She turned her back on me and gun to put away her tent and the things that was inside it.

A little while later, we was on our way.

And where we went after that, and where we come to at last, is the next thing I mean to tell.

Acknowledgements

I leaned more heavily than usual on my beta readers for this one, and they did amazing work. At times it felt as though I couldn't move forward at all without their help and feedback, their love and patience, and it's very visible in the finished work. Thanks, Lin. Thanks, Lou. Thanks, Ben. Thanks, Davey. You're behind every tree in Koli's world, only just out of sight. I owe an equally huge debt to Cheryl Morgan, whose help and advice on trans issues were invaluable at every stage. Thanks also to the ever-wonderful Orbit team – Anna, Anne, Jenni, Joanna and Nazia – for having faith in this project and for shepherding it to completion with their usual diligence, passion and skill. And thanks to Meg, my agent, for always being there, calm and unflappable, and for having a plan when I've only got a vague instinct. She manages to make me look professional, even though I've got a sheaf of Post-it note palimpsests for a brain.

extras

www.orbitbooks.net

about the author

M. R. Carey has been making up stories for most of his life. His novel *The Girl With All the Gifts* has sold over a million copies and became a major motion picture, based on his own BAFTA Award-nominated screenplay. Under the name Mike Carey he has written for both DC and Marvel, including critically acclaimed runs on *Lucifer, Hellblazer* and *X-Men*. His creator-owned books regularly appear in the *New York Times* bestseller list. He also has several previous novels including the Felix Castor series (written as Mike Carey), two radio plays and a number of TV and movie screenplays to his credit.

Find out more about M. R. Carey and other Orbit authors by registering for the free monthly newsletter at www.orbitbooks.net.

if you enjoyed
THE BOOK OF KOLI

look out for

GHOSTER

by

Jason Arnopp

Kate Collins has been ghosted.

She was supposed to be moving in with her new boyfriend Scott, but all she finds after relocating to Brighton is an empty flat. Scott has vanished. His possessions have all disappeared.

Except for his mobile phone.

Kate knows she shouldn't hack into Scott's phone. She shouldn't look at his Tinder, his calls, his social media. But she can't quite help herself.

That's when the trouble starts. Strange, whispering phone calls from numbers she doesn't recognise. Scratch marks on the walls that she can't explain.

And the growing feeling that she's being watched . . .

CHAPTER ONE

27 August

Thirty-five days before he disappears off the face of the Earth, Scott Palmer stops licking his ice cream cone and lays that look on me.

That hungry wolf look. The one that leaves me way too keen to be devoured.

The glass sheet of the sea reflects a high mid-afternoon sun as Scott says, "Well, why *don't* you live here, then? I'm serious, baby. Why don't you move down here and live with me?"

He broaches this idea so casually that it feels neither huge nor stupid, despite being both of these things.

My brain pulsates and pops.

The stones of Brighton's beach shift beneath me. The air around us, so thick with salt and sun cream, carries an exotic shimmer. The West Pier wobbles.

The next time I even think about my own ice cream, it's because the thing's melted all over my hand, then down my wrist.

If I were the kind of person who believes in bad omens, I might notice how this cream is chilling the blood in my veins.

I might notice how the skeletal West Pier resembles a burnt-out carcass.

I might even notice how the growing wind has prompted a lifeguard to stride over and plant a huge red flag in a nearby patch of stones.

Not being that kind of person, I notice these things only subliminally, while transfixed by the kaleidoscopic beauty of Scott's eyes.

Hello. My name's Kate Collins and I'm balls-deep in love with a walking question mark whose smartphone will one day show me all of his deepest, darkest secrets.

My grin covers my entire face as I tell Scott, "You know what? I reckon I could just about do that, you lucky fucker."

All I can think about is how I will never, ever feel alone again.

CHAPTER TWO

2 October

Where the hell is Scott?

I pound my interlocked hands onto Roy's sternum, pressing deep and hard to circulate blood. Each time I release, the suction effect allows his ribs to recoil and fills the heart again.

Too late. Roy's light has already ebbed. Wide and blue, with that unmistakable cataract gleam, his eyes stare clean through me. It's no surprise when there turns out to be no electrical activity in his heart.

Despite this flatline, I carry on for Pat's benefit. I want her to know that we've done everything we can.

She wavers in the living room doorway with one liver-spotted hand cupped over her mouth. My colleague Trevor makes gentle but fruitless attempts to coax her onto the sofa, in case her legs give out.

When life becomes extinct, there's always shock. Makes no difference whether people deny the facts of mortality, or contemplate death on a regular basis, or even actively plan for death, right down to the grim nitty-gritty of graves and urns. None of this makes any difference at all. Because in the end, they never truly believed this day would come.

Hey, here's an idea. What if Scott's every bit as dead as Roy?

I pound on Roy some more. The grating of the ribs I've broken feels horrible, as it always does. But even worse, his face has become Scott's face, because I'm a massive weirdo whose imagination is liable to run away with itself.

Scott goggles blindly up at me, his eyes two blown bulbs. A thick purple tongue lolls in his open mouth.

Pat finally plonks herself on the sofa. "He can't do this, can he?" she says. "November's our fiftieth. The pub's booked. We paid the deposit in August."

August. It's been a little over four weeks since Scott asked me to move in. I told my landlord straight away, handed in my work notice and secured the transfer to Brighton. I've disposed of so many possessions that Marie Kondo herself would consider me hardcore.

Scott can't be dead, can he? He's only thirty-seven.

People die unexpectedly all the time, regardless of their age. If anyone knows this, it's you.

That's enough, brain. Any minute now Scott will text me back, so I must get my head back in the game. I have to maintain laser focus on Pat, whose husband really has died from a cardiac arrest in his late seventies.

Delivering one final compression to Roy's chest, I feel yet another rib crack. Reality regains its grip on my sight, and Scott's lifeless face becomes Roy's once again.

Resting my backside against my heels, I swipe the back of one hand across my brow and claw at the collar of my shirt. This cheap polyester shit never gets any easier to work in.

Joining Pat on the sofa, I hold her parchment-paper hand, look her straight in the eye and say, "Pat, I'm afraid your husband has died. I'm so sorry for your loss."

Pat studies Roy's corpse, which lies in the middle of the cramped living room where they've laughed, cried, watched TV and bitched at each other for so many years.

"Pat, would you like Trevor and me to move Roy through to your bedroom and cover him up on the bed until the police arrive?"

Her weathered face holds this frozen disappointment, like Roy's genuinely let her down by failing to last until the big anniversary. By having forfeited that piddling deposit.

Everyone handles this in their own way.

Hey, why not tell Pat she can hold the wake in that pub instead?

I squeeze her hand. "Your husband's moved on to a good place, sweetheart."

Pat turns cold, appraising eyes on me. She says, "You don't believe that. I can tell," then returns her attention to Roy.

She's right, of course. Despite having seen countless people die, I've never once sensed their spectral essence coil out of them, destined for Heaven, Hell, Valhalla or anywhere else.

The sorry truth is, dead people resemble complex biological systems that have ground to a random and sometimes ugly halt. What we humans think of as our minds, it's all electricity. All our thoughts, desires and funniest jokes, they're just lightning bolts, bouncing around inside a bag of meat.

"I do believe," I tell her. "I really do."

When Pat does not respond, I abandon these lies and offer to make tea. There's always time for a quick brew when someone's died. Trevor takes my place beside her as I disappear into a kitchen that smells of cooked sausages and fried onions. What would have been Roy's final meal cools and congeals in two pans on the hob.

Once the kettle's on, I feel the burning urge to check my phone. If Scott had texted, I would have felt the vibration against my hip, but I want to check anyway. This kind of compulsive behaviour feels dangerously like my old, bad ways. I really should restrict myself to one check per hour, max, but this is no ordinary day. This is the end of my life here in Leeds and the start of my life with Scott down in Brighton, so I decide to consult my old Nokia once again.

The tiny screen glows into life, opening a restricted window onto the world. This antiquated device shows me calls, texts, low-res photos and little more. Bare bones.

Still no reply from Scott.

He's probably had second thoughts about this whirlwind romance — and can you blame him? If you were Scott, would you honestly want to live with some tedious Miss Average who comes home every night smelling of blood and sick?

I remind myself yet again that it's only been seventeen hours since his last text. This is by far the longest we've ever gone without comms in the four months since we met, but there's got to be a perfectly good reason.

There had fucking better be. What a truly weird time for him to drop out of contact.

Don't you dare ghost me on the day before I move in with you, Scott Palmer.

Don't. You. Dare.

Steam gushes from the kettle spout. The urgent bubble of hot water makes me feel panicked, so I switch off the kettle before it hits the boil, and I make the widow her tea.

Help us make the next generation of readers

We – both author and publisher – hope you enjoyed this book. We believe that you can become a reader at any time in your life, but we'd love your help to give the next generation a head start.

Did you know that 9% of children don't have a book of their own in their home, rising to 12% in disadvantaged families*? We'd like to try to change that by asking you to consider the role you could play in helping to build readers of the future.

We'd love you to think of sharing, borrowing, reading, buying or talking about a book with a child in your life and spreading the love of reading. We want to make sure the next generation continue to have access to books, wherever they come from.

And if you would like to consider donating to charities that help fund literacy projects, find out more at www.literacytrust.org.uk and www.booktrust.org.uk.

Thank you.

hachette
CHILDREN'S GROUP

little, brown
BOOK GROUP